DAUGHTER

OF THE SUN

ALSO BY

BARBARA WOOD

Private Entrance

Star of Babylon

The Blessing Stone

Sacred Ground

Perfect Harmony

The Prophetess

Virgins of Paradise

The Dreaming

Green City in the Sun

Soul Flame

Vital Signs

Domina

The Watch Gods

Childsong

Night Trains

Yesterday's Child

Curse This House

Hounds and Jackals

The Magdalene Scrolls

DAUGHTER
OF THE SUN

Barbara Wood

St. Martin's Griffin

New York

DAUGHTER OF THE SUN. Copyright © 2007 by Barbara Wood. All rights reserved. Printed in the United States of America. No part of this book may be used or reproduced in any manner whatsoever without written permission except in the case of brief quotations embodied in critical articles or reviews. For information, address St. Martin's Press, 175 Fifth Avenue, New York, N.Y. 10010.

www.stmartins.com

Library of Congress Cataloging-in-Publication Data

Wood, Barbara, 1947–
    Daughter of the sun / Barbara Wood.—1st ed.
        p. cm.
    ISBN-13: 978-0-312-36368-0
    ISBN-10: 0-312-36368-0
    1. Young women—Fiction.   2. Class—Fiction.   3. Prehistoric peoples—Fiction.
4. New Mexico—Fiction.   I. Title.

PS3573.O5877D38 2007
813'.54—dc22

                                                                                2007016908

First Edition: September 2007

10 9 8 7 6 5 4 3 2 1

This book is dedicated to
my husband, George, with love.

Acknowledgments

Three amazing people deserve recognition. Sharon Stewart, dear friend and assistant; Harvey Klinger, the best agent a writer could have; Jennifer Enderlin, an editor wise beyond her years. Deepest thanks.

BOOK ONE

The Dark Lord

One

THE runner sprinted down the paved road, his heart pounding with fear. Although his feet were bleeding, he dared not stop. He looked back. His eyes widened in terror. He stumbled, fought for balance, and pushed on. He had to warn the clan.

A Dark Lord was coming.

Ahoté could not help his forbidden thoughts. There sat beautiful Hoshi'tiwa, just a hundred paces from where he stood at the Memory Wall, radiant in the sunshine as she spun cotton ribbons for her bridal costume. She looked so happy in front of her small adobe house shaded by cottonwood trees, with the fresh stream trickling nearby. All she had been able to talk about was the coming wedding day. But all Ahoté could think about was the wedding *night*.

His father pinched him.

Under the elder's tutelage, eighteen-year-old Ahoté was reciting the clan history, using the pictographs painted on the wall as a guide. Each symbol represented a major event in the past. And as there were too many events recorded on the Memory Wall—symbolized by spirals, animals, people, lightning strikes—for the clan to remember, it was the job of one man, He Who Links People.

This was the sacred calling to which young Ahoté was apprenticed and upon which he must concentrate. But his mind was wandering.

His father scowled. Takei did not understand the boy's lovesick state. When Takei had wed, years ago, a girl chosen by his parents, he had done his duty, begetting many children on her. He had never wasted his time in moony-eyed daydreaming and sexual fantasies. Sex was for creating children, not for idle amusement. If Takei had ever taken pleasure in the intimate act, he could not recall it.

He glowered at his son. Lovesickness was exactly that—a sickness, and Ahoté's mind was so infected with it, he could not concentrate on his recitations. If only the wedding day could be brought forward, Takei thought, tomorrow perhaps, so the boy could flush the lust out of his system. But the shamans had cast the fortunes of all involved and had declared that the soonest good-luck day was yet three months away!

Takei experienced a ripple of fear. Lust and love seduced a man's mind from his holy works. Was the boy in danger of weakening before the wedding, risking a spiritual pollution that would profane his sacred task?

A dour, unhappy man who believed the gods had singled him out for a life of bad luck, Takei wished now he had not given in to Ahoté's pleas to marry Hoshi'tiwa, wished he had had a matchmaker find a girl in another settlement, one not as pretty and clever as Sihu'mana's daughter. Takei's only hope was that this was just a phase, a matter of Ahoté wanting something he couldn't have. Some men were like that, hungering for the out-of-reach, like desiring a married woman. Hoshi'tiwa was forbidden to Ahoté right now, and that fired the blood. But once he could have the girl anytime he wanted, day or night, the fever would leave him. Or so Takei prayed.

As Ahoté's hungry gaze strayed again to the lovely Hoshi'tiwa sitting in the sunshine, her poppy-red tunic a bright warm beacon, his boy's body stirring with a man's desires as he thought of his coming nights as a husband, another sharp pinch on his arm brought him back to the lesson, and he recited: "And then the people knew the Spring of Abundant Hunting, when elk came down from the plateau to offer themselves as food." The symbol painted on the wall was an elk with arrows in its body.

The last symbol on the wall was a circle with six lines trailing it, marking the sighting of a comet streaking the sky the summer before. No new symbols had been added since because nothing of significance had taken place. As he recited for his father, Ahoté wondered what new symbol would be added next, continuing the clan's long history.

Far down the highway, which cut through the vast plain and between plateaus, the runner fell, his right knee cracking in pain. As he struggled to his feet, he felt in the paving stones of the wide highway the vibrations of the thundering feet of the advancing army. He swallowed in terror, tasted blood and salt on his tongue.

The cannibals were coming.

Hoshi'tiwa looked over at handsome Ahoté at the Memory Wall, his sinewy body gleaming in the sun as he wore only a loincloth, and her heart swelled with love and hope. Life was good. Spring flowers bloomed everywhere. The nearby stream ran with cool fresh water and fish. The clan was healthy and prosperous. And Hoshi'tiwa, seventeen years old, was looking forward to her wedding day.

She sat in the sunshine at the base of the cliff, spinning cotton for her bridal costume. She sat cross-legged as she twirled a wooden spindle up and down her thigh, deftly plucking clean fibers from a basket filled with carded cotton and adding them to the growing thread that would be dyed and woven into a ribbon for her hair.

All around her the clan was going about the daily business of living: the farmers planting corn, women tending cook fires and watching the children, and the potters creating the rain jars for which her clan was most famous.

As she spun her cotton, Hoshi'tiwa did not know that on the other side of the world, a strange race of people had named this cycle of the sun the Year of Our Lord, 1150. She was unaware that they rode on the backs of beasts, something her own people did not do, and used a tool called a wheel to transport goods. Hoshi'tiwa knew nothing of cathedrals and gunpowder, popes and Crusades, nor did she know that those strange people gave names to their canyons and rivers and hills.

Hoshi'tiwa's settlement had no name. Nor did the nearby stream, nor the mountains that watched over them. Many years in the future, another race would come to this place and apply names to everything they saw and walked upon. Two hundred miles to the southeast of where Hoshi'tiwa felt warm sun on her arms, a town would be established and called Albuquerque. The area surrounding it for 120,000 square miles would be known as New Mexico. The young bride did not know that centuries hence, strangers would roam the land to the north of her settlement and call it Colorado.

There was only one place, far away in the southeast, that she knew by name, Center Place, so called because it was the hub of trade and communication for her people, and an important religious center. Even so, centuries hence, the name of Center Place would be changed to Chaco Canyon, and men and women known as anthropologists would stand in the ruins at Chaco Canyon and speculate and argue and debate and theorize over what they called the Abandonment. They would wonder, those people in the far future, why Hoshi'tiwa and her people, whom the anthropologists would incorrectly call Anasazi, had vanished so suddenly and without a trace.

Hoshi'tiwa was ignorant of the fact that she would one day be part of an ancient mystery. Had she known, she would argue that there was nothing mysterious about her life. Her clan had lived at the foot of this escarpment for generations, and in all those centuries, little had changed. Hoshi'tiwa was a simple corn grower's daughter who counted her blessings, secure in the knowledge that tomorrow would be the same as yesterday.

Her thoughts broke like a bubble when she saw Ahoté, while his father's back was turned, gesture to her. It was their private signal. She knew what it meant: At the first opportunity, he wanted to be alone with her.

She nodded in secret response. And her heart began to race.

The runner fell again, stamping his blood into the road's sandstone surface, his knees scraped and bleeding, his bones screaming in pain. He could save himself, he knew, by running to the left, off the highway and down a narrow ravine that would shield him from the approaching army. But the people in the settlement were his kin. They were relying on him as the lookout to warn them in times of danger.

Other families—entire settlements—were now completely gone because they did not have lookouts to warn them when the Jaguars came. If he died at the end of his run, at least his family would survive. And so he pushed on.

Hoshi'tiwa's mother paused in her labor at the grinding stone, where she was turning corn into flour, and squinted up at the sky. The world *looked* right, but it didn't feel right. She glanced around. There was young Maya, sitting in the shade of a cottonwood tree, breast-feeding her great-grandfather. Though her baby wailed in its basket on her back, it would have to wait until the elder was fed. The old man had long since lost his teeth, and now he was having difficulty swallowing gruel. Therefore, after the age-old custom of keeping the precious elders alive—for they alone had memories of what went before—his great-granddaughter nourished him with her own milk.

From the mudbrick dwelling next door came screams through the gaping doorway. Hoshi'tiwa's mother could see, in the darkness, her friend Lakshi, on her knees, her arms over her head with her wrists tied to a rope suspended from the ceiling. Kneeling in front of Lakshi and behind her, two midwives coaxed the babe into the world.

All things normal, nothing out of the ordinary. Yet something was wrong. The air was too still, sounds too muted, sunlight too golden. Was this the day, Sihu'mana wondered, the day she had dreamed about in troubled sleep long ago? Had it come at last? Or was it just a mother's nervousness before a wedding?

Her thoughts were interrupted by a sudden cry.

At the western terminus of the canyon, where the adobe houses ended and a dense forest of cottonwoods began, a cluster of boulders stood upon ground that had been declared sacred generations prior. Here the sun-watcher priest marked the cycles of the sun as it journeyed back and forth between the Solstices. The priest lived in a shelter nearby, never leaving his post, so that today, like every day, he marked the transit of the midday sun until the shadows disappeared beneath the boulders. Seeing this, he gave a shout.

It was time for the noon meal.

Those working in the fields laid down their digging sticks and baskets of seeds, said a prayer to the corn spirits, and began streaming back into the settlement—over a hundred men, women, and children, to be greeted by family members offering gourds of sweet water and places at the cook fires. The men were fed first, by tradition, being handed stacks of thin corn tortillas, or tamales filled with beans and squash, along with roasted onions, chili peppers, and corn on the cob.

Ahoté's father left the Memory Wall, his stomach growling, his mouth watering for the crispy pancakes he would fill with spicy beans. But Ahoté remained. He was hungry—but not for food.

Hoshi'tiwa, laying aside her carding and cotton, gracefully rose to her feet, but she did not join her mother at their cook fire, where her father sank gratefully to the earth after a morning of hard labor and accepted the hot pancakes from Sihu'mana.

Food was not on Hoshi'tiwa's mind. She looked across the golden sunlight at Ahoté, whose eyes were on her. The breath caught in her throat and her heart pounded. When Ahoté spun about and dashed into the nearby cottonwood trees, Hoshi'tiwa lithely sprinted after him.

Chatter and laughter filled the canyon as the men ate their fill and the women and girls served them, but Sihu'mana's eyes followed her daughter into the forest. She felt her heart tighten with fear and dread. Remembering when she herself was young and love had sustained her instead of food, she grew alarmed. Was her daughter going to weaken before the wedding night?

No mother's head rested easy at night while her daughter existed in that fragile state between girlhood and marriage. Once Hoshi'tiwa was under a husband's protection, Sihu'mana, like mothers since the beginning of time, would breathe more easily.

There were two things the marriage partners brought to the union: the man, his courage; and the woman, her honor. Preserving her daughter's virginity had not been easy, because Hoshi'tiwa was blessed—or cursed, depending on how one looked at it—with beauty. Whenever visitors came to the settlement, Sihu'mana kept a close watch on her daughter. Everyone still remembered, although they never spoke of it, the poor girl Kowka who, just days before her wedding, was with her sisters hunting for ground finch eggs when she had strayed upstream and a band of marauders from the north had happened upon her, alone and unprotected. She had survived the attack, but no man would marry her after that because of the clan's complex rules and taboos regarding sex. The elders had declared her *makai-yó*—unclean—and despite pleas of leniency from her mother, Kowka was driven from the village and never heard from again.

The sudden appearance of Kowka in her thoughts now alarmed Sihu'mana, and she quickly whispered words of good luck and traced a protective sign in the air. She had not thought of the unfortunate girl in years. Was it an omen?

Hoshi'tiwa plunged into the dense trees, looking this way and that. "Ahoté!" she whispered eagerly. "Where are you?"

She listened. Birds chirped in branches overhead. The fragrance of spring flowers filled the air. The forest was peaceful and sun-dappled. Hoshi'tiwa tiptoed forward, her ears alert for a telltale sound, her eyes scouring the ground for footprints or a shadow. "Where are you?" she called again, softly, relishing the moment when she found him. This was their private game—hide-and-seek—in which Ahoté pretended to chase her until she let him catch her.

When Ahoté jumped out, she gave a mock cry and turned to run. But he caught her and swung her back, to take hold of her by the waist and pull her to him. He looked into her eyes for a long, breathless moment; then he gently rubbed his nose to hers.

Hoshi'tiwa giggled. "My sweet funny Owl." It had been her pet name for him ever since, one night the winter before, they had been gathered around the fire and Ahoté had been so frightened by one of the storyteller's ghost tales that a five-year-old boy had cried, "Uncle Ahoté, you are so scared, your eyes are as big as an owl's!"

While the women and girls of Hoshi'tiwa's clan wore their hair long, the men and boys kept theirs cut short, hacking it off above the ears with a sharp obsidian knife. When Ahoté jumped out, he had brushed his short hair up into two "owl horns," and Hoshi'tiwa laughed. She now reached up and smoothed his black hair down, bringing her hands to rest on either side of his face, her eyes glistening with love.

As Ahoté touched his nose to Hoshi'tiwa's, and she allowed him to kiss her in this fashion, he burned for more. How was he going to last the three months until their wedding night? When he lifted his hand and brushed his fingers over her breast, feeling the firm flesh beneath the fabric of her tunic, Hoshi'tiwa drew back, suddenly shy.

Although she knew of the private ways between men and women, knew how intimate love was expressed, how men begot babies upon their wives, Hoshi'tiwa was uncertain how she felt about the intimacy she would soon share with Ahoté. Her mother had told her she would find it pleasurable, and Hoshi'tiwa supposed she would, but more important to her was the laughter they would share, the secrets they would whisper late into the night. When she thought of their lives together, she pictured herself cooking for Ahoté, delighting him with food, giving him children, making him proud.

"I love you," he murmured now. "Tell me you love me. It's permissible. We are almost married."

Although she wanted to speak the words, her tongue froze. Hoshi'tiwa had been taught that emotions were powerful magic and therefore must always be kept in check, even such positive emotions as love. To release them by word or gesture was to set free a force that could wreak havoc upon the clan. Everyone knew that words of anger caused sickness, vocalized hatred brought about death; strong emotions destroyed crops and caused miscarriages. Even love, though good, had been known to incite envy, jealousy, and mistrust. So Hoshi'tiwa had been trained, like all her people, to be conservative in actions and speech. But it was all right, her mother had counseled, for husband and wife to exchange endearments—they were encouraged to, in fact, for such tender words enriched the womb and brought forth healthy babies.

Because she could not bring herself to speak the powerful words, Hoshi'tiwa had devised another way to tell Ahoté how much he meant to her. Her hands spoke in clay. Everyone said that when Hoshi'tiwa created a jar, the Cloud Spirits heard her wish for rain. And so, for her beloved, she had secretly fashioned a small, loving memento just for him: a little ceramic owl painted with big comical eyes. She had drilled a hole in it and looped a string so he could wear it around his neck as a constant reminder of her love. And then she had hidden it somewhere in this small forest, as a treat for Ahoté to find.

Sunlight dappled their young bodies as she allowed Ahoté to draw her into his arms and hold her tight. She felt love flood from her body into his, felt their deep bond that could never be broken.

Their love had its beginnings six winters prior. Ahoté was twelve and had begun his apprenticeship as He Who Links People. He and his father were camped in a makeshift shelter at the Memory Wall, away from distractions as they prayed and fasted. The snowfall had been heavy during the night so that morning revealed a white settlement blanketed in deep snow. The people slowly emerged from their adobe dwellings where they had slept huddled against the cold, along with their dogs and turkeys, which they had brought inside for the night, and when it was noticed that one house remained silent, that no one emerged into the cold dawn, the men began to frantically dig the snow away from the wooden plank door.

When daylight flooded the humble interior, they found eight people still in repose, comfortably arranged on woven mats, with puppies and dogs between them—one man, two women, five children. All dead. It was later determined that the smokehole that vented the cook fire through the roof had gotten clogged with snow during the night, asphyxiating the family in their sleep.

Ahoté's father had been inconsolable, screaming and shouting and weeping through the days that followed, while Ahoté had withdrawn into a queer silence. He had stared at his mother, aunt and uncle, and five siblings, lying so peacefully on their mats, small puppies tucked tenderly between them. They had not struggled; they had not known they were dying. But this was no consolation for Ahoté as he slipped into a strange muteness that none of the shamans or medicine men could cure.

After the burials and prayers and mourning rituals, Takei had stiffened his spine, firmed his jaw, and returned to the Memory Wall, where he had a new event to record, grimly painting it upon the rock with his own hand: the pictograph called the Winter of Eight Deaths, and which would be so known down through coming generations. But the tragedy was compounded by Ahoté's continued muteness. No coaxing, cajoling, or threatening could restore the boy's power of speech so that Takei began to panic: What good was a memory man who could not speak?

And then one day, in the spring following the tragedy, twelve-year-old Hoshi'tiwa had found Ahoté by the stream, staring into the shallows. She had just lost her eldest brother to a mountain lion attack, so that she was left with only her parents. Understanding the depths of his sadness and feelings of loneliness, she had wordlessly taken the silent boy into her arms and held him. Ahoté soon began to weep. As he sobbed onto her shoulder, and the tears flowed, the words also began to flow and Ahoté's affliction was lifted.

They were inseparable after that, and when the time came for Ahoté to take a mate and everyone had thought he would seek a bride in a neighboring settlement, Ahoté wanted only Hoshi'tiwa, and she him.

"Tell me," he whispered now in a husky voice against her ear as he moved his hands up and down her back. "Tell me how much you love me."

Hoshi'tiwa felt his arousal pressing against her and, despite herself, began to weaken.

Although he was not far from his destination, the runner turned off the highway to sprint to a small farm where three Wolf Clan families grew beans and squash. Even though they were not his clan, he could not run by without letting them know of the approaching danger. They gave him water as he warned them, between gulps, of the Jaguars' approach.

"Last year they took many of our young men," the elder said grimly, "and two of our maiden daughters."

The runner gasped, "You must run and hide until they have come and gone."

But the elder looked at his frightened wife, and then he scanned the humble settlement that had once been the home of over a hundred people who were now reduced to twenty. "This is our ancestral land," he said in a tight voice, "but we must leave once and for all. To survive, we will depart from this place and never come back."

Their houses were grass shelters that could be abandoned with ease. And the people did so now, quickly gathering up as many possessions as they could carry, hoisting small children onto their backs, and disappearing into the cottonwood trees to leave campfires smoldering and turkeys scratching in the dust.

The runner returned to the highway to dash the final distance home.

Sihu'mana kept her eye on the trees. Hoshi'tiwa and Ahoté still had not emerged.

Recalling the omen that had appeared on the night of Hoshi'tiwa's birth, Sihu'mana's fears returned in full force.

Eight babes had issued forth from Sihu'mana's fertile womb. Two were stillborn, two did not survive the first year, two died before the age of five, and the son, who would have been Hoshi'tiwa's older brother, died when he came of age and went on his vision quest, going into the mountains with only a spear. He had managed to kill a mountain lion, but only after the beast had swiped sharp claws across the youth's abdomen, slitting it open. The boy had run all the way home, holding his intestines in, before dropping dead at his mother's feet.

There were no more children after that, and so for seventeen summers she had loved Hoshi'tiwa and protected her, taught her to walk and talk, to be kind and patient, to be polite and modest, instructing her in the clan's traditions and many taboos, to make sure the girl did not accidentally break a law and bring disaster to the family. But most of all, Sihu'mana had shown her daughter how to "speak" to clay with her nimble fingers, to create the most beautiful rain jars the clan had seen in generations. But the omen she had seen on the night of the birth never left her. For seventeen years Sihu'mana had swallowed her fear with her tortillas, hoping that the omen had been her imagination, the result perhaps of eating too much spice, too many chilies.

But now her blood and her bones were telling her something else. As she watched old Wuki shuffle past with a basket of onions she had just dug up from the garden, Sihu'mana wondered: Is all this about to come to an end?

The gods had always looked with favor upon Sihu'mana's settlement. In the winter, snow lay heavy upon the boughs of cedar and pine; in the summer, rains blessed the tasseling cornfields. Her people always enjoyed a plentiful autumn harvest. While a great portion of the corn was sent to Center Place, demanded by the Dark Lords for as long as the clan could remember, there was always enough left for the farmers and their families. And even though this year the Lords were demanding more, because in the land to the south of Center Place, it was rumored, the clouds had withheld their blessed rain and the cornfields there were growing parched, Sihu'mana's clan were not worried. They would always have rain because their potters made the best rain jars in the world.

Everyone knew that if rain had nothing to fall into, it would not fall. And the more exquisite the vessel, the more the rain would be attracted to it. Therefore, hundreds of jars dotted the landscape at the base of the sheer cliff, in front of doorways, around the kiva, along walls and on windowsills, filling with the precious water that fed the corn crops, the beans and squash, and the drinking gourds of the people. The clan's rain jars were so much in demand by far-flung villages and farms that traders and travelers stopped frequently to exchange sky-stone and meat and feather blankets for the exquisite pottery.

But now, as Sihu'mana's eyes made a sweep of the sandy ground between the adobe houses, and the fields and stream, until they came again to the forest of cottonwoods, she saw the root of her ill-ease.

Hoshi'tiwa had been different almost from birth. As a child, asking questions no child should ask. Hoshi'tiwa could never understand why they had to send their best pottery to the Lords of Center Place. And men, too. Word would arrive that the Lords needed able-bodied workers, and the clan had to send a certain number or suffer swift and bloody punishment. Little Hoshi'tiwa, watching a favorite uncle or cousin walk out of the settlement, would ask why. Sihu'mana had constantly warned her against such inquisitiveness. Questioning fate was an affront to the gods. But Hoshi'tiwa continued to ask, and now it seemed that a day had dawned that felt like no other.

Watching the trees, and thinking that the two young lovers had been in there too long, Sihu'mana's anxiety grew.

The runner wanted to lie where he had fallen on the warm paving stones. He was so exhausted, he thought he could not lift himself up to run the last distance to the settlement.

But his family was there. His grandmother Wuki, and his sister Lakshi. He could not let the cannibals take them captive.

And so, with one final effort, and a desperate silent plea to the gods, the runner pushed himself to his bleeding feet and dashed for the cliffs, where the familiar stream of his home beckoned.

To Hoshi'tiwa's shock, Ahoté dropped to his knees and, wrapping his arms around her thighs, pressed his face to her abdomen. His lips moving against the fabric of her skirt, he said with youthful passion, "I will love you forever, Hoshi'tiwa. I will be faithful to you always. And I promise to keep you safe."

At these last words, Hoshi'tiwa glanced through the trees and was startled to see the men already back at work in the fields.

She frowned. It had not always been so. The midday meal had always been long and leisurely. But the demand for corn was increasing with each year. Would there come a time when the Lords took everything, leaving nothing for her people?

Feeling her body suddenly stiffen, Ahoté rose to his feet and said, "What is wrong?"

With her eyes still on the field where her kinsmen toiled to fill the bellies of other men, she said, "It isn't right that the Lords should take what is not theirs."

Ahoté gave her an amused look. Once in a while, Hoshi'tiwa uttered the most unexpected words. "It is the way of the world," he said patiently, "for the strong to take from the weak. The Lords are stronger than us. We cannot fight them, Hoshi'tiwa."

She wanted to say, "Why not?" but the People of the Sun were not used to questioning the ways of the world.

"Why fret about it, Hoshi'tiwa? We can always plant more corn," Ahoté said with a smile, putting his hands on her waist and drawing her to him again.

She resisted a little, but let him touch his nose to hers, allowed him to brush his lips over her cheek.

"Hoshi'tiwa," he said in a thick voice, "do not trouble yourself with things you cannot change. Think only of us. Tell me you love me. Tell me." And he pulled her against him in a hard embrace.

Hoshi'tiwa's unseemly thoughts vanished. "I have a small surprise for you," she said. "A little gift which you must find."

"How you tease me!" he whispered with a smile. "All right, tell me where to find this love-gift—"

"*Help!*"

They snapped their heads around to see through the trees a man, exhausted and shining with sweat, appear at the distant bend in the stream. "Danger!" he cried, waving his arms as he reached the settlement, where he fell to his knees and pointed upward. "To the safe house! A Dark Lord comes!"

Hoshi'tiwa and Ahoté ran from the forest. The people in the fields, the mothers and children at the hearths, the potters at their kilns— everyone abandoned their labors and ran to the base of the cliff, where ladders stood in constant readiness for swift ascent to the fortress high above. Those who reached the top first lowered ropes to enable more people to hurriedly climb up the sheer rock face wall to safety.

"Hurry!" shouted the runner, who had come from a lookout tower where he had spotted the army in the distance. Two men lifted him up and helped him to a ladder.

A wailing Lakshi was carried by the midwives, the newborn baby lying on her belly, still connected to her by the bloody umbilical cord. Takei came running from the Memory Wall to help raise more ladders. The people scrambled up blindly, assisting each other, calling out to loved ones to hurry, stark fear on their faces.

A Dark Lord was coming.

Hoshi'tiwa's clan was terrified of the Lords of Center Place, having heard tales of torture and human sacrifice. Years ago, at the hearth, Grandfather had whispered of forbidden practices. "The Lords are not of our people, but strangers from the south who came to enslave the People of the Sun. They subjugated us through terror. Our ancestors were forced to build their houses at Center Place, and lay down their wide roads. If we fought back, they came and slaughtered us, they made us die long and painful deaths, and then they cooked us and ate our flesh."

Hoshi'tiwa had thought such tales were invented to frighten children into obedience, but now as she stood on the precipice high above, holding tightly to Ahoté, she stared in horror at the army advancing from the east, the Jaguars' feet thundering upon the paving stones as the soldiers filled the canyon with the roar of their clubs against their shields. In the midst of this sea of savage humanity, the Dark Lord rode high on his throne carried on the shoulders of forty slaves. Up in the cliff house the old women began to wail, the children cried, and the men argued among themselves.

"They are going to eat us!"

"We must escape!"

"They will boil our bones and consume our flesh!"

The frightening mass of men in spotted animal skins, carrying fearsome clubs and spears and shields, came to a halt at the base of the cliff. And the people huddled above fell silent.

No one in Hoshi'tiwa's clan had seen a Dark Lord, but her father's brother, a trader who carried pottery to outlying settlements in exchange for sandals and blankets, had told the family that theirs was not the only cliff dwelling. There were other safe houses like their own, stone chambers and stairways and terraces carved high in the cliff with the only access being ladders and ropes.

In one settlement, Uncle had found the people slaughtered. The men and women and children lay where they had fallen, because there had been no one left alive to bury them. They lay with axes still in their skulls and knives in their breasts. But their arms and legs had been cut off, and Hoshi'tiwa's uncle said he had found those bones, picked clean and boiled to a polish like antelope bones after a feast. Thus they knew the Dark Lords had been there and had feasted upon the inhabitants.

Ahoté and the other men had pulled up the ladders and ropes. There was no access to the cliff house. They were safe. They stared down at the fearsome soldiers called Jaguars. No one in the clan had ever seen a jaguar, but they knew from legend that the jaguar was a spotted cat that lived in a land far to the south. The Dark Lord's soldiers dressed in the skins of this spotted cat, and wore the head of the cat upon their heads. They carried fearsome spears and clubs, and wooden shields painted with bold emblems. In the midst of this frightening army, the Dark

Lord sat upon his magnificent carrying chair, but the people above could not see the Lord himself as he sat beneath a colorful shade canopy.

The wind whistled through the deserted settlement as the people above waited in terrified silence, women clinging to husbands, mothers holding children.

A contingent of Jaguars broke from the main body and began searching the small adobe dwellings clustered on the flat plain. As they inspected every interior, a most remarkable-looking man stepped forward. Hoshi'tiwa's eyes widened at the sight of him, for she had never seen a man so splendidly dressed. Wearing a scarlet cape tied at his throat and a blazing orange tunic that surely was made of cotton, a luxury her own people could not afford, he wore a handsome feathered headdress, and in his right hand held a tall wooden staff topped with a human skull decorated in sky-stone and jade.

He was flanked by two equally astonishing men whose bodies were painted entirely in blue, from their shaven heads to their blue sandals. Draped in blue robes, they played flutes made from human shinbones while the one in the feathered headdress shouted out to the people above, speaking in their own language, his voice rising to the high cliff house: "I am Moquihix, from the Place of Reeds, Bearer of the Blood Cup, Official Tongue of the Tlatoani! Do not be afraid! We come for one of you! Only one of you! The rest, go back to your planting as the gods have decreed!"

Hoshi'tiwa's people looked at one another, their fear turning to puzzlement. *They want only one of us? Why do they want* one *of us? And which one?*

Moquihix's voice rang out over the plain, over the running stream, and up the sheer wall of the cliff. "Send down the girl called Hoshi'tiwa!"

Everyone gasped. They trembled and clung to one another and whispered in fear. *Did we hear wrong? They want Hoshi'tiwa?*

"No!" Ahoté cried, drawing her tightly to him.

The deep, resonant voice called out: "The spirit of the *tlatoani* of Center Place, Lord Jakál from the Place of Reeds, Guardian of the Sacred

Plume, Watcher of the Sky is filled with a thousand sadnesses. The sun does not shine in the heart of your Lord. Send down the girl Hoshi'tiwa, who has been chosen to gladden the heart of her Lord, and we will leave!"

Stark fear stood on Hoshi'tiwa's face. "Mami, what does he mean?"

Her mother's face drained of blood. Horror filled her eyes. And then sorrow. "Daughter," she said in a tight voice. "The Dark Lord has chosen you for himself."

"The tunnel," everyone said, meaning the escape route that led to the other side of the mesa. "Ahoté, take her away. The Jaguars will never find you."

But then they saw the Jaguars pulling an old man from one of the houses. The family cried out as a Jaguar took him by the hair, forced him to kneel, and held an ax to his throat.

"Which one of you forgot to bring Old Uncle up to the safe house?" Sihu'mana hissed in fury.

"Send the girl down," Moquihix shouted, the tall plumes of his magnificent headdress quivering in the wind, "or we will slay this old one."

The women began to wail, for he was their uncle, a spirit-dancer, and without Uncle's Winter Solstice dance, the sun would stay standing still and not resume its journey back to summer.

"Do not go, Hoshi'tiwa!" Ahoté pleaded. "Come with me to the escape tunnel. By the time the Jaguars find a way up here, we will be long gone and they will never find you."

"But why do they want *me*? There must be thousands of maidens at Center Place. I am no one!" Her eyes went round with fear as she saw far below, her uncle on his knees, trembling beneath the ax. She looked over at the Dark Lord hidden beneath the sunshade. His chair stood upon a carpet of woven feathers the color of the deepest sky, which in turn covered a great wooden platform on the backs of slaves. Beneath the edge of the canopy, she glimpsed a bronze-skinned forearm decorated in bracelets made from a metal she had seen only once before, called gold. But the Lord himself she could not see.

Sihu'mana spoke with a dry mouth. "It is because you are favored by the gods, Daughter, and somehow the Dark Lord found out."

And then Sihu'mana saw the stricken look on her husband's face. "I am sorry," he blurted. "I was proud. I boasted."

The air stopped in Sihu'mana's lungs. She barely found breath to say, "Husband—" She could not go on, knowing what came next, what terrible confession he was about to make.

The words tumbled from his mouth—how he had bragged about his daughter to the people in a settlement downriver, the year before, when he had taken rain jars to be traded for salt. They had told him rumors of a drought in the south, where the rain had ceased to fall, and yet in his own region, they said, the rain was abundant. "What is the secret of your rain jars?" they had asked. And he had not been able to resist boasting about his daughter, who had brought rain the night she was born, and ever since their rain jars were always full.

Everyone in the cliff house exchanged worried looks. Word of Sihu'-mana's daughter had obviously traveled the vast network of trade routes until it had reached Center Place, where rain had not been seen in several seasons.

Sihu'mana swallowed painfully and saw, in an instant, the new path her life would take. There would be no grandchildren, no dutiful daughter to take care of her in her old age. Hoshi'tiwa was to leave and nothing would be the same again. The omen had come true.

Knowing that in the years to come her daughter's name, like that of poor Kowka, would never be spoken, Sihu'mana said, "My daughter, you have been blessed with the favor of the gods. The Lord will join his body with yours so that he, too, will share in that blessing."

Hoshi'tiwa could not move. She looked at the Jaguar holding an ax to Uncle's neck. Uncle was needed to bring the sun back from its winter journey. Without the summer sun, the corn would not grow. But then she thought of the Dark Lord hidden beneath the colorful canopy, and the thought of what she must do with him made her heart rise in her throat.

Ahoté, his face red with anger, said, "Let me take her away. They will never find us." How dare another man take his betrothed? Dark Lord or not, the prince in the carrying chair must not be allowed to touch Hoshi'tiwa.

Standing behind Ahoté, his father, Takei, was already, from years of training, disassociating himself from the situation. Future generations relied upon him for their oral history, and so his years of mental and emotional discipline took over, rendering him oblivious of the fear and panic all around him. Takei had already begun to compose the telling of today's event.

He also thought of the new pictograph he would be adding to the Memory Wall. What would he call it? The Day the Dark Lord Came For Sihu'mana's Daughter? He pursed his lips. Too long. And no point in having the clan remember the girl. Especially Ahoté. The boy would attach himself to that pictograph and pine his life away over it. Best to let that detail go forgotten, especially as she was now *makai-yó*. "The Day the Dark Lord Came" would do.

Down below, the official named Moquihix shouted: "You take too long! Your Lord has commanded you to come down!"

Before their horrified eyes, the Jaguar raised his ax and chopped it through Uncle's neck, severing the head from the body.

A terrible silence fell upon those huddled above. Hoshi'tiwa's mother looked at her and whispered, "Daughter, what have you done?"

"Look!" cried Ahoté, pointing. They saw several Jaguars break from the main body and sprint to the far base of the cliff.

"They will find a way to climb up," everyone said, "they will reach us and slaughter us all!"

Sihu'mana said with a heavy heart, "We must all pay tribute to the Lords, whether it is in corn or in daughters."

When Hoshi'tiwa's sobs grew harsh and bitter, Sihu'mana swallowed back her own tears and, remembering the omen of long ago, said, "Listen to me, Daughter. You were born to a special purpose. I do not know what that purpose is, only that you cannot turn from it. You can be brave. You have proved that." The proof of Hoshi'tiwa's bravery lay in three vertical blue lines that decorated the center of her forehead. Hoshi'tiwa had received them during puberty rites when girls were tattooed with the identifying mark of their clan. The ritual was also a test of bravery, as the procedure was painful and any girl crying out brought shame to her family. A sharp bone incised the delicate skin, then charcoal mixed with blue clay was rubbed into the wound. A poultice of aspen leaves soaked in *nequhtli,* a strong alcohol, was applied afterward to ward off the spirits of infection. Brave Hoshi'tiwa had neither winced nor made a sound.

Taking Hoshi'tiwa's face into her hands, Sihu'mana said, "Your life here is over, Daughter. It is in the hands of the gods now. I pray that we will see you again." But Sihu'mana knew it would not be so.

She saw the way the others were looking at her daughter, with the look they had cast upon poor Kowka as she lay recovering from her injuries. Sihu'mana knew that Hoshi'tiwa was now *makai-yó.*

With a lump of fear in her throat, her mouth dry and her heart pounding, Hoshi'tiwa embraced her mother and father, and her beloved Ahoté. But when she moved to embrace her aunts and uncles, they recoiled from her.

Sick with fear and shame, Hoshi'tiwa lowered the rope ladder and when she started to climb down, Ahoté said, "Wait." Lifting over his head a leather thong that hung about his neck, he slipped it over Hoshi'tiwa's head so that the magic talisman lay upon her breast. It was a trophy he had brought back from a vision quest when the spirit of the Great Bear protected him from danger—a bear claw, which Ahoté had found in a cave. Longer and thicker than a human finger, and curved like a half-moon with a hole drilled in the top for the thong to loop through, the claw was sharp and a reminder of the power of bear-spirit. "To protect you," Ahoté said with tears in his eyes. He touched his nose to hers and whispered, "I will find you. I promise. We will not be apart for long."

Overhearing the whispered promise, Takei knew he must not allow Ahoté to fulfill it. The boy had to stay here and memorize the wall. Therefore a marriage must be arranged at once to a girl from a nearby settlement. Perhaps from the three Wolf Clan families who lived down the highway. The wedding, already set for three months hence, would go ahead as planned, just with a different bride.

Hoshi'tiwa shakily climbed down, and at the base of the cliff she paused to look up at the faces staring down at her, and then a rough hand seized her and dragged her to Moquihix, throwing her to her knees. She knelt, trembling, as the high official stood over her.

"You are the girl called Hoshi'tiwa?"

She nodded mutely.

"What are the stars of your birth?"

She kept her head bowed. "S-stars?"

"What stars were you born under?" he asked impatiently. "What planets? What was the position of the moon?"

She bit her lip. "I do not know, my Lord."

"You *are* a virgin?" he asked sharply. "You have not yet lain with a man?"

Hoshi'tiwa's cheeks burned as she nodded.

Moquihix gestured in the direction of the Jaguars, and Hoshi'tiwa watched in astonishment as an old woman materialized from among the soldiers. Bent and aged, she shuffled forward, her facial tattoos identifying her as belonging to Eagle Clan, her necklaces strung with the magic amulets and medicine bag of a midwife. She ordered Hoshi'tiwa to sit.

Perplexed, Hoshi'tiwa complied, sitting cross-legged in the dust until the old woman pressed her backward so that Hoshi'tiwa was lying flat and looking up at the sky. When she felt the old woman's hands on her knees, pressing her legs apart, Hoshi'tiwa suddenly understood what was about to take place. She pressed her hands to her face to keep herself from crying out, which would bring dishonor to her clan.

While the old fingers probed, a hush fell upon the gathered people up in the cliff house. Hoshi'tiwa was overcome with humiliation. She felt violated. In front of her family and this strange man and the soldiers, she was being examined for proof of her virginity. She shut her eyes and choked back the bitter tears.

Finally the old woman rose and pronounced Hoshi'tiwa's purity intact.

"Girl, though you are dust beneath my Lord's feet," Moquihix declared, "you have been chosen by the gods to gladden the heart of Jakál, the *tlatoani* of Center Place."

Moquihix's voice rose up for those in the cliff house to hear. "And if you do not bring joy to my Lord Jakál, you and your clan will be sacrificed to the gods, at the next Solstice, on the altar of blood."

Two

HOSHI'TIWA trudged with the army of the Dark Lord, limping because her bare feet were unaccustomed to the hard paving stones of the road. Gradually her settlement vanished, and she no longer heard the cries and wails of her family in the cliff house. Ahead lay the wide, paved highway the Dark Lords had built, shooting arrow-straight through valleys and between mesas, past settlements and cliff dwellings and farms, a road that led to Center Place and Hoshi'tiwa's unknown destiny.

At the head of the procession, the Dark Lord rode upon his magnificent throne borne upon the shoulders of forty slaves, who were themselves dressed in splendid finery. Hoshi'tiwa could only see the back of the throne, and rising above it, the long green plumes of the Lord's headdress. The high official, Moquihix, also rode on a litter, but a smaller one, carried by only six slaves. He was followed by the Jaguars clad in spotted animal skins and carrying shields and flint-tipped spears—proud and violent men. Bringing up the rear of the procession were slaves bearing food and supplies, their burdens in sacks on their backs with tumplines across their foreheads.

Hoshi'tiwa was filled with terror. Was the terrible act to take place that night? I shall just lie there, she vowed. Let him have his way.

But that would not give him pleasure.

What was she supposed to do? Were the Lords like normal people? She had heard that they were part beast. *Which part?* Icy perspiration broke out on her body and she trembled with fear and sickness.

At dusk the army came to a halt and Hoshi'tiwa was startled to see, at the side of the highway, a vast encampment of people of all ages, tied together, crying or protesting, captives like herself. The Jaguars retreated to the far side of the camp, and the Dark Lord was carried to a type of shelter Hoshi'tiwa had never seen before: brightly colored cloth supported on poles with a doorway cut into one cloth wall. Into this splendid tent the Dark Lord disappeared.

The high official, Moquihix, gestured to an overseer to bring Hoshi'tiwa. But instead of being led to the Lord's tent, she was taken to a campfire where other captives were tied together, protesting and begging to be set free. The official spoke sharply to a slave poking the embers in the fire.

"See that this one does not escape."

"I obey," the slave said, and Moquihix strode away.

After the official was gone, the slave, a potbellied man wearing a stained loincloth and a dirty white cape tied at the throat, straightened and made a rude gesture in the direction of Moquihix; then he fixed a bleary eye on the newcomer. Hoshi'tiwa could not help staring at the man. She had never seen someone without a nose before.

He saw the look on her face. He had seen it many times. "Got it cut off years ago for sneezing in the presence of a Lord."

Producing a rope of yucca fibers, he tied it around her ankle and secured it to a wooden stake in the ground, leaving a tether long enough for Hoshi'tiwa to walk a few paces.

"Is this . . . ," she began, looking around with frightened eyes. In the west, the sun was setting, casting long shadows across the plains and valleys. "Is this Center Place?"

The noseless slave gave her an absurd look and addressed the fire.

An overseer came with corn tortillas, which he threw to the ground, and instantly the captives were upon them. By the time Hoshi'tiwa could get through, there were no tortillas left. He had also brought a gourd of water to be passed around, and when it reached her, it was empty.

"You have to be quick if you want to reach Center Place alive," said the noseless one, who, because he was an overseer—although of a lesser rank—munched on a corn cake and gulped from his own water skin, offering nothing to the girl.

Choking back her tears, Hoshi'tiwa wanted to blurt, "I am not meant to reach Center Place; therefore, they do not care if I am fed or not." But she said nothing, retreating into herself.

Darkness fell, the stars came out, and the plain flared with the glowing lights of campfires. The moans of the captives rose into the air to mingle with the singing of the Jaguars, who had built an enormous bonfire, sparks rising like fireflies to the sky. Hoshi'tiwa had never heard so much noise. It was the sound of collective human agony.

She looked westward toward dark mesas and night-filled canyons, imagining Ahoté already sprinting silently down the highway. *He will come for me. He will save me.*

As her fellow captives jockeyed for space near the fire—most wore only loincloths, and a cold spring night was coming—Hoshi'tiwa could not stop weeping. Noseless, as he was called, snapped at her to keep quiet. He was drinking *nequhtli,* a foamy, thick intoxicating beverage made from the fermented sap of the maguey plant. He drank noisily, wiped his hand across his mouth, and told the girl that she should feel honored. "The Lords are *toltecatl,* because their home is far to the south in a city called Tollan. Your Lord is a *toltecah* and therefore superior to you."

While he spoke, Hoshi'tiwa surreptitiously picked at the rope on her ankle. As soon as everyone was asleep, she was going to escape, meet Ahoté on the road, and run away with him.

Noseless scratched his belly and boasted: "I myself have Toltec blood as I am descended from a long line of *pochtecas,* honorable and crafty merchants who conducted trade over long distances. My great-grandfather owned his own land, we were that respected." Noseless sighed, refilled his cup, and drank. "My ancestor came to Center Place in search of sky-stone. What he found was a simple people who raised corn and lived in plain houses and who were eager to serve. He thought he had found paradise. Word spread throughout his homeland to the south, through Tollan, and as far away as Chichén Itzá—come north where the people are docile, they will grow your corn and give you sky-stone and you will live like kings."

A bloodthirsty howl rose suddenly among the Jaguars on the far side of the encampment. Noseless glanced quickly in their direction, and then away, gulping at his drink. Hoshi'tiwa thought she glimpsed fear in his eyes.

"I have the blood of *your* people in me," he said morosely, "which is why I am an overseer of slaves, because I speak your tongue and understand your ways." His voice rose in false bravado. "But I am more Toltec because Toltec blood is strong!" He thumped his bare chest. "While the People of the Sun were digging pits in the ground, my ancestors were building pyramids to the sky!"

He refilled his cup and glanced nervously in the direction of the boisterous Jaguars again. "It was because of my great-grandfather's success, and that of other brave *pochtecas* like him, that the King sent a *tlatoani* to govern us. *Tlatoanis* have lived here since." His red-eyed glance slid to the colorful tent that was now aglow with light from within.

Hoshi'tiwa could not imagine what the Dark Lord was doing in his magnificent tent, but everyone knew that the Dark Lords cut up human flesh and ate it with corn.

Eventually Noseless fell asleep, and the other captives and even the Jaguars grew quiet as the night grew cold. Giving up on the rope, Hoshi'tiwa curled up and cried herself to sleep, to dream of home and her beloved Ahoté.

She was awakened by a rough hand on her mouth, clamped down so that she could not breathe. Other rough hands were pulling at her thighs, prying her legs open. Her heart jumped in fear. Was this how the Dark Lord did it?

And then she saw the ugly face of the brute who held her down. He was one of the overseeing guards. The grunts of the other two men were muffled as they struggled to hold her down. She felt cold air on her legs as her skirt was roughly pulled up.

Heaving for breath and trying to free her pinned arms, she opened her mouth and chomped down hard on the rough hand, biting into the leathery palm and drawing blood. The guard howled and cursed, and in the brief instant that her mouth was free, Hoshi'tiwa shrieked at the top of her lungs.

"Be silent!" her attacker hissed, but she felt the hands lift from her legs, and heard heavy footfalls thudding away. And then the remaining brute suddenly sat up, a surprised look on his face, and fell sideways, the spear of a Jaguar protruding bloodily through his chest.

Hoshi'tiwa scrambled away as far as the tether would allow, frantically brought her skirt down and dragged her knees to her chest. Through tears she saw Moquihix striding up. He barked an order at two other guards who came and dragged the body away. Then he engaged in a brief, angry exchange with Noseless, who sheepishly said, "Yes, my Lord."

Before returning to his place by the fire, Noseless stood over her and said bitterly, "It seems my job has been made harder, as now I must, in addition to all my other burdens, guard that precious flower between your legs."

On this, she and the repulsive slave agreed. But Hoshi'tiwa had her own reasons for protecting her virtue. Once she was used by the Dark Lord, no man would want her, not even Ahoté. Never marrying meant no children, earning for Hoshi'tiwa the scorn and pity of everyone around her. Not only must she protect herself against every brute that marched with this army, but she had to think of a way to evade the prince's lusty embrace. Perhaps make herself undesirable in some way.

Or would that make the gods angry?

And whose gods? On this Hoshi'tiwa was uncertain. She knew that before the Lords came, the People of the Sun were watched over by invisible benevolent beings who brought rain, made crops grow, and created balance in the world. Hoshi'tiwa's people did not so much worship these spirits as avoid offending them. If nature was thrown out of balance, resulting in catastrophic flood or crop failure, or a disease that wiped out a tribe, then it was because the spirits of balance were unhappy and must be appeased.

But since the arrival of the Lords, long before Hoshi'tiwa was born, new gods had insinuated themselves into the world of the unseen, brought from the south by the invaders, gods that took human form and had names, like Tlaloc, god of rain, and they had tempers and appetites. Some of these superior beings even had families. It was whispered late at night, among the men in her clan, that the spirits of the People of the Sun were being pushed out by the stronger sky-beings, those with names and form and weapons, and that someday the world was going to be so out of balance that it would come to an end.

So which gods must she appease by giving herself to the Dark Lord? What invisible spirits watched over the maiden Hoshi'tiwa and made such a demand of her? Being so far from her village and the sage wisdom of the elders, Hoshi'tiwa had no one to turn to, nowhere to search for answers except in her own young, inexperienced heart.

And then she thought of her family and the shame she would bring upon them if she ran from a trial of courage and bravery. She knew what was expected of her: to sacrifice herself for the honor of the clan.

After the Lord was done with her, Hoshi'tiwa was expected to kill herself.

So went her miserable thoughts, around and around in her head like a poor tethered animal, arriving at no conclusion.

The next morning she awoke to find Noseless cutting the bonds of three captives who had died during the night, salvaging the precious rope.

Overseers moved through the massive encampment, throwing corn tortillas to the captives and handing around gourds of water. Again Hoshi'tiwa had nothing to eat or drink. Good, she thought miserably. Perhaps the Lord won't want to bed a girl who is skin and bones.

Noseless was in a bad mood and complained that demons shouted in his head. As he lined up his charges and retied them ankle to ankle for the day's march, Hoshi'tiwa noticed that he glanced frequently at the Jaguars, who were assembling with their spears and shields. Again, she thought she saw fear in his eyes.

The high official, Moquihix, climbed onto a rock and shouted for attention, his scarlet cloak and deep blue tunic gleaming in the sun, the feathers of his headdress dancing in the breeze. The gathered mass of humanity fell silent. When Moquihix announced the emergence of the Dark Lord, all fell to their knees, pressing their faces to the ground and covering their heads with their arms. The Lords were called Dark because the people did not know what they looked like, as it was forbidden to raise eyes to them. Only the slain had seen the Dark Lords. Yet as the captives prostrated themselves before the figure on the great carrying chair, Hoshi'tiwa could not resist lifting her head to glimpse the Dark Lord passing by, this man who was to seal her doom.

She stared. He was not dark at all, but costumed in such brilliant finery that the scarlets and bright yellows and dazzling blues hurt the eyes. She had no sense of the man, for he was all plumage and flowers, as resplendent as a god.

And then she felt a sharp pain at the back of her head, heard a loud crack, and saw stars and planets before being engulfed in darkness.

When she came to, the sun was high and she was stumbling along the road between two slaves, who had her by the arms. Her head throbbed and she realized she had been struck by an overseer for daring to look upon the Dark Lord. She was hungry and thirsty, and her bare feet were blistered. But the mass of moving humanity did not stop. Overseers came through the lines with tortillas and water, and this time Hoshi'tiwa grabbed her share.

As the river of humanity flowed eastward, mountain ranges gave way to long lines of mesas separated by canyons faced with cliffs of red and golden sandstone. Here and there rose a small island of mountain forest, but they grew fewer and farther between, and lakes and creeks became increasingly harder to find.

Noon brought them to a trickling stream, and overseers distributed empty waterskins to the captives, who were led to the creek with orders to fill the skins. Men came through and sealed each bulging waterskin with pine pitch. As the captives were mustered and moving along the road again, each man, woman, and child now burdened with a heavy waterskin, Noseless said, "Do not dare to drink from that which you carry. That water is for Center Place."

At dusk, the procession halted and the Jaguars broke rank, shouting and banging their spears on their shields, filling the plain with a roar. They immediately began building their nightly bonfire, and commenced their games and dances. Hoshi'tiwa could not see them from her side of the vast camp, but she heard them chanting around their bonfire and playing high-spirited games by torchlight.

She again expected to be taken to the Dark Lord's tent but was once more staked to the ground as water and tortillas were distributed. She could barely eat as anticipation of her night with the Lord made her ill. What was he waiting for?

As the shouts and drums of the soldiers rose to the stars, freezing the marrow in one's bones, Hoshi'tiwa asked Noseless what was happening.

He gave her a blank look, as if she had inquired about the obvious. "These are the Eight Days."

"Eight days?"

His eyebrows lowered over the two holes that served as nostrils. "An uncertain time for the Dark Lord and the Jaguars. A time when," he looked over his shoulder, "anything can happen."

His tone made the back of her neck prickle. "What happens on the eighth day?"

When he didn't respond, she looked around at the hundreds of men, women, and children clustered around campfires. "Why have all these people been rounded up?"

He shrugged. "To serve the Lords."

But a creeping fear made Hoshi'tiwa think the people had been collected for another reason.

And so it went. Each night the Jaguars grew increasingly wild, and during the day Hoshi'tiwa sensed agitation in the way they marched, as if they were barely under control. On the sixth night as Moquihix passed through the small camps, she saw that his body was stiff with tension, his eyes wary and alert. And Noseless drank as if he were afraid of something, until he passed out from the *nequhtli.*

Finally Hoshi'tiwa could not sleep, but lay shivering beneath the stars and wondering once again: What happens on the eighth day?

Three

THEY arrived at a point where the broad highway met another, and the procession turned southward. From there the highway climbed steadily up from the flat plain. They camped that night at the base of a small mesa.

And Hoshi'tiwa knew at once that something was terribly wrong. The Jaguars were silent.

A strange quiet descended upon the vast camp, despite the numbers, despite the glowing campfires. No flutes were played, there was no sound of games of chance, no conversation, not even the ubiquitous moaning and pleading.

Hoshi'tiwa sat with her knees drawn to her chest, rocking back and forth in fear. Her world had become a nightmare. She was far from home, far from the familiar. Her red tunic was torn and her hair had come undone from its maidenly coils. She had managed to bind her injured feet with plant leaves, but the periodic tortillas and water did nothing to stop the hollow ache in her stomach.

"The Lord wants to join his body with yours."

Hoshi'tiwa drifted off to sleep with her cheeks wet with tears, and awoke suddenly from a dream to see a shadowy figure creep from the Dark Lord's tent and disappear into the piñon pines that lined the road.

She stayed awake, and at dawn saw the cloaked figure slip back into the tent. The procession did not move that day, but remained at the foot of the mesa.

Hoshi'tiwa's apprehension grew. The moment was coming. Moqui-hix would stand before her and demand that she follow. The big colorful tent would swallow her like a ravenous beast, and the daughter of Sihu'-mana would be no more.

As they ate noon tortillas, Hoshi'tiwa asked Noseless who it was she had seen come and go from the Lord's tent, and he said sharply, "We cannot speak of such things." So she knew it must have been the Dark Lord himself, for it was forbidden even to talk about him.

Sunset came, and tensions rose with the moon. The Jaguars did not build a bonfire. They did not eat or sing but sat watching the stars. No one could sleep that night, not even the captives who, like Hoshi'tiwa, did not know what was happening but who nonetheless sensed uneasiness in their overseers.

At the hour past midnight, Hoshi'tiwa saw the dark figure steal once again from the Lord's tent and disappear into the piñon forest.

Where did he go each night?

As the next day was spent in apprehensive waiting, the overseers' nerves frayed, everyone on edge, Hoshi'tiwa wondered if she could make a good escape unnoticed.

The sun set and the stars came out, Noseless drank more than usual, his noisy gulps sounding desperate in the hushed silence, as if he were gulping back his fear. This was the eighth night.

The *nequhtli* loosened the old slave's tongue so that he soon grew maudlin and once again lamented about days gone by. Lifting his cup in the direction of the Dark Lord's tent, he said loudly, "Lord Jakál is more than a *tlatoani,* he is the noblest of *tlatoanis,* for his bloodline goes back to the glorious days of Teotihuacan, and there is no greater glory than that!" He gulped the liquor and looked at Hoshi'tiwa with unfocused eyes. "But Lord Jakál has suffered great misfortune. Three years ago his wife died in childbed and since then no woman has gladdened my Lord's heart."

Noseless sobbed loudly and dashed the tears from his cheeks. As he lifted his cup to drink again, Moquihix and two Jaguars materialized out of the night. Without a word, the soldiers seized the startled man by his arms and dragged him away, and Hoshi'tiwa, terrified and speechless, watched poor Noseless disappear into the night.

The next morning, before the overseers brought tortillas and water, Moquihix stood on a tree stump and made an announcement. Someone was being punished for breaking the rule of uttering his *tlatoani*'s name. "You are all to learn a lesson from this." He turned and pointed, and everyone saw what had not been initially visible in first light: a naked man lashed to a pine tree, his bloody face blackened by the horde of flies that feasted there, for it was apparent his tongue had been cut out. He was still alive, and he moaned.

Hoshi'tiwa realized in shock that it was Noseless, and she immediately doubled over, her empty stomach heaving. She sank to her knees and broke out in a cold sweat. The world swam around her. What a monster the Dark Lord was to impose such a punishment on a man. All Noseless was guilty of was bragging about his Lord.

Four

NOSELESS died at sunset, but his body was left on the tree as a reminder of the strict laws of the Dark Lords. Jaguars were stationed next to it, to keep coyotes and vultures away.

Again the night camp was chillingly silent, and the soldiers built no bonfire as they waited in darkness. A day of picking at the rope around her ankle had loosened it. Hoshi'tiwa was free to run. But when midnight came, something stopped her. No one would see her go; no one would miss her. And yet she waited.

When the cloaked figure crept again from the Dark Lord's tent and disappeared among the piñon pines, Hoshi'tiwa knew why she had not run away. She could not resist. She needed to know. After she saw the features of the monster who had destroyed her life, had stolen the hope of her people, she would run and not look back.

Slipping her foot out of the tether, she stepped among the sleeping captives and followed.

As she made her way quietly along the narrow trail, staying well behind the Dark Lord, she reminded herself that Noseless had been killed for having merely talked about the Lord. How much fiercer the punishment to actually look upon him! Yet, although Hoshi'tiwa's neck prickled with anticipation of a Jaguar's sword, she could not turn back.

The trail emerged at the top of the flat mesa overlooking the dark world that stretched away to the horizon. The only light came from the stars and the waning moon. A cool wind blew. No sounds drifted up from the encampment below. Hoshi'tiwa was struck by the notion that she and the Dark Lord were the only two people on earth.

She quietly stole around the edge of the small plateau, remaining hidden in a clump of tall sagebrush. She held her breath as she watched the Dark Lord walk to the edge of the cliff and drop his cloak to the ground.

She was surprised to see that he wore only a simple loincloth, so that moonlight carved hills and valleys along his sinewy arms and legs. His body was tense as he stood erect with arms out, as if to gather the dawn into a lover's embrace. His headdress was simpler than the one he wore during the day, yet Hoshi'tiwa thought it was all the more elegant in its simplicity, for the long plumes that played in the breeze glinted with bright green highlights in the moon's glow.

Hoshi'tiwa had never seen a man like him before. The men of her tribe were short and stocky. But this man was tall, with long limbs and an elongated skull, an impressive nose. In profile, with the plumed head-dress blowing in the breeze, he resembled a remarkable bird. And his ink-black hair was long, flowing over his shoulders and down his back, whereas Hoshi'tiwa's brothers and uncles wore their hair short.

She was confused. The Dark Lord didn't look like a monster at all. He was in fact . . . *beautiful.*

And then she realized: This was not the Dark Lord.

He began to sing, a mournful, high-pitched birdlike song. Every muscle of his lithe, sinewy body quivered. She looked in the direction he was facing, out over the dark plain. She held her breath. And then she saw it: a spark on the dark horizon where the sun was due to appear.

The song changed. It sounded like a chant of triumph, worship, and joy. And she realized these were not sun-worshippers, as her own people were, but rather their god was the Morning Star.

And then abruptly his singing stopped.

Hoshi'tiwa stiffened. Had he sensed her presence?

He turned, his sharp, shadowed eyes searching the darkness. When he found her, and their eyes met, her heart skipped, not from fear but from something she did not, in that moment, understand. To her surprise, he did not fly into an outrage but stood there beneath the night sky, still and silent, dark eyes in shadow until she finally found the courage to slowly back into the trees and hurry down the trail. Now was the time to escape. She would keep running and not stop until she reached her family at the end of the highway.

But when she arrived at the foot of the trail, Moquihix was there with two Jaguars who immediately seized her, tied her arms and wrists, and led her away.

Five

HOSHI'TIWA was sick with fear and thought dawn would never come. The Jaguars had tied her up behind the smaller tent that served as Moquihix's shelter. While she waited for them to come and lash her to a tree, committing her to the same horrible fate as Noseless, she shook and trembled. They had cut out the old slave's tongue for his reckless speech; surely they would gouge out her eyes for having looked upon the Lord.

Yet when dawn broke over the plateau and the valley below, she heard only a great shout from the Jaguars, a tremendous roar as if rising from one throat, and there was jubilation in that roar that she recognized, for her own people cried out with the same joy on the Solstice days and the Equinox rituals. They had been waiting for the first glimmer of the Morning Star.

Hoshi'tiwa realized now why she had not been executed. She had guessed correctly that the man she had spied on was not the Dark Lord. A priest, perhaps. A seer or holy man whose job it was to summon the Morning Star back from its eight days of hiding. She realized something else: that she had not yet been summoned to the bed of the Dark Lord because the eight days were a holy week and the Lord would not pollute himself with a woman. At Center Place, Hoshi'tiwa knew now, the terrible deed would take place.

The procession resumed, but this time in a lively mood, all tension and nervousness dispelled. The day was warm, the sun rose high, and Hoshi'tiwa, burdened once more with a heavy waterskin, was tied up with the other captives.

The main road continued south through a land covered in sparse, scrubby vegetation, and followed the rim of a deep canyon. Far below, Hoshi'tiwa saw farms strung along the course of a waterway that appeared to have once accommodated a wide river but which was now little more than a stream. Thousands of people were camped on the plain all the way to the far cliffs on the other side of the vast canyon, living in shelters made of grass and twig, or crouched around campfires. Directly below, she saw something that made her eyes widen in astonishment.

Abutting the base of the steep escarpment was a massive stone complex that was many times larger than her own village back home. The structure rose in five stories and consisted of apartments, plazas, stairways, and kivas, built in a curved shape, like a great rocky rainbow, alive with more people than Hoshi'tiwa imagined existed. Men on scaffolding were repairing brick and mortar on the immense walls, while others resurfaced with fresh plaster so that the towering walls shone in the sun. Terraces were filled with people working, cooking, socializing. Smoke plumes rose from a hundred firepits. And a bustling marketplace filled the main plaza. It made her think of a beehive.

She recalled something her father had said long ago, when he had returned from a visit to Center Place: "The Toltecs construct large buildings—larger than any you can imagine. They call them rising-splendors, because they are built for the gods and they rise in splendor to heaven. Each is named for a god. The largest rising-splendor, where the Dark Lord lives, is called Precious Green."

When the weary procession descended the cliff and came to a halt in front of the rising-splendor called Precious Green, the Jaguars dispersed to their wooden barracks, and high officials in brilliant robes and headdresses came out to receive Lord Jakál from his carrying chair and accompany him into the building. Hoshi'tiwa tried to peer over the heads of the crowd to catch a glimpse of the handsome Morning Star priest, but the crowd was too thick.

Overseers moved through the captives, ordering them to lay down their waterskins. Servants came running from the stone building to gather the precious skins. The overseers then selected skilled artisans to be sent to respective guilds, workers for the few planted fields near Center Place, and those who would work as servants to the Lords. The remaining captives would be marched southward, where they were to harvest wood, grass, and animal droppings for the many cook fires at Center Place, since fuel had grown scarce on these mesas.

Hoshi'tiwa's eyes were wide as they took in the majestic rising-splendor, the swarms of people, the noise and smoke that filled the canyon. She was struck by the dustiness everywhere, the dryness in the air, the lack of green vegetation. Understanding now why they had stopped at a stream to fill waterskins, which were being hurried into Precious Green, Hoshi'tiwa thought: These people are thirsting.

Released from her bonds, she stiffened her spine and squared her shoulders. Now she would be taken to the Lord.

But when Moquihix and the two blue-skinned priests with their flutes made of human shinbones led her away from the main plaza, through the throng that parted for the official, around to the eastern end of Precious Green, and came to a halt before a pottery workshop, Hoshi'tiwa looked about in confusion.

Inside the cluster of noisy, cluttered rooms, women and girls were at their various tasks, working the clay, coiling, shaping, sanding, painting, or tending the kiln. When the pottery workers saw Moquihix and the priests, they instantly ceased their labors and fell to their knees, pressing their foreheads to the floor.

Seeing the look of confusion on her face, the High Minister said to Hoshi'tiwa, "You are a skilled potter, are you not, from a family of potters who make rain jars?"

"I was brought here to make *pottery*?" she blurted.

"Why else would you have been brought to Center Place?"

Her eyes flickered toward the main building, and Moquihix read her meaning. Over his shoulder he said something in his native tongue, Nahuatl, to the two Jaguars accompanying him and they laughed in an ugly way.

Hoshi'tiwa flushed fiercely. And then she wondered how such a misunderstanding could have taken place. He had clearly said, for all the clan to hear, "Give pleasure to the Lord." He had said nothing about pottery. But as he slid his heavy-lidded eyes back to her, a shocking thought jolted in her mind: He had lied.

She frowned in puzzlement. But there had been the order to Noseless to protect her virginity. And then she realized: It was not for the Dark Lord, but so that her maidenly purity would find its way into the clay, because everyone knew that the work of maidens was ritualistically cleaner than that of women who had lain with men.

". . . to create a jar that will summon rain to Center Place," the high official was saying. "When rain comes, it will bring joy to the heart of our noble *tlatoani,* Jakál from the Place of Reeds, Guardian of the Sacred Plume, Watcher of the Sky, Lord of the Two Rivers and Five Mountains."

Hoshi'tiwa stared at the flat, expressionless face and saw something in his eyes that chilled her to the marrow. It was the look of utter power.

Her heart pounded as she thought: For eight days I lived in shame. I am *makai-yó* for no reason. And I am powerless to do anything about it.

Moquihix rapped his skull-topped staff on the stone pavings and intoned loudly, "Girl from the northern settlement, girl who is dust beneath your Lord's sandals, you will bring rain by the next Solstice, or you and all your clan will be sacrificed to the gods on the altar of blood."

Thus was Hoshi'tiwa's name her destiny, because in the language of the People of the Sun, *hoshi'tiwa* meant "maiden who brings rain." The night she entered the world, the skies poured down a great storm and the farmers and their families rejoiced in the rain. It was why, everyone said, her rain jars were special, because they never failed to attract the rain.

Numb with shock, she watched him go, and then she looked around her new home. The dusty floor of the workshop was littered with scrapers and trimmers and polishing stones. The distinctive pottery of Center Place—white ceramic with black designs—was stacked everywhere: pots, jars, pitchers, mugs, bowls, and figurines. Tupa, a large woman in a long dusty tunic with the insignia of an overseer embroidered on the breast, indicating that she ruled the elite Potters' Guild, inspected the new girl. She wrinkled her nose at Hoshi'tiwa and sniffed. "Filthy," she said, and gestured to a young woman with a yellow feather in her hair.

The girl led Hoshi'tiwa to the patio behind the workshop, told her to remove her red tunic and skirt, and gave her a long white short-sleeved sheath to wear. It was embroidered around the neck and the hem in the distinctive black-thread design of the Potters' Guild, signifying Hoshi'tiwa's rank as a novice. The girl was friendly and said she was sorry Hoshi'tiwa could not bathe, for water was scarce, but the women had filled a stone bin with coarse sand that had been mixed with crushed pine needles. Scrubbing with the scented sand was cleansing and refreshing. Tomorrow, the girl said, she would take Hoshi'tiwa to the potters' kiva, where they took ritualistic smoke-baths to purify themselves.

Her name was Yellow Feather, because of the yellow feather in her hair. "Except that I could not afford a real parrot feather, for that would have taken many pots and we are allowed only a few pieces for personal trade. Still, if you do not look closely, you cannot tell it is a turkey feather dyed yellow," she added with pride. Yellow Feather's blue embroidery indicated she was a middle-rank potter, and the tattoo on her cheek identified her as a member of Owl Clan.

Hoshi'tiwa went through the motions without speaking. She was numb with shock and a sick heart. She was not *makai-yó* after all. And yet . . . she was. Her family believed it to be so; therefore, it was so.

She could not bear to imagine what they were going through. Had Moquihix told the truth, that their daughter had been brought to Center Place for the honor of summoning rain, they would be celebrating. They would be enjoying a feast and recording the event on the Memory Wall. Ahoté's heart would swell with pride. And though Hoshi'tiwa might never return, her clan would rejoice in the knowledge that the gods had chosen her for a sacred purpose. And when word of this reached other people, they would flock to her village to trade for the gods-blessed rain jars.

Instead, Hoshi'tiwa's family wept beneath the cloud of shame. Her mother would die of a broken heart. Word of Hoshi'tiwa's ill fate would reach other settlements, and when they learned she was *makai-yó,* they would avoid her village, they would not come and trade for the rain jars, and the settlement would perish.

She scrubbed herself so vigorously that it hurt. Tears stung her eyes as her skin stung all over, and her mind silently cried: Ahoté will come! He will find me!

But what if he was unable? What if Takei forbade him to leave?

A sob escaped her throat as she sanded her arms and legs until they were raw. *I never told him that I love him. I was unable to speak the words. And my love-gift—the little owl—he will never find it!*

A new emotion was born in Hoshi'tiwa in that moment, springing up from the depths of her heart like sudden, new spring growth. A bitter feeling she had never before tasted: It was called regret.

She was returned to the workshop, where the mountainous Tupa glowered down at her. "Do you know how to sand?"

"I am a skilled potter—"

The willow wand hit her before she saw it coming, leaving a red welt on Hoshi'tiwa's bare arm. "That is not what I asked, insolent girl."

"Yes," Hoshi'tiwa said, fighting back the tears. "I know how to sand."

Sanding pottery was dirty, dusty, and tedious labor that created a soft haze of pottery dust, making the worker cough and sneeze. Back home, all the girls took turns at the unpleasant task so that it never fell to one person, but here it was all left to Hoshi'tiwa, the new girl, who toiled all that first day with dried corncobs, smoothing the unfired pots and bowls and jars that were stacked next to her. It was a delicate business, as one could sand a hole through the unfired ceramic, and rims were particularly fragile. As the day wore on and her hands grew tired, Hoshi'tiwa broke several pieces and felt Tupa's sharp willow wand across her back.

She would not cry. She swallowed down her confusion and grief, and squinted up at the cloudless sky hanging over Center Place. There was not the smallest puff of cloud. It seemed impossible to bring rain by the day of the Summer Solstice.

But she would do it. Closing her eyes, she drew strength from reliving her last moments with Ahoté in the cottonwoods, conjuring up the feel of his hands on her waist, recalling how tenderly he touched his nose to hers in a kiss, and hearing again his words as he had said, "I promise I will love you forever."

Therefore Hoshi'tiwa would create a rain jar that would bring rain to Center Place. By the time Ahoté came for her, the rain would have come and together they would leave this terrible place.

Six

"WHAT has happened?" Lord Jakál asked, rubbing his arms against the cold, as he wore only a loincloth and a cotton cape tied at his throat. He had been summoned to the Star Chamber in great urgency and thus was not attired in the heavy ceremonial robes he would normally wear in the sacred hall.

He was in the Star Chamber—a massive circular structure half-sunk into the earth on the far side of the canyon. Here, priests marked the movements of the stars, phases of the moon, and the risings and settings of planets. Sixty paces wide, making it the largest kiva in the valley, the brick-and-mortar observatory was lined with encircling masonry benches and fitted with four massive timbers, each as thick as a man's body, supporting the roof. Raised floor vaults served as foot drums, which echoed loudly when ceremonial dancers stamped on them, and thirty-four wall niches bore astronomical alignments that made them Solstice, Equinox, and celestial markers. A marvel of Toltec engineering, the sanctuary's entry and exit doors aligned exactly along the north and south axis, and on the Summer Solstice the first rays of the sun shone through a designated window, casting light on a precise spot on the opposite wall where magic symbols had been carved.

"It is about the girl who was brought this morning, my Lord," the Chief Priest said in worried tones. "The one who was brought to make rain jars. Something unforeseen has happened and we fear it is connected to her."

Jakál shivered. Night had fallen, and families across the valley and on the terraces were gathered for the evening meal, people visited with one another, gossiped, and played games until it was time for sleep. So, too, had the Lord of Center Place been relaxing with companions after the long journey to fetch the rain-girl when the unexpected messenger came, saying he must report to the Star Chamber at once.

"Unforeseen?" he said sharply.

The priests glanced at one another. They were afraid to speak, and so Moquihix, who was standing in the shadows—he, too, had been summoned hastily from his dinner—said, "Something catastrophic, my Lord."

Though light was dim in the observatory, the air filled with smoke and sacred incense, Jakál could see the tension among the men gathered there. And he sensed that he had been summoned to make a decision of great magnitude, for only such decisions were made in this Holy of Holies.

"Just after sunset, my Lord, a shooting star was seen."

It was the Chief Star Reader who had spoken. Jakál shot him a sharp look. He could not see the man's expression, as his face was painted with black stripes. The Star Readers were filthy men who never bathed or groomed, having disavowed all acknowledgment of human concerns. Their dirty, matted hair grew down to their ankles, they wore special sandals to accommodate their long, untrimmed toenails, and they stank so badly that people covered their noses whenever the holy men walked by. Among the complex priestly hierarchy at Center Place, the nameless Star Readers were the most revered.

"Where was the shooting star seen?" Jakál asked.

"In the southwestern sky, my Lord."

Southwest! The direction from which rain always came to Center Place. Now he knew why the summons had been so urgent.

Fear was palpable in the air. The Toltecs were terrified of shooting stars. Generations ago, the movements of the stars, planets, moon, and sun had been observed, calculated, and recorded with such exact precision that predictions of night-sky events could be made far into the future. Such astronomical knowledge made for a balanced cosmos and thus brought peace of mind, making men feel they were in control of their destinies. But shooting stars appeared unexpectedly and seemed to follow no law, upsetting the balance and reminding mortals that control was but an illusion. It had been agreed upon long ago that such phenomena were omens that must not be ignored, for what else could they be but signs from the gods?

What did *this* star-sign mean? Appearing in the southwest, the sign must have something to do with rain. But what? Jakál had already conferred with Moquihix and the priests about the girl's trespass upon sacred ground as he had stood awaiting the return of the Morning Star. Such a sacrilege had never happened before, and so they had not known what to do. Moquihix had ventured to say that, since the girl had not been stricken dead on the spot, the god must have allowed her to walk there.

Was Moquihix right, or had the shooting star been sent as a message that he had been wrong and the trespass must be punished?

"My Lord, there is more," the Chief Star Reader said, thin lips parting to reveal rotten teeth.

More? Jakál massaged his stomach, where chipotle peppers waged war. Was this turning into a catastrophic night? He looked at Moquihix. Though the square, flattish face was expressionless, Jakál saw fear in his High Minister's eyes and knew that it mirrored his own. "Tell me," he said grimly to the Star Reader.

"To interpret the shooting star, we consulted the books and found an ancient prophecy that speaks of a coming eclipse, one that we had not calculated for."

Jakál sucked in his breath. "An eclipse of what? The moon? The sun?"

"No, my Lord. It is an eclipse of something much greater."

Jakál frowned. What could be greater than an eclipse of the moon or the sun?

He shivered. An eclipse of the *world*? Since the beginning of time, the world had been destroyed and re-created four times. Everyone knew that this world, which the Toltecs called the Fifth World, would end someday. No one knew when, which was another reason astronomers kept a keen eye on the heavens, watching for signs and portents of imminent disaster. "Does this new eclipse involve the rain-girl?"

"We do not know, my Lord."

The air grew heavy in the Star Chamber. Darkness crowded around the knot of men gathered beneath flickering torchlight. Jakál struggled for breath. First the girl's trespass upon sacred ground. Then a shooting star. Now this prophecy of doom. He closed his eyes. Once again, as had been happening frequently of late, a forbidden yearning crept into his burdened heart: the wish to cast off the mantle of responsibility.

Reminding himself that he was a Toltec—a man who prized honor and duty above even life itself—he swallowed back his secret yearning and faced the new problem squarely.

According to ancient prophecy, a girl child would be born beneath an auspicious conjunction of planets and stars, with the evening star in ascendant—a girl destined to herald in a new age for Center Place. But the specifics of the fulfilled prophecy were unknown.

Jakál paced, his sandals whispering softly on the paved floor. Lord Jakál, the most powerful man in the land, was gripped in indecision. Had he made a mistake? When spies recently reported hearing of a corn grower who bragged about his daughter's magical ability to bring rain, Jakál had ordered her brought to Center Place. But now the Star Readers told him that they had consulted their charts and realized that the celestial conjunction referred to in the prophecy had occurred seventeen years ago. Moquihix reported that the rain-girl had been born seventeen summers prior, at approximately the time of the auspicious conjunction.

Was *she* the one foretold? But what was the eclipse, and what had the girl to do with it?

If only they knew the stars of her birth. Moquihix said the girl herself did not know, merely that she had been born in the spring. Her people did not mark the positions of the stars when a child came into the world, as the Toltecs did. Nor did the People of the Sun count days or give names to the months, unlike the Toltecs, who understood the necessity to name every single day, give every month a title, and assign numbers to the years.

Jakál turned to his High Minister. "She *is* a virgin, you are sure of that?"

Moquihix worked his lips. He had lost another tooth and did not like the feel of the gap in his mouth. Tooth loss was the first sign of a man's decline, a reminder of advancing age and the darkness that awaited on the other side. Probing the vacant tooth socket with the tip of his tongue, Moquihix said, "She is a virgin."

A secret underground passage ran beneath the floor of the Star Chamber, extending from the northern antechamber, passing under the kiva, and emerging at a masonry trench sunk into the floor. Used as a symbolic "underworld" in sacred ceremonies, the subterranean passageway now served a more prosaic purpose: to deliver a newcomer to the scene.

Xikli, Captain of the Jaguars, had not been summoned, but he had spies everywhere. Hearing of an urgent, late-night consultation in the Star Chamber between Jakál, Moquihix, and the Star Readers, Xikli decided his presence was required. His informants had already told him of the girl brought from an outlying settlement and established in the potters' workshop. The rumor was, she would bring rain to Center Place. And now, it seemed, the seers and soothsayers, guardians of Toltec destiny, suspected they had made a mistake.

If he were not in a holy of holies, Xikli would have spat.

Born thirty winters ago, making him twenty years younger than Moquihix and two years younger than Jakál, Xikli was a barrel-chested soldier of grotesque aspect. His face had been sliced by a knife in combat, diagonally from forehead to jaw. The Chief Physician had saved his life by stanching the blood with deer dung and cobwebs, and then stitching the edges of the wound together with maguey fibers attached to a thorn. But the scar had mended in a crooked, puckered line, crumpling Xikli's features into so horrific a visage that children gawked at him in the marketplace, and women looked away. This pleased him. Jaguars were meant to be feared.

The others in the Star Chamber were not surprised at his arrival. As Captain of the Jaguars, Xikli represented Blue Hummingbird, the god of war, and so had a right to be there.

"I, too, saw the shooting star," he growled. "It is a warning." Look at them, he thought, they are like old women fretting over a spoiled stew.

The Toltecs were the most powerful people on earth, and these men were the most powerful of Toltecs. Yet look how impotent they were when their ordered world was thrown off balance. Like ants when the anthill is kicked. And all because of a mere corn grower's daughter! Xikli saw the answer plain and clear: Slay the girl in honor of the gods. Offer her beating heart to Blue Hummingbird and be done with it.

The Captain of the Jaguars was not a complex man. He did not trouble himself with complicated or abstract thinking. Bloodletting was his answer to all problems, and if asked, Xikli would declare that there were not nearly enough human sacrifices taking place on the altar of blood. That was because Lord Jakál was dedicated to Quetzalcoatl, not to Blue Hummingbird, and Quetzalcoatl did not feast on human hearts. Quetzalcoatl preferred flowers and feathers.

Xikli almost grunted with contempt.

But he kept his emotions carefully masked so that no one knew what lurked in his discontented heart. For all their ancient books and star charts and knowledge of omens and prophecies, for all their watchfulness and interpretings, their keen eyes and questing minds—for all their god-given power and spiritual strengths, not one of these men had the slightest clue about Xikli's secret plan to seize power.

That Xikli was Jakál's sworn enemy was known only to Xikli himself. Not even his closest cronies and lieutenants knew of the Captain's secret ambition to someday rule Center Place—an ambition that perforce meant the removal, one way or another, of Jakál. But it was taboo to even think of overthrowing a reigning *tlatoani*. Were this ambition to be discovered, Xikli's head would adorn a spike in the main plaza. Therefore he bided his time and moved cautiously, gathering friends about him, men with power and wealth, as he sought a way to rid Center Place of Jakál and gain the throne for himself.

Part of his plan involved rain—or lack thereof. Xikli was relying on the continued drought to increase his chances of overthrowing Jakál's regime. But now there was this girl who supposedly possessed the magic to summon Tlaloc's Cloud Spirits.

He caught Moquihix's eye on him. Xikli didn't care what the old man suspected. The old fool lived in the past, yearned for the old ways and, given his choice, would return to Tollan like a beaten dog. Xikli had no patience for Moquihix, blind loyal supporter of Jakál. He, too, would be dealt with when the time came.

But first there was the prickly matter of the rain-girl.

"I say the prophecy means that the girl was to be brought here for special sacrifice," Xikli said in a voice grown gravelly from years of barking orders at his men.

"And I say," countered Jakál, "that she was brought here to summon rain."

"But the shooting star—"

"Is a coincidence, nothing more," Jakál snapped. He did not like the Captain of the Jaguars and suspected him of harboring forbidden ambitions.

"A coincidence?" Moquihix asked.

But they all knew that there was no such thing as coincidence. Physical phenomena represented the will of supernatural beings, and earthly men must not question.

Jakál retreated into thought. Was the girl bringing rain *and* ruin? It was possible. The universe comprised duality in all things—good and evil, hot and cold, wet and dry. It was impossible to have one without the opposite other. Even the great god Quetzalcoatl possessed a dual nature, in his contrasting aspects of the Morning Star and the Evening Star. Lord Jakál, trained as a priest of Quetzalcoatl, understood this concept.

He thought about the girl's trespass during his vigil for the Morning Star. The moment had been so deeply spiritual that when he turned and first saw her, he had thought she was an apparition, perhaps a manifestation of his god. And then he realized the truth and it had shocked him. Surely she must have known that she was committing the worst sacrilege and that death would result.

Since returning to Center Place, Jakál had not been able to put the incident from his mind. And now this shooting star!

But there was something else. . . .

It flitted at the edge of his consciousness like a bright moth glimpsed at the corner of the eye, only to disappear when one turned. A flash, but no substance. Jakál sensed that the flitting thought had to do with the rain-girl. More than her trespass. More than bringing rain. What was it . . . ?

Her face, round and pale like a moon, her eyes like luminous twin planets rising above the curved horizon . . . she had looked as if she had been created in that instant by the heavens, all star-shine and moon-glow, as if she had ridden to earth on the tail of a sparkling comet. Not a mortal girl, but a sky dancer from distant nebulae.

"My Lord?" Moquihix said.

"The gods must be consulted," Jakál finally said, forcing the image of Hoshi'tiwa from his mind, and his companions nodded in agreement. He turned to the guard who stood by the southern door, a burly young man carrying a spear decorated with feathers and wearing a leather breastplate painted with a giant butterfly. His wooden helmet was likewise adorned with colorful feathers, indicating his status as a personal guard to Lord Jakál. "Fetch Quail," his master said, and the man exited at a trot.

Quail was a man who kept sacred sacrificial birds, plump spotted-breast quails; it was his sole job, his life's focus, thus his name. If he ever had another name, he did not remember it, because the hour of his birth had taken place three generations ago. He no longer remembered his parents, brothers or sisters, or even where he'd grown up. Brought to Center Place as a boy to apprentice to then-Quail, he had learned the art of breeding and raising the sacred birds, how to weed out the imperfect specimens and to nurture those destined for the holy task of bringing messages from the gods. Living alone in a hut near the Star Chamber, the old and bent reader of omens was always on call. He alone knew the art of handling the bird as he sliced its breast open, to pluck out the heart while it still throbbed with life.

The Star Readers lit special incense and began their chant to alert the gods that a request was coming. Jakál, Xikli, and Moquihix watched in tense anticipation as Quail slit the plump breast of the bird quivering with terror in his hand, and deftly plucked out the still-beating heart. All bent forward to count the number of beats before it stopped.

Seven. The sacred number of Tlaloc, god of rain.

"The gods have spoken," declared the Chief Star Reader, spreading his hands over the dead bird, his long untrimmed fingernails resembling talons. "The girl will work at her craft in the potters' workshop and bring rain to Center Place."

When Xikli started to protest, being of sufficiently high rank and aristocratic blood to question priestly interpretations, Quail held up a bloody hand. Though of low birth and not a Toltec, *he* had sufficient power to cut short even the Captain of the Jaguars. He said, "There is more."

The men circling him stiffened. The air grew heavy with smoke and the stench of sweat from the Star Readers.

"This bird's heart is oversized," Quail said in a hoarse whisper, "which means that after the girl has brought rain to Center Place, she must be sacrificed in the main plaza on the altar of blood."

Across the valley, the workers in the Potters' Guild were sharing a supper of bean stew spiced with chili peppers served on hot corn tortillas. The women laughed and told stories, and groomed one another's hair, while Tupa the Overseer, having consumed four bowls of stew, con-

tented herself with mugs of *nequhtli,* becoming steadily intoxicated, as
Noseless had. Hoshi'tiwa ate in silence and did not take part in hairdressing or songs. And when the potters retired to their sleeping place
behind the workshop, under a roof of willow branches supported on
four poles, Hoshi'tiwa found a spot among the others, curled up, and fell
asleep to dream of Ahoté rescuing her.

Before dawn she awoke and crept outside to relieve herself. The stars
were still overhead, but the sky in the east was turning pale. She stood at
the corner of the southern wall and looked out at the impressive stone
settlement rising in tiers. As her eyes surveyed the hundreds of apartments, the deserted terraces, the empty plaza, and the silent kivas, she
felt the cold wind on her face and thought of the cold eyes of Moquihix,
the terrible trick he had played on her. She must find a way to send a
message to her family that she was not *makai-yó* after all.

She was about to return to the workshop when she heard singing
and, recognizing it, looked to the north where she saw, standing on a
promontory high above Center Place, a figure with his arms open to the
sky. It was the Morning Star priest, greeting the star with a sacred song.

She suddenly felt her heart swell with hope, his song was so beautiful. But then she saw the attendants with him, the robed priests and
Moquihix standing by with a splendid feathered headdress in his
hands—and the carrying chair, its seat empty. And Hoshi'tiwa realized
in shock that the man whom she had spied upon one night prior, when
she had profaned sacred ground, the man she had thought was a Morning Star priest was in fact Lord Jakál, the most powerful man in the
world.

Seven

WAS today going to be a good-luck day or a bad-luck day? Lady White Orchid wondered as she watched the smoke curl up from the incense and drift out the window of her villa.

The morning had already begun inauspiciously. The vague ache in her lower back, the sluggishness in her legs, and mild headache told her that her monthly time was upon her. She would make a pad of dried grass and secure it with a cotton belt to absorb the precious life-blood, which would then be burnt as an offering to the goddess of fertility, along with a prayer to the goddess of fertility.

White Orchid desperately wanted a baby.

Her only child had died when it was a few months old. While she drew some consolation from the knowledge that her tiny son now dwelled in the Nursemaid Tree, the mystical arbor where all babies went when they died, to be nursed lovingly by the tree's milk-filled breasts for eternity, his death weighed on her still. And her arms ached to hold an infant.

However, to get pregnant, she must be married, and Lady White

Orchid was a widow, her husband having perished the year before when he had inadvertently offended the god Xipe Totec and had been punished by an incurable wasting of the bowel. But finding a new husband was not easy. For a highborn lady like herself, the pool from which to draw a prospective spouse was small. Despite the thousands of inhabitants at Center Place, it was forbidden by law for the two races to intermarry. This left only the handful of Toltecs who ruled over the uncountable People of the Sun. And within her own race, the laws of status were strict: While a man could marry beneath himself, a woman could not. Even so, among the membership of nobles and high-born *pochteca* she could choose from, there was only one man in all the world with whom Lady White Orchid wished to tie a knot. Unfortunately, Lord Jakál did not reciprocate the sentiment.

When Lord Jakál's wife died in childbed, everyone thought he would take another wife. He did not, and showed no indication of ever doing so. But White Orchid was determined, and she used every opportunity to let her availability be known. Whenever her path crossed Jakál's, which she made sure was often, at festivals and ceremonies, in the great plaza, attending parties where all the nobles gathered, she managed to be near him, laughing at his wit, drawing his attention, complimenting him on his latest acquisition of birds, shells, sky-stone. Jakál was always polite, but nothing more.

How was she going to ensnare him? Time was trickling like sand, filling her with new urgency. Born twenty-eight summers ago, White Orchid was no longer considered young. How many fertile seasons were left to her?

The household altar held the small effigies of several gods, including White Orchid's personal goddess, Lady Precious Green, goddess of whirlpools and waterfalls, and Huehueteotl, god of fire, patron of the home and of childbirth. To these White Orchid made special obeisance because they ruled her womb.

The small shrine also honored the ancestors and contained a token from each of those who had lived and died in this house—a necklace, a lock of hair, a tooth. The dried umbilical cord from White Orchid's dead baby boy. Her mother's mirror. Grandfather's knife. So many tokens connecting White Orchid to the spirits of those who had gone before.

After Father dies, she thought with a chill, I will be alone in this house. When I die, who will add *my* token to these?

The incense burned down, the smoke drifted out the window, and when she tracked its path, observed how it curled and dissipated, White Orchid made a sound of dismay. The smoke told her it was going to be a bad-luck day.

Leaving the small sanctuary, she returned to her bedroom, where slaves were sweeping the stone floor, hanging up her sleeping mat, and feeding the long-tailed monkey White Orchid kept on a perch.

Two dozen slaves maintained the household of Tenoch the Hero and his daughter. The servants were all People of the Sun who wore rope collars to indicate their nonfree status. Only one freeman worked in the household, the personal bodyguard of Tenoch the Hero, and he was a Toltec.

The villas of the rich, located in the middle of the canyon on what used to be the banks of the river and surrounded by gardens, were spacious and built of adobe brick and wooden beams, and lime-washed so that they shone white in the sun. The lintels over the doorways were painted in bright colors, and each threshold was shaded by a four-post bower of twigs and branches. Inside, gaily painted wooden columns supported the roof, and woven mats covered the stone floors.

White Orchid had been born in this house, as had her mother and grandmother, and she loved it with a passion. There had been a time when the airy rooms were filled with family members and the walls heard female laughter, the shouts of men over *patolli* games. Now it was just her invalid father and herself—a situation that could not be allowed to continue. White Orchid had a duty to her ancestors to fill the house with life.

Two young women rushed forth with hairdressing tools, and White Orchid sat cross-legged on a mat so they could address the intricate taming of her long thick hair, the slaves kneeling on either side of their mistress as they combed and coiled and wrapped the sides of White Orchid's head with ribbons.

While they worked, their mistress focused her thoughts on Lord Jakál.

She recalled the day he arrived at Center Place, eight summers prior. The previous *tlatoani* had been cremated with much ceremony and his ashes placed in an urn to go back to Tollan. The caravan had snaked its way up through the canyon with everyone watching, anxious to know who the new ruler was going to be. When Jakál emerged from a great canopied carrying chair, arrayed in plumes and flowers and robes of dazzling colors, the People of the Sun, numbering in the thousands, fell to their knees and pressed their foreheads to the dust while the nobles of Center Place, and the officials and wealthy *pochtecas,* bowed in respect. Jakál had arrived with his wife, and White Orchid had herself been married at the time. When she had fallen in love with Jakál, she had kept it a secret because adultery was punishable by death. But now they were both without mates.

Surely Jakál did not plan to remain unmarried. The *tlatoani* had obligations to his people. The honor of his family name was at stake. Yet he seemed interested only in writing poetry and watching the skies for signs of Quetzalcoatl's return.

When the slave girls were done, they left White Orchid to inspect herself in a mirror made of polished obsidian. A few wrinkles here and there. She still had all her teeth. No gray hairs yet.

White Orchid proceeded with her cosmetics, painting her face after applying a dusting of fine yellow powder to cover her bronze complexion, and lastly coloring her teeth with cochineal, a dye derived from an insect that lived on cacti far to the south and imported to Center Place at great cost. Few women could afford cochineal, and therefore teeth stained red were a symbol of wealth and status. When she was done, she placed on her tongue a small lump of *tzictli,* a gum made from the sap of a rainforest tree. Flavored with mint, *tzictli* freshened the breath, and White Orchid had developed the habit of chewing it all day long.

She was anxious this morning to get to the marketplace. A new shipment of seashells had arrived, and she wanted to be the first to pick through and select the best. She had a passion for the curious object, which came in many shapes—cone, fan, spiral—and colors, from white to blue to deepest pink. While not sure what seashells were or what purpose they served—White Orchid had never seen an ocean or any large body of water—seashells delighted her eye. Her shell collection was well known, and she frequently invited friends to come and see her latest acquisitions.

Because this was a bad-luck day, which meant being extra careful where she walked, what colors she wore, whom she spoke to, White Orchid chose her attire with care.

Exchanging her nightdress for a brightly patterned skirt of soft cotton, over which went a deep red shift embroidered with yellow flowers, she was ready to leave the house and show the world how well the daughter of Tenoch lived. Because of her high status, White Orchid was allowed to wear sandals (forbidden to the commoners), just as she was permitted by law to wear cotton and jewelry and to paint her face.

Setting her pet monkey on her shoulder, White Orchid made her way through the spacious villa toward her father's suite, where she would pay her respects.

She paused first at the kitchen, as was her daily custom, to check on the preparation of Tenoch's breakfast. This morning she had ordered an egg, and approved now of the way it slowly cooked in the center of a soft tortilla. When beans and chilies were added, it would be taken to Tenoch along with a stone mug of hot *chocolatl*.

She glanced through the door that led from the kitchen to the rear garden, and her eyes fell upon a remarkable sight. An old woman and a lame boy were making their way up the dusty path to White Orchid's house.

The kitchen slaves gathered to watch, and the cook wiped her hands on a cloth, thinking to throw chili powder at the old beggars and drive them off, when White Orchid raised a hand to stop her. She watched the pair approach.

The old woman's crooked body was an extraordinary sight, festooned with strings, ropes, thongs, necklaces, pendants, and bracelets, all adorned with amulets, charms, fangs, small bones, medicine pouches, bits of wood, leaf, twig and bark, feathers and cowry shells, nuts and seeds, pods and roots, snakeskins and maguey ribbons. Like all itinerant merchants, she carried her wares upon her person. The boy was both cane and porter as she leaned on his shoulder for support while he carried on his back a large sack attached to a leather strap across his forehead. They walked with a limping, lurching, shuffling gait, like a grotesque, deformed beast on its last legs.

Such traveling merchants could not afford to buy a mat in the main marketplace, nor could they afford the Supervisor's bribe, so they carried their goods from house to house.

"The blessings of the gods," croaked the old one after bowing low in respect, her body clicking and clacking with its myriad trinkets. She spoke a patois of Nahuatl and her native tongue. "I offer cures for pains, aches, sleeplessness, falling hair, and drooping eyelids. I can strengthen hearts and blood and bowels. I offer salves, powders, teas, purgatives. I am at my Lady's service." She smacked her lips. "All we ask is a cup of water, for we have not had a drink in a day."

White Orchid thought about the coming day, the discomfort in her abdomen, and expressed her need in couched, polite terms. The small wrinkled face, like a nut left in the sun too long, retreated in thought, then the old peddler said, "Only one cure for monthly sickness." She made a circular gesture in front of her abdomen, and giggled.

"I am not married," White Orchid explained, and cautiously added in a low voice, "but I *would* like a baby."

The old woman sniffed the air. She scratched her rump. Looked to the left, then to the right. Then she shocked White Orchid by saying, "To him you are as invisible as the wind."

"I beg your pardon?"

Milky eyes skewered the lady. "There is a man who would give you a child, but he does not see you."

White Orchid made a quick sign to ward off bad luck and turned to go. But the old woman said, "I am not a witch, for I know such creatures must be destroyed. What I am is someone who has lived long and seen much. Your yearning is painted on your face like your cosmetics. There *is* a man you long for, is there not?"

White Orchid whispered, "Yes." And suddenly she wanted to ask, but was too afraid to, if there was an herb, a potion that could be given to Jakál that would open his heart.

The old woman guessed what was in the young noblewoman's mind and said, "I know of something. . . ."

And from those thin old lips White Orchid heard of a remarkable creature that lived in the rain forests far to the south, near Chichén Itzá—a serpent with magical venom that inflamed the hearts of indifferent men. "It is small and green, with a red tongue like fire. The snake lives in a camouflaged hole and rarely comes out. To hunt for this snake is dangerous, my Lady, as the venom is lethal as well as aphrodisiac, and so such a serpent must come at a high price. Are you willing to pay such a price?"

For the love of Lord Jakál, White Orchid would give everything she owned, even her prized seashell collection.

"When the caravan next comes to Center Place," the old woman said, "ask the Master of the Caravan. He will know the snake I speak of. And then soon," the old woman said with a wide grin, "no more monthly sickness, just baby growing in the belly!"

White Orchid instructed her cook to give the itinerant pair a gourd of water, suddenly excited by this glimmer of romantic hope, but as she turned to go, the old peddler suddenly said, "Beware, my Lady!"

White Orchid stared at her.

The old woman frowned and shuffled uncomfortably. "Forgive me," she said. "It is my burden. I am cursed with visions, and when I see them, I must speak."

"Visions? You saw a vision about me?"

"I warn you of a strange, mythical creature with eight arms. It wants to embrace you. Do not let it, for it will suffocate you."

Beneath the highborn lady's skeptical gaze, the old woman sighed with misery. Her name was Pikami and she carried a secret that was heavier than the goods adorning her frail body. She wanted to say to the lady: You see before you a bent old woman, and you think my spine is curved with age. But it is the weight of a terrible crime long ago that has curved my body. For you see, a guilty conscience is the heaviest burden of all.

"How do I protect myself from a mythical creature?" White Orchid asked.

"The vision tells me nothing more," Pikami said, and when she turned to leave, the lady stopped her and began to remove a costly bracelet. But Pikami said, "I cannot accept payment, for it is the will of the gods that when such a vision comes to me, I offer it freely."

After the old woman and her boy shuffled away, White Orchid withdrew inside the house and found her father in the garden, reclining beneath a shade bower, his slaves having just brought him back from the soldiers' kiva, where he had enjoyed his morning sweat-bath, and now he puffed on a clay pipe filled with tobacco, looking out at the parched field of corn his slaves were trying to coax to life.

Lady White Orchid was not so young that she did not recall when the river had come right up to the steps of their villa. In those days, it was a sporadic event, depending on rains and mountain runoff, a joyous occasion with much feasting and celebrating. Her father recalled when the river had *always* been at the steps of the villa, year-round, and water was aplenty, and they had canoe rides and went spear fishing. It was why her people had settled here and conquered the local inhabitants— because this valley reminded them so much of home, far in the south.

Now it was a sandy wasteland, the river trickled a distance away from the villas that had been built upon its older banks, and the people thirsted.

Tenoch looked up at his beautiful daughter, and his heart swelled with pride. White Orchid was named for a rain-forest flower she had never seen. Her name in Nahuatl had many syllables and meant "White Orchid with Morning Dew on Its Young Petals."

"Any news on the caravan from the south?" he asked.

She knelt next to him and stroked his wizened cheek. Like most men of his advanced age, Tenoch had sprouted long wispy whiskers from his chin. Since Toltecs did not have beards, nor shaved their faces, such whiskers denoted a long and brave life and were a badge of honor. "It has not been sighted yet, Father." She tried not to let her worry show. The caravan was late. She prayed it had not met with misadventure. It was their only connection to their homeland far to the south, and now the caravan might bring a solution to her dilemma over Jakál. A snake with aphrodisiac venom! "How are you feeling this morning?" she asked gently.

"My toes itch," he said with a grin that exposed his few remaining teeth. It was an old joke, but White Orchid laughed all the same.

Tenoch had lost his legs during a skirmish with northern raiders who were attacking outlying settlements. The invader's spear had pierced his legs from the side, skewering them together like deer haunches on a roasting spit. When the evil spirits of gangrene infested the wounds, the legs had had to be amputated above the knee. Nonetheless, he was given a hero's welcome when the platoon returned to Center Place, and he had received honors from the *tlatoani,* Jakál's predecessor, a man who appreciated a good battle and a brave warrior.

Tenoch's personal bodyguard, a big-nosed Toltec with faintly crossed eyes, was laying out his master's clothes. Every day White Orchid's father dressed in his warrior regalia, painted his face, combed his hair into a gray topknot, and readied himself to receive visitors. Years ago, the visitors had been an endless parade. They had come for favors, to pay homage, or just so they could brag to their friends that they had sat in the presence of the great Tenoch. That stream of guests had slowed to a trickle, like the river that used to run through Center Place, and now days went by without a single visitor, his old comrades having all died off and the younger ones uninterested in him, only in making legends of themselves.

When I marry Jakál, White Orchid thought as she stroked her father's leathery cheek, I will see that my father's greatness is remembered.

As Tenoch set aside his pipe, White Orchid noticed that he seemed troubled. "What is it, Father?"

He avoided her eyes. "Captain Xikli was in the kiva this morning." White Orchid stiffened. "And?"

"Once again he spoke to me about you."

She shuddered. "Father, please—"

He looked at her directly. "I didn't agree to anything, but White Orchid, you must remarry soon."

White Orchid's devotion to her father, her love and fierce protectiveness of him, was such that she would do anything for him. He had suffered a terrible disappointment in life. Tenoch had wanted his oldest son to follow in his footsteps and enter the ranks of the Jaguars, but the boy was born with a crooked spine, and despite attempts to straighten it, he did not live past his third birthday. White Orchid had tried since to fill those footsteps. But unfortunately, with the death of that boy, the family military tradition, which had begun with Tenoch's great-grandfather when he had established the garrison at Center Place, came to an end.

"Xikli is a loathsome man," she said. Was her father going to ask the ultimate sacrifice of her in the name of family honor? She grasped his hand and spoke quickly. "Father, listen, I have a plan." Dare she tell him about the magic rain-forest serpent? Would he disapprove, call it black magic? "Just give me time, Father, I beg of you."

While she protested, Tenoch's thoughts went elsewhere. White Orchid had misread his troubled expression, and he allowed the error to stand. Regarding Xikli, Tenoch was in fact pleased the Captain was still interested in marrying White Orchid. It was an excellent solution to both their problems. And Xikli was of noble blood, he had a courageous heart, and he was, above all, a man of honor. And he was virile. Tenoch knew that within a year he would be holding a grandchild in his arms.

No, among the troubles that plagued Tenoch on this spring morning, and what he could not tell his daughter, was the shooting star he had seen the evening before, and how everyone was talking about a secret, urgent meeting in the Star Chamber to which Lord Jakál himself had been summoned. But what went on and what was decided beneath the heavy roof of the circular observatory no one knew.

As he gazed out over the waterless fields, the dry riverbed, the villas on the other side and far behind them, the tawny cliffs of Center Place rising sharply to the morning sky, it occurred to Tenoch that this new event did have something to do with his daughter and Captain Xikli after all.

He felt in his old bones that a cataclysm was coming. And he feared he would be dead before it came and his daughter left unprotected and vulnerable. It was his duty as her father, no matter how much he loved her, to see that she was safely married before that catastrophe struck.

White Orchid might be a strong woman, but she was a woman all the same. For now, his name was protecting her and holding the greedy vultures at bay. For this reason, he maintained a semblance of health and vigor. He had commissioned a sculptor to carve two logs of ponderosa pine in the shape of human legs, bent at the knee. Slaves lifted Tenoch onto a carrying chair, the stumps of his thighs meeting the wooden legs, and with a blanket over them, he was carried thus on a litter about the marketplace so that everyone saw how vigorous Tenoch the Hero still was. But after his spirit had flown from its fleshy shell, then what?

Many men had their eye on his daughter. White Orchid lived in a fine villa with its own precious well from which groundwater sporadically flowed (the supply was small and brackish—but it was water, and so a fence had been built around it and guards put in place to keep others from stealing it), and a runoff canal, built a generation ago, crossed her property, also guarded against theft. White Orchid was of high noble lineage, and her father was the great Tenoch. Wealthy traders with ties to Tollan frequently came to him to arrange marriages between White Orchid and their sons, and several high officials in Jakál's administration had also approached him. But Tenoch had always had a soft spot for his only surviving child. He wanted her to be happy and refused to force her into an unwanted union.

Tenoch sighed beneath his burden. He loved her too much. He wanted her to be happy. How did one weigh happiness against duty?

"I will grant you some time," he said at last. "But I will not wait long, Daughter." With a shaking hand he reached for a mug filled with *nequhtli*. As he lifted the liquor to his lips, he avoided his daughter's eyes, ignored the shocked look on her face. Yes, it was only morning and already he was imbibing. But that was his business, not hers. Tenoch needed the alcohol. More and more lately, because of another trouble afflicting his heart, one that was growing, that terrified him, and that, above all, he must not reveal to his daughter.

White Orchid stared at her father, speechless. When had he started drinking so early in the day?

And then she noticed the mug he was drinking from: a ceramic imported from a town on the coast of Yucatán, famous for its whimsical pottery. White Orchid had bought it for Tenoch in the marketplace because of its unusual design—a bulbous creature with eight limbs. The merchant had said it was called an "octopus."

She was staring at it in shock, recalling the old woman's vision, when a slave entered to inform White Orchid she had a visitor. Kissing her father's head, which felt as fragile as a baby's skull beneath her lips, and promising to bring him a treat from the marketplace, she followed the slave into the atrium, where a handsome young man carrying a decorated spear waited. He wore a leather breastplate painted with a giant butterfly, and his wooden helmet was adorned with feathers, indicating his status as a personal guard to Lord Jakál.

"My Lady," he said in low tones. "I have news."

She led him out of hearing of others and turned with an expectant look. While she listened to his report of an urgent and secret meeting in the Star Chamber during the night, consisting of the priests, Moquihix, Xikli, and Lord Jakál, and involving a newly arrived girl named Hoshi'tiwa, White Orchid secretly congratulated herself on having selected this man to be her eyes and ears within the government. He had access to nearly all of Jakál's comings and goings and private conversations, and he could be counted on to be discreet. White Orchid knew the young guard was smitten with her.

She absorbed the news with interest. As each day passed without rain, as the sun beat down on fields where crops withered, more eyes turned to Jakál for a solution. Prolonged drought would weaken him as *tlatoani,* but rain, on the other hand, would bring not only food to

Center Place, but renewed popularity for Jakál and love from his people, as well.

Slipping a gold bracelet from her wrist, she handed it to the guard, saying, "You have done well," and his young eyes brightened with slavish devotion.

"Before you go, pay a visit to my father. Kneel before him and recite his heroic deeds. And then ask his blessing." It wasn't the first time White Orchid had bribed a soldier to pay homage to her father. And she wondered now if that was the root of his new drinking. Was Tenoch aware that his fame was fading? But if that were the reason, then why had the old herb peddler said that the octopus would suffocate her?

Dismissing the puzzling prophecy, and the problem of her father's drinking, she focused on two exciting new ideas: the rain-forest serpent, which she would use to enchant Lord Jakál, and the girl who was to bring rain. For the first, White Orchid would speak to the Caravan Master as soon as he arrived, and arrange for him to bring such a snake up from the south. For the second, she would purchase a small figurine of the rain god, blessed by the priests of Tlaloc, and take it to the potters' workshop to ensure the new girl's success in summoning rain.

As she called for her slaves and carrying chair, anticipating the pleasure of looking over the new shipment of seashells in the marketplace, and eager to hear if the caravan from the south had been sighted, Lady White Orchid smiled. Clearly she had read the incense smoke wrong. Not a bad-luck day, after all.

Eight

HOSHI'TIWA stared in shock at the visitor.

He had come to the workshop with so heavy a waterskin on his back that he walked stooped over, looking at the ground. The waterskin, fashioned from the hide of a doe, was strung from his forehead by a tumpline, and the man sweated and puffed as he shuffled across the workshop floor to where the water urn stood in the corner.

The man was a water-carrier, and Hoshi'tiwa would soon learn that such men were both necessary and despised at Center Place. As he filled the urn, Tupa watched with a careful eye, and when he was done, she checked the measure of liquid and then paid him in six cacao beans, meticulously counted out.

Hoshi'tiwa looked on in astonishment. Tupa was *buying* water!

After the man had left, Tupa announced that the delivery was less this time, and therefore it was necessary to begin rationing water until such time as it was plentiful again. One of the older potters was put in charge of monitoring the workers' visits to the urn, and how much they took.

While everyone made cries of protest, Hoshi'tiwa silently returned to

work. Although rationing water was a concept she could not grasp—
back home water was freely available from the nearby stream—she saw
it was but one more misery in the nightmare she now lived.

That evening after supper, a kindly older woman, whose hair was
not fully gray but whose face was lined with maturity, asked Hoshi'tiwa
why she kept to herself.

Hoshi'tiwa looked into the honest square face. Although the woman's
chin was scored with the blue tattoo of the Mountain Lion Clan,
Hoshi'tiwa saw a resemblance to her own mother, and so she said, "I am
makai-yó."

The woman, whose name was Yani, gasped softly. Her hand flew to
her mouth. Behind her fingers she whispered a magic spell and then
she traced a good-luck sign in the air. She glanced fearfully at Tupa,
who gulped *nequhtli* in the corner while waxing nostalgic over the
three husbands she had outlived.

Yani had encountered only one *makai-yó* in her life, years ago, a girl
who had been caught in a sexual embrace with a son of nobility. The girl
was dragged into the main plaza where, before all the people, she was
stripped naked, declared *makai-yó,* and then led to the stone altar, where
she had been tied down and, while alive and conscious, had her heart cut
from her breast, still beating, for all the world to see.

The girl's lover, Yani recalled with tears, had simply been sent back
to his home city in the south.

She saw now with relief that Tupa had not heard Hoshi'tiwa's ad-
mission; otherwise, the workshop would be turned upside down and
everything within ritualistically cleansed with fire.

"What happened to you, child?" Yani asked, her heart moved with
compassion, because that innocent girl of long ago had been her own
daughter.

Hoshi'tiwa told the woman her story, adding, "I am now *makai-yó*
because of Moquihix's deception. He spoke a falsehood so that I could
never run away and return to my clan. I am a prisoner here now, though
no ropes bind me and no guards watch me. But I do not wish to stay in
this terrible place."

"Terrible?" said Yani. "This place is not terrible. It is wondrous. People from the far corners of the land come here to speak to the gods, to find medicines and clothing, to join with distant relatives. Center Place is the heart of our people, Hoshi'tiwa."

"But it is run by the Toltecs."

"It was not always so, and," Yani lowered her voice, "perhaps it will not always be so. I love Center Place. I was born here. My mother taught me her craft in this very workshop, as her mother taught her. But I am the end of the line, for I have no children. Yet I am content. My bowls and my pitchers are my children."

Her words horrified Hoshi'tiwa, who vowed that she was not going to grow old with only bowls and pitchers for children.

And in the next moment, to her surprise—for what had he to do with children?—the memory of Lord Jakál on the first dawn of the Morning Star, when she had thought he was a priest, suddenly came to her mind.

His face: She had read so many things there—sadness, yearning, loneliness. Hoshi'tiwa recalled that Noseless had said Lord Jakál was unhappy and melancholy. When she felt her heart move for him, she reminded herself that Jakál was an eater of man-corn; he was a cannibal.

And he worshipped the Morning Star. This explained something about her captors. While her own people worshipped the sun and guided their lives according to its predictable and benevolent cycle, the Toltecs guided their lives by a star that wandered, that went this way and that in the sky, that disappeared for periods at a time, a star the people could never be sure would return! This explained their devious and untrustworthy nature.

And yet, Lord Jakál had sung to the Morning Star so beautifully. . . .

Laying a cautioning hand on Hoshi'tiwa's arm, Yani said quietly, "A word of advice, Daughter. Do not let these others here know that you are *makai-yó*." She looked over each shoulder at the women and girls engaged in grooming and gossip, and lowered her voice. "If they were to find out, things would go very badly for you."

Nine

I T was no use, Moquihix thought in frustration.

Pushing the slave girl away, he sat up on his sleeping mat and stared balefully at his limp manhood. Despite the girl's expert ministrations, she had failed to summon Moquihix's virility. Although she was a kitchen worker who spent her days grinding corn, it was also her duty to wake the master in the morning and give him pleasure. This was not the first time she had failed. It was happening too often of late, this alarming impotence. Like lost teeth, it made Moquihix think of the grave.

"My Lord," she began, but he made an impatient gesture that sent her from the bedroom.

Shoulders slumped, Moquihix thought: Without his manhood, is a man really a man? Is this a sign that the gods have forsaken me? Or is it age and nothing more?

Perhaps there was a potion, an herb that would solve the problem. He would speak with Nagual, the Chief Physician, about it.

Putting the vexing problem from his mind, Moquihix wrapped a cloak about himself and slipped outside to trot the short distance from the house to his personal sweat-bath. When he had lived at Precious Green, he had taken his sweat-bath in the large kiva restricted to high officials, and there he had sat in the heat and smoke and suffered the complaints, gossip, and small talk of the Chief Tax Collector, the Builder of Roads, First Architect, on and on, men of such self-importance that the sound of their voices made his ears ache.

Moquihix had been on his way to the Star Chamber, two summers prior, when he had looked at this small stone house tucked at the base of the southern cliff and found it appealing. Though one story with only five rooms and low ceilings, the house was nestled into a quiet niche at the end of a private path, and boasted a cottonwood tree in its garden. That a large family already lived there was of no consequence to Moquihix—People of the Sun, who had inhabited the stone house for generations. He merely had them evicted, all their possessions, dogs, and turkeys set out on the plain, with the startled family milling about in confusion.

They lived there still, having established a camp on the other side of Moquihix's garden wall, as if they hadn't the imagination to move away from where they had lived all their lives.

Moquihix ignored them. He despised the People of the Sun and tolerated them only because they were necessary for growing food, mining sky-stone, building rising-splendors, and serving the needs of their masters.

Inside his private sweat-bath that was not a kiva but had been built in the Toltec style—a curved stone wall hugging the back of the house, with smoke fanned in from a fire maintained by slaves outside—Moquihix sat naked on the stone bench and allowed his pores to open and release refreshing sweat all over his body. He missed the days when the bath consisted of steam instead of smoke, but now there was not enough water. Slapping his back, arms, and legs with a sheaf of aspen wands, hard enough only to inflict pleasant stings and awaken his skin, he finished his bath by scraping his body down with a clamshell and then drying off with the robe.

Returning to his bedroom, he allowed his slaves to commence the complex process of dressing him, braiding and adorning his long hair, and painting his bare arms with the symbols of his high office.

Seated on mats were his scribe—a young man ever-present with paper, pen, and ink, ready to take dictation—and the dream-reader, whom Moquihix consulted every morning before leaving his house.

Many things plagued the High Minister's mind as he sipped a mug of hot *chocolatl* while three slaves attired him in loincloth, cloak, sandals, and jewelry. The Council was meeting that afternoon and several pressing issues were to be discussed, debated, argued about, and most likely not resolved.

A road to the west toward the sky-stone mines had been washed out the previous summer by a flash flood and had still not been repaired, making access impossible. The Minister of Canals and Dams had reported that the northern reservoir was crumbling and would not withstand a heavy runoff, should rain come to Center Place. The Metalworkers' Guild was crying for more charcoal. Captain Xikli was protesting that he had not enough manpower to go to all the farms to enforce tax laws *and* maintain a contingent of soldiers at Center Place to fight raiders. On top of that, two officials who must receive priority—Keeper of Flowers and Keeper of Birds—were demanding their water quota be raised.

Moquihix massaged his temples. He had a headache. Supposedly all these problems were to be addressed by Lord Jakál, who presided over the Council. But truth be told, all Jakál cared about was building his new rising-splendor, leaving the burden of government to his High Minister, who was weary and dreamed of returning to Tollan to spend his remaining days fishing on the river.

The dream-reader was waiting, the Book of Dreams in his lap. Each morning, Moquihix made a point of recalling his dreams immediately upon waking, in as much detail as he could, so he could relay them to the seer, who consulted his book. This morning, however, because of his failed performance with the slave girl, all memories of Moquihix's dreams had evaporated.

"You *must* recall something, my Lord," the man said in mild concern.

To remember nothing at all of one's nocturnal spiritual wandering was dangerous. How was one to know which taboos to avoid that day?

Moquihix concentrated. Narrowed his eyes at the sunlight pouring through a window, and beyond, fields being planted with hope. What had he dreamt during the night? Where had his spirit wandered?

Suddenly it came to him. He had dreamed of the rain-girl, Hoshi'tiwa.

This shocked him. It was good luck to dream of objects and nature, such as cooking pots and trees. But it was bad luck to dream of a person. Did it mean her spirit had visited him in his sleep? He could not recall the details of the dream, only that the rain-girl had been in it.

Once again, Moquihix wondered if bringing her here had been a mistake. They should forget about rain and leave this forsaken outpost of the empire. The Toltecs had stretched themselves too thinly, he believed, in their quest for gold and sky-stone, slaves and power. The previous caravan to come from the south had brought traders who spoke of civil unrest in Tollan and enemies from without plotting an assault on the city. Now was the time to return, Moquihix thought, regroup the army, and strike with force. Save the mother city. Jakál should summon his nobles and the Jaguars, his high officials and priests, and march them all back south, with the People of the Sun in tow, bound together with ropes, to take to the King in Tollan as a blood-gift for the gods.

And leave Center Place to the scorpions and snakes.

Dressed, his hair combed, feathers and headband in place, Moquihix dismissed his slaves and called for his two bodyguards. Because he was in such a bilious humor, he decided to walk to Precious Green instead of riding in a chair. Before leaving the house, he checked the water levels of the kitchen urns, mentally marked them, and informed the cook that drinking water was to be strictly rationed.

Many paths and roads crisscrossed the wide, dusty canyon, connecting villas, kivas, and rising-splendors. Moquihix took the most direct route across to the government center, passing villas of the rich, parched gardens and seared fields struggling to produce food, and the huts and lean-tos of the peasants, his bodyguards protecting him from the beggars with hands held out.

There had not been as many in days gone by, but thirst was forcing people to desperate measures.

The drought was the result of too much ambition in the hearts of men, Moquihix believed, personal desires getting in the way of honor and duty. When the world was destroyed the prior four times, it was because of human hubris, men aspiring to goals beyond their grasp, beyond their station in life, thus angering the gods. Copil, a wealthy tax collector, not content with his envied station in life but casting a greedy eye upon the job of Superintendent of the Marketplace, a plum position in that the Superintendent grew fat on bribes. Xikli, not content with being Captain of the Jaguars, but eyeing the throne as if it were a ripe fruit. Even Jakál himself, not necessarily ambitious but harboring personal desires that conflicted with his duty: wanting only to be left alone to write poetry to his god, Quetzalcoatl.

Whereas Moquihix knew his station in life and accepted it. High Minister was a noble rank, and it made him rich. True, there were others who lived better than he, and had more power—Nagual, the Chief Physician, for one—but Moquihix was content. He would not dream of coveting another man's place.

But he was the last of a dying breed, he feared. The old ways were vanishing. Honor and duty no longer counted as they once did. All men cared about was amassing power and sky-stone. It was going to spell doom for Center Place.

And no rain-girl from the north was going to prevent that.

He scowled. There she was again, Hoshi'tiwa haunting his thoughts. He knew the reason why. If she did indeed bring rain, it would destroy his plans to return to Tollan.

This was the High Minister's secret conflict. Moquihix had sworn an oath of obedience to Jakál, and being Toltec and thus loyal to the bone, he would never betray that oath, not even to save his own life. If Lord Jakál wished rain to come to Center Place, then that should be Moquihix's wish, as well. But it was not. In his heart, he was betraying his *tlatoani* by secretly hoping the girl failed to bring rain. And the conflict was giving him no peace.

He reached the main plaza of Precious Green, the rising-splendor where the chamber of the High Council was housed, where Lord Jakál resided, and also where the main marketplace was located. The sun had broken over the eastern plateau, illuminating a busy population center. A wedding party danced through the throng, but when the air shifted, Moquihix picked up the acrid scent of smoke from a funeral pyre. Life and death within the canyon walls. The cycle never ceased.

He passed a dentist plying his craft, extracting a tooth with people watching and laughing as the patient howled with pain. Jugglers and acrobats were already at their entertainments, hoping to earn a breakfast. And as it was the month honoring Xochipilli, the god of flowers and crops, priests and neophytes danced through the plaza accompanied by drums, rattles, and flutes, bells, and whistles.

As Moquihix threaded his way through the hustle and bustle, making dismissive gestures to merchants hawking wares, he espied Lady White Orchid riding high and lofty in her carrying chair.

Vain, self-centered creature, Moquihix thought. He knew that Tenoch's daughter always took pains with her appearance because she believed people liked marveling at the sight of her whenever she rode through the crowd high on her carrying chair. The populace always bowed low and made signs of respect. Of course, her bearers had to use whips to clear the way, and anyone not casting their eyes down when White Orchid passed felt a taste of the lash.

Moquihix suspected she was conniving to tie the knot with Jakál. Highborn already, and wealthy in her own right, as the wife of the *tlatoani* she would have endless slaves for her amusement, her pick of the best food, and more sky-stone and gold than her body could bear. It was no secret. Anyone with eyes could see how White Orchid laid yearning eyes upon Jakál. The only one blind to her ambition was Jakál himself, who clearly had no idea the woman was weaving a net in which to ensnare him. Jakál was obtuse when it came to women in general. With his head in the clouds and his heart dedicated to his god, Jakál was oblivious of the hungers of the rest of his body.

Moquihix knew White Orchid would never win Jakál's heart. He had loved once and had lost that love. Moquihix thought pining for a dead woman a waste of time. But then Moquihix had no idea what love felt like.

Lust, on the other hand, he knew well. And once again his thoughts returned to his secret impotence. Where was Nagual, the Chief Physician?

When Moquihix saw White Orchid's slaves bring the carrying chair to a halt outside the potters' workshop, he paused to watch as the high-born lady stepped to the ground and, with her bearers sweeping the path with a twig broom, entered the workshop. She carried something in her hands.

The High Minister pursed his lips. Why would Lady White Orchid be paying a visit to the Potters' Guild?

And then he was reminded that he had not paid respects to her father, Tenoch, in a while. Moquihix made a mental note to visit the man later. Heroes of the empire were to be placated because when they died they went straight to heaven and reported to the gods on how others had treated them during their earthly life, and Moquihix wanted his own name to be mentioned favorably.

He didn't like Tenoch. There were few men of their age left in the valley, but that was all the two shared in common. Tenoch had been born at Center Place, he had never seen Tollan, had never visited a real Toltec city, and had only occasionally witnessed a human sacrifice in the main plaza.

Moquihix came upon an awning of brightly dyed cloth, fluttering on four poles. In its shade, a man sat on a stool, flanked by well-dressed servants and two scribes.

Nagual, the Chief Physician.

Tall and ascetically lean, with a personality as cool as winter, Nagual was distinctive from other men in that he shaved his head from ears almost to crown, leaving a narrow stripe of long hair from forehead to the nape of his neck, resembling a rooster's cockscomb. Nagual was of the highest noble lineage, and had studied his art at the great temples of Tollan.

As there was already a line of patients waiting to see the doctor, Moquihix made a mental note to approach him later, to discuss his impotence in private.

Moquihix slipped through the great stone doorway of Precious Green, flanked by handsomely outfitted guards and priests who made sure no bad luck crossed the threshold, and he remembered once again his alarming dream about Hoshi'tiwa.

Pausing in the dim recess of the building, he looked back through the doorway and squinted across the sunlit plaza where, on the far side, hidden by walls and people, the Potters' Guild stood. Unbidden, a memory flashed in his mind: the Chief Priest in the Star Chamber, saying, "We consulted the books and found an ancient prophecy that speaks of a coming eclipse, one that we had not calculated for." Jakál then asking an eclipse of what? The moon? The sun?

The priest responding, "No, my Lord. It is an eclipse of something much greater."

And a terrible presentiment now shot through Moquihix the High Minister.

Ten

A SCREAM shattered the air.

Hoshi'tiwa turned, startled, to see Tupa, large and looming, willow wand raised over her head. "Stupid woman!" she shrieked.

The other potters jumped back and Hoshi'tiwa saw the object of Tupa's wrath: Yani, on her knees, protecting her head from the blows.

"Do you call this a pitcher?" Tupa screamed, her jowly face red with rage. She was brandishing what Hoshi'tiwa thought looked like a nice piece. To Hoshi'tiwa's shock, Tupa threw the piece to the floor and ground it beneath her feet. Again and again the whip came down upon the poor woman, while the others watched in fearful silence, until the tirade ended and Tupa marched out.

After another moment of stunned silence, the others returned to work, stepping around the assaulted woman who lay cowering on the floor. When Hoshi'tiwa made a move toward her, Yellow Feather laid a hand on her shoulder and whispered, "Do not help her. If Tupa were to find out, your punishment would be severe."

Hoshi'tiwa stared at the girl, at the others, who were back to kneading clay, rolling coils, mixing temper, and then at the poor woman whose arms and legs were now covered in angry welts.

Pottery making was not without risks, due to sharp etching knives and a blistering hot kiln, so Hoshi'tiwa knew the workshop must have medicines. She found the supplies, but the others warned her: "Only Tupa is allowed to dispense medicines."

But an older woman, whose hair was entirely white and whose teeth were all gone, the clan tattoo on her face nearly swallowed by wrinkles, declared, "Then we shall not tell Tupa."

As Hoshi'tiwa applied aloe juice to Yani's wounds, and an ointment of herbs and animal fat, she said, "Why did Tupa do this to you?"

The fallen woman was too mortified to answer, so Yellow Feather said quietly, "Tupa's been beating her for months." And Hoshi'tiwa saw now on Yani's arms and legs scars from earlier injuries.

"But why?" Hoshi'tiwa said.

"Because Yani's pots are the most beautiful," said another woman who glanced nervously in the direction of the plaza, where Tupa's large body could be seen pushing through the crowd.

"Yani is the best among us," said Yellow Feather. "And Tupa is jealous."

Yani sat up, murmured, "Thank you," and limped back to her mat where the first coils of a bowl had been laid.

Tupa returned in the afternoon with a fresh skin of *nequhtli* and ignored the workers as she settled on a mat in front of the door to drink at her leisure.

That night, after a supper of tamales stuffed with spiced squash, the women were less animated and spoke in hushed tones. When Tupa began to snore, Hoshi'tiwa said to Yani, "Why does she beat you? Surely it is not just out of jealousy?"

Yani was a soft-spoken woman with pleasant features, who wore her hair in two braids wrapped over her head like a cap, and who reminded Hoshi'tiwa of her own mother. "It is because of this," she said, and she reached into the small leather bag that all potters wore at their belts, and brought out a polishing stone that was so beautiful and perfectly formed that Hoshi'tiwa exclaimed out loud.

Polishing was a difficult skill, it took patience and a keen eye. But most important was the tool. Potters might spend years finding just the right stone that fit just right in the hand, that "spoke" to the dried clay, and that knew how to glide over the molded curves to bring out the shine hidden in the clay. "This has been handed down in my family from mother to daughter back through the generations. Tupa wants it. Her skills are failing and she thinks that my polishing stone will make her own pottery stand out again. But I will not give it to her. And she cannot steal it because the stone would not work for her. As you know, it has to be given freely."

Hoshi'tiwa understood this. Among her own clan, when an artisan died, his or her tools were buried with their owner, for the tools would not work for another. Only tools bequeathed to someone else would work because the spirit of the tool knew it had been passed along freely. Hoshi'tiwa herself had not yet found a tool that would become hers for life, to someday pass down to her own daughter.

"Tupa has brought disgrace to our guild," Yani said, and the others nodded in agreement.

Yellow Feather, who was arranging another woman's hair with ribbons made of woven yucca fibers, said, "Tupa has made us a laughingstock." She explained to Hoshi'tiwa that they carried on a friendly rivalry with the Basket Weavers' Guild, also composed of women and girls. "At every festival we dance in competition for prizes. Now they do not even dance their best, because they know we will always lose. Tupa has taken the heart out of us."

The white-haired woman with no teeth said in a whisper, "Yani was supposed to be the next Overseer of the Potters' Guild, but Tupa paid the Minister of the Guilds a generous bribe. To be an overseer of a guild is a very respected job and people honor those who oversee the work of artisans. But no one respects Tupa, and therefore our guild has lost its pride. We are an honorable profession and a respected sisterhood. But Tupa has brought dishonor to us."

Hoshi'tiwa saw for herself, several days later, the depth of Tupa's dishonor.

It was a clay-harvesting expedition and everyone was required to help. Tupa told them to bring food offerings, which the women purchased in the marketplace by trading pottery they had made.

As local clay sources had been depleted, it was a day's trek to the nearest source, and the potters sang and chanted sacred songs along the way, for clay was sacred as it was a gift from Mother Earth. As the party of women and girls crossed the valley on a beaten path, passing between wilting gardens and small houses and fields lying fallow, they reached an enormous kiva on the other side, built into the base of the sheer cliff: the Star Chamber. Skirting the massive round structure, the procession of potters followed a narrow ravine rising gradually from the valley.

The girls paused on the trail because of Tupa's need to stop and catch her breath, and as Hoshi'tiwa turned her face to the breeze, she gasped in astonishment.

Spread below and as far as the eye could see was Center Place as she had not seen it before. From this high point, on a ridge jutting into the valley like a finger, one could see the entire length of the wide canyon, and now for the first time Hoshi'tiwa saw the true extent of Toltec power.

Seeing Hoshi'tiwa's expression of awe as she looked up and down the valley, Yani said, "It is said that in their homeland, rising-splendors are built in *this* shape," and Yani made a pyramid of her fingers. "Here at Center Place they put square blocks of rooms on top of one another, rising as many as five high. Each has a name. The one to which our workshop is attached, Precious Green, is the largest in the valley. When you look eastward, you see the next rising-splendor. That is Blue Hummingbird. And there to the west is Five Flower."

Hoshi'tiwa saw a glint in one of the canyons across the way and realized in shock that it was a body of water. She had had no idea such a quantity could be found nearby.

"Is that where the water-carriers fill their skins?" she asked, accustomed now to seeing the deliverymen everywhere with their familiar

bent backs and waterskins. They were as despised as tax collectors because they sold what everyone believed was theirs for free. Hoshi'tiwa
felt sorry for the water-carriers. They were men like everyone else, with
families to feed and support.

Following her line of sight and seeing what had caught her attention,
Yani said, "No, the water-carriers fill their skins from a government
reservoir at the other end of the valley. *That* catchment," she said, pointing, "was built by the Lords for their private use. That water is for the
gods. It is not for us to touch."

Hoshi'tiwa murmured, "But did not the gods give us water to drink
and to make our crops grow? How can water be reserved for the gods?"

"It is what the masters have decreed."

Hoshi'tiwa leveled suddenly mature eyes upon Yani, so that the older
woman was slightly taken aback. "Who made them our masters?"
Hoshi'tiwa asked.

And Yani, noticing Yellow Feather nearby, watching them, lowered
her voice and said, "Be careful, Daughter, even the wind has ears." But as
she fell silent, while Tupa called for the potters to resume their trek,
Yani kept her eyes on Hoshi'tiwa, looking at her in a new light.

The potters built a campfire and cooked beans to fill their tortillas,
then they told stories and fixed each other's hair, and slept beneath the
stars, hopeful of a good clay harvest, because their next undertaking was
the sacred rain jars intended for the Solstice festival.

At dawn they dug into the earth and sang and prayed. As the baskets
filled with clods of dense clay, the potters asking permission of Mother
Earth to take part of her body to use in the care of her children, they left
behind offerings of corn and beans and squash. Then, with heavy baskets supported on their heads, the women and girls threaded their way
back down the ravine toward Center Place.

They had gone a short distance when Tupa declared she had left her
leather pouch behind. Ordering the potters to continue down the ravine,
she turned and puffed her way back up the trail. Her curiosity piqued,
Hoshi'tiwa quietly followed, keeping back to remain undetected, and
watched the fat woman collect all the offerings and stuff them into her

leather bag. Hoshi'tiwa was shocked. Tupa was not one of the evil Toltecs. She belonged to the People of the Sun. And yet as she tied the bag to her belt, she patted it and smacked her lips in anticipation of a feast to come.

Hoshi'tiwa lay awake that night, for the first time not thinking of her own wretched condition but of Tupa's shocking transgression and the impact it might have on the guild's rain jars. Clay was a gift from Mother Earth and therefore was sacred. Hoshi'tiwa recalled what the women had said one night at supper: that the gods were angry with the people of Center Place and that was why the rain did not come.

Despite the size of Center Place, the towering stone and brick rising-splendors, the thousands of people coming and going in the canyon, life here was no different from life at home in Hoshi'tiwa's tiny settlement. Gods and ghosts and spirits lurked everywhere, and so people were care-ful in their speech, fearful of causing offense or blasphemy. Good luck and bad luck surrounded them constantly. Since people could not con-trol chance and misfortune, at least they could try to predict them, so that every morning, rising from their sleeping mats, the people checked for omens, from the *tlatoani* down to the peasant weeding his small plot, and every evening, the Chief Astronomer inspected the starry sky for signs.

The gods presided over all activities, patron gods who watched over the potters and basket weavers, the feather workers and spear makers, the cooks and servants and Jaguars and tiny children who toddled about. There was even a god who watched over *patolli* games to whom the players prayed before starting a game. Days were consecrated to specific gods, and the yearly calendar of festivals and feasts and sacrifices was carefully observed by every soul in Center Place.

Therefore Hoshi'tiwa was stunned to discover that there might be people who did not honor the laws. Were there others like Tupa, whose corruption and taboo ways were spelling the doom of Center Place? The People of the Sun believed that the world had been destroyed three times and reborn prior to this, the Fourth World. They also believed that someday this world would also be destroyed, mankind eradicated with just a few survivors retreating underground, as before, to await the world's rebirth. Hoshi'tiwa wondered if she had been born to see the sunset of the Fourth World.

These troubled thoughts were on her mind the next morning as she sanded one of Yani's beautiful two-handled water jars which, after Yani painted it, would turn white in the kiln, its black design standing out in handsome relief. When a shadow fell over Hoshi'tiwa, she looked up, briefly hopeful that it was a cloud crossing the face of the sun, but she saw the silhouette of a man with the brilliant sky behind him.

She realized in shock that it was Moquihix, in a scarlet tunic and deep-blue cloak, the feathered headdress of office on his gray head. As the potters scrambled to their knees and pressed their foreheads to the ground, Moquihix stepped through the doorway of the potters' workshop, accompanied by the two blue-painted priests of Tlaloc. It was their habit to make periodic and unscheduled inspections of the potters' progress with rain jars. However, the women whispered nervously, as they knelt with their faces to the floor, never before had the high official himself accompanied the priests.

He walked about the dusty workshop, frowning at the rows of jars and bowls and figurines, pausing to survey the collection of good-luck amulets and offerings given by hopeful citizens—among them, a handsome statuette of Tlaloc, which Moquihix knew had been donated by Lady White Orchid—then he turned to Tupa, who had remained standing but with her eyes cast respectfully down, and demanded to see the pots the new girl had made.

She shifted on feet flattened from having to carry such a heavy body. "The girl has made no jars, my Lord. She is too worthless for the task."

His command was brisk. The girl was to make rain jars.

After Moquihix left, work resumed and no one mentioned the surprise visit of the high official. Yet everyone sensed a change of atmosphere in the workshop, it was on every potter's mind: Tupa did not like this special treatment of the new girl.

Eleven

THE white clay of Center Place did not agree with her. No matter how Hoshi'tiwa worked it, watered it, kneaded it, spoke to it, and prayed over it, the clay and her fingers did not get along. It would be useless to try to create a rain jar from it. As everyone knew, each potter must harvest her own clay, for only at the source, when she dug into the earth, could she know that the clay would be agreeable. Hoshi'tiwa determined that in order to bring rain so that she could go home, she must find her own clay.

It was a warm spring day, the potters were engaged in various stages of rain jars, and Tupa, having imbibed *nequhtli* with breakfast, made her merry way across the plaza to engage in a friendly game of *patolli* with her cousin, mistress of the Basket Weavers' Guild.

Hoshi'tiwa seized her chance. Slipping out the back way, she hurried around the southern wall, where a family of salt traders was camped, and hurried along the base of the escarpment. The wind shifted, and a stench assailed her nostrils. Three men caught stealing water from a Toltec's well had been hung upside down on the north wall of the plaza for all the populace to see. It had taken them two days to die, and now their naked bodies rotted in the sun.

Hoshi'tiwa chose a path that crossed the canyon, because the potters said the best clay was found in the southern cliffs, and searched along the base of the escarpment where she eventually found, not far from the great round kiva called the Star Chamber, a narrow ravine hidden behind boulders so that she almost missed it. Like everywhere else in Center Place, the vegetation had long since died out, animals had retreated. Yet when Hoshi'tiwa scooped the earth and lifted her face to the breeze wafting down the narrow little canyon, she had a sense that clay was sleeping up ahead.

Her climb was rewarded when she came to a widening where large rocks created a formation that indicated this was a pool during the rains. Empty now, and dry, nonetheless Hoshi'tiwa's keen eye picked out what might have been the banks of a wide stream. Scrub did indeed struggle for survival here, and stunted brush. She even heard birds. Falling to her knees, she drove her fingers into the earth.

And she found it, hard and dry, riddled with debris and gray in color, a clay that spoke to her fingers. It took her all morning to pry the hard chunks from the soil. Later, in the workshop, she would soak the clay, and rinse it, soak it again and rinse it again and sieve out the impurities, and as she did so she would pray and talk to the clay and coax it to become a rain jar that would attract the attention of the Cloud Spirits.

When her basket was full, she made to leave, and then suddenly heard laughter nearby. She looked about, but saw no one. Setting her burden down, she crept in the direction of the sound and came to a dense thicket of sage. Parting the greenery, she saw a glade cradled in the deep bosom of the mesa, hidden and protected, as if it belonged to the gods. Hoshi'tiwa's eyes widened at the sight of the trees and grass, and the spring flowers in thick, full bloom.

And then she saw the young women, dressed in skirts and tunics that were clearly made of cotton, and dyed in all the colors of the rainbow, woven and embroidered with dazzling patterns. The young women were beautiful, and playing flutes, rattling gourds, tapping small drums.

Puzzled, Hoshi'tiwa swept her eyes around the private glade until they fell upon a sight that so astonished her, she gasped, and then quickly covered her mouth with her hands.

She held still, heart pounding, to see if anyone had heard. But she had gone undetected, and so, instead of fleeing, as she should have, she remained on the spot, staring at a sight she could barely believe.

Since her arrival at Center Place, Hoshi'tiwa had not seen Lord Jakál except at a distance, either sitting on a throne in the Plaza, where he judged disputes and criminals, or high up on the promontory, greeting the Morning Star. He had become like a distant god, dressed in glorious raiment, magical and powerful, so that her memory of watching him on the mesa, when he had stood nearly naked before his god—and he had turned and their eyes had met—seemed like a dream, as if it had never happened.

But now she saw the man again, in a startling new manifestation, throwing her thoughts into further confusion. The evil Lord of Center Place was . . . laughing!

He reclined on the grass on a richly woven blanket, his bronze skin gleaming in the sun. His loincloth and the cape knotted at his neck were made of shimmering green and blue cotton, a fabric so rich that Hoshi'tiwa could not imagine how it must feel. His long hair was tied up in a feathered topknot that fluttered in the spring breeze. Upon Jakál's right wrist a magnificent scarlet macaw perched, and the Lord was feeding it pieces of fruit. His tenderness toward the half-wild creature, as he fed it and spoke to it, made Hoshi'tiwa's head swim.

And then she noticed something strange about the glade. The rocks did not appear indigenous but to have come from somewhere else and placed here. The flowers were unfamiliar to her, and different varieties of trees stood bough to bough. It was not a natural glade, it had been *created*.

She caught her breath. The glade was a holy sanctuary. And by standing there, Hoshi'tiwa had committed a taboo act punishable by death.

Twelve

"L IFT your dress and open your legs."

Yellow Feather did as told, and the old woman scooped paste from a jar—a mixture of pulp from the agave plant and magic herbs—and, using her rough, gnarly fingers, inserted it into the girl's vagina.

Yellow Feather was lying on her back in the crude hut while the old peddler of herbs did her work and the lame boy watched with a dull expression. This was not the first time the girl had come to old Pikami for an herbal remedy.

Although, in this case, the gummy concoction was not so much a remedy as a preventative.

Pikami whispered a steady, monotonous prayer as she labored, rocking back and forth on her knees, applying the strong herbal mixture and thinking: Rich lady in the villa wants to make babies, young pottery girl wants to *stop* babies.

Old Pikami remembered a time when no maiden of the People of the Sun would have come to her for such a service. But times had changed, her people were corrupt, they had taken on the ways of their

masters, thinking only of themselves, not thinking of their families or
their ancestors or the balance of nature. Girls stopping babies, having
sex before marriage—what was the world coming to?

Pikami's ancient bones creaked as she heaved a mournful sigh. The
hearts of her people today were filled with greed, vanity, envy. It had not
been so when she was a girl and the world was in balance. Her people
had been led astray and must now be punished. Why else were the
Cloud Spirits withholding rain?

"We are done," she said, wiping her hands down her buckskin dress.
"Clean yourself so the man does not suspect. Afterward, make a tea of
this and drink it." She handed Yellow Feather a small pouch that contained pennyroyal leaves. "It will stimulate your monthly flow."

The girl rose, straightened her dress, and smiled to herself. Now she
was free to give pleasure to the old man and receive his many gifts without fear of getting pregnant.

Yellow Feather was not a virgin, although she told everyone she was.
If the truth were known, she would be banished from the Potters'
Guild. And she would lose the handsome young stone-worker she was
in love with. They planned to marry, she and Falcon, obtain their own
little plot of land in the valley, and build a small house. Stone-workers
were fed well because their strength was needed to repair and fortify the
solid walls of Center Place; stone-workers often brought extra food to
their families. Yellow Feather and her children would eat well, with a
stone-worker for a husband.

As for the fact that he naïvely believed she was a virgin, Yellow
Feather had a plan. When they consummated their union after tying
the knot, she would employ the old trick used by countless women before her: secretly cutting her finger and smearing the blood between
her legs.

Outside the hut, Yellow Feather smiled brightly at the servant who
had been sent to fetch her from the potters' workshop and whom she had
kept waiting. He glowered at her. Instead of going straight away with
him to his master's house, she had insisted on visiting the potters' kiva
for a sweat-bath. And then this visit to the old herb peddler's hut. Now

the girl smiled in a smug way and sauntered at his side, swinging her bottom to and fro.

His master was going to be furious.

Yellow Feather knew the servant was annoyed, but she did not care. She knew that making a man wait increased his ardor and therefore his gifts afterward. Yellow Feather intended to make the most of this unexpected windfall.

High Minister Moquihix was at that moment in a dark humor. Another night of dreams visited by the rain-girl, and another morning of failed performance with a slave girl.

The Chief Physician's remedy was not working.

Upon Nagual's orders, Moquihix made a daily trek down the canyon to the rising-splendor Five Flower, where he sacrificed an unblemished white dove over sacred fire. Such birds were costly, and the priests of Five Flower demanded steep bribes. But Moquihix was desperate. Chief Physician Nagual warned him that the more he worried about the problem, the worse he was going to make it. "Try not to think about it," Nagual had advised.

Easy for you to say, the High Minister had thought bitterly. After the death of his son, Nagual had, for reasons known only to himself, taken a vow of celibacy. So what would he know about these matters? Moquihix was wondering if there were an herbalist among the People of the Sun he might consult, when a slave entered the reception atrium to announce he had brought the girl from the potters' workshop.

Moquihix's secret scheme had come to him during a sleepless night: If Hoshi'tiwa was indeed the cause of his impotence, then something had to be done about her. But first he needed to know what she was doing to afflict him so. How was she making her spirit visit him in dreams? Once he knew this, he could devise a plan to protect himself. Therefore he needed an informant in the workshop. He had singled out a girl with a yellow feather in her hair; she looked the same age as Hoshi'tiwa and might be persuaded to befriend her.

Moquihix looked at the pottery girl with a thunderous expression. "You kept me waiting. I should have you beaten."

"My Lord," said Yellow Feather, "I could not come to you as I was, soiled from the workshop. It would have been disrespectful to you." She ran her hands down her clean white shift. "Am I not more pleasing this way?"

He narrowed his eyes. Why was she acting coy? Her posture, the way she observed him from beneath thick lashes. A strange one—shy and maidenly, yet her gaze was direct and bold.

"There is something you are going to do for me," he said.

She looked around the small reception atrium. "Here, my Lord?"

He blinked. What was the creature talking about?

And then she gave him a smile that was as old as womankind, and he found himself looking her up and down and noting her big round bottom and breasts like melons.

A stirring of life in his loincloth startled him. This was not why he had sent for her. And yet . . . could it be Nagual's prescription was working at last? "Remove your clothes," he said in a voice suddenly grown husky.

When his old eyes beheld her youthful lushness, and he felt his ardor blossom, he gestured toward a doorway with a bright red lintel decorated with pink flowers. Yellow Feather did as told, walking slowly to titillate him, and when she saw the woven mat on the floor did not need to be told to lie down.

Moquihix joined her and was amazed at his performance, his sudden virility and strength. He had not felt so powerful in a long time. It was a sign. Hoshi'tiwa was not stronger than him! He possessed the power to fight her bad magic.

Thus the High Minister's thoughts went as Yellow Feather squirmed and groaned beneath him, Moquihix unaware that as he came to climax, it was Hoshi'tiwa's face that filled his vision.

While Moquihix retied his loincloth and draped a cloak around his neck, Yellow Feather stretched her plump, naked body and said, "I would not refuse a gift, my Lord."

He gave her a trinket, saying, "There will be more if you do another job for me."

She greedily accepted the sky-stone bracelet and slipped it over her hand, turning her wrist this way and that.

"The girl named Hoshi'tiwa," he said.

She gave him an impatient look. Why was everyone so interested in *her*? When Hoshi'tiwa had first arrived at the workshop, Yellow Feather was delighted to have a girl her own age. But in the days since, the special attention given Hoshi'tiwa had stung Yellow Feather's heart with jealousy and envy. Therefore, when a servant had appeared at the workshop that morning, saying the High Minister commanded Yellow Feather's presence, she had thought: At last! *I* receive attention.

Ignoring the petulant frown, Moquihix said, "What do you know of her?"

Yellow Feather thought long and hard. Did he wish to hear good things about Hoshi'tiwa, or bad? How pleased he was with what she had to say would influence the size and quality of his gifts. "She asks questions," Yellow Feather said cautiously, gauging his response.

His eyes widened. "What sort of questions?"

Warming to the subject, Yellow Feather toyed with her new bracelet and said, "She wants to know 'why' about everything. She questions why the Toltecs are our masters."

The alarm in his eyes thrilled her. She had guessed correctly.

"Keep me informed on everything she does, what she says, who she talks to, where she goes." And then, thinking that this stupid girl might get curious about his orders, and talk to others about them, he added, "She is working at a sacred task. It is vital to the well-being of Center Place that she not unwittingly commit a sacrilegious act. It is equally vital that she not know we are watching her. Keep this secret close to your heart and I will reward you well. But speak of this to anyone and I shall make an offering of your beating heart to the gods."

Thirteen

"W HAT are you doing?" Tupa barked, standing over Ho-shi'tiwa with her hands on her plump hips. "Do you call that clay? It looks like antelope dung."

Hoshi'tiwa did not respond, but kept her head bent as she sat cross-legged in the warm sunshine, mixing sandy temper with her newly harvested clay to help counteract shrinkage and to lessen the likelihood of cracking.

Tupa clutched her stomach and bellowed with laughter, telling the others that the new girl had dust between the ears if she thought she was going to create anything from *that* clay. With a belch Tupa went off to inspect the kiln.

Hoshi'tiwa ignored the mockery. Her concentration upon her task put all other considerations from her mind.

Or so she told herself. Yet she could not deny that the sight of Lord Jakál in the private glade haunted her night and day. Noseless had told her Jakál's wife had died and that he would take no other woman to his bed. Yet there were those beautiful young women with him, like colorful, exotic birds. Hoshi'tiwa felt like an ordinary sparrow compared with them.

Her emotions puzzled and frightened her. Why should she care whom the Dark Lord chose for companionship, for he *was* a Dark Lord, and an eater of man-corn. That was something she must never forget.

Nonetheless he visited her in dreams at night, and haunted her thoughts during the day. Her fellow potters saw a silent and determined worker, in the bend of her back as she sat over her coils, in the fixed concentration on her face as she shaped and scraped and formed smooth sides out of the coils. They admired her single-minded attention to creating her rain jars, and wished they themselves were so disciplined. They did not know that the stiffness of her posture and fixed expression were her weapons in a struggle with her unruly mind. Hoshi'tiwa wanted to concentrate on her work—to bring rain so that she could go home—but her mind wanted to concentrate on Lord Jakál.

Why hadn't Ahoté come for her? She had thought he would be here by now. Homesickness was growing within her, and now she was troubled by strange thoughts of the Lord of Center Place. This world was alien and frightening. Here, people bought and sold water. Hoshi'tiwa longed for the little settlement on the stream, for a game of hide-and-seek with Ahoté in the cottonwoods—

A shout tore the air. The potters, startled from their work, looked up to see Tupa holding aloft a bowl Yani had just brought from the kiln. In her other hand was the ever-present whip. "You dare to insult the gods with this shoddy work?" Tupa cried.

The women watched in fearful silence as the fat overseer rained blows upon Yani, who had fallen to her knees with her arms over her head.

"Bad workmanship like this reflects upon this guild!" Tupa cried, the wand coming down again and again on bare skin. "You dishonor your sisters! You dishonor—"

She stopped and stared at the strong hand suddenly gripping her upraised wrist.

Tupa glared at Hoshi'tiwa in outrage. Silence fell over the workshop as the overseer and the novice locked eyes, and the others looked on in fear and apprehension. Then Tupa, feeling the strength in Hoshi'tiwa's fingers and seeing the boldness in the girl's eyes, leaned forward and whispered hoarsely, "You think you are special. But wait until after the Solstice and your jars bring no rain. There will be no one to protect you then."

Hoshi'tiwa held the overseer's gaze for a heartbeat, then averted her own eyes. Releasing Tupa's wrist, Hoshi'tiwa swallowed in anxiety. What was happening to her? She never would have disrespected an elder in this way back home.

As she returned to her work, feeling the astonished eyes of the potters on her, Hoshi'tiwa knew she could not bear to live another day in this place. She must find a way to get a message to Ahoté. He needed to know she was no longer *makai-yó*.

Fourteen

HOSHI'TIWA stared at the misshapen creature.

"You want to buy it?" the merchant asked sharply, sizing up the girl in the attire of a potter's apprentice and deciding she could not afford the little goddess.

"What is it?" Hoshi'tiwa asked, turning the tiny statuette around in her hands.

He snatched it back and placed the effigy on his woven mat with the others—all carved from stone, different shapes and sizes, deities who ruled over luck, childbirth, death, corn, rain, and the heavens. The one Hoshi'tiwa had cradled in her hand was the goddess of looms and weaving. "Move along, make room," the merchant barked, and Hoshi'tiwa was jostled out of the way by other patrons wanting to look at the man's offerings.

It was morning, and Tupa was in the potters' kiva, sweating her bloated body after a night of too much *nequhtli*. As she would not be back at the workshop until afternoon, her workers seized the opportunity to shop in the marketplace, visit friends, make secret assignations with lovers.

Hoshi'tiwa had paused at the mat of a god-seller—a popular man because he peddled hope and the promise of better days—and now she watched in confusion as a woman, identified by her facial tattoo as belonging to Owl Clan, gave the merchant five turkey eggs in exchange for a statuette. Hoshi'tiwa was baffled. Why was a woman of the People of the Sun buying a Toltec god?

In the potters' workshop a small shrine housed an effigy of the patron god of ceramics makers. He looked human. The People of the Sun did not have images of their spirits. Back home, pottery workers prayed to the spirits of clay, water, and fire.

But she had not come to the marketplace to buy something. She was looking for a man to carry a message to her clan.

Ahoté still had not come for her. Each night she prayed for him to be there the next morning, and each day she searched the face of every man she passed, or who walked by the workshop, hoping to glimpse her familiar "funny Owl." Deciding that something must have happened to keep him from coming, that perhaps his father forbade him to come, she had decided to send Ahoté a message.

Although most of the merchants in the marketplace lived at Center Place, Hoshi'tiwa knew that a few were traders who regularly traveled the vast network of trails and roads. She needed to find a man who would be heading north, and when she came upon a salt-seller, his stall wedged between a maker of flutes and a woman offering dyed turkey feathers, Hoshi'tiwa paused.

The man sat cross-legged on a mat, surrounded by bags of salt and goods he had received in exchange. Before him, like a cone of snow, a mound of salt, pure and white, beckoned in the sun. As everyone knew, salt came from the south, where it was harvested along seashores and in marshes.

Upon her inquiry, he averred that in seven days he would be striking off northward for the timber camps in the distant mountains, where he traded salt for pine resin, which he would then bring back to Center Place and sell to the priests of the rising-splendors for their sacred incense.

When she stated her request, he shrugged and said, "Carrying a message is not as easy as carrying a sack of salt. A burden on the shoulder is lighter than a burden in the thoughts. What will you pay me to *remember* your message?"

Her first offer of a small ceramic censer in the shape of a turtle did not interest him. "Have you any water?" he asked, deciding that two waterskins would suffice.

She shook her head. The water in the workshop was rationed by the mouthful. And then she remembered the cotton ribbons in her hair. He examined them to make sure they were genuine cotton and accepted the payment, saying, "I know the settlement you speak of. At the end of the northwest road, they make legendary rain jars. What is your message?"

"Ask for the son of He Who Links People, and when you see him, tell him that Hoshi'tiwa, daughter of Sihu'mana, wishes for him to come to Center Place and find her at the potters' workshop. Tell him . . ." She paused to lick her lips and consider how best to phrase the next, delicate part. "Tell him that the words spoken the day I left were untrue."

The merchant sniffed, wrinkled his nose, and slapped at an insect biting his arm. It was a long message. How was he expected to remember it all? Still, he did have to pass that way, and recalling the beautiful rain jars the clan made there, and thinking that perhaps he could *sell* the message to the son of He Who Links People, the salt merchant said, "Very well," and sealed their bargain by licking his thumb and pressing it to his open palm, to show that he was bound by Toltec honor to deliver her message.

After thanking the man, who was already waving her away to make room for the next customer, Hoshi'tiwa went in search of Yani.

The older woman was on the other side of the plaza, admiring a display of patterned cloth. As law forbade her class to wear colored fabric, she could not purchase any, but Yani enjoyed looking over the rich blues, yellows, and oranges. When she glanced up and saw Hoshi'tiwa in an intense conversation with a salt merchant, she frowned. What business had the girl with him? He was not People of the Sun and therefore not a long-lost kinsman, nor could Hoshi'tiwa afford to buy even a pinch of salt.

Yani watched, deep in thought. Hoshi'tiwa had been on her mind lately, ever since she stood up to Tupa and stopped the beating. It had been so bold and shocking a gesture that even the potters, who gossiped about everything under the sun, did not speak of it afterward. Hoshi'tiwa herself appeared mortified by her actions and for the rest of the day looked neither Tupa nor Yani in the eye.

But the incident had stayed with Yani, and now Hoshi'tiwa was engaged in more remarkable behavior. When Yani saw an object change hands, and she realized the girl was paying for something, but did not then see her receive salt in return, Yani knew she had to get to the bottom of it.

When Hoshi'tiwa stepped away from the salt merchant's stall and looked around the marketplace, Yani slipped behind a blanket display and waited until the girl had gone off in the other direction.

The salt merchant was weighing a small pouch of salt under the keen eye of his customer, a servant from one of the rising-splendors, so that Yani had to wait until he was free. "The girl who was here a moment ago," she said when she had his attention, "wearing the embroidery of the Potters' Guild—"

"What about her?" he snapped when he realized the woman wasn't there to buy salt.

"What did you two talk about?"

His eyebrows arched. Then he studied the embroidery on her shift, recognizing her high rank within the guild, sized up her age and importance, thought of the message the girl had asked him to deliver up north, and decided that, if he couldn't sell this woman salt, maybe he could peddle information.

"Why do you want to know?"

Yani measured the man. She knew such merchants led hard lives, spending much of them traveling from distant southern shores where the salt was harvested, and then hauling it through jungle and over mountain to trade it along the way. He was most likely headed for the timber camps after his rest at Center Place. "Did she give you a message to take to a settlement in the north?"

He scratched a bushy eyebrow with his thumb and said, "What if she did?" He added, "I can't *tell* you," in a tone that implied he was willing to sell the information.

"I do not care what is in the message," Yani said as she scanned the throng for Hoshi'tiwa, finding her in a knot of people watching jugglers, and thinking again of how the girl had stood up to Tupa, if only for a instant before backing down, and how Yani was starting to see the girl in a new light. Recalling a recent conversation in which Hoshi'tiwa had confided that while her betrothed had promised to come for her, she feared he could not because of her *makai-yó* status, and suspecting that Hoshi'tiwa's message was to let her family know that her status had changed, Yani came to a swift decision: Hoshi'tiwa must not be allowed to leave Center Place.

Bringing herself back to the salt merchant, who was giving her an expectant look, she said, "I do not want you to deliver the message."

He spread his leathery hands. "The young lady paid me. I am a man of my word."

"How much will it cost for you to forget the message?"

He licked his lips. This was turning into a most profitable morning. "Two waterskins." He held up a finger. "Government water, mind you. Not that brackish brine that comes from valley wells."

"I have no water," Yani said, "but perhaps this will erase your memory?" She slipped a gold bracelet from her wrist, her only expensive piece of jewelry.

The merchant examined the piece, twisted it, bit into the metal, then nodded, thinking he might close his stall for the rest of the day and seek out a woman of pleasure.

Before turning away, Yani said, "You are sure now you will not deliver the message?"

He grinned at her. "What message?"

Hoshi'tiwa finally found her friend at the edge of the plaza where onlookers were laying bets on a game of *patolli*. As Yani watched her approach, she was startled to see that Hoshi'tiwa's hair had come undone and hung over her shoulders in two black falls. Where were the precious cotton ribbons she had arrived at Center Place with? The salt merchant. In payment for the message he was to deliver to her family.

As they moved away from the crowd to go in search of something to eat, Hoshi'tiwa told Yani about the seller of stone idols. "What is the Owl Clan woman going to do with the statuette she bought?"

Yani said, "She will light incense and pray to it."

"Why?"

Yani glanced about and said evasively, "In time you will learn and understand."

But Hoshi'tiwa had no intention of learning and understanding. She was determined to return home, where the spirits of air, land, and sun had no names, no forms in stone. And where water ran freely and a person could drink whenever she wanted.

"Make way! Make way!"

Well-dressed slaves pushed through the crowd, snapping whips to clear a path for a carrying chair borne on the backs of six men. Hoshi'tiwa and Yani jumped out of the way, Yani lowering her eyes respectfully. But Hoshi'tiwa stared up at the beautiful lady who rode high on the chair. She recognized her as the lady who had brought a jade statue of Tlaloc to the pottery workshop, to encourage him to bring rain. Although colorfully arrayed, her face dusted with yellow powder and her mouth stained red, and wearing more jewelry than Hoshi'tiwa thought a body could bear, the noblewoman did not look happy. As she passed, her eyes straight ahead as if the marketplace were deserted, Hoshi'tiwa saw sadness in her gaze, and a hardness around her mouth.

"Lady White Orchid," Yani murmured after the chair had passed and the crowd closed the gap. "She is a very powerful woman. They say she will marry Lord Jakál."

Such a startled look swept over Hoshi'tiwa's face that Yani said, "What is it, Daughter?"

But Hoshi'tiwa could not herself name the confused emotions that suddenly flooded her heart and mind, like a summer storm that materializes in a clear sky, kicking up wind and darkness, plunging the world into brief turmoil before burning itself out, dying, with the day returning to sun and clear sky.

Tatters of emotions, like the remnant clouds of a storm, swirled in Hoshi'tiwa's mind. Lord Jakál high on the promontory, greeting the Morning Star, looking as if he himself were carved from stone—and yet a handsome man, beautiful, and not at all cold and soulless. . . .

"Yani," she said. "Where will our people be celebrating the Summer Solstice? I have not seen a Sun Watcher, yet surely the time is drawing near." The abrupt change of subject did little to evict Lord Jakál from her mind. Was he truly going to marry Lady White Orchid? But why should she care? Soon Ahoté would receive her message from the salt trader and be on his way to Center Place to rescue her.

"There is a point at the far end of this valley where we used to celebrate the sun's progress," Yani said, pointing eastward where, at the opening of the canyon—a morning's walk from Precious Green—a pillar of ancient mesa rose to the sky. Near its summit, two spirals had been carved into the rock, and on Solstices and Equinoxes the spirals were pierced by a dagger of sunlight. "But it is forbidden for the People of the Sun to hold festival there."

"Why?"

Yani pursed her lips. *Why* seemed to be the girl's favorite word, she spoke it so often. Once again, an idea that had been born just days ago now blossomed in Yani's mind, a suspicion that had been growing into a truth, so that now, in this crowded marketplace beneath yet another cloudless sky, with the stone gods of the Toltecs everywhere and highborn ladies in carrying chairs letting their slaves use whips on the People of the Sun, she came to a decision.

"There is something I want to show you. It is but a short walk—" She froze, her eyes fixed on a point across the plaza.

Following Yani's line of sight, Hoshi'tiwa saw a man standing alone in the shade, a remarkable-looking man. Taller than most men, he wore a shining white robe, his face and arms were painted red, and his hair was arranged in an unusual cut: bald on the sides with a magnificent mane cresting his head from forehead to nape.

"Who is he?" Hoshi'tiwa asked.

Yani whispered, "He is Nagual, the Chief Physician. A very powerful man."

And Hoshi'tiwa thought she heard fear in Yani's voice.

"What did you wish to show me?"

A cloud darkened Yani's face, and then cleared. She composed herself, tearing her eyes away from the formidable-looking physician, and said, "It is a secret. We cannot speak of it here."

As the pair left the plaza and set upon a path that headed toward the west end of the canyon, Yellow Feather stood lazily at the steps of the plaza, eating a tortilla dripping with precious animal fat, a delicacy she could not have afforded before her arrangement with the High Minister. Licking the tips of her fingers, she watched Hoshi'tiwa and the older woman make their way toward an unknown destination. She smiled, thinking of the reward Moquihix was going to give her for this bit of news.

Only the *tlatoani* of Center Place was allowed to use water in his private kiva, to produce steam. And only the *tlatoani*'s kiva had a special, hidden entrance so that he might come and go unseen. As Yani led Hoshi'tiwa on a journey of mystery, and Yellow Feather made her way across the valley to the house of the High Minister, a greatly troubled Lord Jakál hurried along the subterranean corridor to his steam-bath.

He went seeking answers.

Ever since the Star Chamber and news of the foretold eclipse (an eclipse of what, the priests still could not say), Xikli and Moquihix had been pressing him to hold more human sacrifices in the plaza. As a youth, Jakál had witnessed hundreds of blood sacrifices in Tollan, he understood the need for such rituals, and his predecessor at Center Place had offered beating hearts to the gods, whose appetites for human blood were insatiable. But Jakál's personal god made no such demand and therefore, under his rule, the number of sacrifices had shrunk. Now Jakál was beginning to doubt himself. Was it true what the others whispered, that *he* was the cause of the drought?

The kiva was the *tlatoani*'s gateway to the spirit world and thus was cluttered with prayer charms, magic amulets, and sacred rattles, the adobe walls adorned with mystical signs, writings, and pictures. From the wooden ceiling hung spears, arrows, and bows that had once belonged to the gods, and on one of the wooden posts that supported the roof a beautiful golden mask hung. Jakál had added it, having brought the holy relic from Tollan and secreted it down in the kiva. Hammered with the features of a man but with the teeth and nostrils of a serpent, and the golden "hair" coiled into quetzal plumes, the mask had been worn, a thousand years ago, by Quetzalcoatl the man before he became Quetzalcoatl the god.

Jakál stripped off his cloak and loincloth and, pouring water on the hot stones to produce steam, took a seat on the bench and closed his eyes.

He had come because the Star Reader's prophecy was beleaguering his mind and soul. But now, as he inhaled steam and smoke and spicy incense, another prophecy, from long ago, came to his mind.

Back in Tollan, when he was a neophyte in the priesthood of Quetzalcoatl, all the novices had had to spend a week of fasting and engaging in tests of endurance. On the final night, they slept naked on the cold stone floor in the Holy of Holies, waiting for the god to come to them in dreams. The next day, the novices bathed and dressed in fresh robes and were interrogated by the priests, each youth being asked, "Did the god visit you in your dream?"

Young Jakál had been beside himself. Each boy answered that the god had indeed come—each described a different visitation in the dream. But Jakál had dreamed of *chocolatl* and roasted pig, and warm blankets and his mother's smile. He was mortified. Of them all, only he had hung his head and confessed that the god had not appeared to him.

He spent the next days in anguish, knowing he was to be expelled and thus bring shame and dishonor to his family, when he was summoned to the inner rooms of the Chief Priest who declared that Jakál was the most honest of all the boys, as rarely did Quetzalcoatl bother himself with the dreams of youths, so that they had all lied in order to gain favor, whereas only Jakál had had the courage, the integrity, and the purity of heart to confess the truth.

It was a sign, the priest had said, that someday Jakál was going to find favor with his god.

Could that favor be manifested in Quetzalcoatl's return during his reign? It was Jakál's deepest, most passionate wish, and so he kept the rules and tenets of Quetzalcoatl, who was a god of peace. But would the god return to a drought-stricken land? And if Jakál was the cause of the drought, because of his peaceful measures, was he himself thus making Quetzalcoatl not want to return? But if he reinstated mass human sacrifice in order to bring rain, and therefore bid Quetzalcoatl to return, would he not then be breaking from the rules of his god?

The conundrum buzzed in Jakál's brain. His temples throbbed. Sweat sprouted on his forehead. Before the arrival of the rain-girl, Hoshi'tiwa, he had been certain of himself, of his place in the cosmos. Now he was riddled with doubt.

The issue of human sacrifice had to be settled.

Hoshi'tiwa and Yani kept to a beaten path that followed the base of steep escarpments, past thirsting cornfields and withering bean patches. They had long since left the well-dressed nobles behind, the merchants, the wives shopping for the day's food, the entertainers and priests, the men meeting for business, the whole throb and clamor of Center Place. Now the two pottery workers encountered farmers who smiled and waved from their labors, they walked through sparse stands of trees parched and leafless, and finally they passed the rising-splendor called Five Flower, where court musicians, dancers, and poets resided and practiced their arts.

Feeling the warm sun on her shoulders and glad to be away from the workshop, Hoshi'tiwa said, "Yani, why do our people worship the gods of strangers?"

Yani cast her a sideways glance. "There was a time when this was not so, Daughter, a time when the people of Center Place followed the ways of all People of the Sun, no matter where they lived, because here was where the Fourth World began."

Like all her people, Hoshi'tiwa was familiar with the story of how the survivors of the destruction of the Third World had crept up from their underground hiding places and found a new world with sunshine and blue sky. They called this new land Center Place, meaning the Center of the Fourth World, and so she knew that the canyon was very old and sacred.

"But then one day," Yani said, "strangers arrived in this canyon."

Yani looked up at the blue sky and marked the progress of a raven riding thermal currents. "In those days, our people were not here in great numbers. They lived in the small stone houses at the base of the southern cliffs and they were mainly workers of sky-stone. At that time there was only one large stone complex, three stories tall with many rooms. No one lived in this structure. It was used for storage, ceremonies, and a meeting place. This was Precious Green as it was long ago. But then the first Toltec traders arrived and when they saw the abundance of sky-stone mines in the area, they made a deal with our ancestors: Give us sky-stone and we will bring goods from our cities in the south.

"But the Toltecs became greedy and wanted to be masters over the People of the Sun. They came in greater numbers and erected rising-splendors. They built roads and stairways and water channels. And they enslaved our people and demanded tribute."

The raven flew low overhead, the air so still that the *whoosh whoosh* of its wings sounded loud in the morning. "The Toltecs took our homes and our kivas, they forced us to work for them and pay tribute. When the new Lords said we could no longer celebrate our religious festivals but must worship their stone idols, our people complied. After a while, our people began to emulate the Lords. When they saw the Toltec wedding ceremony with the two cloaks tied in a knot, our marriage customs were forgotten and now we, too, tie the knot."

Yani stopped on the path and took a long look at her young companion. "This is why the rain stays away, Daughter. Since the beginning of this world, the People of the Sun have lived the way of peace and balance with the spirits of nature. Now it is a world out of balance, it is *koyaanis'qatsi.*"

She glanced around, at the dry rocks and waterless fields and distant farmers who toiled over barren soil, and added softly, "But it will not be this way forever."

"What do you mean?"

"Where I am taking you is a secret, taboo place. You must promise me with your heart that you will tell no one about it."

Jakál had not asked for this.

He had been happy in his boyhood, studying for the priesthood, expecting to live out his life in one of the temples in prayer and contemplation, and writing poetry to glorify Quetzalcoatl. But then his older brother, who had been slated to rule Center Place, died unexpectedly of a brain fever, and so Jakál had been sent in his place. He had not wanted to go, but he understood duty and honor.

Herein lay his torment. He knew that his destiny was intertwined with the return of the Great God. And he prayed to see the day when he threw himself at the feet of his returned hero and declared, "I have kept the laws you set down for us. I have kept your holy ways." But although Jakál's spiritual duty was to Quetzalcoatl, his earthly obligation as *tlatoani* was to Blue Hummingbird, the god of war. Jakál had been sent to Center Place to gather tribute to send down to Tollan, and to maintain a military and administrative hold on this far-flung outpost.

As a result, he worshipped each god with only half a heart, and knew he should choose either to fight wholeheartedly for Blue Hummingbird, or relinquish his post as *tlatoani* and become the peaceful, dedicated servant of Quetzalcoatl. But because of oaths of duty and obedience, he could do neither, and so he was a divided man.

It was time to choose.

Amid the steam and the heat, chanting sacred prayers in a language so ancient that it was no longer spoken, Jakál readied himself for supreme sacrifice to his god.

He laid out the sharp spines of the maguey plant, and the cup in which to collect his blood.

Hoshi'tiwa and Yani left the path and struck across the canyon at the point where it widened and the wash fanned out on a sandy plain.

"Now listen carefully, Daughter," Yani said as they trudged across the dry riverbed, the rising sun beating down on their arms and heads—two women in long white shifts of woven agave fiber, their feet bare, their arms and necks unadorned. "Our people are scattered, like grain on the wind, each clan growing in its own field, like stalks of corn. We are all the same people, yet we live in our own settlements, live by the rules of our clans, and protect those whom we love. We were not united, as the Lords are. We have no leaders, as the Lords have. But it does not have to be so."

Yani took Hoshi'tiwa's hand as they descended into a narrow ravine where sun and sky were replaced by deep shadow. Her tone grew reverent as she said, "You know, Daughter, that this world will be destroyed someday—all life, all existence extinguished."

Every child born to the People of the Sun was taught this belief. Every man and woman woke each dawn wondering if today was the day the world would come to an end.

"But you also know," Yani continued as they stepped over rocks and brittle brush, mindful of scorpions and snakes, "that this time the world can be saved."

"By the return of Pahana," Hoshi'tiwa said.

"Our long-lost white brother who promised to return someday and prevent the destruction of the Fourth World and bring about instead a new golden age for our people." She paused long enough to face Hoshi'tiwa squarely and say, "But he will not come if the world is in chaos, as it is now," and then she continued along the path.

Yani said nothing more until they arrived at the place she said was sacred to her own clan and was therefore forbidden for others to enter.

"No Toltec has ever seen this place," she said quietly as they followed a path that had grown over from lack of use. She and Hoshi'tiwa trampled through dry brush as she said, "And of the People of the Sun, only those of my clan have seen what I am about to show you."

"But I am Tortoise Clan," Hoshi'tiwa said.

At the bottom of a sharp, vertical cliff lay a hidden cave, hollowed out and worn smooth over the eons by wind and water. Before entering, Yani paused to lay her hands on the cliff wall, close her eyes, and murmur, "Father Rock and Mother Cave, allow us safe entry into this place. We will do no harm. We will treat your hidden gifts with reverence."

The two had to bend low to enter, and when there was room, they straightened. One wall had worn away, allowing light to flood the small overhang.

Yani said, "What I am going to show you, Daughter, was painted by my grandfather's grandfather. It is a record of an event that happened when the first Lords arrived, a strange spectacle in the sky. Since that time, the story of this place has been handed down through my family and is known only to us, for we are the keepers of the prophecy." Yani paused, her face partly in shadow, partly in bright sunlight. "A prophecy," she whispered, "that says a new teacher will be born among our people, who will teach us the ways of balance and harmony and prepare us for the coming of Pahana. This teacher will come from the north and live as a stranger among us. And she will be a daughter of Tortoise Clan."

The pain was sublime.

As Jakál inserted the maguey spine through his shin, and slowly pulled the attached fiber through, drawing blood, he prayed to Quetzalcoatl to accept his pain and blood as a gift.

His voice filled the dark, steamy chamber as he chanted ancient sacred words. He had fasted for two days and a night so that his stomach was hollow, his lips and tongue parched. He prayed for guidance, for visions, for a clear view of the path he must take. He sent his soul out with the pain. His spirit left his body with his blood. He opened his mind to visions.

Suddenly—the face of Hoshi'tiwa, round as the moon with leaf-shaped eyes, swam before him.

He was not surprised. The rain-girl was integral to his conundrum.

Unravel the mystery of the girl, he reasoned, and all else will become clear. He concentrated on her image that was so lifelike, it was as if she were in the kiva with him. She looked benign, not at all like a being who could bring about the end of Center Place (or, if he were to listen to the Star Readers' interpretation of the prophecy—the end of the *world*).

Tell me, Quetzalcoatl, Lord of Breath and Life, his silent mind cried as he rode waves of pain. Has the girl come to Center Place to bring rain or destruction?

Hoshi'tiwa looked at Yani in shock. "Are you saying that I am this teacher? Why me?"

"Because you are not like anyone else here. You are different. I saw it the first night you were with us. Though you try, you aren't like the others, who are submissive when brought here, who comply as good Daughters of the Sun do."

When Yani went on to point out that Hoshi'tiwa questioned the ways of the masters and had dared to look upon the Dark Lord, and Hoshi'tiwa shook her head in protest, Yani said, "I can show you proof of this prophecy." And she pointed upward, saying, "Look."

Hoshi'tiwa looked up at the ceiling of the overhang and was stunned by what she saw.

Jakál grew light-headed. The subterranean chamber swirled around him. He closed his eyes and another vision, sharp and clear, burst in his mind like a brand-new sun, dissolving the face of Hoshi'tiwa and shooting through his brain in blinding light.

He cried out and fell to his knees. *The god was in the kiva with him.*

He had no idea what the vision meant, but he knew in his heart that this was a sign from his god. Three symbols: a ten-pointed reddish star next to a dark red moon crescent, and above them, a white handprint.

Below them, faintly seen, a row of clouds.

Hoshi'tiwa said, "What is it?" unable to take her eyes off the pictograph painted on the rock: a white handprint suspended above a reddish star with ten points and a dark red crescent moon.

"My grandfather's grandfather was He Who Links People for my clan, and he witnessed this miracle in the daytime sky, a star so bright and a moon so clear that he knew it was a portent. The star burned brightly for days and then dimmed once it knew the men below had seen it and beheld its glory. My grandfather's grandfather painted what he saw here on this Memory Wall but kept it a secret within the clan. The star is you, Hoshi'tiwa. The moon is the time when you will unite our people, when you will teach them the ways of balance and harmony, thus preparing the way for Pahana to return. And the handprint is my grandfather's grandfather's promise that what he saw and painted here is all true."

"But how do you know it is I?"

"Look beneath the star and the moon. What do you see?"

The pictograph was unclear. It looked like a row of clouds.

"Those are rain clouds, and you are the rain," Yani said.

How? cried Hoshi'tiwa's spirit. How can the daughter of a corn grower unify a scattered people who have lost their way? I am no teacher!

Pressing her hand to her breast, she felt beneath her dress the reassuring shape and hardness of the bear claw that Ahoté had given her. It was her only connection to home and family, where she desperately wished to be.

In the next instant, darkness engulfed her, and through the darkness a face emerged: piercing eyes staring at her from above a sharp nose like that of a predatory bird. He was so lifelike, it was as if he actually stood there before her. Lord Jakál's lips were moving as if he spoke to her, but no sound came out.

A hot wind blew up out of the stillness then, whipping up sand and twigs, swirling around Hoshi'tiwa's legs like a madly spinning spirit. She closed her eyes against the stinging grit, and when she suddenly felt a sharp pain in her shins, she slumped against the wall.

"What is it, Daughter?" Yani asked, alarmed at the strange wind that died just as suddenly as it had appeared, and the morning was still again.

Hoshi'tiwa looked down at her legs, expecting to see blood. But her legs were smooth and unharmed.

Seated again on the stone bench, with the mist and smoke beginning to dissipate, Jakál finished collecting the blood that dripped from his shins. He was weak and drenched in sweat, but his head was clear. He knew beyond a doubt that the star in his vision was the Morning Star, Quetzalcoatl's physical manifestation. The handprint was that of Blue Hummingbird, reminding the *tlatoani* of his duty to rule Center Place with a strong hand. The clouds beneath were the rain-girl.

And the quarter moon—

No longer of divided mind, he knew what he must do.

For Quetzalcoatl, the girl would bring rain, and afterward she would be sacrificed on the altar of blood. And for Blue Hummingbird, Jakál would hold a mass human sacrifice on the last quarter moon before the Solstice.

With his spirit, and the world, thus in balance once again, Jakál knew that Quetzalcoatl would be pleased.

"You are the chosen of your god," the priest had said to the neophyte long ago. And Jakál, now trembling with passion in his sacred kiva, thought: Yes . . .

Yani said, "There is no doubt of it, Daughter. You are the one chosen to lead our people into a new age."

And Hoshi'tiwa, shivering with fear beneath the prophetic pictographs, thought: No . . .

BOOK TWO

Blood and Clay

Fifteen

"THE caravan! The caravan is coming!"

Lord Jakál, in the middle of his morning *chocolatl,* hastily wrapped his cloak about himself and hurried from the chamber. His bodyguards scrambled to follow while servants ran for his chair, his shade umbrella, his feather fans. Jakál stepped out onto the plaza to find the populace in such turmoil that no one noticed the unannounced appearance of the *tlatoani;* no one fell to their knees in obeisance.

Jakál did not mind. He was trembling with joy and relief. The caravan had come at last.

Having also heard the shouts, Captain Xikli dashed out of the barracks, where he had been drilling his men for the Solstice festival.

Lady White Orchid left her mirror and cosmetics and ran into her father's bedroom. "Did you hear the herald, Father? The caravan has come!"

Across the valley, Moquihix sat up from his sleeping mat and looked down at Yellow Feather, who snoozed next to him in contented slumber. Had he dreamed hearing the cry of the herald? No, his servants were running out of the house, and he heard happy shouts outside.

Priests came running from the Star Chamber and from the rising-splendors up and down the canyon. Nobles emerged from their villas. Merchants and officials struggled into their loincloths and cloaks. The potters in the workshop jumped up from their labors and fled out the door with Tupa waddling as fast as she could into the sunlight to glimpse, at the eastern end of the canyon, the faint cloud of dust that indicated many men marching along the road.

Even the People of the Sun, who were not Toltec and who had never seen the city far to the south where the caravan originated, came out of their huts and shelters, abandoned their cook fires and meager cornfields to rush to the main plaza of Precious Green, where the caravan would halt.

Surrounded by a growing, happy crowd, Yani and Hoshi'tiwa stood in the morning sunlight, smiling at each other. The arrival of the long-overdue human train from the south was a good sign; it meant all was well with the world, that what had gone on before was still going on. And perhaps it was also an omen that rain would come to Center Place.

The sun was high by the time Chief Physician Nagual arrived at the compound adjacent to the barracks to inspect the men being held there—prisoners of war captured during battles with Toltec soldiers, who had been marched to Center Place with the caravan. He noted that they were a pathetic bunch, skin and bone, infested with sores, barely alive.

Captain Xikli shared the doctor's dismal opinion. According to the Caravan Master, only a quarter of the captives had survived the journey from Tollan—an arduous trek through jungle, mountain, and desert—and even those were at death's threshold.

"This one's dead," the Chief Physician said. With a foot luxuriously clad in ocelot-skin slippers, he nudged the body growing stiff beneath the sun.

The captives' moans and pleas for food and water could barely be heard over the din that filled the valley. With the arrival of the caravan, the populace had commenced to engage in lively commerce as merchants displayed new goods, citizens pushed and jostled in good nature, men haggled, business deals were conducted, marriage arrangements discussed. For today at least, the gods smiled upon Center Place.

But for how long? Xikli wondered, sensing that underneath the gaiety ran a current of fear. The caravan, comprising hundreds of slaves, had not brought water, yet now the valley must accommodate all those new thirsty throats.

As he moved among the prisoners with the Chief Physician, he rubbed the thick scar that bisected his face. The caravan this year was noticeably smaller than the previous year's. And this time the caravan had brought not only goods from the south, but news of increased civil unrest in Tollan and enemy armies drawing closer to the city walls.

Xikli squinted up at the sun as he followed Nagual among the men crouched or lying in the dirt of the fenced compound, and he wondered if Tollan, like all great cities before her, was going to fall.

Rather than fill him with fear, as the news did to others, it only heartened Xikli and firmed his resolve to become the *tlatoani* of Center Place.

Because his ambition did not end with this canyon.

It was time for a new empire, the Captain had decided. There was no need for Center Place to continue to be a mere outpost. It could be made into the heart of a new realm, made as great as Tollan, as great as Teotihuacan had once been. There were rich lands to the north where herds of buffalo darkened the plains. To the east and west, mines were filled with gold and sky-stone, and to the south lay an unending source of slave labor.

This was the destiny Xikli had been born to; he was certain of it. To bring the glory of the Toltecs to this bountiful land.

"They need food," Nagual pronounced when he had looked at the last of the wretches in the compound. "Meat. And rest. Let them sleep for seven days. Bring women for their pleasure. And extra rations of water."

Xikli murmured agreement, although his thoughts were elsewhere. Once on the throne, he would implement many changes at Center Place.

Jakál did not extend the aqueducts and canals as Xikli believed he should, but rather expected the rain to come on its own. He imports a rain-girl to Center Place, Xikli thought in contempt, instead of using slaves to build more canals and aqueducts that reach far into the mountains where the rain falls. Xikli would create a corps of engineers to build canals to those faraway water places.

Xikli despised his rival. Jakál could have all the women he wanted, yet he used none of them. He could command venison for his table, yet sated himself with rabbit and pigeon. One would think he was still a priest of Quetzalcoatl, he denied himself so.

If I were Lord, Xikli thought as Nagual barked orders to the men guarding the compound, I would live in the manner that is the *tlatoani*'s right. Girls to share my mat every night. Bison meat on my table.

But seizing the throne was not so simple as just overthrowing Jakál. Xikli needed to prove to the aristocracy and priestly castes that he was a worthy successor. Jakál's bloodline was far superior to Xikli's; therefore, the Captain of the Jaguars needed to form an alliance with a powerful house. There was only one choice: Lady White Orchid, the daughter of a Hero of the Empire, was related to the royal house of Tollan, making her almost a princess. Not a bad-looking woman, if a bit old at nearly thirty. But there was the added bonus of her villa.

White Orchid's land was particularly valuable because of a large masonry-and-earthen dam that had been built across a nearby wash, diverting floodwaters and rain runoff into a canal-and-ditch system that ran through her property. Her father, Tenoch, had cleverly maneuvered this so that he and his daughter controlled the water and could charge a small price to those who received the runoff downstream.

With almost-princess White Orchid as his wife, and Hero of the Empire Tenoch as his father-in-law, and with other powerful alliances Xikli was slowly and secretly cultivating, he saw his future as clearly as he saw the sun in the cloudless sky: He was going to be the richest, most powerful man on earth.

"Captain?"

Xikli came out of his thoughts as the physician's red-painted face came close to his. Nagual's great crest of hair, rising from his shaven head from forehead to the back of his neck, danced in the spring breeze.

Here was another man the Captain of the Jaguars did not like. Nagual had arrived eight years prior with Jakál, the previous Chief Physician having been slain upon the *tlatoani*'s death, as was the custom. Nagual was a taciturn man who doled out his words as if they were made of sky-stone. It annoyed Xikli, who believed that silent men kept secrets.

But men's secrets could sometimes be used against them, and so Xikli, with his network of spies, collected secrets in the same way Lady White Orchid collected seashells.

And the Chief Physician's was an interesting one. Nagual's surprising vow of celibacy had stemmed from the mysterious circumstances surrounding the death of his son. The boy had been caught in an intimate relationship with a common girl, the daughter of a potter. The girl had been slain and the boy sent back to Tollan to train in the guards as his punishment. The boy and his contingent were in the southern highlands when he came to a violent end. Rumors had drifted north that the death was not accidental but a suicide, which was a powerful taboo among the Toltecs. Although the report was but gossip and hearsay, with no proof that the boy had self-immolated, nonetheless it had shamed the Chief Physician into a vow of celibacy as atonement for his son's sin.

And Captain Xikli, always ready to turn another man's tragedy into his own gain, had tucked the information away against the day he might use it to his own advantage.

He strode out of the compound to leave the care of the sacrificial victims, which he had requested of the King of Tollan, in the hands of the physician. In a few days, on the last quarter moon before the Solstice, the peasants in this valley were going to witness the true power of the Toltecs.

He wished he could add the rain-girl to the mass sacrifice. But her turn would come. Let her enjoy life now, in the ignorant belief that once she brought rain she would be allowed to go home. When the day came, her beating heart was going to please the gods indeed.

Jakál's eyes widened as the great paper scroll was unrolled before him and his architects and builders gathered around to shake their heads and make throaty sounds over their Lord's newest project.

A new rising-splendor at Center Place.

The scroll had come with the caravan, and Jakál had ordered it to be delivered to Blue Hummingbird, the rising-splendor to the east of Precious Green—a stone-and-mortar complex of hundreds of rooms, terraces, five levels high—because here was where the offices and archives of his engineers were housed. Here would be the center of operations for the new project.

"My Lord, this plan will call for much wood," the Chief Architect said. A man born in Tollan to old-fashioned parents, his eyes were crossed due to the bead that had been suspended between his eyes during his first year of life. The outmoded practice was once believed to ward off the evil eye and protect an infant from malevolent forces. Many men of his generation were cross-eyed. To some, it was a symbol of prestige. "We will need wood for laying out the foundation, for the scaffolding, for the framework of the steps." He looked at Jakál with an anxious expression.

At Center Place up and down the canyon, small houses, shacks and huts, and the hundreds of thatched shade arbors in the canyon used local wood: juniper, piñon, and cottonwood. For the rising-splendors, however, heavier wood was imported from the mountains far to the north, where the Lords operated timber camps using forced labor—men conscripted from the outlying settlements and farms and marched up into the mountains, there to chop down massive pines, spruce, and fir, cut the logs into predetermined lengths, after which the logs were hauled along the Toltec highways to Center Place. The process was long and hazardous; few timberworkers ever returned to their homes.

The architect repeated, "My Lord, we have not enough wood to commence this project."

But Jakál had already called for more men to be sent to the timber camps. "We will have enough," he said. "Until then, we have plenty of wood in the scaffolding up and down the valley. Take from that."

"But, my Lord," interjected the Master Builder, "we dare not weaken the scaffolding further."

Jakál silenced him.

"And we will need many strong backs—"

"I will get the men," Jakál said, already intending to send out the call for a tribute of ten men to be sent to Center Place from each outlying settlement.

"We will need food to feed so many workers, my Lord. A place to house them. And water, my Lord. Where will we find more water? The reservoir grows low—"

Jakál made an impatient gesture. The rain-girl was going to bring rain to Center Place, which would provide enough food and water to sustain an army of workers. And after she was sacrificed on the altar of blood, Tlaloc in his pleasure would send so much rain that Jakál could build a hundred rising-splendors.

And then Quetzalcoatl, the bearded white savior who had lived among the Toltecs a thousand years ago, teaching them music and astronomy and the art of healing, and who promised to return someday from across the eastern sea, would materialize triumphantly at Center Place.

Time was her enemy.

Lady White Orchid had never thought that her people's passion for understanding time—in their obsession with calendars, months, and years, with naming and numbering every season and day—would be the bane of her existence.

Her father had made it clear: She must marry soon.

And if she did not find a mate, then he would find one for her. White Orchid feared he had the detestable Captain Xikli in mind.

Therefore she paced and wrung her hands, frequently looking out the window for a sign of the Caravan Master, because he was bringing her something that would aid in her campaign to win the heart of Lord Jakál.

Finally he arrived, a squat, bandy-legged man whose back had grown twisted from spending too many months riding on a litter through jungle, mountain, and desert. When he walked, it was with a rolling gait and much puffing of his barrel chest.

White Orchid had to smile and suffer torturous patience while her guest fed himself and spoke of inconsequential matters. The Caravan Master didn't even bother swallowing before stuffing more food into his mouth. And his gluttony for water was beyond belief. With such extreme drought conditions, she was appalled to watch him gulp water as if it were in endless supply. He even allowed the precious liquid to dribble down his chin as he said to his hostess, "I have brought you a gift." And he gestured to a slave who stood attendant in the doorway.

While they waited for the gift to be brought, the Caravan Master helped himself to another roasted pigeon, pulling it apart with his hands.

The trek from Tollan to Center Place, the farthest outpost of the empire, was sixty days of hardship and deprivation, and in that time the caravan leader lost more than men at the wayside—he lost weight. Because he lived well in Tollan, with a fat wife and eight robust children, in a villa on the river so that food was always plentiful, the Master was portly when he started out for Center Place. Sixty days later, he was lean. He would rest awhile here, stuff himself with all the good things Center Place offered and then, plump again, would start back down for Tollan, arriving so lean that his wife would laugh at him.

Thus he always arrived in an advanced state of greed. Only after his appetites for food, *nequhtli,* and sex were satisfied, did he concentrate on amassing sky-stone, gold, buffalo skins, and slaves.

The Caravan Master's servant returned, leading a dwarf on a leash.

"His name is Popo, my lady. He will amuse you." The servant released the rope, and the little man cavorted around the room, making comical faces, doing tumbles and somersaults. When he farted loudly, the Caravan Master roared with laughter, but White Orchid said impatiently, "I don't wish to be amused."

"Perhaps your father—?"

She waved a dismissive hand. As amusing as the dwarf might be for her father, she did not want to be in this man's debt.

He heaved a sigh. No matter. Popo would fetch a good price in the marketplace.

"Did you bring the item I requested?"

"Here it is, my lady." He wiped his hands on his cloak and handed her an object wrapped in cloth. When she opened it and her eyes beheld the rare treasure, White Orchid smiled in satisfaction. She would consult an astrologer for the most auspicious day on which to present this to Jakál.

Now came the awkward moment. She needed to ask the Caravan Master about the aphrodisiac snake the old woman with the lame grandson had told her about. But she was a lady, and Toltec ladies did not bring up such indelicate topics with strangers.

She spoke indirectly, using metaphors and innuendo until the Caravan Master, who knew the ways of the world and especially of women and romance, grasped her meaning and said, "Yes, I have heard of this serpent with the venom that can turn men's hearts."

"Can you fetch me one?"

He gave this some thought and, remembering his wife's lazy brother who needed a new plot of land to feed his growing brood, and thinking that the look in this lady's eye told him she would pay any price, said, "I can procure the snake. But it will be very costly, as hunting the snake is dangerous for the men who hunt it. They will command a high price."

"I will pay it."

"I must warn you, my lady, use of this serpent carries grave risks. You must allow it to strike only once. With a drop of the snake's venom in his blood, the man's heart will belong to you forever. But if the serpent strikes twice, the venom is lethal and the man will die a long and agonizing death."

"I will be careful."

He held up a cautionary hand. "My lady, I must emphasize. This snake is known for striking swiftly in succession. You must be very quick when you apply it to your—*lover*." He had almost said *victim*.

"When next you come from Tollan, bring me the snake."

After the Caravan Master was gone, White Orchid turned her attention to the mess the man had left, when a scream suddenly tore the air.

It had come from her father's bedroom.

She ran, flinging aside the drapery over the doorway, to find Tenoch sprawled on the floor, waving his arms as if to protect himself from a flying creature. "Go away!" he screamed. "Leave me in peace!"

White Orchid dropped to his side. "Father, what is it?"

"Go away!"

She ducked a flailing arm and, with the help of two male servants, managed to subdue the old man. As they carried him back to his sleeping mat, White Orchid detected the strong smell of *nequhtli* on him. It shocked her. Tenoch never drank to excess. And now, the drinking that had begun to alarm her of late was getting out of control. Also—she had never seen such fear in his eyes as he ranted and raved at an unseen foe.

She saw the ceramic mug with the eight-legged creature painted upon it lying beside the mat, a few drops of liquor still inside. *"Beware of a strange mythical creature with eight arms. It wants to embrace you. Do not let it, for it will suffocate you."* The sudden memory of the old herb peddler's prophecy sent a cold shiver down her spine.

"What is it, Father?" she cried. "What ails you?"

"He won't leave me alone," Tenoch whimpered, his eyes darting back and forth at a point past her shoulder.

"Fetch Chief Physician Nagual," White Orchid snapped at one of the servants. "Hurry!"

Tenoch was sobbing on his daughter's shoulder when the somber physician arrived, medicine case slung over his shoulder, a pale-faced apprentice at his side. After hearing a brief account from White Orchid, Nagual slipped into the bedroom, closed the drape behind himself, and left Tenoch's daughter to wait with the apprentice.

From the other side of the drapery they heard sobbing—bitter, wretched weeping—and what sounded like a mumbled plea, or a desperate confession. The words were incoherent, but the tone and emotions were recognizable. Tenoch the Hero was a man in torment. White Orchid's stomach tensed with fear. Had an evil spirit taken possession of her father?

When Nagual emerged a short while later, he wordlessly retrieved his case from the apprentice and made to leave.

"What of my father?" asked White Orchid, stopping him at the door.

Nagual leveled cryptic eyes upon her and weighed his thoughts. Though she was Tenoch's daughter, it was unthinkable that Nagual discuss the man's problem with her. Nonetheless, seeing the fear and worry in her eyes, he said, "I shall undertake his cure."

She wrung her hands. "Will he be all right?"

"That is up to the gods. But listen to me, woman. You are never to speak of this night. You are never to ask your father what troubles him. These are grave matters that are not your concern." And with that, the physician disappeared into the night.

Sixteen

ALTHOUGH she knew she walked upon taboo ground, Hoshi'tiwa could not stop herself. Lord Jakál was there, waiting to greet the dawn, and she needed to ask him a question.

Since her arrival at Center Place, she had not been able to get out of her mind the fact that he had allowed her to live after she had trespassed upon sacred ground and had looked upon the most powerful man in the land while he was at his sacred prayers. Poor Noseless had been horribly executed merely for speaking the Lord's name. Yet Jakál had not had her killed. Why? She decided she would simply ask him.

When she reached the mesa high above Center Place, to stand on top of the world with only the stars between herself and the gods, she looked for him, her eyes scanning the scrubby brush, boulders, and paltry cottonwoods. She found him standing at the edge of the plateau, facing east. Jakál looked exactly as he had that first night, and he was singing now, as he had been then, a most beautiful, high-pitched song, as if his throat were a flute. His arms were outstretched, bathed in starlight, with his long hair streaming down his naked back.

Hoshi'tiwa held her breath. Strange sensations filled her. When she had

observed him that first forbidden night, she had known only fear and apprehension. But this time, new feelings swam in her blood. Exciting, terrifying
feelings.

Jakál turned suddenly, his dark eyes seeking and finding her in the night.
He did not seem surprised to see her there. Nor was he outraged, demanding
she be punished for sacrilege. Instead his gaze remained on her, secretive and
alluring.

Her feet moved on their own, carrying her across the sandy ground until
she came to stand two arm-lengths from him. When Jakál's eyes traveled up
and down her body, and his lips lifted in a smile, Hoshi'tiwa looked down at
herself and saw in shock that she was naked. What had she done with her
clothes? Strangely, she felt neither embarrassed nor shy, but only a sweet excitement that thrummed in her veins.

"You have a question," he said in a soft voice.

"Why did you not have me killed when I trespassed upon sacred
ground?"

His eyebrows rose, as if her question were an absurd one. "I cannot kill
you."

"Why not?"

He blinked. "Because I am the blood and you are the clay." Stated
matter-of-factly, as if she should already know this.

"What does that mean?"

Jakál held her eyes with his for a long moment, then he stepped toward
her until he was close, and she could see starlight in his pupils, feel warmth
emanating from his body. When he bent his head and touched his nose to hers
in a gentle kiss, Hoshi'tiwa did not draw back. She felt no alarm or fear. And
when he brushed his lips over her chin and cheeks, she leaned into him, feeling the heat intensify within her.

Jakál took her into his arms and Hoshi'tiwa bent to him. His skin was
hot. He smelled of sage and pine. His hands sent delicious tremors through
her flesh. Suddenly she could not breathe. She put her arms around his neck,
so filled now with desire for him that she thought she would die if he did not
lie with her right then, in that moment before the Morning Star rose.

He lowered her to the ground, and she was surprised to feel a fine cotton

*cloak beneath her bare back, protecting her from the coarse sand. Jakál's long
hair fell forward, brushing her shoulders and breast. Hoshi'tiwa's heart galloped like a wild antelope.*

*His hands explored her body. She was a willing prisoner of his intense
gaze. Holding her with his eyes, he sent his hands downward, gliding over
her trembling skin until—*

Hoshi'tiwa cried out. Her eyes snapped open and she found herself
staring up at the underside of the workshop bower until she realized it
was night and she had been dreaming.

She lay still on her mat, listening to the respirations and gentle snores
of the potters, fearful that her sighs and moans had disturbed them. But
her sister potters slumbered peacefully on.

Hoshi'tiwa breathed deeply to calm her racing heart. What had just
happened? Never in her life had she been visited by such a dream. Never
had her body been inflamed by such desires. Her skin burned. Her heart
galloped. And deep within her abdomen, a sweet ache . . .

Jakál. She closed her eyes to hang on to shreds of the vanishing
dream. Were these feelings normal? Was the dream a betrayal of her
love for Ahoté? Should she feel ashamed?

And then she thought: Yani will know.

Realizing that she was not going to sleep for the rest of the night,
and driven by emotions she did not understand, Hoshi'tiwa left her
sleeping mat to tiptoe between the others, hoping that Yani would not
mind being wakened, and would have a way to help Hoshi'tiwa through
her confusion and feelings of guilt.

But Yani's sleeping mat was vacant, her cloak gone. Thinking she
was outside answering nature's call, Hoshi'tiwa went to the edge of the
arbor and peered into the night. There was Yani, wrapped in her cloak,
but hastily making her way across the valley. Hoshi'tiwa was shocked.
Only the extremely brave or extremely foolish ventured forth at night,
when ghosts and demons walked the land.

Briefly forgetting her dream, Hoshi'tiwa wondered where Yani hurried off to, at such a dangerous hour. She knew Yani had no family in the
canyon, and that her close friends were either potters or basketmakers,

with a couple of friends who were servants at Precious Green. Yet the cloaked form was making its way unmistakably across the canyon, nearly running, and following a dusty path that cut through cornfields and eventually ended at the mysterious building called the Star Chamber.

With the chill air biting her skin, and remembering that she herself was exposing herself to evil spirits, Hoshi'tiwa quickly ducked back under the bower and into the safety of her sleeping sisters. Bewildered, she returned to her mat, thinking what a strange night this was, marveling at the new heat that burned within her. She was thirsty, but the water urn was off-limits until morning. Anyone caught stealing a sip during the night was severely punished.

As soon as Hoshi'tiwa lay down, memories of the dream returned in full force. Her heart jumped; her body came alive. As the image of Lord Jakál filled her mind, a new and startling thought occurred to her: that the Lord's spirit visited her in her sleep.

Had the Lord of Center Place in fact *shared the same dream?*

Seventeen

A S the Solstice festival drew closer, the atmosphere in the potters' workshop grew tense, for it was their ceramics that the rain-god priests were counting on to bring rain. Even Tupa lowered her bulk onto a mat and put her hand to clay, helping with the scraping and forming, the sanding and polishing, and mixing vegetables and minerals for the final paint.

Hoshi'tiwa concentrated on her work so that she did not have to listen to her thoughts. Yani's words about a terrifying prophecy continued to ring in her ears. Hoshi'tiwa was *not* the teacher Yani had spoken of. Yani was mistaken; it was another daughter of Tortoise Clan they were expecting. But it *was* her fault that Yani had drawn the erroneous conclusion, because Hoshi'tiwa had acted inappropriately by standing up to Tupa—to go so far as to grab the overseer's wrist while she was administering punishment to one of the guild members.

Hoshi'tiwa must fight such impulses. Even though she had been unfairly snatched from her family and home, she nonetheless must comport herself like a true Daughter of the Sun, with modesty, patience, and obedience. She was *not* different from everyone else. She wanted only to bring rain and go home. Therefore, she vowed on her mother's love and on the bear claw that lay upon her breast that from now on she would control her emotions and do as she was told.

Above all, she silently vowed, she would not think of Lord Jakál and the frightening, erotic dream.

Eighteen

"TUPA! Tupa, come quickly. Mouse is ill!"

The overseer waddled over and looked down at the woman lying prostrate on her sleeping mat. "What's wrong with her?"

"She says her chest hurts, and her skin feels like fire."

Tupa drew no nearer, but stared at the potter for a moment—this one was good with delicate figurines, and the guild could not afford to lose her—then ordered two workers to go out and bring back the old herbalist named Pikami.

But as the two pottery workers searched the marketplace for Pikami, asking her whereabouts, news of the sickness in the workshop reached Moquihix. And because rain was the number one priority of the Lords, sickness could not be allowed at the Potters' Guild.

When he strode unannounced into the workshop, the workers ceased their labors and dropped to their knees. Although the sick one was the reason he had come, the High Minister could not help searching the curved feminine backs for that of the girl who continued to plague his dreams.

Hoshi'tiwa was in the corner, crouched on her knees, her forehead pressed to the floor. To see her in such a posture created a stirring in his loins, and he cursed her anew for the black magic she was working on him. The plump one, Yellow Feather, was crouched nearby, her familiar wide hips high in the air. His arousal increased at the sight of her as well, and the old adage that it never rains but pours came to mind. After months of impotence, he felt as virile as a young man again.

Tupa led Moquihix to where the groaning woman lay. He stared down at her, and then snapped an order at one of his attendants to bring Nagual the Chief Physician to the workshop.

One of the prostrate women let out a gasp. Moquihix looked around, but could not tell which had made the sound of surprise. When the High Minister strode out, Yani heaved a shaky sigh of relief.

The Chief Physician arrived, tall and lean, with a magnificent crest of hair, plugs in his ears that had stretched his lobes so that they brushed his shoulders, and a jade plug in his nose that gave him a ferocious aspect. The women and girls retreated in his presence, but Hoshi'tiwa noticed that Yani most of all seemed terrified of the man as he knelt over the ailing woman.

What had Nagual done to her, Hoshi'tiwa wondered, that made her so frightened of him?

The Chief Physician had been trained at the great learning center in Tollan, under the strict tutelage of Toltec priests. He now followed precisely the protocol he had practiced in the years since. A physician never spoke to the patient or asked about symptoms, since how could a sick person give the right answers when those must come from the gods? The physician, though a healer, was above all a sorcerer, but a benign one, practicing only good magic.

He had brought with him a sacred jar filled with holy water, and upon the water he threw a handful of grass seeds while chanting magic spells and reciting the sick woman's name over and over. He closely observed how the seeds sank and at what rate.

After reading and interpreting the answers in the seeds, he looked up at Tupa and spoke with urgency. "The spirits possessing this woman wish to possess all of you and keep the rain from coming. Carry her at once to your kiva, place her there with no food or water, and no companions. She must be alone in the kiva, for when the spirits leave her body they will seek another vessel. If she is alone, they will ride away on the smoke and leave this valley. Hurry now."

Yani and Hoshi'tiwa were chosen to hold vigil outside the kiva, and when night fell and the stars came out, Hoshi'tiwa found the courage to ask, "Yani, why are you afraid of the Chief Physician?"

The older woman's eyes widened. "Why do you say that?"

"I have seen it on your face on two occasions when you beheld the Chief Physician. You are afraid of him."

Yani bowed her head and stared at her hands. "I told you that my daughter was found in the arms of a noble youth. That she was executed for taking pleasure with him, a Toltec boy, and you know that such unions are forbidden."

She lifted shimmering eyes filled with moon-glow and said softly, "That boy was the Chief Physician's son." She paused, then added, "It is whispered that the boy took his own life on his return to the city in the south, and now great shame has fallen upon the Chief Physician."

Tupa arrived the next morning, and when they lifted the cover of the kiva, found the woman dead. Nagual pronounced it a good cure. The spirits of sickness were gone, he said. The potters were safe.

Nineteen

FINALLY the day of firing was upon them. The potters had not slept the night before, and Tupa was in a particularly foul mood as the success or failure of today's firing would be laid at her feet.

This was the most precarious stage. If the clay had not been properly dried, or if air pockets existed, those days of previous effort would be rendered worthless. The women gently laid their rain jars on the stone racks in the kiln while Tupa oversaw the building of the fire underneath. Then heavy leather covers were laid over the top of the stone oven to intensify the heat inside.

They prayed and chanted and watched the kiln, nervously listening for the telltale sound that meant a pot had exploded. Finally, Tupa lifted the cover to peer in, saw the ash and dying embers, and declared it to have been a successful firing.

One by one the new vessels were brought out into the light—dazzling white bowls and jars and pitchers painted with stark black designs. Yani's pitchers, Yellow Feather's bowls. All perfect. Tension mounted with each new ceramic lifted from the ash, for a broken pot would be the worst omen.

Hoshi'tiwa's was the last to emerge from the kiln. The women held their breath as Tupa reached in with wooden tongs, for this was the piece made of homely gray clay, and it was created by the new girl, who was untried in the guild. Tupa placed the jar on the yucca mat and gently brushed away the ash.

Everyone stared in shock, for the ceramic was not white like the others, but had turned a beautiful hue, the orange-gold of a summer sunrise, and the design was not black but red, like a blazing autumn sunset.

There was not another like it in all of Center Place.

Twenty

T HE priests began the purification of the main plaza before dawn, making a circuit with their drums and flutes and rattles, bowls of incense held high, the drone of their steady chanting sounding like a swarm of bees.

Everyone knew the significance of the sacred rite: Today was the day the captives who had been brought by the caravan were to be sacrificed to the bloody gods of Center Place. Many had seen the ritual before, but not in such numbers, and the anticipation filled all with both fear and excitement.

A hundred beating hearts were to be offered to the gods today.

For this special occasion, the gods themselves were brought out from their sacred sanctuaries—men and women carved in stone riding high on colorful litters, with names that held no significance for the People of the Sun: Xipe Totec, Huitzilpochtli, Quetzalcoatl. Barely recognizable as human, the stone idols were decked out in feathers and cloaks, paint and jewelry. The Toltecs gave cries of wonder and obeisance when the pantheon was paraded in the plaza, while the People of the Sun looked upon the gods and goddesses as lifeless blocks of stone and nothing more.

When the plaza was declared ready, the various priestly brother-hoods took their places around the perimeter, along with the Jaguars who had dressed in their finest, complete with padded armor and blood-stained weapons. Next came the high officials arrayed in their most im-pressive ornaments and headdresses, and then the nobles and their wives. Lady White Orchid and her father, Tenoch the Hero, enjoyed seats of honor next to the priestesses of Precious Green. Down on the plain, from the foot of the plaza and stretching out, the People of the Sun formed a sea of humanity, so hushed and silent that the pennants of the gods, flying from terraces and rooftops, could be heard snapping in the breeze.

Lord Jakál assumed his throne with his High Minister Moquihix on one side, Captain Xikli on the other. Chief Physician Nagual took his place beside the altar of blood, where the first victim was now brought, dressed only in a loincloth, and laid out on his back, with a priest hold-ing each wrist and ankle. The man had been among those collected in the fenced compound where Nagual had ordered food and drink and women. For seven days the victims had lived well, knowing their fate because it was the glorious fate of all those captured in battle to be sacri-ficed to the enemy's gods.

The man did not resist. He was dazed with drugs. This was neces-sary for the procurement of a beating heart, as a terrified man died when the knife slashed his chest. It was Nagual's responsibility to see that just enough of the elixir had been administered—too much and the victim slept through his sacrifice; not enough and he died of terror.

The Chief Priest of Tlaloc, a man with a shaven head and painted blue from head to foot, raised the obsidian knife high, brought it down, and, with expert skill honed over the years, slit the man's skin, muscle, and breastbone the way Quail sliced into his birds, leaving the man still alive to watch as a second priest swiftly reached in with both hands and plucked the beating heart from his chest and held it aloft for all to see.

A roar erupted from the throats of the Jaguars, who pounded their spears on their wooden shields, causing such a thunderous sound that the people on the plain thought the cliffs would crumble and fall.

The heart was thrown into a special sacrificial bowl, and the next victim was brought, and then the next, the knife coming down, the Jaguars roaring, until the sun reached its zenith and then began its slide into the west, and the stone vessel filled with hearts and blood to the glee of the gods and to the horror of the People of the Sun who stood as pillars on the plain, wondering how the world had gone so far out of balance that it had come to this.

One who watched in the crowd was neither terrified nor filled with sorrow—old Pikami, who leaned on the lame boy as the sun beat down on their heads and filled the day with the stench of blood. Her attention was not upon the sacrifice in the plaza, nor upon the victims. She was thinking of another day of horror, long ago, when her life had changed forever, and the burden of guilt had begun to weigh upon her spine.

The sun had been shining then, too, on that fateful day. But there had been water in the seasonal river, and the air was fresh, filled with birdsong and breeze. The memory filled her mind so sharply and with such poignancy that it blocked out all else. Oblivious of the mob around her, Pikami was back at the river, young again, and the memory caused such pain that when she cried out, those around her thought it was in sympathy for the men being slain on the sacrificial altar.

No one knew the chant that haunted her guilt-ridden mind: I turned my back for but a moment . . . but a moment . . . a moment . . .

Others in the crowd, however, watched the slaughter, unable to take their eyes away. Hoshi'tiwa, standing with her sister potters, wanted to weep for the poor men led staggering to the altar of blood, wanted to shout out her anger at this injustice, wanted to turn and flee to the peace and harmony of her little farm in the north, but knew she could do none of these, that she was as helpless as the men on the altar of blood.

And through the haze of her confused emotions, she watched Lord Jakál on his throne, recalling her dream about him, now sick with shame that she had, even if only in a dream, enjoyed pleasure with him.

Twenty-one

THE sisterhood of potters cleaned their bodies with pine-scented sand and donned new shifts with the distinctive embroidery of their guild. They took extra pains in dressing each other's hair, and fasted and prayed and waited for the priests of Tlaloc to come for the rain jars.

The Solstices were always tense times because they symbolized extremes: Days and nights were either very long or very short, temperatures were either very hot or very cold. It was why the People of the Sun loved the Equinoxes, when day and night were equal, and even if it was hot or cold, everyone knew that milder days lay ahead. Equinoxes were times of order and balance. Solstices were not.

In the potters' workshop, the new rain vessels were lined up on a workbench, gleaming in the sun. Hoshi'tiwa's stood out from the rest. Her own family made the traditional black-on-white pottery to trade with other settlements, but for themselves they made the golden bowls, but there was only enough clay for their own use. This was why one had never been seen in Center Place.

Hoshi'tiwa prayed the rain-god priests would choose hers. And then her bowl would sit out in the plaza beneath the cloudless sky, gleaming in the sun, and the Cloud Spirits would not be able to resist coming to take a look. Never had the rain been able to resist Hoshi'tiwa's pottery. The spirits would see its beauty and symmetry and design, and the desire to fill the bowl would be irresistible.

Thus were Hoshi'tiwa's thoughts when Moquihix arrived in his scarlet cloak and brilliant green tunic, accompanied by the blue-painted, blue-robed priests of Tlaloc. The potters fell respectfully silent, permitted on this one day to remain standing. Even Tupa, who was rarely quiet, held her tongue as the high official and holy men made a slow inspection of the rain jars. Their expressions were unreadable as they walked along the line of newly fired ceramics, but when they came to the end, the three men stopped and frowned in puzzlement.

They were staring at the golden jar.

When Tupa saw on Moquihix's face that he was impressed, she boasted, "I found the clay myself, Lord, I saw the color of sunlight in its homely gray."

Moquihix fixed Tupa with a sharp eye. "You made this jar yourself?"

She lifted her chin. "Well, no. I am after all too busy. You said the new girl was to be given a chance, and so I gave to her the job of working with the new clay."

Hoshi'tiwa's heart galloped. She felt color flush her cheeks. Moquihix had already betrayed his admiration of the jar—and now he knew it was hers! What would he do next? Would pride make him grind it beneath his feet, or would his loyalty to the Lord and the need for rain make him swallow that bitter pride and choose her jar for the plaza?

He conferred with the two priests, and when it was obvious they were also impressed with the golden bowl, Tupa added eagerly, "I can make many more like this one, Lord."

Moquihix frowned. "There is only the one?"

"The new girl is slow, Lord. My guild turns out numerous vessels and figurines a day. But this lazy creature takes her time. She *dreams* while she works."

Moquihix gestured to a rain-god priest to hand him the jar, and as the priest picked it up, the jar fell apart in his hands.

Silence descended upon the workshop as everyone looked in horror at the two equal halves, one in each hand. It was the worst luck for a new pot to break, especially one that was to be dedicated to the gods. Hoshi'tiwa was also shocked, but only for a moment, because in the next instant she realized what she had done.

She had approached the making of the jar with the wrong sentiments in her heart—selfish sentiments that were driven by homesickness and a longing to escape. Instead of keeping her thoughts holy and pure, thinking only of the welfare of the people, she had desecrated her holy task by spinning fantasies of running away with Ahoté. That was why the jar broke. Hoshi'tiwa was suddenly ashamed and filled with regret.

Perhaps she was *makai-yó* after all.

When a shadow darkened the doorway, the potters were instantly on their knees, pressing their foreheads to the floor. This time, Hoshi'tiwa joined them.

Lord Jakál rode a small carrying chair, hoisted upon the shoulders of two slaves. His attire was more resplendent than that of Moquihix and the priests, his wrists and ankles bound in gold bands, his long hair woven with beads of silver and sky-stone. He carried a fan of green and blue feathers, with which he concealed his face as he stepped from the chair, his splendid leather sandals, inlaid with sky-stone and silver, touching the dusty floor. He said something to one of the priests, and the man took Hoshi'tiwa by the arm to lift her to her feet. Jakál's dark eyes, peering over the fan, studied her, his thick eyebrows knotting in a frown.

His frank scrutiny embarrassed her, calling to mind the erotic dream that had visited her again. And yet, the way he looked at her now, she saw no sign of recognition in his expression. Was it possible his spirit had not visited her in her sleep, as she had feared? If so, then the forbidden dream had been hers alone. While this brought relief, Hoshi'tiwa next wondered if he recognized her as the girl who had interrupted his Morning Star ritual. If he did not—if, in fact, he did not even remember the incident—then that, too, should make her feel relieved. But, to her surprise, she felt the opposite—hurt, almost, and disappointed in a way she could not define.

Jakál kept his eyes on the girl, taking in a posture that was both modest and proud, mildly impressed that she met his gaze so frankly. But puzzled about her as well. She was a pottery maker. A mere girl, the daughter of corn growers. Yet she visited his thoughts at the most unexpected times, her face floating into his mind to distract him from his work, his prayers, his meditations.

Setting aside the fan, he held out his hands and snapped an order for the priest to give him the two halves of the broken pot.

The moment stretched as Jakál studied the two halves, first the right, then the left, turning them in the sunlight, bringing them close to his face, then piecing the edges together to form the seamless golden bowl. He deliberated for a long moment, during which Hoshi'tiwa thought her heart would thump right out of her chest. Surely this disaster was a sign of bad luck.

But the Lord of Center Place was not thinking of luck, rather he was marveling at the astonishing ceramic in his hands. The color was beyond description—the hue, perhaps, of gold as it catches a sunset, or the sunrise bathing an orange lily in early morning glow. The texture was unusual, too, so smooth that the fired clay felt like obsidian. The delicacy of the design, painted in bloodred, showed not only a steady hand but also an inspired mind, making Jakál think that the creation of this jar was surely guided by the gods.

Lifting his eyes from the rain jar and settling them upon its creator, he looked at Hoshi'tiwa again—this time in a new way, and he felt a stirring in his heart that he had not felt in a long time.

Abruptly, Lord Jakál ordered Tupa to her feet. He pointed to the sheathed etching knife hanging from her belt and gestured to the priest to hand it to Moquihix. Tupa's face drained of color as the priest unsheathed the obsidian blade and handed it to the high official. Moquihix then held the blade up to the sunlight so that Lord Jakál could inspect its edge.

Running his finger along the flat blade, Jakál held up his fingertip for the others to see the fine coating of pale orange dust. And when he wiped his fingertip on the broken pottery, the dust blended in.

Tupa immediately fell to her knees. "I did it to save the guild, my Lord! The girl has created jealousy and rivalry. We cannot get our work done without—"

Tupa's own blade went deep into her neck, and she was dead before her body hit the floor.

Throwing the dagger away, Moquihix conferred briefly with the priests over the appointment of another woman to take her place.

Although in shock—Tupa's execution had been so swift—Hoshi'tiwa spoke up. "My Lord, if I may?"

The other women gasped and Lord Jakál shot her a sharp look. Yet no order for punishment of the insolence was given, so Moquihix gave her an expectant, if disapproving, look.

Hoshi'tiwa's mouth was dry and her pulse raced in fear. But she had to make things right. Laying her hand on Yani's arm, she said, "This woman deserves the position of Overseer of the Guild, my Lord, for she reveres the gods and obeys the Lords and her pottery is the most beautiful in all of Center Place."

Moquihix studied her, and Hoshi'tiwa waited for him to see the new humility in her eyes, and understand that the silent feud that had existed between them—of which surely only she herself was aware—had ended.

Then he looked at Jakál, who returned a slight nod.

Lord Jakál then said something to Moquihix, who in turn instructed the priests to bring the girl with them. When Hoshi'tiwa stifled a cry of alarm, Moquihix barked, "You are not to be killed, stupid girl. You are to continue your work elsewhere. You are being honored."

When she turned a startled face to the High Minister, she saw the corners of his mouth twitch in an unpleasant smile, and she read the message in his hard, flat eyes: *I made you makai-yó. Now I make you honored. I can kill you or spare your life. I have complete power over you.*

Hoshi'tiwa wondered what she had done to make the High Minister hate her so.

And then suddenly she wondered where they were going to take her—to continue her work "elsewhere." As Lord Jakál returned to his chair and was lifted high, she saw his eyes upon her again, the same cryptic gaze from the dream. Her heart thumped and her mouth ran dry. The moment stretched—what thoughts were harbored behind that masked look? She parted her lips, she wanted to ask, "What does it mean, you are the blood and I am the clay?" But the slaves turned and bore the carrying chair, and Lord Jakál, from the potters' workshop.

As the priests started to lead Hoshi'tiwa away, Yani reached into the leather tool bag on her belt and brought out the fabled polishing stone. Placing it in Hoshi'tiwa's hand, she said, "I have no daughters, so when I die this stone will be buried with me. But you have gifted hands, Hoshi'tiwa. This stone, who has been my dear friend in life, will be happy with you. And together you will bring rain to Center Place."

Hoshi'tiwa kissed the older woman and wished the blessings of the gods upon her and the workshop, and as she stepped into the sunlight to follow the High Minister and his slaves, Hoshi'tiwa was unaware that she left behind two sister potters whose hearts were troubled by her removal from the guild.

Yellow Feather, who panicked as she saw her lucrative arrangement with Moquihix suddenly come to an end; and Yani, for reasons she could reveal to no one, especially not to Hoshi'tiwa.

BOOK THREE

Cloud Spirits

Twenty-two

"I AM frightened, Grandmother," the lame boy said as he pulled himself along the difficult trail.

"There is nothing to be afraid of," Pikami replied, puffing with
exertion as she struggled up the secret path that had once carried rainwater to the canyon below, but which now was dry and dusty and devoid
of plant life. "But we must take care that no one knows what we are about."

Yani had cautioned the old woman on the strict need for secrecy, but
Pikami was already aware of the Lords' injunction against the People of
the Sun worshipping any other than the Toltec gods. Death would be
long and painful for those who disobeyed.

She had heard about the secret cult from Red Crow, a Master Potter
who worked with Yani. "You will find comfort and solace," Red Crow
had promised, even though no one knew of Pikami's secret burden, the
guilt that had plagued her for years. Perhaps Red Crow said that to
everyone she confided in as she spread the word about the new underground religion taking root at Center Place. "Comfort and solace," Red
Crow had said, nodding as she said it, because that was what *she* had
gone seeking, and had found.

Pikami was skeptical. She was coming to the secret ritual only out of curiosity, harboring no high expectations of relief from her own inner pain.

She looked at the poor boy struggling ahead over rocks and brush, his withered leg dragging as he supported himself on a crutch. The sight of him reminded her of the pain and suffering she had caused one fateful day long ago. The tragedy had not been intentional, and so, even though it *had* been her fault, the clan had forgiven her. But Pikami could not forgive herself, and so to put the world back into balance she had embarked upon a life dedicated to healing and easing the ills of others.

They came to the end of the trail to find Yani outside the secret cave, her white shift glowing in the sunlight as she greeted arriving celebrants. Pikami and the crippled boy were the last. "Welcome, Old Mother," Yani said, helping the elderly herb peddler inside.

Pikami was surprised at the size of the crowd, but when she saw that they were almost all elders like herself, she was not surprised at all. These were men and women who, like herself, hungered for the rituals and spiritual sustenance of their childhoods, the rites and prayers and gods that had been banned at Center Place.

While torches flickered and sent shadows dancing on the limestone walls, Yani lit a ball of incense and the fragrance filled the air. From somewhere within the cave came the sound of a rattle and a flute. And then a man's voice, speaking in an ancient tongue, cried, "*Haliksa-i!* Listen now!" And he began to recite. . . .

Yes, thought elderly minds as the disembodied voice echoed up to the limestone ceiling, I remember this. The celebrants joined in the ancient chant that was not only a memorized prayer, but a story—the myth of how Corn Maiden flew down from the sun every year in her golden raiment to make newly planted seeds germinate in the fields. The elders filled their mouths with the sacred words while in their hearts and minds they were children again, and tucked in the comforting circle of family and friends.

Even Pikami was moved by the remembered song from childhood, and she joined in the chant, forming each precious sound and syllable.

When a spirit suddenly appeared among them, materializing out of the cave's shadows, the first-timers in the audience cried out. The spirit was dressed in golden garments, her apron embroidered with a spiral symbol to signify the womb of Mother Earth. In each hand she held a gourd of water, and her face was covered with a painted mask.

Those who had been here before knew what to expect, but newcomers were amazed, staring wide-eyed as the woman costumed as Corn Maiden performed a familiar dance around the cave, her body bowing and straightening as she symbolically sprinkled water on the imaginary field beneath her feet. To the accompaniment of rattles and flutes, the audience clapped and made sounds of wonder, their faces alight with joy.

When the ritual ended, many were weeping or murmuring among themselves, nodding, saying what a good thing this new religion was, wiping their eyes and clearing their throats, trying to remember when a religious ceremony had been so satisfying.

"These are kachinas," Yani explained, "spirits sent to give us help and guidance. Though kachinas are sacred beings who dwell in the supernatural realm, they take temporary possession of humans so that we may accept them more easily." Raising her hands in benediction, Yani said, "Go in peace now, brothers and sisters. Do not all return to the valley together, or at the same time. Follow different trails. Make sure you are not seen. And speak of this cave and its spirits to no one except those whom you love and trust, and bring them with you next time."

Yani surveyed those gathered with satisfaction, pleased to see Pikami and other newcomers. The group was growing. And although for now the crowd comprised mostly old people, Yani had a plan to attract young people, who had lived all their lives under Toltec rules and had even adopted Toltec ways.

Going to the cave entrance and squinting into the bright sunlight, she peered down the dusty trail that led through the scrubby arroyo to the canyon below. She could not see the great kitchen of Precious Green, but she pictured it, saw the people laboring there—one in particular, Hoshi'tiwa, working alone on her rain jars, whom Yani would bring into the secret cult.

Hoshi'tiwa would be the first young member and then other young people would follow. Hoshi'tiwa did not know it yet, but she was destined to be the heart of the kachina religion, bringing the People of the Sun together in one belief. She was to be the catalyst between the old and the new, the bridge between the generations.

But the time was not yet right. Hoshi'tiwa was untried, immature. The girl needed to grow, and then she must pass a test. What that test would be, Yani could not guess, but it would be a trial of courage and honor so that Tortoise Clan daughter would fulfill at last a prophecy from long ago.

Twenty-three

THE astrologer had selected five auspicious days on which Lady White Orchid might give Lord Jakál the special gift that had come with the caravan—a rare antique book of poetry. Unfortunately, the first of the five days was over a month away and White Orchid did not have the luxury of time.

Her father was growing impatient for her to marry.

As she rode toward Precious Green in her high carrying chair, White Orchid thought of her conversation with Tenoch that morning.

"It is your duty to continue our line," he had barked grumpily, claiming to have spent a bad night due to phantom pain in his nonexistent legs, although White Orchid suspected his new truculent mood was due to his supply of *nequhtli,* on Nagual's orders, having been cut off. "You must put your personal wishes aside, Daughter. Find a husband. Give me a grandchild."

As she neared the kiva—one of many sunk into the floor of the main plaza—she prayed it was unoccupied. White Orchid was not in the mood for company. She could not stop thinking about her father's drunken fit when she had had to send for Chief Physician Nagual. Tenoch had not spoken of it since, but there were shadows around his eyes, and sometimes she caught a haunted look on his face. What had the secret confession to the physician been about?

She climbed down the ladder and looked around. The subterranean chamber was empty. Although White Orchid normally welcomed the company of her friends, and was secretly proud of her popularity, she was not in the mood for them this morning, especially Malinche, now in her eighth month of pregnancy, who would sit there naked like a bloated toad to show off her fecundity. Nor was she in the mood to hear Copil's wife brag about their son, down in Tollan studying to be a Star Reader. Or the pompous Lady Toci, who insisted her eldest daughter wove the most exquisite cloth in the empire. Endless, empty talk. Not one of White Orchid's friends possessed a dream beyond her own hearth. They would certainly be shocked if they were to find out about her secret ambition to rule Center Place at Lord Jakál's side.

Sighing with relief—she needed the silence and solitude to think—she stripped off her tunic and skirt, fanned the embers glowing in the fire pit, added dried herbs and spices to create an aromatic smoke, then took a seat on the circular stone bench. Luxuriating in her nakedness in the heat and darkness, she leaned against the mudbrick wall and draped a cloth over her face to protect her complexion from the smoke. She closed her eyes, and as she felt the perspiration sprout over her body, she became aroused. Brushing her moist skin with her fingertips, she imagined it was Jakál's hand, and she smiled with warm pleasure.

As she began a delicious fantasy in the arms of Jakál, the silence was suddenly jarred by shrill laughter from above. White Orchid groaned. The other members of this kiva—which was restricted to ladies of her high rank—had arrived and now they descended into the pit, chattering like birds.

"Does anyone believe Jakál had the rain-girl moved to Precious Green so he could keep an eye on her progress with the rain jars?" It was the sharp tongue of Malinche, who was the first down the ladder.

Her companions laughed.

The voice of the tax collector's wife rose above the others: "Maybe it's not his *eye* he wants to keep on her."

More laughter, followed by lewd comments. As the women exchanged greetings with White Orchid and began to remove their clothing, White Orchid struggled to hide her shock. Although there was a marriage ban between the two races, there was no law against Toltec nobles taking pleasure with the peasant girls, and in fact it was done frequently.

White Orchid was suddenly alarmed. Would Jakál stoop to such a level, as her friends were intimating? She had not thought so, but if he found pleasure that way, then what inducement would he have for getting married?

As her friends drew her into a dialogue of news and gossip, White Orchid kept up a friendly, smiling face and made a swift decision: to go against the advice of her astrologer and give the book to Jakál on a day not deemed auspicious.

For her own survival, she must risk the bad luck.

Twenty-four

Y OU there, girl!"

Hoshi'tiwa looked up. The Master Cook stood holding a pitcher of water. "Take this to the Lords."

She looked behind herself, to see whom he was addressing.

"I'm talking to *you*."

Rising from her mat where she had been working on a rain jar, she stared at the cook. Surely he did not mean for *her* to go into the Lord's private apartments? In the two weeks that she had lived with the kitchen workers, since the day Tupa was executed and Yani named Overseer, Hoshi'tiwa had been left alone to concentrate on creating rain jars.

"Are you deaf?" he barked. "You know we are shorthanded due to summer fever. Take this!"

Timidly taking the water jug, she peered down the corridor that led from the kitchen to the inner rooms, the way lit by torches. She had never ventured into the interior of Precious Green.

"Hurry!" said the Master Cook, and Hoshi'tiwa delivered herself into the forbidding corridor.

Life in the main complex was different from living at the potters' workshop, which was located on the far side of the south wall, away from the heart of the governing center. The potters worked in isolation, whereas this warren of rooms and apartments was a-bustle with guards, scribes, porters, cleaners, servants, all coming and going, carrying the tools of their office, wearing the cloaks and headdresses of their rank. As the governor of Center Place, Lord Jakál lived in the largest apartment on the first level, with doors opening onto the great plaza. Hoshi'tiwa enjoyed no such luxury, but shared a hearth protected by a partial wooden shelter with the kitchen workers (uncomfortably close to the Jaguars' barracks, she thought, even though the soldiers were hidden behind a high wall. She could hear them in their fenced compound, playing their vigorous ball games, or training with their spears and clubs).

She was not supervised, she was not even watched, but was free to work her ceramics on her own, free to come and go. Free to run away. She had thought about it. She could leave with the many visitors and traders arriving and departing from Center Place, and by the time her absence was noticed, she would be far away.

But Hoshi'tiwa would not do that. When she left Center Place, it would be to return home to her family and Ahoté with honor, to tell them she had been commanded by Lord Jakál himself to bring rain, and that she had done just that.

Another, less certain reason kept her from seeking freedom. Hoshi'tiwa could not put her finger on it; the idea would not coalesce beyond a vague, troubling thought. It had to do with Tupa's execution, the shock of Tupa's desecration of a rain jar, and the shadow the incident had cast over the Potters' Guild. As she worked alone in the kitchen, surrounded by noisy workers, Hoshi'tiwa felt an invisible connection to the workshop on the far side of the plaza and Precious Green.

A serving girl carrying a platter of tortillas went ahead of Hoshi'tiwa down the corridor. The girl walked fast, and Hoshi'tiwa nearly ran to keep up, the sound of the fresh water sloshing in the jug making her lick her lips. She thought she could drink the whole of it down. Or at least take one sip.

But stealing from the Lords was punishable by death.

Hoshi'tiwa had seen Lord Jakál almost every day since she had been brought to the kitchen, where Moquihix had instructed the Master Cook to give her space for her pottery work, and to build her a kiln next to the kitchen's large, beehive-shaped ovens. Lord Jakál passed by daily because part of his administrative duties was to sit in judgment on cases involving disputes between parties, or crimes of sacrilege and blasphemy.

Every afternoon Lord Jakál came out into the plaza, his men setting up a throne and laying down a carpet, and the people with business before the Lord lined up. Here Jakál dispensed justice, collected taxes, tallied the census, and invoked the laws and the gods. People trembled as they stood before him. Jakál's justice was swift and brutal. If he judged a man guilty, punishment was carried out at once. Hoshi'tiwa had watched as a farmer accused of urinating during a religious ritual was found guilty of sacrilege. Upon a signal from Lord Jakál, a Jaguar soldier stepped forward and with one sweep of his sword, cut off the man's head. When the business of the day was concluded and the crowd dispersed, the family of the executed man were permitted to claim the body and carry it off.

But the people looked to Jakál for more than upholding the laws and appeasing the gods; the people themselves needed to be reassured in these uncertain times. When word went through Center Place that a farmer had found a live two-headed snake in his field, panic quickly spread. The man was ordered to deliver the creature to Moquihix, who retreated into the inner chambers with high priests and Lord Jakál. Everything came to a standstill while the Lords deliberated. Even work in the potters' shop ceased. Silence fell over the canyon as the people waited nervously for a verdict on the snake: Was it a good omen or a bad omen?

Finally, Lord Jakál entered the plaza and all had fallen to their knees, pressing their foreheads to the ground. It was Moquihix who spoke, his voice ringing out to the stone walls, over the Jaguars' barracks, to the distant cliff on the far side of the canyon: The two-headed snake was a good sign. The people, much relieved, returned to their business.

But mostly the people relied on their *tlatoani* for water. With the canyon's many arroyos dry and dusty, and only a few wells delivering up artesian water, the government reservoir, high in the mesa and heavily guarded, was the main water source. But rumors spoke of the level dropping alarmingly low, and rationing had been implemented so that the water-carriers were more despised than ever because they delivered smaller quotas to households and no amount of bribery or threat would induce them to pour a few drops more. Hoshi'tiwa felt sorry for those men, but understood also the people's ire. They were growing desperate. Thirsty children were given pebbles to suck on. Fights broke out over wells. Succulent cactus plants were stolen from private gardens.

And Hoshi'tiwa, corn grower's daughter from a small northern settlement, was pressed to produce no less than twelve rain jars before the Winter Solstice.

The corridor seemed to go on forever until finally the serving girl came to a halt, drew aside a bright red-and-yellow rug, and entered the torchlit chamber. Hoshi'tiwa followed. The room was high ceilinged with brightly painted ceiling beams, the walls whitewashed with borders trimmed in painted flowers, the stone floor covered in woven mats. Torches flickered in sconces.

When Hoshi'tiwa saw Jakál, an instant recollection of her forbidden dream made her cheeks burn. Twice more, the *tlatoani* of Center Place had visited her in her sleep and bestowed upon her a phantom kiss. Hoshi'tiwa tried not to look at him as she brought the pitcher inside.

Lord Jakál was reclining on a woven carpet, resting on one arm as he engaged in *patolli,* a game of chance played on a reed mat painted with squares and figures. *Patolli* had been brought up from the south by the Toltecs and was so popular that throughout Center Place the roll of beans and the cries of winners and losers were always heard. Hoshi'tiwa's own father and uncles and male cousins were passionate players, moving the colored pebbles in friendly but heated competition. As men rarely went abroad without their *patolli* mat, a game could break out anywhere at any time, the people's obsession was that keen.

When she saw who Lord Jakál's opponent was, her heart rose in her throat. Moquihix, the High Minister, who wielded complete power over her.

As she set the pitcher among the offerings of sweet prickly pear, beans and squash, and jugs of *nequhtli,* Hoshi'tiwa tried to keep her hands from shaking. She stole a quick glance at the two men, who were laughing as they rolled beans and moved colored stones, like two friends. Even Moquihix was smiling—Hoshi'tiwa had not thought him capable of it. They were dressed in richly dyed cotton tunics and cloaks, their hair tied up in the topknots of noblemen. Hoshi'tiwa wondered where the beautiful young women were, whom she had seen in the secret glade.

As Hoshi'tiwa straightened from her task, Moquihix glanced up, and what she saw in his eyes startled her. Older than Lord Jakál, with deep lines etched in his face, and gray in his long hair, Moquihix bore a somber countenance at the best of times. But in that instant, when his eyes skewered Hoshi'tiwa, she felt something cold and dangerous rush through her.

He believes I should have been killed with Tupa. He thinks I am bad luck. Moquihix put her on edge. He was the one who had swiftly and wordlessly plunged the dagger into Tupa's neck. Moquihix was like a venomous snake, coiled and watchful, and one never knew when he was going to strike.

The serving girl departed just as another servant entered, walking over the woven mats on bare feet, bowing low and murmuring something to Lord Jakál. A brief exchange and the servant left, immediately upon which Moquihix reached for his cloak and said the hour was late.

As the High Minister quietly slipped out, Hoshi'tiwa was wondering what she was supposed to do when another person materialized in the doorway. Hoshi'tiwa recognized her as Lady White Orchid, dressed in brightly patterned cotton with yellow cosmetic on her face, her mouth stained scarlet.

Hoshi'tiwa watched as Lord Jakál rose to his feet and received his visitor warmly, speaking in soft tones so that Hoshi'tiwa could not make out what they were saying. The lady spoke an order to her companion, and the woman came across to where the food and drink were laid out.

Hoshi'tiwa saw in shock that the attendant's tattoo—three vertical lines in the center of her forehead—identified her as belonging to Tortoise Clan, and Hoshi'tiwa nearly cried out with joy.

The servant, however, did not share the sentiment. As she snapped an order for two goblets of *nequhtli,* the Tortoise Clan woman ignored Hoshi'tiwa's hopeful smile, and when she accepted the two drinks, gave Hoshi'tiwa a disdainful look before turning away.

The Lord and his guest sat on a woven mat, accepting the drinks, while the female companion retreated into the corridor. Hoshi'tiwa remained where she was, not knowing what to do, but feeling invisible and insignificant as the pair spoke in low tones and laughed their secret laughs.

Hoshi'tiwa envied their familiarity with each other, the friendly intimacy, as she no longer experienced such moments herself. Lord Jakál and Lady White Orchid reminded her of herself and Ahoté, back home, or Hoshi'tiwa with her female cousins as they shared stories and jokes and laughed about amusements they held in common. Since coming to Center Place Hoshi'tiwa had found no one with whom she could enjoy such moments.

Had the salt merchant reached her settlement with her message? Was Ahoté at that moment on his way to Center Place?

Hoshi'tiwa watched Lady White Orchid give Lord Jakál what appeared to be a gift. He unwrapped the cloth, and when the contents were exposed to the torchlight, he exclaimed in delight. Hoshi'tiwa could not make out what he held in his hands.

She wanted to leave but did not know if she was allowed to. Being ignored in this way was humiliating; it was worse than receiving a look of contempt from a servant. So she closed her eyes and willed herself far away in the north, where her clan were peacefully tending the cornfields and making their famous rain jars. She was in the cottonwoods once more with Ahoté, and this time she was uttering words she regretted not having spoken before.

On the other side of the room, White Orchid watched the rain-girl. She had chosen this evening to give the gift to Jakál, instead of waiting for one of the astrologer's five propitious days, because she needed to know the truth about the rain-girl. White Orchid had come expecting to ask innocent, amiable questions, perhaps discuss the weather with Jakál, and the progress of the rain jars. But when she had walked into the room, she had been shocked to see the girl there—alone with him!

Her alarm rising, White Orchid focused her attention on Jakál, pleased with his reaction to her gift.

Jakál's delight in the book of poetry was complete. It was obvious in the way he slowly unfolded the bark paper and gazed at the pages, his eyes drinking in the colorful glyphs and symbols, tracing them with a long index finger, his lips moving to the rhythm of the poetry written there. And when he looked at White Orchid there was such joy and gratitude in his eyes that her heart leapt, and she knew that it had been well worth the expense and the long wait for the Caravan Master to search for and locate this rare collection of ancient poems written to Quetzalcoatl.

When Jakál reached out and softly touched her arm, White Orchid's skin burned and her body blossomed into sweet ache and desire. She wished she could linger and take this further, but propriety and rules of etiquette demanded that she now take her leave. It was his turn to reciprocate, and all she could do was go home and wait.

As she rose to leave, she caught Jakál staring across the room at the rain-girl. The look in his eye, the way the moment stretched too long—White Orchid felt something cold and lethal steal into her heart.

If her suspicions were true, the girl was an obstacle to her plan to marry Jakál. An obstacle that needed to be removed.

Twenty-five

WHEN Yellow Feather was five summers old, her father bundled her onto his back and walked six days from his farm to Center Place. There, like many desperate fathers with too many mouths to feed, he went from guild to guild, offering his daughter for the price of three sacks of grain. The Potters' Guild had lost three artisans to fever that summer and needed to replenish their ranks. Thus was Yellow Feather inducted into the sisterhood of pottery workers.

She had never really been happy in the Potters' Guild, feeling that she deserved better things. Therefore when the High Minister selected her to spy on Hoshi'tiwa and report back to him, she had thought her dreams had come true.

In the weeks since, she had received many nice things from Moquihix, and she had thought she had worked out the perfect life until, because of Tupa and the broken bowl, Hoshi'tiwa had been taken from the workshop and put to work in the kitchen, away from the prying eyes of Yellow Feather. With nothing to report to Moquihix, she no longer received gifts.

Which was why, on this warm summer morning as Yellow Feather crossed the canyon to the High Minister's house, she was proud of herself. It had come to her the night before: Why fret that she had nothing to tell Moquihix when she could invent a story? He would be just as happy and give her a nice gift, and he would never know that it was not the truth.

She was admitted into the small stone house at the base of the mesa as always, and escorted to the reception atrium where the High Minister received his reports before sending her to the bedroom where he joined her. This morning, however, he seemed distracted. "I will not be needing you anymore," he said as he removed a jade plug from one of his earlobes and tossed it to her. "That is your final payment. Do not come back again."

"But why, my Lord?"

"You are no longer useful. Hoshi'tiwa does not live or work with you. You seldom see her. You are of no use to me."

"But I come with an interesting report, my Lord," Yellow Feather said hurriedly, mentally scolding herself for not having thought of the lies sooner, for having come twice to the High Minister only to hang her head and confess she had nothing to tell him, and to be sent away with no gifts.

He narrowed his eyes. "Tell me."

She opened her mouth but, because it was an invented lie and not the truth, and because she was in a panic, she forgot her story. She knew that if he would give her a moment she would remember it, but because she fumbled about and stammered and wrung her fingers, he guessed the truth.

He said, "I can get the information I need from others." As he turned away, Yellow Feather said, "But have I not pleased you in other ways?"

He flicked his wrist high in the air and said, "Your kind is as numerous as pine seeds."

She stood rooted to the floor, stung by his insult, and watched him retreat into the bedchamber, and as the doorway hanging parted and then fell back into place, she saw, supine and naked on the sleeping mat, one of the kitchen workers from Precious Green.

Through tears of anger and disappointment, Yellow Feather found her way back across the valley, following a beaten path between two fallow cornfields toward Blue Hummingbird, which lay a short distance to the east of Precious Green. The western wall of the five-story complex was being shored up after mortar had started to crumble the winter before.

It was to this wall that Yellow Feather now headed, pushing through people, wiping away her tears so that no one would know she had been crying.

She came to a halt at the foot of the rickety scaffolding that groaned beneath the weight of many men climbing up and down all day long. A new team worked there today, removing poles and planks from the already precarious framework, carrying them off to the area that had been cleared for Lord Jakál's new rising-splendor.

Shielding her eyes against the sun, Yellow Feather found Falcon by his laughter. He was the most cheerful of workers, and everyone loved him. Calling out, she caught his attention, and the young man swung down from platform to platform monkeylike, to drop to the ground with a gap-toothed grin. He had lost his front teeth when he won a game of *patolli* against a poor loser.

Yellow Feather's heart expanded at the sight of him, and she told herself she would forget the old toad across the valley. "Let us tie the knot," she said impulsively. "We wait too long."

Falcon's grin stretched. She did not have to persuade him.

Her disappointment at Moquihix's house forgotten, Yellow Feather hugged a wonderful secret to herself. She had a surprise for Falcon.

Land ownership was another custom the People of the Sun had adopted from the Toltecs. At first they had asked, How can a person own land when the land belongs to Mother Earth and therefore to all people? Nonetheless, in the valley of Center Place, lines had been drawn between dwellings, borders had been laid around gardens. Secretly, with the gifts she had received from Moquihix, Yellow Feather had taken possession of a small stone house at the western end of the valley. It came with a plot that grew beans and squash, and because it stood in the shadow of a great mesa, was cool in the summer, and protected from cold winds in the winter.

Of course she could not tell Falcon the truth of how she paid for the house. She would tell him that the previous owner, who wished to return to his ancestral land in the north (that part was true), had accepted four of her most exquisite jars in exchange.

Yellow Feather told herself now that she was in fact pleased Moqui-hix no longer wanted her. She need not visit the old herbal peddler for her medicine against pregnancy anymore. Instead she would buy fertility charms and drink potions that encouraged conception. She would forget the High Minister and Hoshi'tiwa. She would work in the potters' work-shop and mind her own business, and cook beans and squash for her hus-band and wait for the babies to come.

Once again, Yellow Feather's life was perfect.

Twenty-six

HOSHI'TIWA had never prayed so much in her life. She
prayed before she slept, when she awoke, and as she worked,
praying for the gods to favor her rain jars and bring life-giving
clouds to Center Place.

On the day of the Summer Solstice, the Cloud Spirits had not come.
The special rain jars set out in the plaza by the members of the Potters'
Guild had not attracted them. Although everyone said the potters were
not to blame, that the bad luck was the result of one woman's actions,
the evil Tupa, nonetheless the proud Potters' Guild felt the sting of
shame, and it greatly troubled Hoshi'tiwa. For the first time since being
taken from her home, she worried about someone else's welfare before
her own.

While she still looked for Ahoté in the crowded marketplace, and
asked if anyone had encountered a young man of Tortoise Clan inquir-
ing after her, Hoshi'tiwa found herself thinking of the reputation of the
guild, and the low morale among the girls and women who had become
her friends. And again, the feeling of separation from them haunted her.

She was so deeply mired in her thoughts as she laid down clay coils that she did not at first see the scarred legs come to a standstill before her, did not notice the richly embroidered hem of a cotton cloak. But then the kitchen workers cried out and were immediately on their knees, and she squinted up at the man silhouetted against the sky.

Hoshi'tiwa did not move as Lord Jakál transfixed her with penetrating eyes. "Where do you find this clay?" he asked impatiently, tapping the clay-filled basket with a leather sandal inlaid with sky-stone. Hoshi'tiwa, who had walked barefoot all her life, stared at the magnificent sandal.

"I asked you where you found this clay."

Her heart skipped a beat. Did he know she had once spied on him in the secret garden? Did he know she had tried to spy on him again, returning to the end of the trail on the pretext of harvesting more clay, but really in the hope of glimpsing him once more? Did he know that she now had a surplus of clay, that what he was looking at was far more than she needed because she had gone so many times to the glade hoping to see him again even though she knew it was taboo and that if she were to be discovered it would mean instant death?

"A potter never reveals the source of her clay," she said, finding the courage to speak.

His eyes flickered. As he looked down at her, his expression unreadable, Hoshi'tiwa felt the kitchen, the workers, Center Place, and all the world fade away. She knew she should not meet the Lord's eye, yet she was compelled to do so, and between two heartbeats a question rose in her heart. What does it mean, she wanted to ask, you are the blood and I am the clay? And do you know that you come to me in dreams?

Then the world came back, the kitchen and its workers, and the din of Center Place, and in the next heartbeat, without another word, Lord Jakál turned and walked away, his retinue following. The kitchen staff, rising from their knees, looked at Hoshi'tiwa with expressions of curiosity, envy, and mistrust.

Twenty-seven

THE glade no longer brought joy. The beautiful women, the colorful birds, the sweet fruit, the fragrant flowers—it was all as dust.

Jakál could not fathom his feelings. Every day he was surrounded by servants, government officials, Moquihix and the Jaguars, highborn ladies seeking his company and bringing him gifts. So how could he feel lonely? And the beautiful handmaidens who served the gods—Jakál could take his pleasure with them whenever he wished, and he did every now and then, but it seemed an empty pleasure. A physical connection without joy that only increased his sense of loneliness.

Morosely picking through the platter of nuts and berries, while the temple dancers laughed and sang and played their musical instruments, Jakál's melancholy mood conjured up his mother, when he was a boy back in Tollan, a woman as lovely and remote and untouchable as a goddess. His most poignant memory was of kissing her perfumed cheek and being rewarded with laughter. He would glimpse her as she swept through the palace with her retinue, a palette of colors, a chorus of high, feminine voices. When he was old enough to understand such matters, he knew what she meant when he had overheard her say to his father, "I am done with that service to you, my Lord. I have given you four sons." So Jakál knew that he was the result of "a service" and nothing more. He accepted it as the way of the world. But it was a sad way, he thought, and sometimes wondered if he would treat his own children thus, should he ever again sire a child.

When such thoughts came to his mind he would look out at the people in the plaza of Center Place and note how like animals they were, carrying their young on their backs, playing with their children, expressing love and worry. And yet they were inexplicably happy, like the peasants back in his own Tollan, who crowded the marketplace with their noise and coarse ways, women with babies at their breasts, men with boys on their shoulders.

We nobles are above that, he would tell himself, and then sink into deeper melancholy.

And now there was the girl who was invading his thoughts. Although he had decided her fate, in the kiva when he had offered up his blood to Quetzalcoatl and had settled the question of sacrifice, and although he had plunged himself into his new project, spending each morning with his architects and builders, reviewing the construction site, noting the progress of the laying of the foundation, and although he prayed more than ever to his god, and wrote poetry that he hoped would please Quetzalcoatl—despite all of this, the rain-girl remained dominant in his thoughts.

Hoshi'tiwa, whose hands brought forth the most beautiful pottery he had ever seen. Where did such golden ceramic come from? How was it possible for a corn grower's daughter to create such exquisite perfection?

When Hoshi'tiwa looked at him, there was no shyness in her gaze. Her face was like the moon, he thought. Round and flawless, except for the three lines on her forehead. Tortoise Clan, he had been told. On days when he sat on his throne in the plaza to listen to complaints and to dispense justice, he would find himself searching the crowd for her, and he would see her with her friends, watch how she laughed, the swing of her hips, the *freedom*.

Why was she haunting him? Why did he want to know the details of her simple life?

He knew why. On the final dawn of the Eight Days, when he had stood stripped and humble before the horizon, awaiting the first sign of his god, the girl had been there, watching him. Such a taboo had never been broken before, not in Jakál's lifetime or, as far as he knew, in the lifetime of his people. It had so stunned him, to see her standing there, that he had not known what to do. Her smooth round face illuminated in the pale dawn, leaf-shaped eyes watching him—Jakál had felt a strange presentiment creep through his chilled flesh. And he thought, to his surprise: This is meant to be.

But what? That part of the mystery he did not know. The girl had not been instantly struck dead by the rising god, as she should have been. Instead, Quetzalcoatl had allowed her to look upon a taboo scene and live. Was it because she had been brought to Center Place to call forth the rain?

Or is she here for another reason?

"My Lord?"

He looked up at the beautiful face framed by a blue sky, and struggled to bring himself back to the present.

"My Lord," the Chief Dancer repeated. "We are finished."

He looked around and saw the petals and fruit rinds scattered in the grass. The musical instruments were silent; the dancers had ceased their movements. The sacred rite was over.

And Jakál had been elsewhere through the whole of it.

He shot to his feet, mortified. And angry with himself.

Why had he had her moved to the kitchen of Precious Green? He had told himself it was to keep from having another bowl maliciously broken. But that was a lie. He knew the other potters would not dare touch her rain jars after the swift execution of their overseer. When Hoshi'tiwa had suddenly appeared at his chambers, carrying the pitcher of water, he had been so stunned that he had barely been able to control himself. Moquihix, too, had been visibly disturbed. The cook who had recruited her as a servant had been sent to work in the rock quarry as punishment, and orders had been given to all kitchen workers that the rain-girl was not to be called upon for kitchen or serving work.

It was his own fault, Jakál realized in hindsight. Why did he not listen to his conscience at the time?

"The dead are alive, my son," his father had said when Jakál was ten summers old and had stolen a toy that had been given to one of his brothers. When the theft was discovered, his father had sat Jakál down and said, "When you contrived to steal the toy, did you not hear a voice in your head that told you it was wrong?"

The penitent boy nodded.

"My son, when you think an improper thought, or set out to do something wrong and your mind tells you otherwise, this is called conscience. Conscience is the dead speaking to us, to keep the living from doing things that we should not. A man without a conscience is a man who cannot hear the dead. Do you understand?"

Jakál had said he did, and then silently accepted his punishment, which was to be suspended upside down over a fire of chili peppers and forced to inhale the burning smoke.

He never stole after that, and took care to listen to his conscience. But in the case of Hoshi'tiwa, he had been deaf.

"We must hurry, my Lord," the Chief Dancer said, a look of concern on her face. The ritual was over, the gods had been summoned to the sacred glade, and now the humans must leave.

But Jakál fumbled with the knot of his cloak and searched for sandals that were right there by his feet. Why was he reluctant to leave?

The clay in her baskets. Too much of it. Why did she come here so frequently, so unnecessarily?

And then he realized he was looking for her, as he had looked for her in the plaza and in the kitchen, wondering if she might come by.

The dancers and musicians hurried from the glade, which was now occupied by spirits who might become jealous of the humans' presence. Jakál, too, hurried out, suddenly aware of his verge upon sacrilege, aware of his itinerant thoughts, his lack of control.

He knew what had to be done. Move her from the kitchen. Out of his sight. But to where? She could not go back to the Potters' Guild, because he did not trust the other women. And he had to keep in mind the sacredness of her task.

As he joined his attendants who waited outside the glade, and walked with them down the path toward the valley, his mind worked on the problem of where to put the girl so that he was not committing sacrilege, so that she could continue her work but at the same time be out of his sight and not a constant reminder.

Yes, that was the answer. Lock her away where she could not distract a man from his sacred thoughts and duties. Hide the girl away completely—from all eyes, including his own, until she had accomplished her holy task.

Twenty-eight

FALCON says that he will bring his monthly ration of meat home for me to eat. Stone-cutters are fed well, you know."

Yellow Feather was bragging, but her sister potters did not mind. In six days she would be a bride, and then a wife, and then—the gods willing—a mother. There had not been a wedding in the Potters' Guild for many seasons; excitement was at a fever pitch as all the girls and women looked forward to their roles in the ceremony and festivities afterward. The celebration was going to take place at Yellow Feather's new little house.

She had not been able to keep her secret for long. After informing Falcon of her clever transaction, she had taken the entire Potters' Guild across the valley to exclaim over the small dwelling with its own little garden (telling her friends the same story she had told Falcon, that she had purchased the house with her best jars). There, in the larger of the two rooms, Falcon and Yellow Feather would tie their cloaks together as a sign that they would be partners for life, and all their friends would feast and sing and bless the new couple.

Yellow Feather no longer gave thought to Moquihix or Hoshi'tiwa. They had ceased to be her concern.

"Falcon says that his overseer has praised his work," Yellow Feather went on as she laid clay coils for a cooking pot, "and said that he might be sent to work on the Lord's new rising-splendor and—"

Crack!

All heads snapped up.

Cra-ack!

"What was that?" Yellow Feather said.

Another cracking noise followed by a roar.

The potters jumped to their feet. "Thunder!" cried one. "The Cloud Spirits have come!" shouted another.

They ran outside, joyful faces lifted to the sky. "Where?" said Yani, spinning in a circle, her face upturned. "Where are the thunder clouds?"

And then they saw people running past, shouting and pointing. Yani turned in the direction they were headed and saw a cloud of dust rising to the sky. Was it a caravan? But there was no road there. She could not see the cause of the cloud because the mesa jutted out, blocking her view.

More people ran by, shouting, waving their arms. Yani stopped one— a *nequhtli*-seller who had abandoned his mat—"What is it?" she asked.

"A scaffold has collapsed!" he gasped and hurried on. "At Blue Hummingbird," he shouted over his shoulder.

Yellow Feather broke into a run. Yani and the others sprinted after her, joining a mob of panicked people.

They came upon a horrific sight—a grotesque jumble of broken platforms, poles, and timbers at the base of the western wall—and through the dust and powdered plaster they saw bloody arms and legs protruding from the wreckage, and heard the moans and cries of men.

Yellow Feather looked frantically about for Falcon. She called out his name. She ran back and forth as people fell upon the wreckage, swarming over it to pull up planks and beams and drag injured men to safety.

"Falcon!" she shrieked, rushing to each victim, looking at his face, running back to the wreckage, stepping over rocks and chisels and brittle logs.

Officials arrived, moving at a more stately pace but white-faced with shock and worry. This was a very bad sign. Part of Blue Hummingbird's wall had come away when the scaffolding collapsed. The god was going to be angry.

Moquihix scowled as he drew near, recalling his warning to Jakál that it was unsafe to remove wood from existing projects for his new rising-splendor. But Jakál had not listened.

Hoshi'tiwa came running with the kitchen workers and stopped short, her hands flying to her mouth when she saw the enormous wooden pile that looked like a Winter Solstice bonfire, knowing that hundreds of men were buried underneath.

Wives and mothers came running, throwing themselves into the chaos to pull away rocks and debris in search of loved ones. Those who had been working on the topmost platform survived with injuries, but the stoneworkers who had occupied the middle and bottom tiers had been crushed.

Hoshi'tiwa joined the pottery workers, who scrambled this way and that in search of Falcon.

Yellow Feather clawed at the broken beams until her hands bled and stung with splinters. Through eyes filled with tears she saw cut and broken limbs. One man had been decapitated. Another had been severed through the torso. A roar of shouts and wails filled the canyon, and shrieks of joy when a worker was found alive.

The sun began its descent to the west as more mangled corpses were pulled out and laid in a row, with family members moving among them, seeing familiar faces reposed in death, or moving through the mob and saying, "Have you seen my boy?" "Where is my husband?" "I am looking for my brother."

Sobbing and heaving with fear, Yellow Feather scrambled over a mound of stones and mortar, blindly digging, praying to the gods that Falcon had been sent on an errand and was far from here, or that he had already been transferred to the new construction site, when her hands pushed through pulverized mortar and she felt something soft and cool.

A man's shoulder.

"Here!" she shouted. "Another one!"

People ran over to lift bricks and wood away from the body. When the victim's head was exposed, they saw the mouth frozen open in a silent scream, the front teeth missing because of a game of *patolli* between a lucky winner and a poor loser.

He had no hands.

Yellow Feather cradled Falcon in her arms and would not let him go, rocking back and forth, calling his name over and over, until Yani and Hoshi'tiwa gently drew her away and assured her that Falcon was now with the Great Spirit and at peace in the eternal fields of corn.

It was well past sundown when the last of the bodies was recovered. By order of Lord Jakál, the dead were dumped in a pit and set afire while the relatives of the victims wailed and tore their hair.

Eighty-two men perished that day and scores more were injured, some so severely that eventually they would succumb, or die when the spirits of infection invaded their wounds. Few who survived were able to work again, and the invalids would become a burden to their families.

Yellow Feather's sister potters sat with her through that first night, consoling her, praying, lighting incense to the gods. She stayed at the potters' workshop for seven days, during which no work was done, but on the morning of the eighth day, she declared she wanted to move into her new house.

They walked with her to the little stone dwelling where she planned to live until another man wanted her—a silent, sorrowful procession that snaked its way across the canyon, walking between silent abodes where other mourners grieved for lost sons, brothers, and husbands. Yellow Feather hung her head and walked as if in a dream. Where were Falcon's hands?

After the bodies had been removed, men were brought in to clear the wreckage, and Yellow Feather visited the site every day for seven days, hoping to find her beloved's hands. But such body parts as were uncovered were immediately thrown onto a fire, as they were taboo and might draw evil spirits to Center Place.

As the group neared the little house, Yellow Feather paused to give each of her sister potters a token in remembrance of Falcon—clay figurines, colored stones, turkey feathers dyed blue, green, red. She said in a voice still wooden from shock, "Here I shall live, but I will come to the workshop each day and I will do my guild proud by making the best jars I have ever made. I will do so in honor of my beloved Falcon, may the Great Spirit give him peace."

"What's that?" one of the younger girls said, pointing past Yellow Feather.

She turned and saw smoke spiraling through the roof of the kitchen.

"And what is that?" another asked, pointing to a string of chili peppers drying on a wall.

Hurrying along the rest of the path, they now saw what had not been visible before: children and dogs playing in the small garden.

When they reached the threshold, a large man came out. He was well dressed in a clean loincloth and white cloak knotted at his throat, but the clan tattoo on his chin identified him as belonging to the People of the Sun, and he wore the rope collar of a slave.

"What business have you here?" he bellowed, and the potters saw that he carried a club. "My master is not home."

"What master?" Yellow Feather cried. "This is *my* house."

He spat and wiped his hand across his mouth. "Stupid woman, our people do not own land. Go away."

Yani stepped forward, dignified and calm. "Can you tell us, please, who lives here?"

He looked her up and down and, recognizing her high rank as the overseer of a guild, said, "My master came up from Tollan with the last caravan and has had to suffer living in temporary quarters until he found this empty house."

"But it was not empty! I put mats in there, and a corn grinding stone!" Yellow Feather shouted, and Hoshi'tiwa silenced her with a touch.

She looked at the club in the man's meaty hand, noted how well fed he was, how clean and decently dressed, and knew the new master of this house was a high official, possibly even a noble.

A Toltec had taken what belonged to Yellow Feather, and there was nothing she, or any of them, could do about it.

Twenty-nine

HOSHI'TIWA came to the glade seeking answers. But answers to what, she did not know.

Late summer was upon them and the thirsting populace anxiously watched for rain, as the corn in the fields was now at the critical stage, upturned leaves waiting for the blessing from the sky. Rain dances had begun in the main plaza and would be performed for days.

Hoshi'tiwa had tried to stay away from the secret garden. She should be at her sacred task of creating rain jars. Yet here she was. She crept up and peered through the foliage. The glade was unoccupied. Just ferns and grasses and flowers. As she surveyed the beautiful scene, it occurred to her that while this hidden glade was green and lush, the valley below was brown and parched. Here, dew glistened on petals. There, the earth gasped for water. When she recalled seeing, on her first clay gathering expedition, a secret water reservoir across the canyon, she wondered: Was that water brought here for these ferns and flowers? Did slaves with bursting water skins sprint past arid fields and children with blistered mouths to pour the precious liquid onto these plants?

Koyaanis'qatsi, she thought. A world out of balance.

Like a noble stealing a girl's house.

Like Lord Jakál ordering wood to be removed from a scaffold so that it would be used for a new rising-splendor. And all those boys and men perished as a result.

She drew away, heavy of heart, realizing that the glade did not itself possess answers, rather it *symbolized* the answers she sought. Which made those answers all the more elusive and unreachable. She remembered her vow to suppress such thoughts, to drive away words such as "why" and "unfair" whenever they tiptoed into her mind. Entertaining such ideas, she knew, would lead to disaster.

Vowing never to return to this place, to concentrate on her rain jars and the day she would return home, she turned toward the upper end of the ravine where she would harvest one last batch of the special clay and looked straight into Lord Jakál's piercing gaze.

The breath caught in her throat. It was as if her thoughts had created him on the spot out of damp soil and tree bark and sunshine. His bronze skin gleamed, gold bracelets glinting upon each wrist, gold earrings, necklace, and hair ornaments casting off bright lights. The blue of his cloak and tunic was deeper than the summer sky.

Strangely, he was alone.

Hoshi'tiwa dropped to her knees and pressed her forehead to the ground. She did so automatically, conditioned after weeks of living at Center Place. But while her posture was one of obedience, there was no subservience in her heart.

"Why are you here?" he asked.

Hoshi'tiwa lifted her face and gave him a questioning look.

A flick of his wrist and she rose to her feet to stand with dignity. But her heart thumped with fear as she looked around for the Jaguars and their spears. "My Lord, I am on my way to harvest more clay. I thought—"

"*More* clay?" he said, and she knew he was referring to the baskets of raw clay he had seen on the kitchen patio.

She grew uncomfortable beneath his unwavering gaze; then she took a breath, tipped her chin, and said boldly, "You *did* order me to make twelve jars. That is a lot of clay."

To her surprise, lines of amusement appeared at the corners of his eyes.

He was mocking her. Anger flared in her heart so that she blurted a question she wished she could call back as soon as she uttered it: "Why is there water for this glade but not for my people?"

His brows arched. He took the measure of her tone and stance and saw no challenge or defiance there, but an open, honest face asking an open, honest question. "This glade is for the gods."

"Your gods live better than the people do?"

"Of course," he said, as if it were a ridiculous question.

Jakál did not hide his sudden impatience. He had come here to be alone, for peace and reflection, and recalled now his decision to hide the girl away from all eyes, including his own, until she had accomplished her sacred task. But so many things had demanded his attention, foremost being the foundation for his new rising-splendor. He avoided the kitchen and thus thought he could avoid the girl.

Knowing he should send her away, perhaps even punish her for this trespass, Jakál felt an inexplicable compulsion to repeat himself and follow it with a question: "It is necessary that our gods live better than we do. Do your own gods not live well?"

"They do not live as people do."

Jakál knew nothing of the beliefs of the People of the Sun, nor had he ever inquired. "What do your gods look like?"

"We do not know."

"Then how can you carve their statues? How can you worship them and make sacrifice to them?"

"They are spirits. There is Mother Earth and Father Sky, and we were created by Grandmother Spiderwoman. They exist everywhere and are not in one place. We pray to them and scatter corn to the wind."

Jakál remained silent, as if what she had told him needed deep consideration. While he stood looking down at her, being so much taller, the air around them underwent a subtle change, and a sense of time at a standstill came over Jakál. He noticed that, as they stood beneath a leafy bower with sunlight dappling through, shedding diffuse light in the sylvan thicket, the ribbons in the girl's hair appeared to be changing colors. Sounds grew muted, as if birds and wildlife had retreated. The air became heavy and warm. Jakál felt as if he walked in a dream. "Why does it concern you how we revere our gods?" he finally asked.

Hoshi'tiwa had felt an imperceptible shift in the bosky atmosphere, the muting of sounds, the heaviness of the air. The back of her neck crawled as she thought: Spirits walk here. Knowing that she should turn and go, run from this enchanted ravine and away from this man who had the power to cast spells over her, she could not stop herself, the words poured out: "Because you forbid my people their sacred ceremonies and I fear Pahana will not return while my people are living in a state of disharmony."

He frowned. "Pahana?"

Hoshi'tiwa had been braced for the back of his hand, or for the sting of a whip from an unseen Jaguar. But she saw no fury on the Lord's face, sensed no indignation in him. So she said, "He is someone who walked among us long ago. Once, there were two brothers who became separated. The red-skinned brother remained here, while the white brother, Pahana, traveled east, toward the rising sun, with the promise to someday return to help his brother to prevent the destruction of the Fourth World and bring about a new age of peace and brotherhood."

A queer look stole across Lord Jakál's face as he stood motionless in the dappled sunlight. Overhead, but sounding far away, a hawk cried. "What does this brother look like?" Jakál asked.

"He is pale-skinned, and he has a beard."

A perfumed breeze played through the foliage, rustling fronds and leaves and the long green feathers of Jakál's headdress. Hoshi'tiwa could not read the expression on his face, but when he spoke, there was wonder in his voice. "We Toltecs believe the world was destroyed and reborn four times and that we now live in the Fifth World. We believe that a man will come and prevent the destruction of this world and bring a new age."

Hoshi'tiwa listened, her face upturned to his.

"Long ago," he said, "when my ancestors lived in a city called Teotihuacan there reigned a benevolent king named Quetzalcoatl. He was born of a virgin mother, the goddess Coatlicue, and he gave us astronomy, the calendar, and corn. He taught us that cultivating flowers was a sacred task. He was also a healer. When Quetzalcoatl died he threw himself on a fire and his ashes became the Morning Star and he promised that he would one day return from across the ocean in the east, to bring a golden age so that the world will never again face destruction. His risings in the morning and in the evening remind us of that promise."

Hoshi'tiwa stared back. Then she, too, frowned. Did Pahana go by another name? Or did they speak of two different men? "My Lord, what does Quetzalcoatl look like?"

"Our books tell us that he is a tall white man with a beard."

They both fell silent, absorbing the significance of what had just been said. Neither had seen a truly bearded man. The men of Hoshi'tiwa's race did not grow facial hair, except for the elderly, who sprouted long wisps in their later years. It was the same with Jakál's people, and so such a beard made a man unique and set him apart from his people. That was why the Toltecs knew they would recognize Quetzalcoatl the moment he appeared, because he would look so different from other men. The People of the Sun said the same of Pahana.

Jakál felt strange new feelings steal through his body. Was this why the girl had been foretold in the Book of Fate, and why she had been brought here? Did her presence at Center Place have to do with much more than mere rain?

He looked into her eyes and saw no guile there, and for reasons he could not fathom, Lady White Orchid came into his mind—beautiful, aristocratic, wealthy—a woman of his own race, but whom he did not for one moment trust.

His thoughts startled him. He stepped back. "Be on your way," he said quietly. "I wish to be alone."

But when he started for the glade, Hoshi'tiwa's arm shot out, and she cried, "Wait, my Lord!"

He looked down, shocked to see her hand on his bare arm.

Hoshi'tiwa was stunned, too, to see her hand on his arm. To touch a *tlatoani* meant instant death. But she had acted impulsively, out of instinct. She pointed to the ground with a shaking arm. Jakál looked down, and froze.

A column of sunlight illuminated the bulging triangular head, the fat scaly body covered in a diamond pattern, the tail pointing skyward, shaking and sounding like the rattle of a priest of Tlaloc, and the two eyes like hard, black beads that fixed on Jakál and the girl as a forked tongue flicked in and out—a rattlesnake, coiled and ready to strike.

Jakál's eyes widened. He had not heard the warning rattle. Nor could he believe the snake had been there just moments prior. What witchcraft was this?

Nonetheless, it *was* a real snake, enchanted or not (he would consult with priests and seers later, to divine the meaning of its appearance here), and so, whispering a protective oath, Lord Jakál slowly and smoothly stepped sideways to stand in front of Hoshi'tiwa, placing himself between her and the snake. He spoke in a calm, soothing voice: "We come in peace, Brother Snake. We mean you no harm. If this is your home, forgive us the trespass."

Hoshi'tiwa was startled. She had thought Lord Jakál would try to kill the creature; instead he had spoken as the People of the Sun would, addressing the animal with respect.

She raised her hand and lightly placed it on Jakál's back, where she felt, through cotton and skin, muscle and ribs, the pounding of his heart. She had never been this close to him before. She smelled the fragrance of sage about him. And her dream came back in full force, stunning her with a new question: Was it perhaps not a dream at all but rather the vision of a future event? And was that event *now,* this moment?

Was Jakál going to turn and touch his nose to hers in a kiss?

He continued to speak calmly and respectfully to the snake, and the moment stretched until the creature finally lowered its head and slithered away.

When Jakál turned and looked down at her, Hoshi'tiwa caught her breath and felt her heart rise in her throat. "Are you all right?" he asked.

"Yes," she said with barely breath in her lungs.

Jakál looked down at Hoshi'tiwa with confused thoughts. She had saved his life. If she had not cried out and stayed him with her hand, he would have walked right into the striking range of the snake. Why had she done that? He was the one who had snatched her from the arms of her family. And he was the one who would give the order for her sacrifice on the altar of blood.

Suddenly, he sensed a power within her, a power that perhaps not even the girl herself was aware of. What would it take to waken that power, Jakál wondered, and what would she do with it once she was aware of it?

He looked down at the ground where the serpent had been, and a tremor rocked his body. In all his years of coming to this glade, he had never seen a snake here, not even the most harmless kind. And rattlesnakes never emerged during the day in the summer months.

The snake was one of Quetzalcoatl's earthly manifestations. Had this been a message from his god?

When he brought his eyes back to Hoshi'tiwa, he felt another emotion jolt him, one entirely new and disturbing—the impulse to take her into his arms.

A dark look fell across his face and he said abruptly, "You have enough clay."

She blinked, swallowed, sensing the dangerous threshold at which they both stood. "Yes, my Lord."

"Do not come back here again."

"Yes, my Lord," she whispered, and she felt the enchantment of the forested ravine vanish, and all the noise and sounds of the mesa—birds and insects and wildlife—rush back in.

Hoshi'tiwa marveled at how quickly he changed moods, the way a man changed cloaks. Earlier, when she had said she needed more clay, she had seen amusement around his eyes. And then just a moment ago, when he turned and asked her if she was all right, there was concern in his eyes. Now, this thunderous look. Jakál was a mercurial man, of shifting moods. Like a river that, from a distance, appeared to be a solid, unmoving thing, but step to its edge and one saw the swift current, the different colors from shallow to deep. Step in, and one felt the power of the current. Lord Jakál was like that.

They heard footfalls on the trail. Moquihix appeared with four Jaguars. "We have been searching for you, my Lord."

Without another glance at Hoshi'tiwa, Jakál turned and fell into step with his men. Striding away from the enchanted wood and the perplexing rain-girl, he told himself that above all else he must address the task of finding a hiding place so that the girl would be sequestered from the world—and most especially from himself—until the Winter Solstice.

Thirty

LTHOUGH the potters were jealous of Hoshi'tiwa, envying her move to the rising-splendor kitchen, where she had a more comfortable sleeping place and plenty of food, they always received her with smiles and open arms because she never failed to bring gifts and gossip and a welcome diversion from their daily toil in the summer heat.

For this morning's breakfast Hoshi'tiwa brought a basket of roasted pigeons, left over from a feast the night before when Lord Jakál had entertained his highest officials in his private chambers. Even more welcome, she had brought a small skin of water.

As Hoshi'tiwa set out the offerings, she glanced at Yellow Feather and noted in alarm that the girl did not look well. Since Falcon's death, and losing her house, the girl had lost interest in everything. She slept poorly and ate little. Hoshi'tiwa was startled, in fact, to see how much weight she had lost, her shift hung so loosely on her frame.

As they passed the waterskin around, each savoring a mouthful as if it were sweet nectar, the conversation turned to gossip, another gift Hoshi'tiwa brought from the Precious Green kitchen.

"They say that the wife of Copil, the Chief Tax Collector, is so desperate to have another child that she has sought the services of old Pikami."

"It is the end of the world indeed," cried Red Crow, one of the older potters, her mouth full of food, "when a Toltec lady asks for help from one of us!"

They all laughed and nodded, prideful of the fact that because this was *their* ancestral land, and though the Toltecs be their masters, whenever the wives of the Lords needed help, they came to the women of the People of the Sun.

"What will Pikami do for her?" asked a young girl who had been with the guild for six months and so far was good only for sanding.

The older women glanced knowingly at one another, exchanging secretive smiles, and then Red Crow declared, "She will put chili powder on her husband's corncob," punctuating her remark with a lewd gesture that brought even louder laughter.

Yellow Feather cried out suddenly and shot to her feet. Grease had dribbled down the front of her shift. When tears sprang to her eyes, Yani said, "It is nothing, Daughter. We can clean it."

But Yellow Feather turned and fled the gathering, leaving a sob to fade on the air.

Yani shook her head. "She has not been the same since the misfortune."

"It has been two months," Red Crow said with an unsympathetic sniff. "It is time she thought of the guild. Her work has been poor."

Hoshi'tiwa excused herself and went to console Yellow Feather, but when she stepped under the shade arbor at the back of the workshop where the potters slept, she stopped short.

Yellow Feather had stripped off the soiled shift and was reaching for a fresh one, so that she stood naked in the thin beams of sunlight that streamed through the twigs and brush overhead. Hoshi'tiwa nearly cried out. The girl's arms and legs were like sticks, but her breasts were full, her belly rounded.

Seeing Hoshi'tiwa in the doorway, Yellow Feather pulled the clean shift to her chest and looked at her friend with pleading eyes. "Please don't tell Yani," she whispered.

Hoshi'tiwa was so stunned, she could not at first speak. And then she found her voice. "But you cannot hide this forever. Soon your condition will be obvious."

"I can wear bigger shifts. I can say I am gaining weight. When my time draws closer, I will leave, I will say I am going to visit my family. Please do not tell anyone. I beg of you."

Hoshi'tiwa held out her hands as words escaped her. What Yellow Feather had done, and was doing, was unthinkable. "You *must* tell Yani."

"She will banish me!"

Hoshi'tiwa chewed her lip. It was true. Yani would say that Yellow Feather brought bad luck into the guild by committing a terrible sin. She had taken pleasure with Falcon before they were married. She had broken her vow of chastity and obedience.

"I was *almost* married to Falcon. Our wedding was six days away—it is not my fault that Falcon is dead."

Hoshi'tiwa rubbed her forehead. Was it possible Yellow Feather was unaware of the enormity of her transgression? No, she was aware of it, Hoshi'tiwa decided, because she was trying to hide the result. "Yellow Feather, listen to me. When you were initiated into your clan, you took a vow of purity, promising to stay chaste until you married. We all do, as Daughters of the Sun, as we were taught by our mothers. Yani and the others—" Her voice broke. Was there no end to poor Yellow Feather's misfortunes? "They will say that you have committed a terrible desecration by breaking a vow to the gods, that your pottery is defiled, that perhaps *all* of it here is. This is very serious. Yani must be told."

"Please do not tell her. I can pay you. I will give you whatever you want if only you will stay silent—"

Suddenly, Yani was in the doorway. "I must be told what?" she began, and then she saw Yellow Feather's nakedness as she tried to hide her secret behind a clutched dress. "By the gods, Daughter," Yani whispered, "what have you done?"

When Yellow Feather began to weep, Hoshi'tiwa said, "She and

Falcon were betrothed. Perhaps . . ." But then she was remembering her mother's words not long ago: "Though you and Ahoté are betrothed, the gods demand restraint and purity until the wedding night. If you transgress, you bring bad luck upon us all."

"Yellow Feather," Yani said, "you have to think of Center Place. Think of our people toiling in the fields, the children crying for water. If you put your contaminated rain jars out in the plaza at the next Solstice, the Cloud Spirits will be so offended, they might never bring rain again! The Potters' Guild might never recover from it."

A pain shot through Yani's heart. She was fond of Yellow Feather, and felt sorry for her. But Yani's duty was to the guild, and to the gods. For the sake of bringing honor back to her potters, and to appease the Cloud Spirits, she must declare Yellow Feather *makai-yó* and banish her from the sisterhood.

Without another word, Yani returned to the others, told them the terrible news, and gave the order. The women and girls, understanding what must be done, set about to smashing Yellow Feather's ceramic pieces, lifting them high and dashing them to the floor—beautiful jars and pots and figurines, painted black on white, pleasing to the eye and certain to attract the Cloud Spirits, but defiled now and a danger to the workshop and Center Place.

Yellow Feather, clothed in a fresh shift, watched in dismay as her sisters retrieved the larger fragments and began flinging them at her with such anger and force that she threw up her arms to protect her face. The women and girls pelted her with sharp shards that struck her head and cut her skin. Pleading with them to forgive her, Yellow Feather backed toward the front door and stumbled through it as the shower of ceramic pieces stung her body. The potters drove her from the workshop—thus hoping to drive away her bad luck—shouting protective words and spells and calling upon the gods of good luck and good magic for help.

Hoshi'tiwa watched in horror, unable to move as the women threw broken pieces of Yellow Feather's rain jars at her, striking her hard, drawing blood, and making her cry out.

After Yellow Feather finally turned and ran, sobbing hysterically until she disappeared in the fields, the potters burned her sleeping mat, her ribbons, her comb, her shawl, and her food bowl. They destroyed everything she had touched—the clay, the paints, the paintbrushes—and then Yani sent for a priest from Blue Hummingbird to come with his sacred incense and charms and prayers to purify the workshop again.

In her distraught and frightened mind, Yellow Feather reasoned that Moquihix would take care of her. He was the father of the child, and he was a Toltec noble dedicated to duty and honor.

"Get away from here," the High Minister snapped when she stood at his door and told him what had happened. She had caught him in the middle of morning preparations before he headed toward Precious Green and his day's many duties. He wore only a loincloth, his paunch hanging over it, and his long gray hair lay upon his shoulders and down his back. It occurred to her that he was not so impressive without his feathers and cloak.

"But my Lord," she said, thinking he had not heard her. "I am with child."

"I told you never to come back here," he said sourly, scratching his arm. He had spent another bad night on his sleeping mat, the rain-girl once again haunting his dreams. Why had Hoshi'tiwa been outside the sacred glade with Lord Jakál? And why did Jakál continue to tolerate her disobedience?

As Moquihix started to turn away, Yellow Feather threw herself at his feet and cried, "But my Lord, it is *your* child."

He narrowed his eyes. "How do I know this?"

"I have not lain with another man."

She saw him hesitate and mistook it for a weakness she could use. As he turned away, she shot to her feet and said, "I will not bring this child into the world. I will purge it from my body."

He whipped around. "You would dare to do that?" Inducing a miscarriage was one of the worst sins among both races that lived at Center Place.

She lifted her chin, confident that her exploitation of his one weakness would work—that, like any man, pride in his powers of procreation would force him to take her in. "I would do that."

Emotions rippled across his face and Yellow Feather almost smiled, until Moquihix seized a whip hanging by the door and lashed at her. She fell back, startled. He advanced and struck again, leaving a red stripe across her upper arm.

"My Lord!" she cried, retreating as he struck her again and again, the whip laying angry welts across her arms and stinging her belly and breasts as she screamed. She tripped, falling to the ground, shielding her head with her arm. He flew at her, snapping the whip over her body, shouting at her to get away from there and never to fill his eyes again.

Curling into a ball, she lay in the dirt as Moquihix spent his anger, and when he saw thin stripes of blood seep up through her white dress, he finally dropped his arm, spat on her, and marched back into his house.

Although slaves and servants peered through windows and doorways, having heard her shrieks of pain, no one came to her aid, and after a while Yellow Feather struggled to her knees, then to her feet until she managed to stagger, dazed, away from the house of the High Minister.

Wandering in shock, she found a pool of shade at the mouth of a ravine and, collapsing there, wept until she had no more tears, no more breath, and lay in the sand oblivious of the flies, heat, vultures.

Night fell, the stars came out, but there was no moon to lend relief to the darkness. Like all people of her race, Yellow Feather feared the night. This was the time when ghosts walked the land, and evil spirits bent on possessing an unsuspecting human. While the populace retreated indoors, or under crude shelters, clustered around comforting fires and huddled together on mats, Yellow Feather searched desperately for shelter.

When she saw the great circular structure called the Star Chamber, silhouetted like a giant rain jar against the stars, she knew she would be safe there, for no evil spirit would dare venture closely to so holy a place. Crawling into a niche between two boulders, mindless of snakes or scorpions that might inhabit the spot, Yellow Feather curled up and cried herself to sleep.

In the morning, filthy and bloody, she went to the villas of the rich, hoping for a handout. But she was driven off, as news of Yellow Feather's disgrace had spread through the valley. She was now a pariah, with no home, no family.

That night she crossed a field of struggling cornstalks and came upon a humble altar upon which a hopeful farmer had placed a bowl of corn. Making sure she was not observed, she took the bowl and ran away with it.

As she crouched once again in the protection of the Star Chamber, Yellow Feather gobbled the sweet kernels and wept bitterly. There was no more wretched creature on earth than she. She had stolen food meant for the gods, corn intended for Mother Earth.

She could not go on like this. Yellow Feather knew she would starve if she didn't find someone to take care of her. But there was no one.

And then she realized there *was* someone.

In a camp far above Center Place, at the end of a hidden trail, lived a group of outcasts who had been cut off from society for crimes not serious enough to be punished by death. They were men who had deserted their families, or cheated at *patolli,* or disrespected a Toltec master; men without honor or conscience and lower in status than common beggars, and who were not permitted to walk among normal citizens.

Their camp was known to be a lawless place and thus it was avoided by normal citizens, and overlooked by the Jaguars as a necessary evil in the world. And as they were men who hunted and trapped and sustained themselves, Yellow Feather knew they would not take in another mouth to feed who could not herself bring food to the group—especially one who had a baby growing in her belly.

But Yellow Feather had something to trade in exchange for their protection.

As she started across the valley, thinking of the vile men who would be using her body so that she could eat and have a safe place to sleep, and give her baby a chance to be born, dreading the days and months to come and wondering if she would even survive, Yellow Feather looked back at Precious Green, where torches flickered, windows and doorways glowed with light, and people laughed over cook fires on the terraces. Her emotions were like a night sky filled with shooting stars, each a painful stab: anger, bitterness, remorse. But none stung so deeply or sharply as her intense hatred for the person who had brought about this terrible fate.

Starved and frightened, Yellow Feather's skewed and confused thinking led her to believe that someone had to be blamed for her circumstance, *someone* must be the focus of her rage and hatred. It could not be Yani, who had only done her duty as overseer of the guild, and the others had only acted under Yani's orders.

That left Hoshi'tiwa. If she had not walked in on Yellow Feather while she was dressing, if she had not spoken in such a loud voice, if she had not attracted Yani's attention, everything would be all right now. Yellow Feather would simply be wearing a clean shift, sharing dinner with her sister potters, with no one the wiser.

As she wept bitter tears and whispered bitter oaths, Yellow Feather fueled her starved body with the thought of revenge, and it brought her such solace, no matter how paltry and sour, that she shouted in her confused, despairing mind: Yes, Hoshi'tiwa is the one to blame!

Thirty-one

THE day of the Autumn Equinox was upon them. Festivals and ritual dancing had been going on for days, and now it was time to bring in food for the winter ahead. The corn harvest had been poor, and the corn tribute from the outlying farms had been lower than expected. Now the focus was on meat. Because the forests around Center Place had been thinned, the larger game had vanished.

Dawn saw the entire population gathered at the western end of the canyon, where the dry riverbed fanned out onto a plain. High on the mesa above, Lord Jakál sat upon his throne flanked by Chief Physician Nagual, Captain Xikli, High Minister Moquihix, Lady White Orchid, and her father, Tenoch, a robe hiding his wooden legs. The rest of the nobles and officials of Center Place were lined up on the ridge, to observe the great hunt below.

The People of the Sun spread out and proceeded in an orderly if excited fashion, in anticipation of the feast to come.

A line of children went first, beating bushes and burrows with sticks, screaming and shouting and stamping their feet. Behind them came the line of young men bearing spears and bows and arrows, to shoot the game that the children had scared into the open. These were followed by older men with digging sticks and axes, and lastly came the women with baskets, bending and moving with great exertion.

An enormous, organized mass of humanity made slow progress across the plain, growing louder and more animated as they took every living thing in their path—rabbits, gophers, snakes, prairie dogs, and lizards of every kind. Nothing escaped; even birds were brought down with stones and arrows. The kills were left where they lay for the women who brought up the rear to scoop every little bloody carcass into their baskets.

Later, the sun dipping in the west, the carcasses were skinned, flesh was roasted, and entrails were boiled. Everything that was not eaten became the center of industry as women cured leftover meat for the coming winter. Bones were fashioned into tools and weapons, new bowstrings were made from animal sinew, feathers and fur became new clothes and blankets, while beaks, teeth, talons, and claws were turned into amulets, talismans, and jewelry. Not a scrap was wasted as the populace of Center Place busied itself with preparations for the coming cold months.

In all this industry, no one dared whisper the dark fear that was forming in their hearts: that this year's hunt had produced less than last year's, and that last year's had produced less than the year before. Already the people were thinking: Next year there will not be enough.

Thirty-two

THREE days before the Winter Solstice, the Morning Star vanished. Quetzalcoatl had descended to the Underworld, where he would dwell for fifty days before reappearing as the Evening Star. It felt strange to Hoshi'tiwa, in those first days after the disappearance of the Morning Star, not to see Lord Jakál on the promontory over Center Place every morning before dawn, greeting his god. It had become a comforting sight, and Hoshi'tiwa had begun to understand that as long as there was a Lord on the promontory to greet the dawn, all would be well at Center Place.

She also realized she missed seeing the *man* up there every morning, and that Lord Jakál was becoming something more in her mind than the *tlatoani* of her people. She could not forget the day at the glade, when they had encountered the rattlesnake and Jakál had placed himself between Hoshi'tiwa and danger. She told herself he was only protecting Center Place, that she was needed to call forth the Cloud Spirits. But sometimes at night she would waken from a feverish dream, throw off her blanket, and think long and deep about the Lord of Center Place.

Now the eve of Winter Solstice was upon them. Tension was high as

Moquihix and the rain-god priests returned to the potters' workshop, where Hoshi'tiwa's twelve rain jars, in varying tones of gold and yellow and orange, had been placed with the black-and-white pottery of her sisters.

Moquihix and the priests grimly inspected the pottery, examining each for flaws, for weaknesses, as a second-rate pot would insult the gods. Not all of Hoshi'tiwa's were chosen, only those with the most even hues, as some of her pieces ranged from pale red to golden on one jar. The blue-painted priests of Tlaloc played their human-shinbone flutes and chanted as they made the selections, and then, with great ceremony, in front of the gathered populace, the chosen vessels were set out in the plaza, and a night of prayers to the Cloud Spirits began.

Hoshi'tiwa returned to her sleeping mat in the kitchen, but it was not to sleep. She would hold vigil all night, deep in prayer, pleading with the Cloud Spirits to come. She shivered during the night, not from the cold—although the night was freezing—but from fear. There had been no clouds at sunset. How could rain be produced overnight? Nonetheless, she would not allow doubt to enter her heart. Silently reciting the prayers of her ancestors, sending them up to the stars, where she hoped the Cloud Spirits would hear and come to her aid, Hoshi'tiwa made a promise to herself: When the rain came, she was going to ask Lord Jakál to let her go home.

The settlement awoke cautiously that morning, the whole canyon subdued as people crept from their blankets and huts to see if the gods were still ignoring their prayers. And as the first rays of a pale dawn broke over the surrounding mesas, people rubbed their eyes and squinted in puzzlement.

Center Place had turned white.

Lord Jakál strode out into the plaza draped in a heavy cloak of buffalo hide, and stood at the edge of the stone masonry to look out at the plain. It was white as far as the eye could see. More light broke over the escarpments, exposing white-coated boulders and scrub, pockets of white on the sides of the cliffs, and a layer of white on the terraces and stairways of Center Place.

"It is not enough, my Lord," Moquihix pronounced solemnly. "The pottery did not bring snow, merely frost. The gods are angry. We must restore balance. We must give them a beating heart." And he gestured to the stone altar in the center of the plaza. It had been a long time since the stone had drunk the blood of a sacrificial victim.

Jakál said, "It is not snow, as you say, my friend. But it is frost, and frost means moisture." Already people swarmed the plain, falling to the earth to scoop up frost and press it to parched mouths. Every crystal of frost was saved and placed in jars. Water, though in small amount, had come to Center Place. "It is a sign from the gods that rain will follow."

As Hoshi'tiwa stood at the edge of the plaza with her sister potters, and overheard Jakál's words, her heart leapt with hope. Would this promise of future rain be enough to reward her? Would he let her go home?

But in the next instant, as she stood happily shivering with the other potters, Hoshi'tiwa realized she did not want to go home. Not yet. But there *was* something she wanted. When Lord Jakál turned to retreat into Precious Green, Hoshi'tiwa dashed forward, crying, "My Lord!"

He spun about, startled.

Throwing herself to the frozen ground at his feet, she pressed her forehead to the frost-covered limestone and said, "May I make a request, my Lord?"

While Jakál looked down at her in surprise, Moquihix stepped forward. "Such insolence!" he barked, and gestured for guards.

But Jakál stayed them. "What is it?" he said sharply, displeased with her impertinence, yet curious to hear her request.

Remaining on her knees, Hoshi'tiwa lifted herself up and said, "May I please be allowed to return to work at the potters' workshop?"

His eyebrows arched.

"We brought frost," she added quickly, gesturing to the others who stood uncertainly at the edge of the plaza. "But if we are allowed to work together, and pray as we work, and call upon the favor of the gods—so many voices in unison—we can bring rain."

His dark eyes studied her. He shifted beneath the heavy buffalo robe.

He thought of his decision to move her out of the Precious Green kitchen because he did not like her proximity to his own comings and goings. And he heard good sense in her request.

"No," he said, turning on his heel and striding away.

Thirty-three

Y ANI was in a baffling mood.

Hoshi'tiwa had come to the workshop to visit and share the evening meal with her sister potters, and now it was time to return to the warmth of her mat in the Precious Green kitchen.

But she was worried about her friend. Yani's distracted mood, which was so unlike her, reminded Hoshi'tiwa of a strange occurrence that had taken place at the kitchen a few days earlier. She had been busy at work, sanding her new jars, when the feeling of being watched had made her look up. She had been startled to see Chief Physician Nagual standing in the entry of the large, bustling kitchen, his hooded eyes fixed on her.

No one paid him any attention, as it was not required to kneel to the earth for anyone less than the *tlatoani* and certain high priests. While kitchen workers came and went, the Chief Physician stood motionless in the doorway, the great crest of hair on his shaven head backdropped against a clear blue sky. When Hoshi'tiwa's eyes met his, she had thought he would turn away, having been caught staring. But he did not. Those enigmatic eyes remained on her until she began to grow uncomfortable. Such a stare could almost be taken for witchcraft, and were it any other man, she would have whispered a prayer and traced a protective sign in the air.

It was only when one of the cooks needed to step outside that the physician finally left, but the sense of his presence lingered, filling Hoshi'tiwa with a nameless dread.

Recalling now that it was the Chief Physician's son with whom Yani's daughter had been caught, that it was because of Nagual's son that Yani's daughter had been executed, she wondered if the anniversary of that death were drawing nigh, and perhaps it was a dark reminder to them both.

"Are you all right?" Hoshi'tiwa asked, not wanting to leave until she had inquired after her friend's well-being.

Yani sighed and said in a melancholy tone, "We should be allowed to celebrate the Solstice in the way of our ancestors." She was clearing up after the evening meal, gathering bowls and sweeping the mat. The potters took turns at housekeeping and Yani executed her duties this evening in a strangely disinterested manner.

Quickly looking around to make sure no one heard, Hoshi'tiwa said, "Be careful what you say, Yani."

Yani's eyes seemed to look inward as she said wistfully, "I was a child when the last sacred ritual was held at the Sun Dagger. I remember the joy and jubilance of our people when the sacred dagger moved across the spiral and we were assured that the world was in balance again. And then our new masters outlawed the ritual and forced us to celebrate the Solstices and Equinoxes in Toltec fashion." She looked at Hoshi'tiwa. "This is why the world is out of balance. And for this reason I fear Pahana will not come to prevent the destruction of the world."

Hoshi'tiwa was shocked at Yani's bold talk. She wanted to say more, but realized it could only lead to a subject Hoshi'tiwa avoided—the prophecy recorded on the cavern overhang, and her own supposed part in that prophecy—so she said, "Yani, please watch what you say. As you once warned me, the walls have ears. I bid you good night, may the gods keep you until morning."

As she made to leave, the older woman touched her arm, staying her, and gave her a long thoughtful look. Yani knew Hoshi'tiwa wondered at her strange mood, and wished she could confide in the girl: that the kachina cult was growing and would soon need a stronger leader than herself. But Yani feared that Hoshi'tiwa was not ready. And now she lived at Precious Green, dangerously close to Lord Jakál and his advisers. Yani dared not risk sharing the secret with the girl yet.

"And the gods be with you as well," she said.

The cold night air pinched Hoshi'tiwa's skin, making her wish she had brought a blanket with which to warm herself for the trek across the plaza. The warm kitchen where she lived and slept seemed a long way from the potters' workshop, now that the plaza was dark and deserted and the winter wind blew.

As she hurried to round the high wall that was the eastern edge of Precious Green, Hoshi'tiwa glanced back, wondering if she should return to the warmth of the potters' workshop, when she saw someone emerge from within.

Yani. Bundled in a blanket. Hoshi'tiwa saw her friend pause to look around, as if not wishing to be seen, and then steal quietly into the freezing night.

Staring after her, Hoshi'tiwa recalled rumors she had heard of a new religious cult that had been brought to Center Place, one that was making the priests of the Toltec gods grumble to Lord Jakál. Hoshi'tiwa prayed that her friend was merely on a late-hour visit to acquaintances in the valley and nothing more.

With the chill reminding her that she was unprotected, she looked again across the deserted plaza where a merciless wind cut through like sharp knives, and she made a quick decision: to take a shortcut through Precious Green.

Hoshi'tiwa had not been inside the rising-splendor since the night she had taken a water pitcher to Lord Jakál's private chambers. She had not been recruited for servant work since. However, no one had said she was forbidden to go inside. And it would be a warm way to reach the kitchen.

Slipping through a small doorway used by lesser officials who came and went during the day on their many errands, she found herself in a corridor so dark that she had to feel her way along the wall.

It was surprisingly cold inside the massive stone complex. Hoshi'tiwa had thought there would be small fires to give the rooms and corridors warmth. But her breath formed a plume in front of her face, and when she rubbed her bare arms, she was shocked at how cold her skin was. She was also dismayed to discover that she did not know which way to go. In the darkness, the corridors and chambers formed a maze.

Many rooms had two doorways, and the darkness was so complete that she was blind, forcing Hoshi'tiwa to go this way and that, feeling her way, not knowing if she were moving forward or backward, if the doorway she had just entered was one she had entered before. The back of her neck prickled with fear as she expected at any moment a guard with a spear to catch her trespassing.

Belatedly wishing she had turned back to the warm workshop, or taken her chances in the cold wind across the plaza, she stepped up her pace, her hand running along the wall, coming to an end, not knowing if it was the end of the corridor or just another doorway, so that she went in, following her own hand as it crept along cold stone and mortar.

Where were all the people?

They lived on the upper tiers, she recalled. The ground level was for administrative activities only—bustling with life during the day, but deserted and eerie at night. Did ghosts rush in when mortals left?

One person did live on the ground floor, Lord Jakál, but Hoshi'tiwa recalled that his private chambers were closer to the kitchen.

Finally she saw a light up ahead. A doorway. Did it lead to the kitchen? She had made so many turns, and had even backtracked, that she did not know which way was which.

She went to the light, moving slowly, listening, wondering if that was the way out or if she were venturing into a forbidden area.

She paused before the doorway, drew a breath, and pushing the blanket aside, looked into a room filled with golden light. And Lord Jakál, his long black hair streaming over his shoulders and cascading down the blue and green feathers of his cloak, sitting cross-legged on the floor, his head bent over a puzzling occupation.

He looked up and smiled. Then, seeing who it was, frowned.

Months ago he had decided the girl must be removed from Precious Green and hidden away. But it had turned out not to be an easy task to accomplish. Jakál realized he couldn't place her in a house or any of the dwellings in the canyon because she needed a proper kiln and only a kitchen could provide that, and anyway she was about a sacred task and must not be distracted by the daily activities of family life. He had considered sending her to Blue Hummingbird where there was a large kitchen, but she still would not be hidden and he made frequent trips to that rising-splendor. To Five Flower, he had wondered, where she would be sequestered with the dancers and musicians? But there were the frequent rehearsals, the constant music. Set her up in a small house by herself in the valley? But might Tlaloc not take offense at such prosaic treatment of a holy endeavor?

In the end Jakál had decided to leave her where she was. And now, he realized in surprise, *here* she was, realizing also that his heart had jumped with pleasure at the unexpected sight of her.

Hoshi'tiwa hesitated in the doorway, not knowing what to do. When he had first looked up, he had smiled. Now he frowned. Had he thought she was someone else?

Perhaps Lady White Orchid, whom, it was rumored, he was going to marry.

He was not alone in the chamber filled with golden light. Two handsome young men sat in the corner playing flutes. One played harmony; the other, melody. A simple tune, but a haunting one. The young musicians were also blind.

"I'm lost," she finally said to Lord Jakál.

"Lost," he whispered, and the word seemed to resonate in his eyes.

How had she found this private sanctuary, where not even his High Minister was allowed, where only blind musicians were permitted to enter? Jakál did not believe in coincidence. There was no such thing as chance. The gods guided every step taken by a man.

Or a rain-girl.

He rose, his magnificent cloak covered in shimmering green and blue feathers catching the torchlight in colorful sparks. Sensing their master's movement, the musicians ceased playing. Jakál strode to Hoshi'tiwa, who stood frozen in the doorway. His eyes roamed her body and settled upon her bare arms. "You shiver," he said.

"It is very cold," she whispered.

His eyes met hers, held there for three heartbeats; then he brought his hands to the knotted rope at his throat, untied it, and lifted the heavy cloak from his shoulders. When he swung it around and brought it behind Hoshi'tiwa, she caught her breath. As he settled the heavy garment on her shoulders, and she felt the weight of it, the warmth it still held from his own body, she thought she would never breathe again.

Turning away, Jakál said something to the musicians in Nahuatl, and they resumed playing. As delicate flute melodies filled the air, Jakál gestured for Hoshi'tiwa to enter. When he resumed sitting on the woven mat, surrounded by paper, brushes, and pots of paint, Hoshi'tiwa hesitated. To move beneath such a heavy cloak was a strange sensation. But she was also spellbound to think that the garment had only moments before adorned the body of the most powerful man in the land. His warmth was now warming her, driving away the chill and replacing it with a heat that astonished her.

And then she realized that it was not just the cloak that was warming her. Jakál wore only a loincloth—dazzling and colorful and bejeweled, to be sure—but a loincloth all the same, so that the rest of him was exposed to the flickering torchlight, and Hoshi'tiwa could not take her eyes off him.

He looked up, and then gestured to her to join him.

Clumsily, trying to manage the heavy cloak, she sank to the mat and crossed her legs. She could not help but stare at the curious object in his lap. It was called, she had learned, a book.

"I am composing a poem," he said.

Hoshi'tiwa frowned at the shapes and lines and colors. "What is a poem?"

"It is like a song that is not sung, or a prayer that is not chanted. I will read this to you."

> *Flowers die.*
> *The quetzal bird dies.*
> *Does any man really live on earth?*
> *Not forever on this earth.*
> *Flowers are brief,*
> *The quetzal bird is brief,*
> *Man is brief.*
> *Not forever on the earth, only a short time here.*

Hoshi'tiwa said, "It is very sad."

"This is a poem to my wife. She died several summers ago."

"I'm sorry."

Looking at the pictures on the folded paper, she thought of Ahoté, standing at the Memory Wall, learning how to record events on the rock face, using paints and carving tools, and able to read the stories recorded there by previous men. And she wondered once again if he had received her message from the salt merchant.

"Symbols have meaning," Jakál said quietly as he laid aside the paper and reached for a paintbrush. "When we paint these symbols on paper, or upon a wall, we give them life, we give them power."

To her shock, he shifted about to face her and, without a word, took hold of her right hand, turning it palm upward. Dipping the brush into a pot of black paint, Jakál traced an outline on her palm.

Hoshi'tiwa feared she was going to faint. It was too hot now in the chamber, and the cloak weighed upon her. But it was Jakál's nearness that made her head swim, and the feel of his hand as it cradled hers.

She looked at his bent head. His hair, not drawn up in the usual topknot but hanging loosely, was shiny. She had heard that the Dark Lords were fastidiously clean. She suspected Jakál bathed in water, the only person at Center Place permitted to do so. She herself had bathed in the stream back home, and knew the freshness such cleanliness brought to the soul, the new life it gave to the spirit.

From his hair, her eyes roved to his shoulders and arms, the hills and valleys of his sinewy muscles. There was no fat on him. Lord Jakál was as lean and strong as a hunter.

Her heart quickened.

Laying aside the brush, Jakál picked up another, dipped it into the pot of blue paint, and filled in the outline on her palm, saying, "I am giving life to this symbol now, as I paint it on your skin."

"How?" she said, surprised that she could find breath and voice.

"If you show this symbol to any man who can read, he will recognize it. He will speak the symbol's name. Whereas it did not exist before, now it does, and so it has life."

She studied the painted figure on her palm. "What is it?"

He lifted his face, close to hers, and murmured, " 'Water.' "

"Water," she whispered, and when she lifted her eyes, and saw how close his face was to hers, she felt the floor fall away beneath her and imagined she floated on a hot cloud far above the earth. Jakál's deep-set eyes held a thousand mysteries. His thin-lipped mouth contained a thousand secrets. She wanted in that moment to open her breast to him, to hand him her heart, and say, "Take my spirit, keep it always."

He leaned forward, as if to inspect a mote on her eyelash, or to share her breath, or speak in silence. The blind musicians played their flutes, but the melodies could not drown out the thumping of her heart, which Hoshi'tiwa was certain could be heard out across the mesas and rivers to the ends of the earth.

She thought he was going to kiss her.

And then suddenly he looked at her in shock, like a man startled out of a deep sleep. Jakál blinked, his eyes widened, and he drew in a sharp breath. Whispering something in his native tongue, he shot to his feet, as if he had just encountered a scorpion.

The flutes fell silent.

Hoshi'tiwa, struggling to find herself, her own feet, her equilibrium, managed also to rise and felt the cloak slip from her shoulders as Jakál took it, the magic moment having passed, his eyes no longer mysterious or secretive but sending a clear message: She was to leave.

And once again she thought of the river with its changing currents and tides beneath a placid surface.

He ordered the musicians to escort her to the kitchen and then turned his back on her as the three left the room and Hoshi'tiwa stumbled out behind the blind boys wondering what had happened, why the magical moment had taken place, why it had so abruptly ended.

Jakál remained rooted to the floor as he heard her footsteps fade down the corridor. He was mortified.

A pottery maker! The daughter of a corn grower! A girl who could neither read nor write, nor grasp mathematics, nor interpret the stars. *He had enjoyed her company.*

What was happening to him? He should have hidden her away when he had the chance. He wished he could send her back to her farm. But he needed her. He knew Xikli had eyes on the throne of Center Place. The Captain would never dare to assassinate a seated *tlatoani,* but there were other methods. If he could rally all the nobles, officials, priests, and Jaguars to his cause, they could force Jakál to abdicate and he would have no choice. In order to keep his throne and be the reigning *tlatoani* when Quetzalcoatl arrived, Jakál needed Hoshi'tiwa and her powers to summon the Cloud Spirits. The frost and light snow were evidence that her presence there was working.

That was the reason—the *only* reason—why he must keep her at Center Place. But he would send her back to the potters' workshop, he decided grimly, where she belonged. And it would be only until the next Solstice, and then her beating heart would be offered to the gods. As he had promised.

Thirty-four

THE party was a triumph.

White Orchid had told her guests that the feast was in honor of her father, but the real reason was more personal and had only marginally to do with Tenoch. It had been a way to get Lord Jakál to visit her home.

After she had given him the book of poetry and he still had not reciprocated by paying her a visit with a comparable gift, White Orchid had devised another way to lure Lord Jakál to her house. And as it must be so fabulous an event that he could not possibly decline to come, she had invited every noble and high official and wealthy *pochteca* in Center Place, a crowd so large that she had had to evict a neighboring farm family so that she could use their field to accommodate all the guests, musicians, entertainers.

After all the preparation and great expense, sleepless nights, worry, and much hand-wringing, after making sure her guests enjoyed a day of gorging and drinking, laughing and telling stories, playing heated games of *patolli,* receiving gifts from their hostess, and ensuring that they would speak of this celebration for years to come, her secret plan had succeeded beyond her highest expectations.

White Orchid had spent the day getting herself ready, scraping the hair from her body and massaging honey into her skin to make it supple and smooth; tweezing her eyebrows with clamshells and painting them back in; braiding no less than fifty perfect sky-stone beads into her hair. The orange-and-yellow pattern of her dress was flawless and brilliant. Her perfume came from the crushed leaves of a rare flower. And she stained her teeth red, making sure she smiled frequently. All to catch the attention of Lord Jakál, who had arrived with an entourage and, after presenting White Orchid with a beautiful gift, had been the regal center of attention for much of the evening, before graciously departing to attend to prayers at the shrine of Quetzalcoatl.

The only shadow cast upon the otherwise perfect evening was Tenoch.

Before the first guest had arrived, her father started drinking. He had had his slaves carry him to the seat of honor in the main room, and there he had sipped steadily from his octopus-mug until finally, too intoxicated to hold his head up, he had had his slaves carry him to his private rooms. But Captain Xikli went with him, which worried White Orchid. He was in there still, after the last of the guests had staggered home. White Orchid suspected Xikli was working on a way of persuading the drunken old man to agree to a marriage contract.

What troubled her even more was Tenoch's startling setback after a long spell of abstinence. Since the frightening episode when he had screamed and flailed his arms at a phantom attacker, and White Orchid had summoned Chief Physician Nagual, Tenoch had been sober. What had caused this relapse?

Wondering if she should send for Nagual—he had politely declined an invitation to her party and so had not been among the revelers—White Orchid went into the kitchen where slaves were cleaning up, scrubbing the hundreds of pots and bowls and platters, using sand instead of water, and went to the open doorway to look out into the night.

A horrific scene was unfolding at the edge of her property, and she observed it in disgust.

For the feast White Orchid had managed to procure a large mountain sheep, which her servants had roasted on a spit for two days. Her guests had reduced the carcass to bone and gristle but with enough meat left on it for her servants and kitchen staff to enjoy. When they had finished, they tossed the remains beyond the boundary of her property, where a crowd had been gathering for days.

Word of a nobleman's feast always attracted the poor and hungry hoping for scraps, and the mob now descended upon the remains of the sheep like starving ravens, shrieking and fighting.

As she watched them squabble and fight, with more arriving in hopes of a mouthful of meat, White Orchid thought she recognized a girl in the crowd: skinny and very pregnant. Hadn't she once worked in the Potters' Guild? She had worn a yellow feather in her hair, White Orchid recalled, and was surprised to feel a stab of envy. The girl was obviously an outcast—filthy, malnourished, with hollow eyes. Nonetheless, there was the babe in her belly.

She is barely more than an animal, White Orchid told herself as she turned away from the sight in disgust. The People of the Sun were barely one remove from the dumb beasts that lived by brute instinct.

As she left the kitchen, thinking of the skinny pregnant girl fighting for carcass scraps, White Orchid absently placed her hand on her flat abdomen. Another winter had passed, adding another year to her life. Time was rushing past like the river that used to rush through this valley. If only marriage and a husband were not a prerequisite to motherhood. And although adoption was not unheard of among the lower classes of Toltecs, it was out of the question for a noblewoman. Bloodline and ancestry were all. And she owed it to her father to give him a grandchild of his own flesh.

Thinking of Tenoch, she left the kitchen and glanced in the direction of Tenoch's bedroom. Captain Xikli had been in there a long time. What promises was he making to get Tenoch to agree to a marriage arrangement?

White Orchid was not worried. She had elicited a promise from her father that he would do nothing about her marital situation until the caravan had arrived. Like all Toltecs, Tenoch was highly superstitious with deep beliefs in magic and luck. When she told him she had asked the Caravan Master to bring her something special from Tollan that would guarantee her being wed to Jakál, Tenoch believed her. And so her future, her life depended upon the arrival of the caravan and the master bringing the serpent with the love-venom.

Moving through the rooms of her villa, where slaves were sweeping up, restoring order, White Orchid thought how well everything was working out. Jakál had come to the feast. He had presented her with a beautiful gift—a mantle spun from rich, deep blue cotton—and when he left, he had complimented her so that all could hear, warmly and with sincerity.

The only obstacle to attaining her goal was the rain-girl who continued to live at Precious Green. Although White Orchid's secret spy, Jakál's personal bodyguard, reported that nothing untoward was happening between the Lord and the rain-girl, White Orchid's suspicions still remained high. The girl had to be removed.

Once that was taken care of, and the aphrodisiac venom had done its work, White Orchid would move into Precious Green as Jakál's wife.

Hearing a booming voice that, in its familiarity, turned her stomach, she saw Captain Xikli emerge from her father's bedroom. The man never walked; he strode. And he reached White Orchid in three long paces, bowing his head in an almost mocking way, and said, "Your father and I enjoyed a fruitful chat."

"It's late," she said. "You are the last to leave."

Placing his fists on his hips, his legs set apart, Xikli looked about himself as if taking stock. He was impressively dressed in jaguar skins, with gold and sky-stone adorning his arms, his face painted in black and white stripes, his long hair gathered into a feathered topknot.

Bringing himself back to his hostess, Xikli sized her up as well, as if she were on the slave block; then he seized her arm and pulled her to him. He smelled of liquor.

"Let go of me," she said.

His face, grotesquely distorted by the pebbled scar that ran diagonally from forehead to jaw, twisted into what served as a grin. Pulling her to him, he growled, "I will have this villa, I will have the throne of Center Place, and I will have *you*."

White Orchid boldly met his eyes, looked into them with loathing, then pulled her arm free and said in a cold voice, "It is time for you to leave."

He laughed as he strode out. White Orchid watched him go; then she turned toward her father's bedroom, where she heard him snoring loudly beyond the covered doorway. Why had he imbibed so heavily tonight after such a long period of sobriety? A chilly draft swept through the house, causing her to shiver and rub her bare arms, and feel her prior joy and giddiness swiftly dissipate.

Something was wrong.

She pulled aside the hanging over the bedroom doorway and peered around it. Tenoch was slumbering fitfully on his mat, his blanket thrown off. She tiptoed in and knelt to restore it. Suddenly his eyes were open and he whispered, "Omaya!"

"No, Father," she said gently. "It is White Orchid." Omaya was her mother, dead these many years.

"Omaya, Omaya," he moaned in a raspy voice, his rheumy eyes wandering without focus, his head rolling from side to side. "What did we do?"

"Hush, Father, go back to sleep." White Orchid hated what liquor did to him. She would definitely seek Nagual's counsel first thing in the morning.

As she started to rise, he seized her wrist in a surprisingly strong grip. "We were wrong!" he rasped. His eyes sought her face but settled on a spot above her shoulder. His words were slurred and spittle ran down his chin as he said, "Tenoch . . . haunts me. Bedroom . . . every night . . . says I will be punished. I cannot take it anymore!"

White Orchid frowned, and then she realized he was referring to the *first* Tenoch, who had founded the bloodline when he arrived at Center

Place generations ago. Following Toltec tradition, the eldest son was named after the first male ancestor of the bloodline. White Orchid's own little boy, dead at six months, had been Tenoch also.

"Why does he haunt you?" she asked gently, to calm him, wishing he would drift off to sleep. It had been a long day and she was exhausted.

"Angry. Blood—bloodline at an end . . ."

She patted his shoulder. "Do not fret, dear Father. I will give you a son, I promise." So this was the root of his urgency to have her marry Xikli. He was having bad dreams.

As she started to leave, she saw that he had urinated in bed. "Oh, Father," she sighed. "Why did you drink so much tonight when you have been sober for so long?"

"I don't blame you, Omaya," he groaned. "I know how badly you wanted a daughter. I gave you sons. But no daughters . . ." His head lolled from side to side. "Ashamed! But . . . my love for you—was great . . ."

White Orchid stared down at her father. He clearly had no idea of place or time, or whom he was talking to. Nor was he really talking—it was the incoherent babbling of a drunkard.

And yet . . .

"Father," she said softly, leaning close, "what are you talking about? You did give Omaya a daughter. You gave her White Orchid."

His bloodshot eyes darted from side to side, not focusing on her face as he said, "Yes, I did! After the man came . . . in the night . . . I was uncertain . . . it did not feel proper. . . . But when I saw the delight on your face, how you smiled—when I placed the little girl in your arms . . ." He sobbed loudly and dragged an arm under his nose. "I gladly paid the stranger the price he asked. But now I am being punished! My ancestor knows of my deception. He says I will suffer for it!"

A creeping chill began deep in White Orchid's bones as her father's words sank in, and their terrible meaning. But it could not be. He wasn't speaking clearly. She was hearing incorrectly. "Father, you had . . . *another* daughter? Where did she go? Did she die?"

"No other daughter, only White Orchid! And I do love her, even though she is not of my blood, may the gods forgive me."

Tenoch continued to ramble, his sentences fragmenting into bits and pieces, about a Toltec wife, no longer fertile, who so desperately wanted a daughter that her husband, a Hero of the Empire, secretly purchased a baby from a stranger—Tenoch and Omaya staging a pregnancy in which Omaya was confined to the villa, allowing few visitors, so that no one knew of the deception.

"It is not possible," White Orchid whispered with a dry mouth, her heart thumping. She glanced over her shoulder, imagining a thousand eyes watching. But the night was silent. The servants had retired to their mats.

Tenoch began to weep uncontrollably, pushing a fist into his eyes. "Don't know where the baby came from! Stranger . . . didn't say!"

White Orchid heard liquor-soaked words fly from his mouth like evil creatures: "Orphan . . . abandoned . . . stolen. Don't know."

It wasn't possible. He was hallucinating. Poisoned by alcohol. A sob escaped her throat. Sober men keep secrets, but drunkards blurt the truth.

The moment stretched, the silence deepened as shock kept her rooted to the spot, a cold horror dawning on her. Memories: the morning of her three-day puberty celebration, when she had started menstruating and her mother had inducted her into the secrets of womanhood, young White Orchid passing through the house and catching words in worried tones behind a covered doorway, Omaya saying, "We should take it from her and replace it. Give her another one."

Suspecting that they were talking about her, White Orchid had moved closer, but had not been able to hear clearly as other family members had resided in the villa in those days, and the rooms were filled with voices. On the other side of the tapestry, her father had said, "No, she must keep it. It connects her to—"

White Orchid had not been able to make out the rest of her father's sentence. He had spoken two words. What had they been?

And what had her parents been arguing about? "We should take it from her. . . ." Take what? White Orchid had not known, but now, years later, in the sudden intuition that truth sometimes brings, she sensed that the contentious subject had been the amulet she had worn since she was a baby. Everyone wore a protective charm, even the lowliest slave. White Orchid's was a beautiful pale pink stone incised with a magic symbol, given to her by her father when she was born.

Her hand now rose to her breast where she felt, beneath the fabric of her dress, the comforting amulet lying against her skin.

"It connects her to . . . ," her father had said. To what?

Suddenly she knew, as if her father's voice continued to echo within these walls from that day to this, waiting for the right moment for her to hear.

"It connects her . . . *to her people.*"

Tenoch drifted into unconsciousness and White Orchid rose shakily to look down at this man she had loved and worshipped all her life. She would not call for slaves to clean him and dress him in fresh clothes. She would let him lie there and find himself thus in the morning.

Tomorrow she would figure out what to do. She must make certain no one learned the truth. Tenoch had managed to keep his awful secret for nearly thirty years, but now he was being haunted by his great-grandfather. Whether the haunting was real or imagined, it was driving him to drink and causing his tongue to loosen. White Orchid must make sure the secret was never exposed—

Chief Physician Nagual.

"Blessed Lady Corn," she whispered in a panic. Nagual knew! Would he tell Jakál? As Chief Physician, would he be bound by honor to warn his *tlatoani* that the daughter of Tenoch was not of his blood-line, that in fact she did not *know* her bloodline?

And then, like a bolt of lightning, a far more terrible revelation burst upon her mind. Taking Tenoch by the shoulders, she cried, "Father, what are the stars of my birth?" But he slumbered on.

She wrapped her arms about herself and rocked back and forth. All these years, going to the astrologer, having her horoscope cast—what were the stars she had been using? The stars of the night the stranger had brought her to the villa? *Not* the stars of her birth?

White Orchid was immobilized. Terror flooded her soul. Without knowing the stars she was born under, how was she to lead her life?

Suddenly everything that had tied her to the earth was severed. She felt as if she were flying up to the sky. She was no longer connected to the man lying on the urine-soaked mat, or to his ancestors, or to anyone she knew, or to the stars or the land and all the creatures on it.

She struggled to her feet. The bedchamber tilted. The floor heaved up. The walls began to spin. She staggered to the doorframe to catch herself. When her foot hit something, she bent to pick it up.

The octopus-mug. The old herb peddler's prediction had come true. White Orchid could not breathe. She was being suffocated by a terrible truth.

Running blindly from her father's chamber, she flew through the silent and sleeping house and out into the night, on the other side of the villa from where the obscene feasting upon a sheep's discarded carcass was going on, to the cornfield side of the villa, and there she dropped to her knees, sobbing.

She gasped for air, her lungs tightening in pain, her chest heaving with spasms. The *nequhtli* mug lay in the dirt, the eight tentacles of the octopus shining in the moonlight, as if the sea creature were there, waiting to strangle her.

Words swam through her mind: stolen . . . abandoned . . . orphaned . . . Toltec or People of the Sun, we do not know . . .

In the shimmering moonlight, the eight tentacles moved on the mug and wriggled up toward White Orchid, reaching for her throat. With a cry she grabbed the evil vessel and shot to her feet. Swaying beneath the cold and impersonal stars, she raised her hand high, drew back her arm, and flung the mug with its odious creature into an arc through the air, to hear it crash to the earth, shattering into a thousand pieces.

Thirty-five

CAPTAIN Xikli strode from his quarters in the Jaguar barracks and scanned the cloudless firmament with a dyspeptic eye. Another cycle of the moon and still no rain. And now the fifty days were coming to an end. In three days, the Evening Star would appear.

It was time for a man-corn festival.

His soldiers had been celebrating for nights around their bonfires, working themselves up as they thumped their shields and shrieked to the stars, and now they were mustering in the plaza, splendid in their skins and plumage, with their fierce javelins and spears, and devilish howls that made everyone's blood run to ice.

Striding dramatically out onto the plaza, knowing that the sight of his platoon struck fear in the hearts of all who watched, Captain Xikli took his place at their head. The priests blessed them, Xikli shouted a command, and the Jaguars went running out of the valley. People turned their backs as the army passed, and raised their voices in high keening sounds because they knew that, in a settlement not far from Center Place, a slaughter was to take place, followed by the ritualistic eating of man-corn.

Captain Xikli and the Jaguars returned three days later after having feasted well, proof of their success seen in the human heads they displayed on their spears. Xikli had taken them south, where the rain was good, and so they had ingested people who had been blessed by rain.

As they paraded around the plaza, before the eyes of the People of the Sun who knew that another of their clans had been sacrificed, Captain Xikli sought out White Orchid among the nobles gathered in welcome. He found her sitting next to Tenoch on honored chairs. She was pale and stiff. She looked as if she had lost weight. Xikli grinned, his lips still caked with human blood. His promise, on the night of her party, that she would be his, had clearly had an impact.

He enjoyed a feeling of immense satisfaction. When he caught her eye, his grin sent her a silent message: *See how great my power is.*

Thirty-six

YELLOW Feather awoke from fitful sleep and knew at once that her worst nightmare was about to come true.

Far worse than having to live among vile outcasts who existed beyond the fringe of society, barely more than animals, who had used her body for their own amusements, who had shown her no tenderness or compassion, nor care for the child she carried, who had let her starve when the whim struck them, who had forced her to cook and grind corn and skin rabbits, and travel with them when they raided nearby farms—far worse than the depravity she had sunk to was the onset of labor pains.

She must get away.

When she had first joined the outcasts in their isolated camp, Yellow Feather had thought only of her own survival. But now she was thinking of her child. She knew they would take the baby after it was born, and sell it—there were barren wives in Center Place who were known to secretly pay for an infant. Or perhaps they would take it to the witch who lived in one of the ravines and who, it was whispered, used babies in her black magic.

In these past months Yellow Feather had given no thought to escape, because where could she escape to? Where could she go, what house could she visit, what path could she walk where people would not throw stones at her for fear of catching her bad luck? And so she had stayed with the rapists and thieves, the liars and cheats, because at least there was shelter here, deep among the boulders high above Center Place, warm cook fires and protection from the cold, and there were scraps of food the men occasionally threw to her.

But now she had to leave. Where she headed, as she climbed down the trail shivering in the spring night, she did not know, but was driven by an instinct older than time—to save the infant above all costs. Whenever the men had used her, Yellow Feather had sent her mind far away, sent her soul up to the sun and stars, and left her body for as long as she could. Therefore her thoughts, as she made her way down to the valley, were incoherent, without solid form or direction, and yet somewhere at the back of her numb and beleaguered brain a voice whispered: Leave the baby on the doorstep of a rich man.

Hoshi'tiwa tossed and turned in a disturbing dream. Lord Jakál painting a symbol on the palm of her right hand—an owl, which suddenly came to life, taking wing and flying up to the sun.

She woke abruptly and stared up at the wooden arbor covering the patio adjacent to the kitchen of Precious Green. She listened to her pulse, and lay still until it slowed and she was breathing normally again.

Ahoté. Coming to her in dreams instead of in real life. He was never going to come after her; she knew that now. He had promised, but it was a promise he had no right to keep, for he was dedicated to the clan's Memory Wall.

And Lord Jakál, painting an owl on her hand, setting it free. What did it mean?

The Lord of Center Place was in her dreams by night, her thoughts by day. She thought of the Jaguars, returning from a bloody rampage to the south. Hoshi'tiwa had expected Lord Jakál to accompany them, yet he did not. Therefore she had assumed his portion of the man-corn would be brought back. Instead, a festival had been held in the absence of the Jaguars, to bring attention to the gods that a human sacrifice was taking place, and in this way did Hoshi'tiwa learn that Lord Jakál was not a consumer of human flesh, nor was Moquihix, nor any of the Toltecs who lived at Center Place.

And with this new knowledge, her curiosity about Lord Jakál—and her budding, forbidden desire for him—flourished and grew.

Wondering what had wakened her, she listened to the night and, hearing a strange sound, sat up. A queer, high sound. An animal in pain? Rising, she enfolded herself in a blanket and looked out into the chilly spring night.

The valley slept beneath darkness and silence. Had it been the moan of a ghost? The back of her neck prickled with fear.

And then she heard it again. Human! Someone was hurt.

She debated for a moment—to venture into the night was dangerous and foolhardy—but the cries came again and she realized it was a woman.

Heading out, walking briskly, she followed the cries for help until she came upon a dusty path that cut across the canyon. The sounds grew louder as she pushed through low, brittle brush, the last remnants in the valley that had not been plucked for cook fires and shade arbors. When she came upon a ghostly white shape on the ground, Hoshi'tiwa thought she had been deceived. An evil spirit had lured her to this hidden place with the intention of stealing her soul.

She was about to run away when she saw that it was a woman in a dirty white shift, lying on her side and gasping in pain.

Yellow Feather!

Hoshi'tiwa cried out with relief. After Yellow Feather had been banished from the guild, Hoshi'tiwa had searched for her. But no one knew where the girl had vanished to. Hoshi'tiwa had prayed that Yellow Feather had somehow found her way back to her family and had been received with a warm welcome.

But now here she was, lying on the ground clutching her abdomen, her eyes shut in agony. Hoshi'tiwa saw the bruises on her arms. When Yellow Feather grimaced, Hoshi'tiwa saw missing teeth. As she felt her heart stir in her breast, a strange thought entered Hoshi'tiwa's mind: I was once declared *makai-yó* through no fault of my own. It was an unjust judgment. Yellow Feather had done nothing more than to fall in love. She and Falcon had been betrothed, their wedding was only days away when he died. Was that not almost like being married?

Reaching down, she lifted Yellow Feather to her feet. "Where shall we go?" she asked, reasoning that Yellow Feather had been on her way somewhere.

The girl looked at her rescuer through blurred vision. Her eyes widened. "Hoshi'tiwa?" She looked around wild-eyed, and then down at herself, at the great mound of abdomen from which pain was radiating. "I do not . . . know . . . where to go. . . ."

Hoshi'tiwa had a sudden idea. Drawing Yellow Feather's arm across her shoulders, and supporting her around the waist, she encouraged her to walk, and together they stumbled down the path.

Because old Pikami was a healer, she was therefore holy and thus her hut would be safe from evil spirits. But Hoshi'tiwa was dismayed to find the crude shelter deserted. Not even the lame grandson was at home. However, embers glowed welcomingly in the fire pit and the hut was warm.

Easing Yellow Feather to the woven mat, Hoshi'tiwa surveyed the roof made of branches and brush but found no beam from which to suspend a rope to tie around Yellow Feather's wrists. Even if she did, she feared her friend's weight would pull the whole structure down. The hut looked as if it had been blown down and reconstructed many times, with new wood strapped to old, new twigs tucked between old boards. The round floor space was wide enough for two people to lie lengthwise, end to end; there was a grinding stone for corn, a pile of surprisingly nice blankets, and a few jars containing beans, corn, and chilies.

However, what set this shelter apart from the hundreds of others dotting the canyon were the medicines and herbs hanging from the low rafters. Tied on the ends of strings were bunches of leaves, petals, stems, and roots; bags of seeds, nuts, berries; pouches filled with powders and pebbles; and magic talismans. It was like being inside a magical forest with all the wealth and beneficence of nature sprouting overhead.

But Hoshi'tiwa had no idea which of this would help Yellow Feather in childbirth.

Where was Pikami?

Yellow Feather cried out and said that the baby was coming.

Hoshi'tiwa looked at her in fear. Wasn't it too soon? Back home, first babies took a day to arrive. Perhaps it was because she was so malnourished, or had lived, judging by her condition, so harshly these past months. Perhaps the baby was eager to enter the world and start a life in service to the gods, for that was sometimes said of bastards and other unwanted babies.

"Help me!" Yellow Feather gasped.

Hoshi'tiwa clutched the bear claw that hung about her neck and prayed to the bear spirit for strength. Then she placed her hands under Yellow Feather's armpits to assist her to a squatting position. "Put your hands on my shoulders," Hoshi'tiwa said. She had witnessed enough births to know what was going to happen next. As Yellow Feather screamed with each contraction, Hoshi'tiwa knelt with her hands out, and she chanted, ready to receive the new life.

The baby came swiftly, crying lustily despite its small size, a boy with a pink face and shock of black hair. Hoshi'tiwa cut the umbilical cord with her teeth, wishing she had a bowl of cornmeal in which to pour the last of the umbilical blood to later plant in a field. Then she helped Yellow Feather to ease back against the wall of the hut, the infant at her breast.

Hoshi'tiwa sat for a moment, overcome with emotion and the curious elation that came with bringing new life into the world. She looked at Yellow Feather, filthy and bedraggled and malnourished, but smiling as she suckled her new son. Love swept over Hoshi'tiwa—of a sort she had not felt before. A new connection to Yellow Feather, a bond that was strong the instant it was formed. Hoshi'tiwa smiled and thought: my sister.

And suddenly the girl who had never had sisters and barely remembered her brothers felt her connection to the sisterhood of potters deepen.

She left the hut and returned with handfuls of dried grass and sand with which to clean the new mother and the mat upon which she had given birth. These would have to be buried far from the hut so that evil spirits weren't attracted by the smell of blood.

As they waited for the afterbirth to be expelled, Hoshi'tiwa said, "Tell him his father's name. Quickly," she added because Yellow Feather hesitated for some reason.

Yellow Feather opened her mouth, but no sound came out. Hoshi'tiwa frowned. "What is wrong?"

"Nothing . . ."

"Then quickly speak his father's name or an evil spirit might whisper one and deceive him."

Yellow Feather licked her lips.

"Falcon," Hoshi'tiwa prompted.

But Yellow Feather knew she could not lie at such a moment. She said, "Moquihix," and Hoshi'tiwa stared at her.

Had she heard wrong? Or had Yellow Feather, in her exhaustion and malnourished state, misspoken?

But when she saw the shameful look on Yellow Feather's face, the way she hung her head and would not meet Hoshi'tiwa's eyes, the truth hit her. Yellow Feather had lain with a Toltec Lord.

And suddenly, to her shock, Lord Jakál sprang into Hoshi'tiwa's mind.

"Please do not tell anyone," Yellow Feather pleaded. "For then my child will be cursed."

"Do not worry," Hoshi'tiwa said gently, pushing Lord Jakál from her thoughts, wondering why he had come to her mind at such a moment. "I will tell no one. The matter of the boy's father is between you and the gods."

"We must leave before Pikami returns," Yellow Feather said urgently. "She will say I have brought bad luck to her medicines."

But Hoshi'tiwa stayed Yellow Feather, pressing her back against the wall. "I will speak with Pikami. I will pay her if I must, but I will persuade her to give you and your child shelter."

As she watched Yellow Feather cradle the small newborn in her arm, Hoshi'tiwa felt a new understanding stir within her. Like the new life in Yellow Feather's arms, or new life that struggles in the shallows of a stream, seeking to define itself, to find its place in nature's complex order, within the breast of Hoshi'tiwa, whose thoughts and emotions had been struggling for order, this new life breathed and grew and stretched its fresh wings. And it brought a revelation.

In the days since Tupa's death and Hoshi'tiwa's removal from the workshop, she had felt the need to return to the workshop, had asked Lord Jakál to permit her to return, but she had not fully understood why this need was in her. For the combined power of the potters, she had told herself and Jakál. To help the guild overcome the stigma Tupa's evil ways had cast upon it, she had said.

But now, looking at Yellow Feather and suddenly feeling an intense connection to this girl, a fellow potter—no, not potter, *sister*—Hoshi'tiwa recognized the true nature of her desire to return to the workshop. She had come to feel about them as if they were her sisters, as surely as if they were her blood.

This was what had been haunting her since Tupa's death, the vague notion that had danced at the edge of her mind and which she could not define, which kept her from running away from Center Place. She had been unaware of the bond that was forming between herself and her new "family." And now that she saw it for what it was, she understood her need to return to the bosom of the workshop.

In the next instant she was surprised—and then not at all surprised—to sense *another* new and growing connection, a bond not just with Yellow Feather and the potters, but with Center Place and all its people.

Thirty-seven

SHE was being watched.

Hoshi'tiwa could not say how she knew. She had no evidence, had not spotted anyone hidden in the brush. Yet, as she bent at her labor harvesting the sacred clay, she knew someone—or something—was watching her.

She straightened and looked around. The small rocky canyon was dappled with late afternoon sunlight. A few feeble spring flowers struggled up through the dry rocks and boulders that, in rainy season, would create a pond but which had not held water in years. Hoshi'tiwa saw no one. Yet she could not shake the feeling of being watched.

A ghost? The back of her neck crawled. Did ghosts walk by day?

She prayed it was not an evil spirit, because she was laboring at a holy task. After the appearance of the Evening Star, shining bright in the western sky, the spiritual rhythm returned to Center Place, with rituals and festivals honoring the many gods who watched over the people. Hoshi'tiwa worked with single-minded dedication on the rain jars, for next would be the Summer Solstice and the hope, once again, for rain.

Although she had vowed to stay away from the sacred glade, this time she really did need more clay, and so she had a right to be up in this narrow ravine. But when her basket was full and she should have headed straight back to Center Place, the small trail that forked off to the glade beckoned.

Was Lord Jakál at that moment in the glade? Were *his* eyes the ones she had felt on her?

Creeping close to the edge of the sacred glade, careful not to approach too near—even though no one would observe her trespass, the gods would know—she looked in and saw sunlight everywhere, blinding, golden light that hurt the eyes.

And there he was, among the flowers, wearing only a loincloth, his body gleaming in the sun.

She held her breath and stepped closer. She blinked. Something was wrong. Jakál's hair was short now, cropped just below the ears. And he was slimmer than before. She watched him as he moved about, inspecting the blossoms, and as he stepped from a ray of dazzling sunlight, she saw that it was not Lord Jakál at all.

Ahoté!

Thirty-eight

HOSHI'TIWA cried out.

Ahoté turned, his expression puzzled, and then he broke into a smile. "There you are!"

"Come out now. Quickly!"

"I was told I would find you—"

"Ahoté, this is a holy sanctuary! *The gods live here!*"

He ran from the forbidden glade, and they flew into each other's arms. Hoshi'tiwa held tight and closed her eyes. She never wanted to let go. "You came," she murmured. "You kept your promise."

He held her close, murmuring her name, pressing his lips to her hair. Ahoté had pined and yearned and agonized through spring, summer, autumn, and winter, torn between his duty to the clan and his love for Hoshi'tiwa, refusing to marry a girl chosen by his father, earning the displeasure of the elders but determined to find Hoshi'tiwa until his father conceded that the boy could not go on like this, that for the sake of the Memory Wall and the clan Ahoté be allowed to find Hoshi'tiwa.

And now he had her and was never going to lose her again.

She drew back, tears of joy in her eyes. He was not just Ahoté—he was her family, he was the adobe houses, the cottonwoods, and all the happy memories of her young life. And then she saw the little figurine hanging on a string against his bare chest. "You found it," she said.

Ahoté looked down at the comical owl she had made for him. "I searched every tree and bush and branch, I overturned every rock and stone. It took me days, Hoshi'tiwa, but I found it."

"How did you know I would be here?" she asked, filling her eyes with the sight of him. Ahoté, a year older, perhaps wiser, whom she had feared she would never see again.

He explained that he had gone to the Potters' Guild, as that was the logical place to find her, and was told that she was harvesting clay. "A woman named Yani told me how to find the trail. And here you are!"

Hoshi'tiwa was glad now she had confided in the older woman. "In case anything happens to me," Hoshi'tiwa had said to Yani, "you must know where the golden clay is found." But she had told Yani nothing about finding a hidden glade, and twice encountering Lord Jakál there. "Look," she said, reaching under her dress and bringing out the curved, sharp bear claw. "I have not removed it once. I have kept you against my heart all this time."

"We can go away now," Ahoté said. "We can go where the Lords and the Jaguars will never find us."

Hoshi'tiwa's smile faded. A year ago she would have run off with him. But things were different now. There were her sister potters and the honor of the guild—and Lord Jakál—and all the people at Center Place. Somewhere in the year she had been away from home, Hoshi'tiwa's allegiance had shifted. It was not a betrayal of her own family, she knew, simply an aligning of herself with a new one, like a bride moving away to a new village, still loyal to her family but bonding with the new.

As she opened her mouth to reply, another sound intruded into the silence, a loud snapping noise, like something being broken. Or stepped upon. Hoshi'tiwa turned and saw Moquihix standing behind her, flanked by two Jaguars.

She fell to her knees. "Please, my Lord, we did not trespass upon the sacred ground!"

But Moquihix wordlessly pointed to Ahoté's left hand, and Hoshi'tiwa saw the forbidden flower he still grasped—a yellow marigold freshly plucked from a bush dedicated to the gods. In three long strides a Jaguar in spotted skins and cat skull on his head, with formidable club and spear—a tall, powerful man with a face painted in stripes and spots—reached Ahoté, took a handful of the boy's hair, and yanked him to his feet.

"Tomorrow the gods will drink your blood," Moquihix declared.

Turning to Hoshi'tiwa, the High Minister stared long and hard. She could not read the emotions on his face, was unaware of the turmoil behind his eyes—that an internal debate was taking place between his heart and brain, that lust had surged suddenly within him while his thoughts commanded him to punish the girl for sacrilege.

If she were dead, he reasoned, she could no longer haunt his dreams or afflict him with recurring impotence. She could no longer cast spells upon Lord Jakál, weakening him. But she was a virgin and so he could not kill her. Not even the High Minister could cross such a taboo line.

Then let the gods decide.

He pointed to the ground, and with the tip of his staff he brushed aside a pile of leaves to expose the bloody remains of a fox. "What a mountain lion does not finish," he said, "she covers up and returns to later. You see how fresh this is. The lioness was here last night. She will come again tonight. But she will receive a surprise. Something more tasty than a fox will fill the mountain lion's belly."

Hoshi'tiwa fought her captors as they dragged her to a young aspen and forced her to the ground. With her back to the slender trunk, Hoshi'tiwa's hands were tied behind, roughly and tightly so that the agave cord cut into her skin. Moquihix towered over her. She saw no malice or pleasure in his eyes, just a flat stare empty of emotion.

"You need me to bring rain," she said with a dry throat.

He paused, licked his lips. He liked her there, at his feet in supplication. Perhaps . . .

"You have not yet brought rain," he said, strengthening his resolve.

"Tomorrow, the beating heart of this boy will please the gods, and *that* will bring rain."

She watched them disappear down the ravine, Ahoté stumbling, looking back at her in terror. Hoshi'tiwa struggled against her restraints. The twine was strong, the knot complicated. She twisted this way and that, pulled her arms, lifted her shoulders, panting with the exertion of the labor until she rubbed her wrists bloody trying to free herself.

When the sun went down and darkness fell, she grew fearful of the ghosts and spirits and supernatural beings that came out at night. She imagined every shrub and rock to be a menace, every shadow and movement to be a demon. She thought: The kitchen workers will wonder where I am. They will come looking for me.

But not at night. They will wait until morning when it will be too late.

As the spring moon sailed across the black sky, she heard, in the distance, the sound of the big ceremonial drums. A steady, rhythmic beat that the people of Center Place seldom heard. It was the priests readying themselves for their most sacred act. Hoshi'tiwa knew they would be fasting and cutting themselves, drawing maguey fibers through their tongues to spill their own blood before spilling the blood of their sacrificial victim.

Ahoté! What were they doing to him?

Movement in the brush.

Hoshi'tiwa held her breath and listened.

More movement. The big cat was prowling nearby!

Frantically she renewed her efforts to free herself, aware that the blood she drew from her wrists would only attract the beast. She dug her feet into the soil and pushed, to topple the young aspen. But its roots remained steadfast.

The cat drew nearer. Hoshi'tiwa could hear the deep rumble in its throat as it picked up her scent, heard the soft pad of large paws crushing underbrush.

Her terror grew. Sweat poured down her back. Her heart thumped. Please, she thought to her gods as she twisted and turned, the tree bark digging into her back, her wrists screaming with pain. Please save me!

And then she felt something behind her, on her wrists. Ants? Something tugging, nibbling. She tried to look back, to see what beast had attacked her from behind while the big cat crept closer from the front. But all she could see were the dark boulders.

She held her breath and listened. Drums in the distance, and closer in—brush snapping beneath huge feline paws.

But something was at her hands, gentle, persistent.

Suddenly her hands were free. She jumped up and whirled to see a desert tortoise at the foot of the aspen, calmly munching on the rope. She stared with wide eyes. Since coming to Center Place, Hoshi'tiwa had not seen a single desert tortoise, the totem spirit of her clan. Yet here he was. He had emerged from his winter burrow and managed to find Hoshi'tiwa in this hidden little canyon, finding her wrists in the dark, to nibble at the rope without harming her with his sharp, curved beak.

Hoshi'tiwa smiled. "Thank you, Grandfather Tortoise," she whispered, and then, before the lioness could enter the clearing, she began to leave.

She stopped. By moonlight, Hoshi'tiwa saw that there was very little for the tortoise to eat. He would not touch the few clumps of creosote that struggled up from the dry soil. And there was no water.

As she sensed the lioness circling, listening, Hoshi'tiwa quickly searched the boulders and saw, high above, fresh green dandelions growing out of a crevice. Hastily climbing up, she grabbed a handful and brought them back to the desert dweller. He immediately turned his old gray face to the offering. Hoshi'tiwa knew that the yellow blossoms would nourish him, the stems and leaves would provide him with water. With a final prayer of gratitude, she quickly hurried down the ravine, leaving the lioness far behind.

Dawn broke, and priests blew trumpets made from the horns of wild mountain sheep, alerting the people that a blood sacrifice was to take place. Farmers abandoned their fields and wives their cooking hearths to come running to Precious Green, where the altar of blood had dominated the plaza for as long as everyone could remember. The priests thrummed upon drums crafted from large gourds stretched across with human skin; they shook rattles and played flutes as the new sun shed morning light across the plaza.

By the time Hoshi'tiwa crept back to Center Place, making sure she was not seen, people had come from great distances to witness the holiest of ceremonies.

They came with divided hearts. The altar of blood belonged to the Lords, not to the People of the Sun, whose own altars were those of corn. Yet they dared not defy the summons of the powerful Toltec priests who demanded that everyone, from the youngest to the very oldest, even the blind and the lame, witness this most precious offering to their gods: a human life.

As the morning grew brighter, Hoshi'tiwa saw that every inch of brick and mortar was occupied by men and women and children as they packed the terraces, crammed onto the rooftops, and lined every available space on the walls. The plain, too, was a mass of humanity, and although those out there could not *see* the ritual, they heard well enough because the curved design of the complex enabled the priests' voices to carry as if from the throats of giants.

The altar stone stood between two great kivas, on the raised side of the plaza. When not in use, the stone was covered so that on market days people milled about the draped mound and gave it no thought. Today the rock was exposed, and everyone saw the decades of blood that had soaked into it. Originally gray, the rock was now a dull red, but soon to be brightened by the fresh blood from today's victim.

Hoshi'tiwa went first to the potters' workshop, where she cleaned her wounds, applied ointment, and bound her wrists in yucca fiber bandages. Then she exchanged her filthy, bloodied shift for a fresh one, sliding the cool dress over her head with care. Finally, she took the time to fix her hair. She knew the sacrifice would not take place yet, as the priests and Jaguars were performing their complex marches around the plaza, to gain the attention of the gods.

The coils on the sides of her head had come undone. Hoshi'tiwa combed her long hair and twisted it back up into "squash blossoms," holding them in place with ribbons. She did not want her hair to hide the embroidery of her tunic that identified her as a first-rank potter in one of the most prestigious guilds. The people would know she was someone of status.

As she prepared herself, she tried not to think of Jakál. Whatever her feelings for him—curiosity, sympathy, admiration (and deeper: fear mingled with desire)—she hardened her heart against them, and against him, for surely he knew that Moquihix had left her on the mountain as a sacrifice to a lioness. As she tied the agave fiber belt around her waist, she told herself that Ahoté was all that mattered. And when she was ready, whispering prayers to the peaceful gods of her people, and silently thanking Grandfather Tortoise once again for rescuing her, she stepped out into the blinding sunlight and felt as a warrior must on the eve of battle.

This time, she was not going to suppress her rebellious side.

The spectacle in the plaza momentarily took her breath away—the drums and horns, the Jaguars marching, the priests lined up in their feathered headdresses and robes of patterned cloth, and the nobles sitting in chairs while smoke and incense rose to the sky. Hoshi'tiwa recognized Lady White Orchid, who sat with her father, Tenoch the Hero. She also saw Chief Physician Nagual, at his post beside the altar. Captain Xikli stood at attention with his fearsome Jaguars. On the far side of the plaza, as if they had come early to grab a good viewing spot, were old Pikami and her lame grandson. With them was Yellow Feather, her baby strapped to her back in a basket. Pikami had needed no persuading to take the pair in. The old woman had taken one look at the newborn and, feeling her heart soften, had insisted they share her hut.

Statues of the gods had been brought from their holy sanctuaries, wearing feathers and cotton, and perched upon pedestals. Hoshi'tiwa saw Lord Jakál seated upon his high throne, looking like one of the stone statues, the shimmering green quetzal plumes of his headdress fluttering like pennants in the breeze. Handsome, beautiful even, she thought, but the man, Hoshi'tiwa reminded herself, who was to officiate the bloody ritual.

She made her way cautiously through the tightly packed crowd, insinuating herself between people whose attentions were fixed upon the plaza. On the other side of the barracks wall, a roasting spit was being prepared. Upon it, the body of the sacrificial victim would be cooked for the Jaguars' feast.

Jakál rose from his throne and called for silence. All fell still. Not even a cough, not the scrape of a foot was heard. Overhead, a lone hawk circled, his sharp eye looking this way and that for something to swoop upon.

Hoshi'tiwa crept closer, moving one person at a time, like fish she had observed hiding in the shallows of the stream back home. She stopped suddenly when a contingent of priests emerged from a doorway, dragging their hapless victim between them.

Ahoté, blinking in the sunlight.

He was naked, and blood streamed between his legs. Hoshi'tiwa stifled a cry. The purification that she had feared had already taken place. Without his manhood, Ahoté was now as innocent as a child.

With great solemnity they led him to the altar and stretched him, on his back, over the stone. Four priests held his wrists and ankles while the fifth wielded the sharp obsidian knife that would pierce Ahoté's breastbone. Chief Physician Nagual stood by, holding a golden cup. If the boy lost consciousness before his chest was cut open, he would be revived with a tonic because only when the sacrificial victim was awake could the heart be removed.

The priest with the obsidian knife stepped up to Ahoté and began a droning incantation in Nahuatl, which only the Toltecs understood. Incense and tension filled the air. Among the onlookers, women wept and men shifted nervously. Unlike the prisoners of war who had been sacrificed the year before, this victim was one of their own, a healthy son bearing the tattoo of the Tortoise Clan.

Rumors had run through the populace that he was an apprentice to a Memory Man and would one day become He Who Links People. A troubled undercurrent rippled through the crowd. No one could kill a Memory Man. It was the same as killing a clan itself. But the Toltecs did not care. Men who were farmers, traders, woodworkers, and brickmakers curled their hands into fists as they watched the helpless boy struggle under the hold of the four priests. But no one dared question the decision of the overlords.

As the knife rose high, Hoshi'tiwa broke through the crowd and dashed up the steps to the plaza before guards could stop her. She stood before a startled Lord Jakál and said, "This boy did not commit sacrilege, my Lord. He did not know the ground he walked upon was sacred. When I told him, he left at once. He obeyed the law."

Several Jaguars moved forward. Moquihix rose from his smaller throne, startled to see her alive. The priest holding the knife stopped his incantation and looked over, puzzled.

Jakál raised his arms for silence. Standing on a dais, he towered over Hoshi'tiwa. Like the priest, he was puzzled. But for different reasons. The girl who had crowded his thoughts these past months had had the audacity to break a taboo, and yet she had spoken in humble, almost pleading tones. Even now, though she boldly looked up at him, her posture was respectful.

"The matter has already been decided," he said, his mind racing ahead. Her actions shocked him. Yet he also admired them. She should be punished, yet he could not turn her over to the Jaguars.

Her hands create ceramic that looks like gold. She is being guided by the gods.

"But you do not know the truth, my Lord," she said in the tone of a supplicant.

"You were *there*? At the sacred glade?"

"I was nearby harvesting the clay for my sacred rain jars," she said pointedly, reminding him of his own edict the first time he had found her at the glade and had said: "If your sacred clay is nearby, then the gods give you permission to walk this path."

"Nevertheless, the boy desecrated holy ground. The gods demand a sacrifice."

The words tumbled from Hoshi'tiwa's lips: "My Lord, you brought me here to summon the Cloud Spirits, but my heart was divided while creating rain jars, for I have been homesick and yearning to see my family. This is why my rain jars have not brought rain. But if I know this

boy is safe and back with his family, my heart will be filled with gratitude and it will be at peace, and the clay will know this and make a jar to
bring rain."

He studied her. The moment stretched as a sea of humanity stood
eerily silent upon the plain, in the plaza, on the terraces and rooftops and
walls. The *tlatoani* of Center Place, Jakál from the Place of Reeds,
Guardian of the Sacred Plume, Watcher of the Sky, Lord of the Two
Rivers and Five Mountains held private counsel with himself as he took
the measure of the girl before him. Finally, with challenge in his eyes, he
said softly, "It is not enough."

She met his eyes. The wind picked up, whistled through the plaza
while the shadow of the hawk swept over the onlookers. "Let the boy
go," Hoshi'tiwa said, "and I will serve Center Place." She paused. Her
heart skipped a beat. "I will serve *you,* my Lord."

"Blood must be spilled!" boomed Captain Xikli, and his men banged
their clubs upon their shields.

When the thunder died down, Hoshi'tiwa held out her arms and
cried, "Spare this boy, my Lord, and take my life instead."

Jakál raised an eyebrow. "You would die for him? What is this boy to
you?"

"We are betrothed, my Lord."

Jakál's eyes flickered. The long graceful green plumes of his headdress
quivered for a moment. She could not read his look—disappointment?
Bitterness? But when he turned and raised his arm to give the order for
the knife to descend, Hoshi'tiwa rushed forward, reaching for Jakál.

In a move so quick no one saw it coming, he swung his arm and
struck her jaw with the back of his hand, in such a powerful blow that it
sent her flying backward to sprawl on the pavement.

Hoshi'tiwa saw an explosion of stars and planets, and when her head
cleared, as she lay on the stone floor of the plaza, she looked up and saw
an expression of revulsion on Jakál's face. She hated him for it. And then,
in the next instant, she pitied him, because she realized the revulsion was
not directed at her but at himself.

Keeping her eyes locked on his, she rose to her feet, swaying slightly, unaware that blood ran from a cut on her chin. She straightened her spine and shoulders and said in a voice that rang out over the silent crowd, "If you want rain, my Lord, let this boy go." No longer in a supplicating tone but spoken as a demand.

Captain Xikli bellowed out and strode forth, javelin raised. Lord Jakál stayed him with an upraised hand. Moquihix shot his *tlatoani* a dark look while, at the altar, the priest stood over the quaking Ahoté, knife ready to plunge.

Hoshi'tiwa stood her ground as she boldly faced the Jaguars and the Lords. She recalled what her mother had said as they had huddled in fear up in the cliff house: "You were born to a special destiny." And then Yani, insisting that she was a girl foretold in the stars, to be a teacher to her people.

No, she thought now with a thumping heart. Hoshi'tiwa did not believe in prophecies. All she wanted at this noon hour was to save the boy she loved.

Moquihix spoke next: "You desecrate a holy sacrifice!"

To her own surprise, she turned on the High Minister, whom she greatly feared, and thrust out her arm to point a finger at him. "And you hold secret, *unholy* sacrifices!"

Unraveling the bandages around her wrists, Hoshi'tiwa raised her arms aloft and slowly turned for all to see. "This man tied me to a tree as a sacrifice to the mountain lion god. He recited no prayers, offered no incense, but left me as a miserable offering to a god he did not respect. But my clan totem, Grandfather Tortoise, chewed through my bonds and set me free!"

A murmur rippled like a wave through the crowd as everyone marveled at what she said.

Hoshi'tiwa trembled with a sense of victory. But when she faced Jakál again, a pain shot through her heart, because a victory for her would be a defeat for him, and she had no desire to defeat him. And yet, for Ahoté, she must.

Suddenly, another voice rang out. All heads turned. It was Yani, Overseer of the Guild of Potters, having the audacity to climb the steps up to the plaza, where she took her place next to Hoshi'tiwa. It was not necessary for her to speak. Everyone knew Yani, a highly respected woman, and not without status, even among the Toltecs.

She stood shoulder to shoulder with the younger girl, and the silence stretched as everyone waited for the next move. Then, one by one, the pottery workers climbed up to the plaza to stand with their sisters to send the overlords a silent threat: Kill the boy and there will be no more rain jars.

The air became charged with tension. The Jaguars gripped their spears and clubs, ready to cut the people down like an autumn harvest. Everyone waited with held breath, wondering what the Lord was going to do next.

Jakál remained as still and silent as the ancient gods on their pedestals watching the drama with empty stone eyes that had witnessed countless dramas since the beginning of time. He observed the restlessness of the crowd, rippling through them like an undercurrent in a placid lake. An uprising would spill much blood, which the Jaguars wanted. But it would also leave no one to plant crops.

Lord Jakál had never questioned his destiny. He had been born on the tenth day of the month, the day governed by the Dog, and everyone knew that a child born under the Dog sign was gifted with great powers of leadership. Although he had expected, in his youth, to be a leader of priests, he had obediently accepted the role of *tlatoani* of Center Place. But now, as he stood before the bloody sacrificial altar, all eyes upon him, with an impossible decision to make, he wished, for just a moment, that the mantle of leadership be lifted from him.

Jakál was not a dictator like the King of Tollan, but a *tlatoani,* a ruler who needed the support of the nobles and high officials, the Jaguars and the powerful guilds. If he went ahead with the sacrifice, he would have a peasant revolt on his hands. If he canceled the sacrifice, he would forever be perceived as weak and he would lose his authority to Captain Xikli. Either way, it was a defeat for him.

His power hung by a thread.

Everyone watched as tension filled the silent air: Lady White Orchid, her heart racing, finding the moment strangely erotic and sexually arousing; her father, scratching a wooden leg and wishing Jakál would get on with it; Chief Physician Nagual, hooded eyes observing the scene with no opinion written on his cryptic face. In the crowd, old Pikami was unimpressed. She had seen bravado over the years and what did it ever come to? Yellow Feather, shifting her shoulders beneath the papoose straps, silently urged: Kill the boy and then kill *her*.

An idea came to Jakál. "We will let the gods decide," he cried out over the heads of all gathered. "We will put the question to the gods and listen for their reply."

"Which gods, my Lord?" Hoshi'tiwa had the impertinence to ask.

He gave her a dark look, this creature with a face like the moon who bedeviled his thoughts and his dreams and who now put him to a test before all the world. "Whichever gods are watching over us this day."

He looked at the pottery workers: "Do you agree to this?"

Yani stepped forward. "We do, my Lord."

"And you will accept the decree of the gods and abide by their decision?"

"We will."

He engaged in a murmured exchange with Moquihix, who, with a sour expression, gave an order to a lesser priest. The man sprinted into the main complex and emerged a moment later with a fur-wrapped bundle. With great ceremony, Jakál opened the bundle as the priest held it out to him, and lifted a dark object for all to see.

"This is the Guiding Stone," he called out, turning slowly, as Hoshi'tiwa had turned when displaying her wounded wrists. "The ancient Guiding Spirit that brought your Lords to Center Place."

When the first *pochtecas* ventured this far north, they had followed a talisman that held them to a true path, eventually bringing them to this canyon. In the generations since, the Guiding Stone had been kept in a place of honor within the stone walls. This was the first time, since the arrival of the original Lords, the stone had seen the sun.

The collected mass of humanity watched in tense silence as they saw Lord Jakál release the dark object, letting it fall to the ground. Everyone cried out when the object stopped before it hit the floor of the plaza. The Guiding Stone was suspended on a thread, which Jakál held in his right hand.

Hoshi'tiwa had never seen such an object. It looked like stone, yet it shone like metal. The length of a man's forearm, the Guiding Stone was narrow and shaped like the slender fish who lived in the stream where she was born. One end of the stone was larger than the other, so that it did indeed resemble a fish floating in the air.

"I will spin the Guiding Stone. The gods will choose where it stops. If it comes to a rest pointing north, the boy goes home, for his home is in the north. If it points to the south, he will be taken to Tollan as a slave on the next caravan. If it points east or west, he stays here and is sacrificed on this day on the altar of blood."

With the stone suspended for all to see, Jakál placed the forefinger of his left hand on the larger end, gave it a firm push, and the stone spun wildly on its string.

No one moved. No one blinked. All watched the spinning object, wondering where it would stop, while the traders and farmers and wood-workers in the crowd silently laid bets, being gamblers at heart, to see if they could guess the will of the gods.

The stone began to slow. Slower. Then it swung this way and that. Jakál held the thread as the Guiding Stone swung to the south, then back to the north. South . . . north. Until finally it came to a rest.

Pointing north.

"The gods have spoken!" Jakál declared. He turned to the priests at the altar stone. "Release the boy."

The crowd on the plain erupted in a jubilant roar that was joined by those on the terraces, rooftops, and walls, men and women screaming with relief and joy because the release of Ahoté meant that it was *their* gods who had guided the spirit-stone—it meant that the gods of the People of the Sun had not abandoned Center Place.

When the priests let go of Ahoté's ankles and wrists, he rolled off the altar and lay unconscious on the ground. Hoshi'tiwa ran to him. He was still alive, but shockingly cold and pale. While the Jaguars looked at their

Captain with displeasure, and the priests turned to Moquihix for guidance, and Jakál marched angrily back into Precious Green, Hoshi'tiwa gestured to Yani and the others, who rushed forward, gathered Ahoté's limp body, and as a group, carried him out of the plaza.

The crowd on the plain broke up, people heading back to their farms and camps and duties, while the priests clustered like colorful birds in the plaza, arguing and debating the consequences of what had just happened, and the Jaguars, sullen and silent, having been deprived of a man-corn feast, returned to their barracks. Xikli the Captain strode up to Moquihix and growled, "This is not over."

Thirty-nine

THE women carried Ahoté to Pikami's hut, where they gently
laid him on a buffalo hide blanket and stepped back to let the
old woman do her work. Although he had suffered a great
shock, after examining him she declared he would live.

While the rest of the women retreated outside to commence a vigil
of prayer, Hoshi'tiwa remained at Ahoté's side. She was surprised when
Pikami produced a small doll made of sticks and string, dressed in a
rudimentary costume, with twig-hands clutching herbs and grass. As
she moved the doll over the unconscious boy, murmuring a prayer,
Hoshi'tiwa whispered, "What is that, Grandmother?"

"She is a spirit of healing," was all Pikami said. The doll was in fact
a kachina, given to her by Yani. The old herb peddler was now a regular
attendee at the forbidden rituals, and had brought in new members, all
of whom were finding comfort and solace in the prayers of their youth.
Pikami herself, though she would never be entirely rid of her guilt, had
found a little solace, a small easing of her pain.

Not that she expected ever to be forgiven for her crime of long ago.
There should never be total peace for a woman who had caused the ex-
tinction of an entire clan.

Forty

THEY want revenge. They will carry it out with their own hands. They will bring disaster to us all.

Such were Moquihix's troubled thoughts as he hurried through the chilly spring night, bundled in a cloak made of rabbit fur. He wore no headdress, no gold bracelets or ceremonial paint. He was on a secret errand and did not want to draw attention to himself.

The revenge that was in his thoughts was not that of the gods, but of the Jaguars.

Blood should have been spilled that day. If not the boy's, then that of another victim. Lord Jakál had not handled the incident wisely. Likening the Toltecs to a brick wall—solid, unified, and unbreakable—Moquihix saw his *tlatoani* as a loosened brick in the foundation of that wall. The peasants of Center Place, incited by the girl, had only to loosen a few more and the whole edifice would come down.

"She had offered her own life in exchange for that of the boy," Jakál had said earlier when Moquihix had gone to him with worries that an incorrect decision had been made that day. "I myself have never known such love," Jakál had said, as if it mattered, making his High Minister

wonder what he was talking about. "What does it feel like to love someone or something so much as to be willing to die for it? Do you know,
my friend?"

Moquihix's thoughts had been in such a turmoil, he had barely been
able to answer. By what supernatural intervention had the girl escaped
from her bonds at the aspen tree? Now she would walk in his dreams
again, and he would waken impotent once more. He finally said, "You
cheated the gods and you cheated your people."

Jakál had averred this was not so.

"But, my Lord, the Guiding Stone always points north."

No one knew the origin of the strange metal object. Centuries ago,
the tomb of a noble near Tikal had been plundered by invaders, and the
fishlike stone was found within. How it came to be there, no one could
say. Legend told of men who had come from across the eastern sea in
boats many generations prior, and who had brought the north-facing
metal with them.

"Just because the Guiding Stone has always pointed north," Jakál
had countered, "does not mean it cannot point in any other direction. It
simply means that the gods have always made it point north. Today the
gods had the power to make the stone point in another direction. Once
again they chose north. There was no deception."

This had shocked Moquihix because he had thought Jakál would see
what he was saying, and the fact that he didn't meant he was being
blinded by the girl.

Action needed to be taken, and therefore Moquihix's secret visit this
night to the Captain of the Jaguars.

He did not come with a clear conscience, however. He did not like
acting behind Jakál's back. For in truth, he was fiercely devoted to his
tlatoani.

When Jakál first arrived at Center Place, Moquihix had not realized
how hungry he was for home. Instantly drawn to the new young leader
like a bee to a flower, he could not ask enough questions about Tollan,
could not fill his ears enough with news of what was going on in Court,
what new trade was transpiring, what new battles were being fought and

won. It was as if Jakál wore the smells and sounds and colors of Tollan like an invisible mantle, and Moquihix was drawn to that mantle, desiring to feel its texture, to close his eyes and remember the villas on the river, the temples, the fabulous gardens. Tollan was the center of the world; in Tollan a man felt tied to the earth, *belonging*. Not like here, living in an outpost where a man felt cast off. Jakál was not just a man or a *tlatoani,* he was the very essence of all that Moquihix believed in and held dear.

And yet, as High Minister, with the welfare of Center Place as his primary concern, Moquihix must disobey Jakál. And so he went on this late-night errand with a conflicted heart.

A sentry stood by the locked gate in the barracks wall, which was constructed of logs that had been transported a great distance from the mountain forests in the north. Few people were allowed inside the domain of the elite Jaguars. Recognizing the high official, the guard opened the gate and locked it immediately behind. Moquihix hurried across the compound that was deserted at this late hour but which, by day, served as the training field for the soldiers as well as the game court for their highly competitive and bloody sports.

As he slipped through another doorway, his shadow joining others on the walls where torches burned in sconces, Moquihix felt again a stab of guilt over his secret errand tonight, feeling it was a betrayal of his love for Jakál. And then he reminded himself of the disaster his *tlatoani* had brought upon their heads.

That was Jakál's terrible mistake. By playing a trick on the populace, he had insulted the gods.

Captain Xikli was reclining on a blanket, idly rolling beans on a *patolli* mat (although no one played opposite). But his thoughts were not idle. Something strange was going on at the house of Tenoch.

The old man had stopped drinking and was less malleable, insisting that White Orchid have a say in whom she married. And White Orchid herself did not look well these days. Xikli's spies told him she was paying visits to the priestesses of Lady Corn, but they had not been able to learn why.

Xikli gave his spies orders to get to the bottom of this new turn of events. He was determined to marry White Orchid. Not that he was in love with her. Xikli didn't believe in love. He was contemptuous of men who "fell in love." Love was for women. For weaklings. Love drained the heart and emasculated a man. Women were good for only two things: producing children and taking care of a home.

Unlike most of the other Jaguar knights, who had homes and families, Xikli had lived his entire military life in the barracks. The others rotated through the garrison, living there, drilling, practicing martial arts, and then they went home to live heroes' lives and to see that their forefathers' bloodlines were continued.

Xikli's memories of mother and home were dim because, like all Toltec boys, he had left home at the age of ten to take up residence in the bachelor lodge, where youths lived and studied and trained until they left to enter professions, marry, and establish their own houses. Xikli had taken to the life at once, enjoying the company of boys, relishing the constant competing, the frequent victories. He neither drank liquor nor smoked tobacco. Xikli's drug was power. To control the lives of other men was intoxicating. And he was never satisfied. The higher he rose in rank, the more he strived to go yet higher. Once he was Captain of the Jaguars, he set his sights upon the throne. And once he had the throne, he would not be satisfied with anything less than building an empire that would rival that of Tollan.

His thoughts went back to White Orchid. He might not love her, but he was looking forward to intimacy with her. Xikli had never had much direct contact with White Orchid because, even though they were both nobles, they moved in different circles. The women he used for pleasure were whores who came to the barracks for quick, nameless couplings and small payments in return, but he never grew attached to any of them. Having a highborn lady in his bed would be a novelty.

The Captain did not look up as Moquihix came in, shrugging off his fur cloak to discover that it was cold even in the Captain's private quarters.

Xikli himself wore only a loincloth. Like all soldiers in the Toltec

empire, he prided himself on his stamina and immunity to extreme temperatures and pain. As further evidence of his bravery, his nose had been
broken multiple times and he was missing several teeth. Xikli wore his
hair in an intricate style, with a topknot on the crown of his head,
straight bangs across his forehead, a trim cut over his ears, and a long
"tail" down the back. To maintain such a style required daily attention.
Xikli and his men were like birds, Moquihix thought, always preening.
They plucked hair from their bodies with clamshells, they shaved their
eyebrows and painted them back on, they wore plugs in their noses, ears,
and lips, changing them each day from bone to sky-stone to gold to jade.
When not preening, they were in the training compound fighting among
themselves, or strutting about the plaza with their arrogant chests puffed
out. But Moquihix did not despise the muscular, scar-faced Captain.

In fact, he loved him.

Moquihix had come to Center Place thirty summers ago, when he
was a young man of twenty-five. He had left behind a wife and son, for
whom he sent five years later, when he was established as the High Minister. He had soon gotten his wife pregnant and the following year she
gave birth to a baby daughter. And then tragedy struck. They lost the
daughter, and Moquihix's wife suddenly hated Center Place. Declaring
herself divorced from Moquihix, she returned to Tollan.

"What took you so long getting here, old man?" the Jaguar Captain
said contemptuously as he rolled the marked beans and studied how
they landed on the mat.

Moquihix sighed as he sat down. He was second only to Lord Jakál,
yet this soldier felt free to address him thusly. It was a fact of life that no
matter how high a rank a man achieved, there was always a rank higher,
therefore leaving room for *someone's* disrespect. In this case it was the
Jaguar Captain, who answered only to the King of Tollan, the supreme
leader of all Toltecs.

Long ago, as a boy, Moquihix had dreamed of becoming a Jaguar.
But such lofty rank was awarded only to the swiftest, bravest, and most
agile. Sadly, he had fallen short and had had to find his way in government administration. When he was offered a post far to the north, at

Center Place, Moquihix had accepted in the hope of one day being the *tlatoani* of this land. That, too, fell beyond his grasp as the prize post went to the son of a family more noble than Moquihix's. He did not begrudge Jakál his position. Jakál was a good man, and just. If weak in the head these days.

The Jaguar spat contemptuously. Although Moquihix was the second most powerful man in the government of Center Place, the ferocious soldier had no patience with men of letters and books and pens and paper. "The boy should have been sacrificed. We have the right to spill blood. We are of noble lineage." He thumped his scarred chest. "It is that accursed girl. Lord Jakál allows her to look at him! She will steal his soul with her eyes."

"He believes the gods brought her here to summon the rain," Moquihix said simply, not to defend the girl or Jakál, just to state a fact. He kept mute about his own fears regarding the girl—the power she wielded over his manhood.

The Captain rolled the dice again, this time with a different flick of his wrist. "She is but the daughter of a corn farmer!"

"She found the sacred sanctuary," Moquihix said musingly, finding Xikli's preoccupation with the way the beans fell a strange pastime for a soldier. "In all the generations we have been here, no one has ever found the sacred glade."

"She is but a nosy girl!"

"You have seen the rain jars she makes. They look as if fashioned from gold. And the special clay she uses is near the sacred glade. It can be no accident that clay which transforms into gold is found so near to the place of the gods." Moquihix didn't know why he was defending Hoshi'tiwa to Xikli. He feared her and hated her as much as the Captain did. He wished the mountain lion had consumed her.

But he could not put her face from his mind, the vision of Hoshi'tiwa standing in the plaza, proud and defiant.

"She is making our *tlatoani* weak," Xikli said. "The people's strength comes from the Lord. If the Lord is weak, the people are weak. The girl must be sacrificed. Give her to us, and we shall sacrifice her in a manner most befitting." He smiled grimly. "We will see that she takes days to die."

"Have you forgotten," Moquihix snapped, "that she is working at a sacred task? That she has the eyes of the Cloud Spirits? Have you forgotten," he said, his voice rising, "that she is a virgin and that it is taboo to take her life?"

Xikli's lip curled in a sneer. "Didn't you attempt just that, tying her to a tree?"

Moquihix shot to his feet. He would not spar with this man. What did Xikli know of the finer points of religion, of the thin lines between duty and sacrilege? Moquihix would not have killed her; the lion would have. And as it was, she was spared. Another sign from the gods that she was special.

Xikli narrowed his eyes at the High Minister and said, "Nonetheless, what you say is true. The girl's power lies not only in her skill to bring rain, it lies also in her virginity. But if she were no longer pure, then the rain jar would not be sacred and the Cloud Spirits would not come. Is that not so? And without rain, our people will thirst and starve. Therefore, should she lose her virginity, she must be sacrificed to avert disaster."

Moquihix sighed with relief. The visit was a success, his twofold mission accomplished. Xikli had played right into his hands. Moquihix dared not kill the girl himself, nor would he demean himself by asking Xikli for help, and so he had contrived to have Xikli come up with the solution on his own. The Captain would see to the girl's destruction, and Moquihix would be rid of her once and for all. And at the same time, the threat of a Jaguar rampage was for now averted.

"Very well," he said. "At the Solstice, whether rain comes or not, I will see to it the girl is delivered to the barracks. You and your Jaguars can do with her as you wish."

The Captain made a dismissive gesture, and Moquihix picked up his cloak and took his leave. But not without a heavy heart. He so desperately wanted to say something to this man who, despite the scars and broken nose, resembled Moquihix's beloved wife Xochitl, who left him years ago. But the gap was too wide now for new bridges. Therefore, as he left, although part of Moquihix was proud that Xikli had risen to the rank of Jaguar Captain, part of him was sad, too, to have earned Xikli's contempt. But who could blame him? No son should outrank his father.

Forty-one

WITH Pikami's help, and her magic herbs and elixirs, Hoshi'tiwa nursed Ahoté back to health, and when he had recovered from his wounds and it was time for him to return home, he begged her to go with him. But Hoshi'tiwa said she must stay at Center Place. "I promised to serve these people and Lord Jakál. I promised to bring rain."

"Is it because I am no longer a man?"

Hoshi'tiwa's throat tightened with emotion. She had saved his life, but what sort of life was it going to be? With words he had said he would dedicate himself to the Memory Wall and to serving the clan as He Who Links People. But with his eyes he had told her of the deep sorrow and suffering in his soul.

Taking him into her arms, Hoshi'tiwa held him tight. "You will always be my first and dearest love, my funny Owl. But before you came I had already decided I must stay here. Although I have a duty to my clan, I have new duties here, to the people of Center Place, to my new sisters in the Potters' Guild. I cannot go home without bringing rain to Center

Place, for that would dishonor my family. And no one knows when the rain will come. But you must go back because they need you."

They rubbed noses in a tearful kiss, suspecting they would never see each other again. She tried to give the bear claw back to him, saying it was rightfully his, but Ahoté insisted she keep it so that part of him would be with her always.

As she stood in the plaza and watched him go, traveling with a band of merchants and hired guards, Hoshi'tiwa felt a curious sense of freedom steal over her. She thought of the Potters' Guild and the work she wanted to do there, she thought of her new sisters, of her desire to join them and become part of their family—and the sense that one stage of her life had ended with a new one beginning started to fill her heart with fresh purpose.

As Ahoté disappeared down the path at the far end of the canyon, Hoshi'tiwa vowed to plunge into her work to the exclusion of all else. She would croon to the clay as she kneaded it, whisper to it, tenderly press out the bubbles, dry it to perfection, and sing as she polished the rough jar until it had the brightest sheen, painting it with the symbols of rain and clouds and sky and wind, her hand the steadiest it had ever been, the yucca brush an exact width, the lines straight and unwavering, with not a flaw, not a mistake anywhere: a perfect jar.

And while she silently rededicated herself thus to her work, with Ahoté walking out of her life, Hoshi'tiwa was not surprised to see Lord Jakál walk into her mind, for he was Ahoté's benevolent liberator. In her mind's eye, Jakál looked upon her with a melancholy gaze and filled her head with his deep, resonant voice. She pictured his strong limbs, the shape of his jaw, the curve of his nose—and when she felt a strange, exciting warmth swim through her veins and throb deep in her belly, Hoshi'tiwa wondered where her new road was going to lead.

Forty-two

THE day of firing was upon them. The potters prayed and held vigil as they waited for the fire to die down to ash. And when Hoshi'tiwa's jar emerged, gently golden like a sunrise, its painted design like a blazing red sunset, everyone exclaimed it was the most beautiful rain jar ever created.

With great ceremony Hoshi'tiwa laid her jar with the others, but this time, while the rain-god priests praised Hoshi'tiwa's rain jar, Moquihix stood in silent counsel, a strange look on his face that Hoshi'tiwa could not interpret.

Rain dances were performed continuously in the plaza, where sunlight blazed down from a cloudless sky. The people chanted and sacrificed their meager portions of corn to the gods while the high priests, surrounded by nobles and Jaguars, laid a sacrificial victim—a poor wretch destined for the sky-stone mines—over the stone altar, and offered his beating heart to the gods.

Dancing and ritual continued late into the night as a hundred torches were lit and blazed up to the clear, starry sky. And then Center Place grew quiet. People retired to their reed mats and small shelters, curling up beneath a sky that was too clear and too empty of clouds. Tomorrow was the Summer Solstice, a day that was longer than the night, harbinger of weather too hot. Extremes. Nature out of balance. While the corn thirsted in the fields.

In the hour before dawn of the Summer Solstice, Hoshi'tiwa dreamed of Ahoté—his body not broken by the priests of Center Place but whole again, and a man. She saw him follow the dusty road to the protected canyon where their settlement had stood for generations, saw her mother look up in joyous surprise, and Ahoté's father, and all the uncles and aunts running to him, embracing him and laughing and giving him food and water and drawing him excitedly to the hearth to hear stories of Hoshi'tiwa and Center Place. It was such a heartwarming scene that, in her sleep, Hoshi'tiwa wept. Tears poured from her eyes and dampened her cheeks. Tears rolled onto her reed mat and soaked it. So many tears that even her clothes became wet so that when she awoke suddenly, it took her a moment to realize that it was not she who was crying but the sky, for the stars could no longer be seen behind dense storm clouds as a torrential rain poured down onto Center Place.

She jumped up and ran with the others, with all the people of Center Place, to cram into the plaza and laugh and dance and sing, holding their arms up to the downpour, tilting their faces up with open mouths to drink the blessed water. Across the plain, people placed jars and bowls and waterproof baskets beneath the rain, they waded into the narrow stream that was now running swiftly and growing wider, they stripped off their clothing and pranced beneath the deluge.

In his private chambers deep inside Precious Green, Jakál still slumbered. In his dream, Quetzalcoatl appeared before him, a tall pale-skinned man with a beard and wearing dazzling white robes. Jakál was so overjoyed, in his dream, to see his god in his earthly reincarnation, that he ignored the shouts of people all around him. "What are you saying?" he cried to his god, because Quetzalcoatl's mouth was open, his lips moved yet Jakál could not hear him for the noise all about him. "Silence!" he shouted, knowing that Quetzalcoatl was bringing an important message and Jakál did not want to miss it. But the noise grew, the shouting rose until, in his frustration, Jakál snapped open his eyes and realized in sharp disappointment it had only been a dream.

But then he realized that the shouting was *not* a dream. Precious Green thundered with the voices of people raised in joy and excitement.

Hastily dressing, Lord Jakál strode into the plaza and held out his arms, his magnificent feathered headdress running with rain, his feathered cloak glistening. Torches sputtered and winked out so that there was little light, but everyone saw the figure of their Lord, his gold armbands glinting through the downpour. He began to chant, and other voices joined him until all the throats in Center Place, thousands of throats, joined to create one thundering voice in thanks to the gods for bringing rain.

As Hoshi'tiwa was embracing Yani and her sister potters, a Jaguar materialized in the downpour, his face paint running, his cat skins drenched. He took her by the arm and forced her through the crowd, people stepping away to make room, ogling the girl being dragged by a Jaguar, and then resuming their dancing and merrymaking.

To her surprise, he took her straight to the main doorway of Precious Green, the entrance that only Lord Jakál used, pushed her inside, and then turned to face the plaza and stand guard.

After her eyes adjusted to the light from torches that burned in sconces, she saw Lord Jakál sitting on a magnificent chair of ornately carved and painted wood. His headdress and feathered cloak had been removed so that he wore only a loincloth of scarlet cotton lavishly embroidered in gold thread. His bronze chest, still wet from the rain, was festooned with necklaces of silver, gold, and sky-stone. Two slaves attended to his long hair, combing it out dry, draping it over his shoulders and down his back.

"There you are!" he cried, jumping to his feet and startling the slaves. "You brought rain!"

"So did my sisters in the Potters' Guild, and the priests who chanted for rain, and the rain-dancers, and all the people who prayed, my Lord."

He laughed. "I will never understand the People of the Sun, who abhor boasting and believe that all people are equal! In Tollan we praise the gifted artisan and raise him, or her, above all others. In Tollan, smart and successful citizens are richly rewarded and all the rest are but dust beneath our feet."

She barely heard the rain beyond the door, her heart pounded so. Had he forgotten their showdown two weeks prior, when her victory had meant his defeat? *When he had struck her with such force, he had split open her chin?*

The slaves left, and Hoshi'tiwa was alone with Lord Jakál in a chamber she had never seen before. Here was the heart of the government of Center Place, where the *tlatoani* received distinguished visitors and met with high priests, held counsel with his nobles. Woven tapestries hung on the walls; colorful reed mats covered the stone floor.

"You may choose your reward for bringing rain," he said with a smile. Lifting a torch from a sconce, Jakál beckoned her to follow.

Hoshi'tiwa was familiar with the plan of the lower tier of the stone complex, but Jakál led her to a stairway, and as they climbed, she wondered where they were going.

The way was reached by narrow tunnels with steps so that they no longer heard the rain or the chanting of the populace. She had a hard time keeping up, Jakál was so energetic in his climb, taking the steps two at a time and laughing as they ascended. She followed him upward and upward, and she realized in that moment that she would follow him anywhere.

The outdoor terrace of the fifth level was where middle-status servants lived, but the inner rooms were closed off and forbidden for any but the Lord to enter. They emerged briefly into the open, and Hoshi'tiwa gasped at the sight of rain-swept Center Place below, the people happily bathing and drinking and playing in pools of water, dancing in the downpour while the priests chanted nonstop to the gods. "This way!" Jakál said, and led her into the first of several chambers, each more splendid than the last, inviting her to choose her reward.

The first was the House of Feathers, where one wall was decorated with feathers of a brilliant yellow, another with radiant and sparkling hues of blue, woven into tapestries and placed against the walls in graceful hangings and festoons. The remaining walls were hung with feathers of brilliant reds, and plumage of the purest and most dazzling white.

Next came the sky-stone storage chamber, filled from floor to ceiling with the gemstone in every color, every shape, and every form it came in, raw, shaped, polished, some chunks as big as a man's fist.

And then the Gold Room, and the Silver Room, until finally Jakál took her up to the roof of the fifth level, where a willow-branch overhang kept the rain off them as he showed her the aviary, a giant cage of willow and birch, housing a collection of the most fantastic birds Hoshi'tiwa had ever seen.

"Make your choice," he said magnanimously, holding his arms out as if offering her the world. "She who brings rain shall have any treasure she wishes."

Hoshi'tiwa could only stare at him. The smile, the energy—as if he could flap his arms and swoop up into the sky. It was infectious. She felt herself start to laugh.

And then suddenly he was somber. "I did that," he said softly, and she felt his fingertip touch her chin. Though the wound had healed leaving only a small scar, his touch felt like a bolt of lightning. "I do not know why I struck you." His thick brows met in a frown, as if the incident he was recalling had taken place many years ago, and the details eluded him.

But Hoshi'tiwa did not want to talk about that day. It almost seemed as if the confrontation and the outcome of victory for one and defeat for the other had happened to two other people. She looked at the birds in the cage and said, "They remind me."

Jakál's eyes were as stormy as the night as he, too, brought himself back from the debacle of two weeks prior, when he had thought he had lost his power altogether. But now, the rain restored it. Hoshi'tiwa had restored it. "They remind you of what?"

"The young women who assist you in the ritual in the glade. They are so beautiful. I am a sparrow in comparison."

"But the sparrow is the hardiest of winged creatures. They live in snow and heat and rain, in drought and famine. The sparrow is strong and determined and a survivor. *These* birds," he gestured toward the exotic creatures on their perches, feathered in all the colors of the rainbow, "for all their beauty and plumage, are delicate and would perish were it not for our careful guardianship of them."

He paused and looked at her, and said, "But you are not plain, though you compare yourself to a sparrow. And remember, the sparrow is a songbird, delighting us with her presence."

The rain fell all around them, creating a wall between themselves and the outer world, so that this inner world, dry beneath an arbor, was the only one that existed. Jakál stood close to Hoshi'tiwa. She could see the details of the prince whom she had once hated and called "monster"—the tiny scars on his body, damp strands of black hair, the collarbone still glistening with raindrops.

And Jakál could not take his eyes off this girl who called herself a sparrow yet who possessed miraculous hands and the magic to create gold out of clay.

And he thought: She brought rain! Now Quetzalcoatl will surely come to Center Place. Jakál's joy became so complete that he thought he could fly up to the sky and ride the rain clouds like a god himself.

Impassioned by a need to reward her in this special moment, he lifted a small gold medallion from among the necklaces festooning his chest. "This flower," he said, "which is *xochitl* in my native tongue, was given to one of my ancestors by Quetzalcoatl himself. It contains a drop of the god's blood." He laid it in the palm of her hand, where he had once painted the symbol for water.

Hoshi'tiwa marveled at the exquisitely crafted blossom, with six perfect petals of gold and a bead of striking blue sky-stone in the center. Behind the bead, Jakál said, was a small compartment where the drop of sacred blood was contained.

"This is too precious," she whispered, holding it out. "I cannot accept."

"But you must!" he cried, and he suddenly, impulsively, pulled her to him and pressed his lips to hers.

A jolt shot through her. A cry filled her throat.

Stunned, Jakál stepped back and stared down at her, a look of confusion on his face.

"My Lord," she whispered, touching her lips with trembling fingers.

The rain picked up, the wind blew sharply, as if nature had been excited by the impulsive, forbidden kiss.

Feeling as if she had been struck by lightning, Hoshi'tiwa held out the golden *xochitl* and dropped it into his palm. Jakál restored the precious amulet among his necklaces, rearranging the strands and strings in an effort to compose himself—what had he just done?

Hoshi'tiwa said, "My Lord—" The brief, intimate contact had thrown her off balance. She needed to set the moment straight. Words were needed. Any words. *The feel of his lips upon hers*... "May I ask a question?"

He looked at her with shadowed eyes, a furrow between his brows. He looked at her mouth, and then away.

"My Lord, why did you let Ahoté go? You did not need to consult the gods."

"It was for the good of the people," he said quietly, while his mind shouted: Why did I kiss her? "I released the boy to bring rain." Because of the dark day and curtain of rain, Hoshi'tiwa did not see the yearning in his eyes, did not know the confusion in his heart as he wondered once more at a love so strong that a mere girl had been willing to sacrifice her own life for that of the son of corn farmers.

He thought of his wife, a highborn lady chosen by his family to be his consort and who had died in childbirth but who left him no legacy of love or grief. Jakál could not recall a time when his heart had been moved by another. He certainly could not think of anyone for whom he would sacrifice his life.

He stepped closer and, placing his hands on her shoulders, said solemnly, "It is no accident that you came here. The gods are at work, guiding you."

Her heart rose in her throat as she feared—*hoped*—he might press his mouth to hers again. "I am just a humble potter, my Lord. The gods are barely aware of my existence."

But Jakál's grip on her shoulders tightened and he said with passion, "You are an enigma to me, Hoshi'tiwa. I have thought about you every day since you were brought to Center Place. On the surface, you are the daughter of a corn farmer, but with hands and skills that surely came from the gods. Your golden jars are the most beautiful I have ever seen, surpassing even those made in my city of Tollan, and *they* are considered to be the most beautiful in the world."

He took her hands. "What a miracle these are," he whispered.

She could barely speak, his touch and nearness petrified her so. And what she asked next startled her, yet hearing the words she realized it was a question that had been in her heart for months. And now she needed to know the answer. She needed to know because of *him*. "Why do Toltecs kill people and eat them?"

He gave her a surprised look. "It is in the natural order of things. The mountain lion eats the antelope, does she not?"

"But I do not think mountain lion eats mountain lion."

This gave him pause and she realized that he did not think of her people as beings like himself, as equal to himself, but inferior, as the antelope was to the mountain lion.

He could not understand why she found the practice repugnant. It was something his people had always done. "It is what the gods demand. They ask for blood. It makes them strong."

"*My* gods ask for corn."

It was on his tongue to tell her that her gods were weak, but then he remembered how she had defeated him in the plaza when she forced him to resort to a magic trick in order to save face, although she did not know about the trick. He wondered now if her gods had had a hand in his decision that day. And if they were spinning a spell around him and the girl now, as they stood beneath the rain-soaked arbor, alone in the world with only their two bodies, two hearts.

He looked into eyes that reminded him of polished stones in a running stream, leaf-shaped eyes that made him think of the mountain forests back home, and he realized that she was beautiful. Not like the ladies of Tollan, exquisite creatures who were pampered and spoiled. This girl made him think of cornfields and ripe soil and the life-giving rain that was falling just then on Center Place.

His heart moved in a way it never had before. And his loins stirred with feelings he had thought died long ago. And then he remembered the wide gulf between them, a chasm too wide to be bridged. They were from two races, spoke two different tongues, worshipped different gods and followed different customs—he was a prince and she made pottery! And now she belonged to the gods so that she was unreachable even for the *tlatoani* of Center Place.

Reluctantly, he released her hands and took a step back. "Choose," he said in a voice as soft as the whispering rain. "From any of what I have shown you, as my reward to you."

She beheld him against the stormy backdrop, the power of nature complementing the power of the man—or so it seemed to Hoshi'tiwa, who was speechless in the presence of such force. Jakál made her heart rise in her throat, the breath struggle in her lungs, the pulse throb in her veins. Her emotions confused her. When his dark eyes remained on her, she felt her spirit leave her body and soar to the sky.

"I want to go home," she said.

Rain and wind lashed around them, lifting Jakál's long hair like the black banners on the Jaguars' spears. She thought she saw anger in his expression. She did not know that his own heart suddenly thumped fearfully at the thought of losing her, that he realized just then what he had not known before, that he would gladly give her all he had shown her—the feathers and sky-stones and precious birds—if she would stay.

But freedom was the one thing he could not give her, because she now belonged to the gods. And then a strange thought came to him: Just as leadership had been thrust upon him, so had the responsibility of bringing rain to Center Place been thrust upon this girl. She had been brought here against her will, as had he. So alike were they in that moment.

And this terrified him most of all.

"I cannot let you go," he said, and Hoshi'tiwa was not surprised. Nor was she disappointed. It was the answer she had expected. "Then let me return to the potters' workshop and live with my sisters."

His eyes flickered, and for an instant, Hoshi'tiwa thought she saw a hurt look in his eyes. But surely she had imagined it. And then, without a word, he turned on his heel to lead the way back down.

Hoshi'tiwa followed. Was he going to let her go back to the workshop? But of course! He had offered her "any reward" for bringing rain. She couldn't wait to tell Yani the good news.

In the downstairs chamber, servants brought mugs of a hot brew made from beans grown in the jungles far to the south, a brew that was thick and brown and bitter, and which Hoshi'tiwa did not care for. Jakál called it *chocolatl*.

But he did not drink with her. He had duties, he said, with the priests of Tlaloc, but said that she could remain in the shelter of this warm chamber.

While she sat and drank, and listened to the rain beyond the walls, she tried to sort the jumble of emotions, like a weaver sorting yarn in preparation for making a blanket. But her thoughts and feelings were a tangled mess. They left her exhausted until she fell asleep on a reed mat. When she awoke later, she found herself covered in a rich feather blanket.

Lord Jakál was nowhere about.

Creeping through the warren of rooms, she emerged onto the plaza in eager anticipation of a wet cloudy day, and could not believe her eyes: The sun was blinding and there was not a cloud in sight. The ground was dry, as if the earth had been so parched, it gulped down all the rain and left none for the people. Even the stream running through the canyon was slow and narrow again. The only rain that had been saved was in the vessels that had been placed all around, but with the day growing warm, the precious water was beginning to evaporate so that people ran about collecting the vessels and carrying them indoors.

Lord Jakál stood in the plaza, a furious look on his face. Hoshi'tiwa went to his side.

"Collect your possessions from the kitchen," he said without looking at her, and then he strode away.

Even though the rain had been brief, it was rain all the same, and the women and girls of the Potters' Guild were celebrating a victory when Hoshi'tiwa arrived with her small bundle of possessions.

They greeted her with open arms and warm embraces, happy to have their sister back in their midst. Hoshi'tiwa, her eyes shining with joy, went straight to Yani and said, "You were right, dear friend. My destiny is here at Center Place. Although I am not the girl prophesied on the ancient wall, I *was* brought here for a reason. To bring rain." Myriad emotions swirled in Hoshi'tiwa's mind and heart—Lord Jakál and the feel of his lips upon hers—but she would sort them later, when the others were asleep and she was alone with her thoughts. For now, she was home. "I am here to stay," she said.

Yani could barely suppress her joy. The rain was the sign she had been waiting for. When Hoshi'tiwa had stepped up onto the plaza and confronted Lord Jakál—successfully winning Ahoté's freedom—Yani knew *that* was the test of courage and honor Hoshi'tiwa must pass. And now the gods had revealed their pleasure, by sending rain.

Tomorrow Yani was going to take Hoshi'tiwa to the secret cave and introduce her into the kachina cult.

Runners came back from the mesa lookout points to report no clouds from horizon to horizon. The rain had been but a brief squall. When Jakál finally retreated inside, Moquihix joined him with a dour look on his face.

"Last night," the High Minister said, "I saw a *coyotl* in the downpour. The trickster god was laughing. Coyotl played a joke on us."

Jakál lashed out at him, startling him. "You mock the gods, Moquihix. The girl brought rain."

"But my Lord—"

"Not another word!" Jakál bellowed. "The Cloud Spirits listened to her. You will not speak of Coyotl or tricks."

Jakál clapped his hands and servants came running. In a bellowing voice, their master called for an emergency meeting of the Council. "*Now,* my Lord?" said Moquihix. The Council never met until Star Readers and astrologers chose an auspicious day.

"At once!"

The nobles and officials arrived in haste, accompanied by the Jaguars who had been sent to fetch them, and as they lined up in their places in the great Council Chamber, they asked one another what this was about. The filthy Star Readers were also there, as well as priests from as far away as Lady Corn.

Jakál entered the hall and all fell silent. He wore his feathered cape and quetzal headdress of office, and walked with purpose, his lean frame drawn up tall and straight. Jakál strode back and forth in front of the gathered company, stretching the silence, creating tension and anticipation as the men shifted on their feet and avoided his gaze as if he could read their thoughts. Jakál had been trained, in the great temple of Quetzalcoatl in Tollan, the tricks and techniques for reducing the most stubborn and fearless of men into a state of nerves.

Finally, sensing the rising anxiety in the chamber, he snapped at a pair of guards, "Bring the girl."

A bewildered Hoshi'tiwa was thrust before the Council by the rough handling of a Jaguar, having been snatched from the homecoming party at the workshop. She did not know why she was here, now facing this august body.

The gathered men knew of the plan to execute her after she brought rain. Was the deed to take place *here*?

Captain Xikli, standing at the head of the two rows of nobles, smiled to himself. The rain had been brief, and he, too, had heard of a *coyotl* in the downpour, the earthly manifestation of the trickster god. He took it as a sign that Jakál's power would also be brief, and that the gods were playing tricks on him.

Moquihix, however, suspected that something else was afoot.

All waited in respectful and nervous silence as Lord Jakál proceeded to declare a new law that, by his mere speaking it, had to be obeyed beyond question. As his scribes hastily recorded his words, the *tlatoani* of Center Place informed all in the council hall that the rain-girl Hoshi'tiwa was from this day forward *tiacápan*.

A collective gasp filled the hall. The men looked at one another. Had they heard correctly? So rarely was the distinction of *tiacápan* placed upon someone—"first born, favored of the gods." Did Jakál have that power?

The Chief Star Reader stepped forward and said in a respectful tone, "By what right do you do this, my Lord?"

"By my right as the messenger of Quetzalcoatl, whose will is not to be ignored." Jakál had thought about the dream he had been enjoying when the rain arrived, analyzed it, consulted with a dream interpreter until he had convinced himself that what Quetzalcoatl was trying to tell him in the dream, and which Jakál could not hear above the shouting, was that Hoshi'tiwa was to be awarded an elevated status at Center Place and that she was untouchable to all men.

The Council members, officials and Jaguars, High Minister Moquihix, Captain Xikli, and Chief Physician Nagual listened in shocked silence. One of the scribes was so stunned, he forgot to keep writing. And Jakál's personal bodyguard, standing nearby, carefully memorized every word his master spoke so that he could later repeat it verbatim to Lady White Orchid.

Because Jakál spoke in Nahuatl, Hoshi'tiwa did not understand what was being said. But the reactions of the nobles and officials, the shocked faces and low angry voices frightened her, and she knew that her fate was being decided in that moment.

"Let every man from horizon to horizon know that the girl will no longer be known as Hoshi'tiwa. From this day forward she is Summer Rain," Jakál said in a ringing voice, and more gasps erupted throughout the chamber. "She will take up residence in Precious Green, to live as a Toltec, in chambers of her own, with servants of her own. She will be allowed to wear cotton and sandals. And all are to show her proper respect as one blessed by Tlaloc and a messenger of the gods."

Jakál swept his fierce gaze over the faces of those present, taking in their awe, confusion, stupefaction, searching for signs of disobedience or dissent. Finally, his eyes met those of Captain Xikli, who stood in a defiant pose. Jakál's eyes were like blazing firebrands as he shouted in a sonorous voice filled with authority and finality, "Quetzalcoatl has spoken!"

BOOK FOUR

Summer Rain

Forty-three

WHITE Orchid was so blinded by rage, she could barely see. As she stepped from the carrying chair and set her soft leather sandals upon the path that led to the rising-splendor Lady Corn, she was oblivious of the people around her, the sun overhead, the smoke and noise filling the canyon. She saw only the face of Hoshi'tiwa.

Summer Rain.

Living in Precious Green! Bearing a Toltec name! Elevated beyond her station and receiving special treatment from Jakál!

Bile rose in White Orchid's throat. She could not recall when she had hated another so. Or been so consumed with anger and resentment. And the passionate desire to strike out.

As she hurried down the path, anxious to find answers within the stone chambers of Lady Corn, she thought back to the spring evening when her life had reached a giddy, joyful zenith—when Jakál had come to her party and paid attention to her and given her a fabulous gift— only to drop to its nadir when her father had drunkenly blurted the truth of her birth. Since that turning point, nothing in White Orchid's

life had been the same. Nor had she ever felt such hatred as now blackened her heart.

The rain-girl with her clan tattoos, who knows her parents and her
grandparents all the way back to her distant ancestors. Barely one step
above being an animal, and yet she has something I do not.

Bloodline. Ancestors. Family.

And now she stood in the way of White Orchid marrying Jakál.

As she entered the courtyard of Lady Corn, White Orchid drew her
cloak about herself. It was the rich, deep blue mantle Jakál had given to
her the night of her party—both of which everyone still talked about.
She wore it to remind herself of Jakál's affections, for that was how
White Orchid chose to interpret his attentiveness that evening. She wore
it also to remind *others* of her special relationship with Jakál. Never
mind his surprising move with Hoshi'tiwa. Never mind that gossips
speculated on a more intimate arrangement between the *tlatoani* and the
rain-girl. Jakál belonged to White Orchid, and nothing was going to get
in the way of her attaining that goal.

But she must not act recklessly. The girl was working at a sacred
task. Hoshi'tiwa could not be killed, or kidnapped and taken away from
Center Place. Nor could White Orchid have her injured in a way that
might render her unable to work, such as crippling her hands or blinding her.

White Orchid had thought long and hard about the problem, had
consulted the stars, fortune-tellers, and her own conscience. Finally, she
had realized the solution was a simple one. The girl must be made displeasing to Jakál in some way.

If Hoshi'tiwa were horribly disfigured, Jakál would no longer look
upon her with pleasure. But this presented White Orchid with a fresh
set of problems. How to render Hoshi'tiwa unpleasing to the eye? Slash
her with a knife? Burn her face with fire? A knife might cause her to
bleed to death. Or the spirits of infection could sicken her and make her
die. To burn her face might also damage her sight, and a blind potter did
not create rain jars that pleased the Cloud Spirits.

No, White Orchid thought in frustration as she entered the cool, dark reception room of Lady Corn. To make Hoshi'tiwa displeasing was going to take something special.

"How may the goddess help you?" the young priestess asked of her distinguished visitor. Although the guardian of Lady Corn was not personally acquainted with White Orchid, she had seen the daughter of Tenoch at many public events. And it occurred to the priestess, on this warm summer morning, that the lady did not look well.

"I wish to draw up a genealogy for my father," White Orchid said crisply. "A gift for his birthday."

"It pleases the goddess to grant you your wish," the young woman said and, turning, led the visitor deeper into the building.

Lady Corn was the goddess of paper and writing, wind and good luck. Among the duties of the handful of priestesses who resided there was to oversee the manufacture of paper, ink, brushes, and books. While such industry was conducted outside beneath shade bowers, inside the small building was a storehouse of records on bloodlines and family lineages.

The folded books were stored on shelves made of wooden planks and filled several rooms. As White Orchid followed the slender young woman in the ink-stained robes, with the symbols of her sacred calling hanging from her belt—pens, brushes, and knives for sharpening them—she scanned the hundreds of volumes that rose from floor to ceiling, and thought of all the souls recorded there, people connected to parents, grandparents, great-grandparents, all the way back to the very first Toltecs who came to this canyon. White Orchid knew her birth was recorded here, somewhere among these many pages.

What was she going to find? Writing was sacred; written words possessed tremendous power. Would Tenoch, who was devoutly religious, have asked a priestess to write a special protective formula next to the Nahuatl symbols that meant "White Orchid with Morning Dew on Its Young Petals"?

With a racing heart, she gave the priestess the name of her bloodline, and the name of the month, the name of the year, and the number of the day of her birth.

"A genealogy is a precious gift," the priestess said as she read the tags on the shelves. "We have many fine scribes here. We can create a beautiful book for your father."

"It is in honor of his sixtieth winter."

"Sixty winters," murmured the priestess, who was herself only twenty-three. "The gods smile upon Tenoch the Hero."

White Orchid hated lying to a holy woman, but she could not tell the priestess the truth: that she needed to find out who her real parents were. Because surely Tenoch would have told the truth to the birth recorder thirty years ago. To do otherwise was blasphemy.

While the priestess searched through the records, White Orchid tried to calm herself with the knowledge that at least one of her initial fears had been allayed.

Seeking a consultation with Chief Physician Nagual on an invented complaint of lower back pain, she had engaged him in conversation, being circumspect in her purpose. Casually, she had brought the subject around to how a physician handled the private things a patient divulged to him.

"It is kept confidential, my Lady," the Chief Physician had said as he wrote a magic healing spell on a small piece of cactus-fiber paper.

"You tell no one?"

"No one, my Lady."

"Not even—"

"No one," he had said pointedly, handing her the magic spell that would cure her back pain. "A patient's secrets remain a secret with me."

His assurance brought some consolation—Nagual was not going to reveal her father's secret—*her* secret—to Jakál.

And her father was sober again, since the night of the party. He had been wretchedly sick for two days after and had no memory of his blurted confession. But now at least he was off the *nequhtli* and back under Nagual's care, so that his tongue was guarded once more.

She anxiously watched as the priestess came to a halt and reached up to a shelf, lifted a pile of folded books and drew one out. The young woman smiled and gestured for White Orchid to follow.

As torches were not permitted inside due to high fire risk, all manual labor, writing, and reading were conducted in the forecourt, in the sunlight. White Orchid followed the young priestess to a shaded bower, where they sat cross-legged on a reed mat. Two other visitors sat beneath the bower, bent over a folded book with a priestess and murmuring what they wanted recorded there. Was it a birth? A death? A marriage? White Orchid did not care. Her eyes and ears and mind were focused only on the Bloodline of Tenoch of Tollan, starting on the distant date of 12 Flint in Year Rabbit.

She watched the priestess's ink-stained fingers as they reverently opened the book, the young woman whispering a sacred chant as she unfolded the long sheet of fig-bark paper. White Orchid's eyes widened at the many symbols painted there, the oldest ones faded and in an archaic script, with more recent ones, as the accordion-fold book opened all the way, richer in color and bolder in design. Where the symbols ended, blank pages followed, ready for future names.

When the priestess ended her holy chant, she said, "Shall I read this for you?"

"I can read," White Orchid said impatiently, taking the book from her.

"How would you like the genealogy to be arranged? And have you a kind of paper in mind? Animal skins are the most durable."

White Orchid had no intention of creating so precious a gift for her father, with whom she was still furious. Studying the glyphs, she saw the name of her own child, his death and birth, others in the family who had died or married and moved away, until finally, with her heart pounding in her ears, she came to the recorded birth of "White Orchid with Morning Dew on Its Young Petals."

She braced herself. Had Tenoch divulged her mother's name, if he knew it?

She had tried to discuss the issue with her father. "I need to ask you about my mother," she would begin, and he would turn away, saying, "The subject of my beloved Omaya is too painful." Or she would say, "I want to ask you about the night of my birth," and he would close his eyes and clamp his mouth shut, like a child.

White Orchid suspected he knew what she wanted to ask about, but as long as she could pretend she didn't know, then he didn't have to face the truth. And so she had come to Lady Corn, because only truth could be written on the sacred paper of the goddess. At least here, informing the priestesses of the arrival of a new daughter into the bloodline, Tenoch could not turn away from the truth. He could not lie.

She studied the vital page, following the glyphs of her name to those of her mother and father. She froze. The parental names listed were Omaya and Tenoch.

White Orchid closed her eyes. Tenoch had lied.

"Are you all right, my Lady?" came the young priestess's soft voice.

Nodding, White Orchid opened her eyes and stared at the symbols next to her name, designating the stars and planets, moon and sun, and numerals stating year, month, day, and hour of her birth.

More lies. All of it. Her whole life—a lie.

Riding high in her chair with slaves shouting to make way along the road, White Orchid was blinded by fear, rage, and feelings of betrayal.

First Jakál. And now her father.

She found Tenoch in his private suite, playing *patolli* with an old friend. Stiffly asking the guest to please excuse them, with Tenoch protesting and the guest shocked at her rudeness, the man gathered his cloak and left.

"What is the meaning of this?" Tenoch thundered. "How dare you drive my guest out of the house. How dare—"

"I have just come from Lady Corn. I saw my birth record."

He tipped his chin defiantly. "So?"

"Is it the truth, what I saw written there?"

He made an impatient gesture and called loudly for a slave.

"I have tried to talk to you about this, Father, but you refuse. I will not let you ignore me this time. On the night of the party, you were so drunk you thought I was Omaya, and you talked about buying a baby from a stranger."

The slave came running in, and before Tenoch could give an order, White Orchid dismissed the bewildered man.

"The insolence!" Tenoch shouted. "I am still Tenoch and a Hero of the Empire! I will not allow such disrespect. I can still take a whip to your back for such insolence."

White Orchid stood her ground. Retrieving the amulet from beneath her dress, she held it before his face and said in a sharp voice, "Did you give this to me?"

He looked away.

"Did you give this to me?"

Tenoch thought for a moment; then he turned a different face to her, one filled with sorrow. "Why bring all this up now? It is a beautiful day. The gods sent birds to sing in our cornfield. Let us go and sit together—"

"Where did this amulet come from? What is the meaning of its symbol?"

He finally hung his head and looked at his hands, one still clutching the *patolli* beans he had been about to roll when she had come in. Relaxing his fingers, he let the beans fall to the floor. "It was around your neck when you were brought to us," he said softly.

White Orchid compressed her lips. "What do you know about my birth? Did my mother sell me? Was I kidnapped?"

He shook his head. "We were told nothing. Your mother got her baby girl, and that was all that mattered."

"My mother? You mean *your wife*."

He lifted eyes filled with sadness. "Omaya loved you as if you had come from her own body. Honor her memory, White Orchid, and the love she bore for you."

But White Orchid honored no one in this house, least of all herself. "So," she whispered, "it is all true then."

"Yes," he said miserably, "it is all true."

She slipped the amulet back beneath her dress. Later, she would try to find out what it meant, if it was Toltec or People of the Sun, and what magic it contained. At the moment, a more pressing issue crowded her mind. "I need to know the stars of my birth."

He slumped. "White Orchid, please—"

"Did the man who brought me tell you the stars that were in the sky the night I was born?"

Tenoch looked at his daughter, and when he saw the naked hope in her eyes, her desperate need to be told that, yes, those were the stars of her birth—he felt a sharp pain in his chest. "No," he said sadly. "The man could tell me nothing. He received you from yet another man. You were a few days old when you came to us. The stars by which you have guided your life, my dear daughter, were the ones in the heavens the night you came to us."

White Orchid swallowed painfully. Her worst fear had been confirmed. And now a darker fear grew within her—that it was only a matter of time before Jakál learned the truth about her bloodline. Which suddenly made it all the more urgent she get Jakál away from the rain-girl's enchantment.

"If you will forgive me," Tenoch said, "I must answer nature's call. I really must have my slaves."

White Orchid wasn't listening. Her thoughts were going round and round again, embroiled in the conundrum of getting Hoshi'tiwa out of the way without actually getting rid of her.

As slaves came in and went swiftly and silently about their business—Tenoch could not attend to the chamber pot on his own—White Orchid looked on with disinterest. But when the loincloth came away and the two strong men lifted Tenoch and placed him on the chamber pot, White Orchid looked at his useless stumps with new interest.

Suddenly, she knew what to do. And it made her smile grimly, because the solution to the problem of Hoshi'tiwa had been in front of her all along.

Forty-four

THEY met in secret.

Three men who stood in a close knot, like conspirators, feeling the weight of the Star Chamber bear down on them. Torches flickered and incense filled the air. Although the ceiling was high—as tall as six men standing foot to shoulder—the three ducked their heads and spoke in low tones. A Star Reader, in his filthy black robe and matted hair that grew down to the floor, was performing his morning ritual of chasing out the night's bad magic and purifying, with his smoke and chants, all the nooks and crannies of this holiest of subterranean chambers. He made special obeisance at the secret underground passageway that ran beneath the foundation, extending from a masonry trench sunk into the floor and out to a northern antechamber. The subterranean causeway was used as a symbolic "Underworld" in mystical rites and must be ritualistically purified daily.

"Why did you call us here?" Moquihix said, displeased with having been summoned by Captain Xikli. The Jaguar's arrogance was growing. No one summoned the High Minister except Lord Jakál himself (although, deep in his heart, Moquihix was secretly proud of his son's audacity).

Xikli had called the meeting because of the shocking incident in the Council Chamber with "Summer Rain." It was a sign of Jakál's increasing weakness, Xikli believed, and the powerful men of Center Place must be prepared to take action in the event of government collapse. He knew that, since all people, Toltec and People of the Sun alike, lived with the constant fear of the world coming to a sudden catastrophic end, the collapse of Jakál's regime might trigger chaos and complete anarchy. Xikli wanted to be ready to seize rulership of Center Place and avert disaster.

But he had to make sure support was in place.

"The rain-girl was to have been sacrificed on the altar of blood," Xikli growled. "Her beating heart was promised to the gods. Now Jakál elevates her and keeps her close. And he has been acting strangely since. What else can it mean, if not Jakál breaking his own taboos? By his own edict she is untouchable."

"But we are certain he is not taking pleasure with her," Moquihix said hurriedly. "Servants, under the knife, do not lie."

"But can it be far off?" Xikli countered. "He is a man, after all. And he dresses her like a Toltec woman. It is an insult to us all!" Xikli thumped his chest.

"Jakál said Quetzalcoatl spoke to him in a dream," Moquihix countered, "instructing him to keep her alive and to treat her as *tiacápan*."

Xikli spat. "Quetzalcoatl! It was the one-eyed god in Jakál's loincloth that spoke to him."

"Be careful," Chief Physician Nagual cautioned. "Your words verge upon blasphemy."

Xikli turned on him. "You dare to warn me of blasphemy? What have you done about the heretics?"

There was talk of a seditious new religion taking root among the peasants and farmers in the valley—new gods who had nothing to do with the pantheon of the Toltecs or with the spirits of the People of the Sun. But as everyone knew that new gods, by their novelty, always conquered, the followers of the forbidden sect needed to be ferreted out and extinguished.

"Jakál does nothing about it," Xikli said. "If left to grow unchecked, the people will embrace new gods, and then who will worship our gods and make sacrifice to them? This is a dangerous situation."

"I have heard of this new religion," Nagual offered. "I have a way of finding out the truth."

His two companions looked at him and conceded that Nagual, because of his office, had entry into areas where Xikli and Moquihix had not. The Chief Physician moved freely among all people; he had their ear when they were sick or fearful or troubled by conscience. Only Nagual walked through doors without permission and entered chambers without asking. "We will leave it to you then," said Moquihix, who had too many other things on his mind to worry about a few more gods crowding the valley.

Nagual fingered the edge of his rich cotton cloak, deep in thought, but not about the new gods or heresy or even Lord Jakál and the rain-girl. Nagual's thoughts were upon his son. So devoted had Nagual been to the youth, that when the boy was caught committing a taboo act with the potter's daughter, Nagual had thought his own life had come to an end. And when the boy was sent away in disgrace, Nagual's heart left also. The Chief Physician had thought life could not be bleaker until news came back that the boy had died en route to Tollan, under mysterious circumstances and possibly by suicide. Afterward, Chief Physician Nagual, of impressive bearing and such power as to control life and death at the altar of blood, had moved through his days and nights like a man made of stone.

"Son," Nagual had pleaded after the lovers were caught, "all you have to do is tell them that the girl tricked you, she seduced you, you were her victim." But the boy had refused, declaring he was in love. The girl, daughter of Yani, now the Overseer of the Potters, had been executed on the altar of blood, while Nagual's son had been sent away in shame to meet an infamous end.

When he realized the other two were staring at him, Nagual cleared his throat and said, "I have men already looking into it. Whoever is at the root of this seditious cult, I will find him." Or her. "I will put an end to the heresy."

Moquihix nodded absently. He was in a dyspeptic mood. The girl, Yellow Feather, was on his mind. She had taken up with the old herb peddler and her lame grandson. It was difficult to avoid seeing them in the marketplace, the girl with the baby strapped to her back. *His* child. A boy, he had heard. His son. He looked at Xikli and felt no warmth from him. Why did men say that sons were a blessing?

Moquihix had had a daughter once, long ago, a baby girl whom he had not had the joy of watching grow up. After his daughter was taken from him when she was an infant, Moquihix had often wondered if daughters were the greater blessing.

His thoughts segued to the problem at hand: Jakál's strange behavior of late, acting suspiciously, as if he were concealing a monumental secret. *Was* he taking pleasure with the rain-girl? When Moquihix felt a stab of jealousy, he was immediately disgusted with himself. Hoshi'tiwa continued to haunt his dreams, causing him to wake up sexually aroused. Why her? he wondered each time. With so many beautiful women in the valley, why did his blood boil for the rain-girl?

Strangely, even though she was now *tiacápan*—favored by the gods and therefore untouchable—his ardor had increased. Moquihix's back, beneath his knotted cloak, was striped with scars from self-flagellation in the kiva, where he tried to sweat out his poisonous desires and whip the lust from his body.

Hoshi'tiwa had obviously bewitched Jakál in the same way. How long, the High Minister wondered, before she enchanted every man at Center Place?

"What is that sound?" Nagual said suddenly, turning toward the subterranean tunnel through which outside noise sometimes filtered into the kiva.

"Trumpets," Moquihix ventured.

"Warning signals!" Nagual said, and the three immediately pulled their cloaks about themselves and, making gestures of respect toward the Star Reader, hurried from the observatory and into the noon sunlight.

They hastened across the valley with everyone else who followed the call of the ram's horn trumpets, until they reached the growing crowd at the base of the main plaza of Precious Green. Priests were lining up, and Jaguars were forming ranks—to Xikli's surprise, as he had not been informed of a muster.

When Jakál strode out into the sunlight, green quetzal plumes shimmering brightly, the green and blue of his magnificent feathered cloak swimming about him like mountain lagoons, every man, woman, and child dropped to the earth to press their foreheads to the ground. Only Xikli, Moquihix, and Nagual remained standing, and they did not like what they saw. Such theatrics were out of character for Jakál, as was impulsiveness. First the edict about the rain-girl, and now this.

Bad omens indeed.

To their astonishment, Jakál shouted out over the silent, prostrate throng to rise to their feet and "behold with your own eyes the power and majesty of Quetzalcoatl, God of the Breath of Life!"

Xikli, Moquihix, and Nagual stared in puzzlement as a procession emerged from the inner rooms of Precious Green. Their puzzlement turned to shock when they saw that, riding on a platform carried on the backs of twenty slaves, was no less than the god Quetzalcoatl himself, arrayed in such splendid finery that the people could not remain respectfully silent. A rumble raced through the crowd as sounds of awe and fear erupted from throats. This was no ordinary Toltec god carved from cold stone, but a shining, blinding being whose face was brighter than the sun, with teeth whiter than snow, and hair streaming up to the sky in brilliant green feathers.

It was the sacred mask of Quetzalcoatl, which Jakál had brought from Tollan to Center Place and kept hidden in his private kiva. A mask so old that no one knew its years, a mask that Quetzalcoatl himself had worn when he was in his earthly incarnation.

While the People of the Sun marveled at the radiant sight, the

Toltecs looked on in fear and horror. Few had ever looked upon the famous mask of Quetzalcoatl; not even Tenoch the Hero had seen it. And yet here it was, out in the open for all to see.

The god was brought to a rest beside Lord Jakál, who smiled in admiration at this manifestation of his beloved deity, which was in fact a stone idol hidden beneath robes and the gold mask. But the spirit of the god resided in the stone, Jakál knew, and the gold mask was the exact likeness of Quetzalcoatl himself when he was a man.

Xikli hissed, "He cannot do this!"

Nagual, a man of few words, murmured darkly, "He can do anything he wants."

Moquihix was again of divided heart. Loyal to his *tlatoani,* he felt surprising admiration for Jakál. At the same time, deeply religious and superstitious, Moquihix wondered if this outrageous act was going to bring about the end of the world.

And yet, despite their personal fears and wondering what Jakál was up to, the three men could not deny that they felt the power of Quetzalcoatl there on the sunlit plaza.

With a gesture, Jakál began the procession moving again, out of the plaza and eastward toward the Blue Hummingbird rising-splendor, a stately parade of Jaguars and priests and nobles, with musicians thumping drums and blowing flutes as Quetzalcoatl led the way high on his litter and Lord Jakál walked humbly behind.

As the god's platform was brought to a halt on the level ground that had been cleared and made ready for the first bricks of Jakál's new rising-splendor, Moquihix, Xikli, and Nagual noticed with disapproval that the rain-girl Hoshi'tiwa-now-Summer Rain, dressed in a flaming orange tunic and skirt, had been given a prominent position among the honored dancing girls from Five Flower.

And then the eyes of the three men, as well as those of the thousands amassing in the valley, turned to a puzzling structure in the middle of the cleared field: a tall wooden tower constructed of poles and planks and branches, topped with an enormous basket. Like all good administrators of foreign outposts, Jakál had learned to speak the tongue of his subjects so that he never had to rely on translators, who might not be trustworthy. He addressed the people now in their own language, and such Toltecs as were newly come to Center Place struggled to follow his speech.

"All men know that the world has lived through four previous cycles," he announced in a resonant voice, "each of which flourished with life and spirit, each of which underwent a catastrophic devastation to be reborn again. All men know that this fifth cycle must also come to an end. But this time the destruction can be prevented by the arrival of one man, Quetzalcoatl, who will save the world and bring about a golden age."

A buzz rippled through the crowd as the People of the Sun recognized the description of their own Pahana.

As Jakál recounted the story of Quetzalcoatl who, centuries ago, had died a fiery death and who had promised to return, the crowd listened in rapt interest. But Xikli was unimpressed. This outrageous performance was not intended to dazzle the people or the nobles, he suspected, but just one person. Jakál's head had been so turned by the rain-girl that he was acting recklessly.

Moquihix was troubled. To put the sacred mask of Quetzalcoatl on display in front of the common people! What blasphemy. The High Minister would not have been surprised had the mesa, rising steeply behind Lord Jakál, suddenly broken apart and come crashing down on him.

Yellow Feather, carrying her baby on her back, was uninterested in the Lord's long speech. She looked about and saw Yani, the woman who had banished her from the Potters' Guild and forced her to live among the outcasts. Yellow Feather's sharp eyes noted that Yani was not looking at the golden mask or at Jakál but to the left, across the crowd, her eyes fixed on Chief Physician Nagual. Yani looked terrified. Yellow Feather wondered what she was so afraid of. Recalling that Nagual was conducting an investigation into a new cult, rooting out the heretics with a plan to execute them, Yellow Feather smiled to herself and decided to watch her old rival over the next days, perhaps to find out something interesting about this woman who had once declared her *makai-yó*.

Only Hoshi'tiwa's thoughts, during the long speech, were not upon gods or the end of the world. She was still marveling at her reversal of fortune. One day she had brought rain, and had expected to be returned to the potters' workshop—and then that very same day had been declared a favorite of the gods and given residence in Precious Green with her own slaves.

She was still in shock, still unused to the feel of cotton on her body, sandals on her feet. She felt unworthy of such luxury and yearned more than ever to be returned to the company of her sisters.

And yet, to her surprise, the desire to stay at Precious Green also tugged at her heart.

As she filled her eyes with the splendid vision of Lord Jakál, she remembered the feel of his mouth upon hers in a gesture so intimate that it shocked her, because the People of the Sun did not kiss in such a manner. However, as she lay awake at night in her new quarters, unable to sleep, she felt her lips tingle and the restless desire to be thus kissed again.

Coming to the end of his recitation of the holy saga, Jakál pointed dramatically to the basket atop the wooden tower and shouted, "Behold the sacred fire that consumed the earthly body of Quetzalcoatl, Lord of the Breath of Life!" All faces shifted to the basket that held no fire but stood cold and silent atop the tower.

"Behold the sacred fire that transformed Quetzalcoatl into the Morning Star! Behold the sacred fire that will herald his return! Behold the sacred fire that promises us the world will never again be destroyed! *Behold!*"

And in that instant, before the eyes of the flabbergasted onlookers, a fire suddenly erupted from the basket, flaring hotly so that tongues of flame shot up to the sky. The crowd fell back, crying out.

As the fire continued to burn brightly, the people moved restively in fear, awe, and curiosity. Where had the fire come from? No man had ignited it. No man even stood nearby!

It was the work of Quetzalcoatl, they began to reason. And then they whispered it among themselves. Powerful Quetzalcoatl had set the fire with his invisible hand!

As the farmers and merchants and blanket-weavers and onion-sellers marveled and wondered, Moquihix narrowed his eyes. He knew how Jakál had engineered the "miracle." The secret of the magic light-fire powder had been learned from the ancient Mayan priests of Chichén Itzá, who had themselves learned it from the gods. The magic powder called light-fire was obtained from a residue of evaporated urine—a white solid that glowed in the dark. Jakál had only to create a base of flammable oil and dried paper and then gauge the heat of the day as the sun rose during his long speech. Pointing to the tower was calculated on chance: Jakál would have uttered "Behold!" a thousand times until the fire finally ignited spontaneously, making it look as if he himself had brought forth flame.

Moquihix glanced at his two companions, who also knew how the trick was done, and realized the three of them had been wrong in thinking Jakál's power was being weakened by the rain-girl. By the reaction of the crowd to the fire trick, it was clear that Jakál was more powerful than ever.

After the shock died down and the fire burned itself out, Jakál drew himself up tall and erect again, paused for silence and for total effect, and called out in a voice that sailed off to the southern cliffs: "Know then, all of you present, that I consecrate this ground to the Lord of the Breath of Life. And know also that what we build here will be no ordinary rising-splendor. For the great and divine Quetzalcoatl, Lord of the Breath of Life, we will build a mighty pyramid, the likes of which have never been seen in this land or in any other!"

"By the gods," murmured Nagual, a man who rarely uttered oaths.

Xikli curled his fingers around the shaft of his weapon so tightly that his knuckles turned white.

And Moquihix, seeing the shocked and angry faces of the Jaguars and priests, thought in sudden fear: Jakál invites a holy war.

Forty-five

WHITE Orchid thought the Caravan Master would *never* arrive.

From the moment runners from the south had announced sighting the caravan's approach, she had been breathless with anxiety. Everything had changed. She no longer wanted to marry Jakál merely because she was in love with him, or because she coveted power. It was because being his wife would give her an identity, it would anchor her to the earth. He would link her to his own bloodline and she would no longer be alone.

White Orchid and her father had not spoken since the day she confronted him after discovering his lie in the records at Lady Corn. The villa of the house of Tenoch had grown strangely silent as the two residents went about their daily activities without interacting. And then the caravan had finally arrived, and now the Caravan Master was coming up the dusty path to the villa, carrying a mysterious box. Once Jakál was under the magic spell of the serpent's venom, she could leave Tenoch's house and never speak to the old man again.

"My Lady!" the Caravan Master effused as a slave admitted him to the house. "The blessings of the gods be upon you and your father."

Wishing to grab the box and send him on his way, White Orchid forced herself to be civil and go through the motions of endless amenities and rules of etiquette before they were allowed to discuss business.

With great pains she listened to the Caravan Master describe his long and arduous trip from the south, speaking as usual with his mouth full, and wasting precious water as he drank, letting it dribble down his chin. Finally, her patience at an end, she said, "Tell me about the snake."

He had brought the aphrodisiac serpent as promised, and now, at long last, White Orchid held the key to Jakál's heart, and her own future, in her hands.

She did not handle the creature directly. The exotic snake lay coiled in a small mahogany box with holes drilled in the lid and magical symbols painted on the sides. "What does it eat?" she asked as she held the box in her lap and imagined slipping a few kernels of corn inside.

"All snakes are carnivores, my Lady. They prefer mice."

"Mice!" Well, she would be feeding it for only a few days before she presented the box to Jakál as a gift. After that, once it had injected its venom and Jakál was hers, the snake could be killed.

She was about to say something further when a warm breeze wafted in from the fields, bringing the scent of sage and dust, evoking a painful memory. The Caravan Master's voice faded as White Orchid was taken back to a day like this, not long ago, when she had awakened in the morning and gathered her baby to her breast, and she had noticed that his eyes did not look right. Had they changed from the night before? Or was it only her imagination?

Over the ensuing days it had become apparent that her son's eyes were starting to protrude. She consulted Chief Physician Nagual, who advised her to sacrifice an unblemished white dove to Lady Corn and provide the priestesses with a banquet.

White Orchid complied, but the baby's eyes continued to protrude. And then she noticed his brow ridge was beginning to bulge. Seeking

Nagual's counsel again, she was told to make a sacrifice of two unblemished white doves and another banquet for the priestesses.

When White Orchid realized that her baby no longer looked up at
her, that his eyes no longer tracked movement as they once had, she sent
for the midwife who had delivered the baby. The Toltec woman laid her
hands on the infant's head, which Nagual had not done, and gently felt
around. "You summoned me too late," she said at last. "Had I come in
time, I could have used a knife to cure this problem. But the bones in
your baby's skull have fused before their time, and I cannot remedy it.
There is no room inside his skull for the brain to grow, and so it presses
against bone. The brain is dying, and so is your child."

The Caravan Master's voice came back. "But you need not feed it a
mouse a day, once a month will—" He stopped and stared.

White Orchid felt something on her cheek and realized in embar-
rassment that it was a tear. "I understand," she said, thinking of the baby
that had lived another month, his features twisting and distorting out of
shape as the prematurely hardened skull plates pulled on the facial bones
until his tongue protruded and he could no longer nurse. "I will have my
servants round up some mice at once."

"A final caution, my Lady," the Caravan Master said, uncomfortable
with her sudden tears. It was bad form to display emotions, particularly
negative ones, in front of a guest. "The snake undergoes different phases
during its yearly cycle. There are months when its venom is powerless.
You must be certain to use the serpent only during its active periods and
when the moon is at its fullest. You will of course wish to consult with
your astrologer for the most auspicious alignment of your stars with
those of your intended lover."

My astrologer, she thought in disgust. Her horoscope was meaning-
less now. "Which phase is it in at the moment?" She had hoped to take
the serpent to Jakál's private chambers within a day.

"It is dormant. It sleeps during the summer months. You must wait for
the Autumn Equinox, and then select the most auspicious days after that."

The food platters empty, his mug of *nequhtli* drained dry, the Caravan Master announced his departure. As he rose, wiping his greasy

hands on his cloak, he said, "I will not be coming again. The trek has become too dangerous. There are brigands and thieves along the route because the King of Tollan cannot send soldiers to guard the way. He has his hands full with defending the city and suppressing civil unrest." The Caravan Master belched, and then sighed. "I doubt you will see another caravan from home at all," he added, noting that his hostess was not listening, her attention riveted on the magic serpent, her thoughts no doubt flying ahead to the day when her intended "love victim" was bitten and then smitten. The Toltec empire was being threatened with collapse, and all this woman thought about was a partner for her sleeping mat.

White Orchid rose and bade the Caravan Master farewell. Before he stepped through the door and into the warm summer day, he turned and said, "Remember, my Lady. The snake must strike only once for romance to occur. If it should strike twice, the man will die a most agonizing death."

Finally, for dramatic effect, he pointed a greasy finger at the box and said sternly, "Above all, keep your own hand out of there."

As White Orchid watched him go, her mind a whirlpool of thoughts, a slave came up and quietly informed her that a messenger had just come from the marketplace. The seller of seashells had a new shipment of pink conches and pearl abalones.

White Orchid immediately called for her carrying chair and traveling mantle. She would not be going to the marketplace, however, because the message had not come from the purveyor of shells. As she could no longer risk her spy—Jakál's personal guard—coming to the house, she had devised a secret signal for him to alert her when he had new information.

Or, in this instance, when he had found a man to take care of a certain delicate job.

They met in secret at the Shrine of the Nameless God.

The tumbledown brick structure, consisting of one room and a dusty courtyard, was conveniently deserted. No one ever visited the stone effigy that had been placed there in the first days of Toltec habitation at Center Place, to appease any god the Toltecs might have overlooked. There were no offerings, no incense, no inscriptions on the walls, and there was no priesthood. With hundreds of gods in the Toltec pantheon demanding attention, the Nameless One was neglected.

Leaving her slaves with the carrying chair, White Orchid hurried through the small musty room and out the door at the back, where the young guard waited beneath a broken-down bower that offered little shade.

The handsome young man was not carrying his usual decorated spear, nor was he wearing the leather breastplate painted with a giant butterfly, nor his wooden helmet adorned with colorful feathers that indicated his status as a personal guard to Lord Jakál. In a plain white loincloth and white mantle, his head bare in the dappled sunlight, he looked ordinary and insignificant. But White Orchid knew otherwise. The young guard had provided her with vital information since the day she had recruited him to be her eyes and ears within the government, and specifically in Jakál's private life.

This afternoon, however, she was using him for another purpose.

On the day White Orchid had visited Lady Corn and had seen the record of her birth, and afterward had confronted her father about the truth, the solution to the problem of the rain-girl had come to her. White Orchid had watched her legless father being lifted by his servants onto a chamber pot—the utter humiliation and indignity of it—and had realized that to make Hoshi'tiwa undesirable was simple. No man wanted to lie with a woman who was useless from the waist down.

"What do you have for me?" she asked now, looking around to make sure they were neither seen nor heard. But the Shrine of the Nameless God was tucked at the base of the southern cliff, far from rising-splendors, far from pathways and foot traffic.

"I have found a man," the young guard said as he glanced over each shoulder, relishing the danger of the moment.

Although his position as Jakál's bodyguard was prestigious and carried honor, and although it made his parents proud and caused women to look at him with interest, the young guard had found it to be a boring job. After all, what man would dare to harm the *tlatoani* of Center Place? Being Jakál's bodyguard was like being protector of the sun. Everyone was respectful of the sun and no one could come close to touching it. The young man had started seeing himself as a symbolic guard only, an ornament at court, when this intriguing lady had approached him with a proposition. He had accepted, and his life had not known a dull moment since.

But there was more to it: He was drawn to White Orchid's power. Strong women excited him, and the daughter of Tenoch was the strongest woman he had ever met. Although there could never be physical pleasure between them, nor did he even entertain such a fantasy, merely receiving a summons from the great Lady, doing her bidding and earning her gratitude, excited him in a way no other woman could.

"I have found a man, my Lady. He has agreed to take care of your problem for a small payment."

She narrowed her eyes. "What man?"

"His name is Bone Snapper, because that is his specialty. Captain Xikli uses him to persuade men to talk under interrogation, and also to mete out certain punishments."

"He knows what is expected of him?"

"He will approach Hoshi'tiwa from behind, seize her by the neck, and apply enough pressure to render her unconscious. Then he will snap her spine—"

White Orchid held up a hand. She did not want the details. "Her legs?"

"She will be as crippled as—" He caught himself. He had almost said, "Tenoch."

But White Orchid understood. It was her father who had inspired the idea in the first place. "When will it be done?"

"Bone Snapper will determine the time. But soon."

"Tell him to make sure it looks like an accident."

"He understands. After the deed is done, he will place her at the foot of stairs to make it look like she fell. The whole of it will be executed so swiftly that not even the girl herself will remember what happened. She will not know she had been attacked but will most likely believe that she did indeed fall."

The young guard smiled and his chest puffed out when he saw the look of approval on White Orchid's painted face. "Do not worry, my Lady," he added. "One morning the sun will rise and Hoshi'tiwa will walk no more."

Forty-six

HOSHI'TIWA knew she was living an envied life, having a room of her own on the top tier of Precious Green, with a slave to cook for her and look after her needs. She worked each day on her rain jars, sitting on the terrace in front of her door, cross-legged and bent at her sacred task, while below, the rising-splendor dropped away in four stories, with the great bustling plaza spreading before it and, beyond, the valley filled with humanity and life.

The monsoon season had begun, when storms were supposed to blow up from the southwest and drench the land. But the sky remained maddeningly clear and blue as the summer heat beat down upon Center Place, and not a raindrop was felt anywhere. But Hoshi'tiwa was not worried. Her new jars would bring rain.

Even though she lived far above the main populace, she sensed the troubled undercurrents in the valley. The caravan had come and gone, leaving in its wake an unsettled mood. It had been the smallest caravan yet, and rumors persisted that the master had declared he would not return, nor would any other caravan. As this was an insupportable thought for the Toltecs, who regarded being cut off from home as being cut off from their gods, they threw themselves into festivals and prayers and rituals, and into watching the progress of Lord Jakál's new building project, telling themselves that Quetzalcoatl was a beneficent god who would show favor upon the men who erected a pyramid in his honor.

Hoshi'tiwa had heard that Captain Xikli and the followers of Blue Hummingbird strengthened their vows to the god of war, and the Jaguars brought victims back from outlying farms, to march them to the altar of blood in the plaza and offer their beating hearts to the gods. And in the middle of this growing rivalry between Quetzalcoatl and Blue Hummingbird, a new secret cult flourished—of which Hoshi'tiwa believed Yani was a member—quietly attracting followers who chose to believe in helpful spirits called kachinas.

While everyone talked about the rain and searched the heavens for clouds, the eternal sunshine and heat and absence of clouds did not disturb Hoshi'tiwa. In her heart she knew rain would come and then all would be well in the world, life would be in balance again, and Lord Jakál's god, desiring to live in so harmonious a world, would come.

Jakál had convinced her of this when he had stood so magnificently arrayed in precious feathers, as brilliant as the golden mask of Quetzalcoatl, and summoning fire from out of the air, showing the world his great power—she had never believed she could admire a man so. Not even Sun Watcher back home, who was an impressive priest, had inspired such awe in her.

If only he would permit her to return to the potters' workshop and labor in joy with her sisters.

As she climbed down the four ladders that led from her room on the top level to the plaza below, smiling at people on the terraces as she descended—women at grinding stones or weaving cotton, cooking over fires, making tortillas—she thought how well this new life should suit her. It did not. Without her sisters, she realized as she struck across the plaza where the market was alive with noisy commerce, she was incomplete.

Which was why, at this first opportunity since being moved into Precious Green, she was resuming her visits to the Potters' Guild. As she neared the workshop, however, she was surprised to hear no calls of welcome when she stepped through the door.

Moving from the bright sunlight into the cooler darkness of the workshop, she looked around in puzzlement. The women and girls remained at their various tasks. When a few glanced furtively at her and then away, she was startled by the coldness in their eyes.

"Daughter," said Yani, coming with hands outstretched.

Relieved to see her friend, Hoshi'tiwa placed in the two brown, callused hands the gifts she had brought for her sisters: shells and feathers and ribbons and even a small skin of precious water.

Yani took the offerings and set them down and led Hoshi'tiwa from the main workshop to the covered patio in the rear. "They will not accept your gifts," she said quietly. "You must take them back."

Hoshi'tiwa blinked at her. "I do not understand."

Yani studied the younger woman's face, privately weighing her thoughts. Was it possible Hoshi'tiwa had no idea what people were saying about her? That, because the Dark Lord gave her a Toltec name and dressed her in rich cotton, she must be Jakál's woman? If not, then certainly *some* man's woman?

Yani was sick over this unexpected turn. On the Day of the Brief Rain, as it was being called, when Hoshi'tiwa had come with the news that she was to be moved back into the workshop, Yani had decided to introduce her to the kachina cult. But then Jakál had shocked everyone by declaring Hoshi'tiwa untouchable and favored by the Toltec gods. Yani had decided not to divulge the secret of the kachina cult to Hoshi'tiwa just yet, not until she was certain the girl could be trusted.

"They are jealous," Yani said. "You are dressed very finely and you look as if you eat well, and yet you are a potter, like the rest of us."

Hoshi'tiwa stared in horror at her friend, the woman who had given her the magic polishing stone that made her rain jars shine. "I have no choice," she whispered. "It is Lord Jakál's order. How can I refuse?"

Yani nodded in sympathy. Hoshi'tiwa was not the first woman of their race forced against her will to comply with the wishes of a Lord.

"And Lord Jakál is not entirely a bad man," Hoshi'tiwa said. "He let Ahoté go free."

Yani looked closely at the girl and came to an unhappy conclusion. Hoshi'tiwa might not take pleasure with Jakál yet, but Yani suspected it was in her heart to do so. Yani was suddenly filled with urgency. Hoshi'tiwa, the prophesied one, the Tortoise Clan daughter destined to save their people, must not be allowed to fall from grace.

Red Crow passed through the patio, and as their eyes met, Hoshi'tiwa was stunned to see the look of contempt on the older woman's face. Did they not know how desperately she wished to return to the workshop? "Yani," Hoshi'tiwa said, "I want to come back. When I stood in the plaza that day with Ahoté's life in the balance, and you and my sisters joined me, to stand by my side, united against the Lords, I had never felt such love, such connection with other human beings. My heart is here, Yani."

The older woman, wise to the ways of the world and the hearts of young girls, laid a hand on Hoshi'tiwa's arm and said quietly, "Is it?"

"What do you mean?"

Yani thought, then shook her head. Hoshi'tiwa was not yet aware of her budding feelings—the feelings of a woman—for Jakál. So Yani would not, on this cloudless and rainless summer morning, plant the idea there. Hoshi'tiwa must be allowed to concentrate on creating her sacred rain jars.

When Red Crow appeared again, to pass back through the patio, she paused to glare at Hoshi'tiwa, making her resentment known, and then to the horror of both Hoshi'tiwa and Yani, Red Crow spat at Hoshi'tiwa's feet.

Hoshi'tiwa stared down at the droplets of spittle on the floor, and when the full implication of Red Crow's action swept over her, gave a cry of pain. Without a word she turned and fled, her heart in such agony that she could barely breathe, and as she hurried down the path toward Blue Hummingbird, she looked back at the workshop, where she saw the women and girls throwing her gifts into the dust.

———————

When Jakál turned away from his Chief Architect and saw Summer Rain approaching the construction site, he reacted first with a sudden leap of his heart, his lips curving in a smile, and then with a deeper reaction, less physical and harder to define, but possessing much more power.

Both reactions troubled him.

Watching the sway of her hips as she followed the beaten path where workers and slaves toiled beneath the sun, Jakál recalled their conversation the day before, after a sacrifice at the altar of blood, and Summer Rain had had the audacity to question the ritual. Although Quetzalcoatl did not demand blood sacrifice, the other gods did, and so Lord Jakál permitted the sacrifice of beating hearts. When Hoshi'tiwa had quietly voiced that it was wrong, he had explained that human blood and the human heart were the most precious things that could be offered to the gods.

"*Corn* is the most precious thing we can offer the gods," she had countered, but with respect.

He had replied, "To offer corn is an insult to the gods."

"To offer blood is savage," she had said, and her audacity had almost made him smile. "The gods gave us blood and hearts so that we should *live*. It goes against the balance of nature to spill that blood and still those hearts."

"But the victims go willingly, Summer Rain. They know that through a sacrificial death they go straight to heaven and dwell there with the gods."

But when Hoshi'tiwa had said, "What if the men you kill don't believe in your gods?" it had given him pause.

Summer Rain not only occupied his thoughts and haunted his dreams, now she made him *think*.

Just as Hoshi'tiwa struggled with unwanted thoughts and suppressed forbidden ideas, so was Jakál beleaguered. Not a day went by in which the voice of his conscience did not whisper that he rationalized his actions with Hoshi'tiwa because he harbored a secret desire for her and that he was inventing excuses to keep her near. But the voice lied, he told himself: Quetzalcoatl had come to him in a dream to deliver a clear message that the girl was not to be sacrificed on the altar of blood but to be kept at Center Place to bring more rain. Yet the voice persisted, accusing Jakál of keeping the girl close to himself so that he could have her without crossing the taboo line.

When Hoshi'tiwa came to the end of the path, she stopped abruptly and stared in surprise at Jakál, dressed in a blue cotton loincloth and a red cloak knotted at his throat. She was startled to realize where she was. When she had fled the potters' workshop she had run blindly, with no direction in mind. Now she saw that she had run straight to Lord Jakál.

She quickly made to leave because she knew that women were forbidden to walk upon this consecrated ground, but Jakál surprised her by saying, "I am glad you came, Summer Rain. There is something I wish to show you." And he turned, indicating that she should follow.

Feeling the hard eyes of the architects and engineers upon her, and the enslaved men of her own race as they watched her walk behind Lord Jakál toward a colorful pavilion, the pain of Red Crow's actions wounded her anew, and she sensed now the jealousy and resentment of her kinsmen.

The pavilion consisted of four sturdy poles supporting a colorful cotton roof, with patterned cloth stretched along two sides to provide privacy and a windbreak. The walls flapped in the wind as Jakál held up a sheet of bark paper covered in sketches and plans for rainspouts that were to decorate the four corners of the pyramid—images of Quetzalcoatl in his plumed-serpent manifestation, mouth open to reveal fangs and tongue and through which rain would run.

"Can you do this?" he asked, and while Hoshi'tiwa shyly took the paper to puzzle over it, the voice of Jakál's taxed conscience whispered: For shame, Jakál. This is but a pretext. The girl has no business being here. Nothing good can come of your charade.

"I make pottery, my Lord," she whispered, handing the paper back and feeling her heart grow small and tight in her chest, not knowing the cause of it—the potters throwing away her gifts, or Jakál standing so near.

"I do not ask you to *make* these, Summer Rain, for they will be carved from sacred stone. But I want your blessing to be upon them. You will oversee the harvesting of the stone as you do your sacred clay, for is stone so different from clay? And you will guide the hands of my stonemasons in the same way you guide the paintbrush upon your golden jars."

She looked up at him, and Jakál thought of a type of flower that grew high in mountain boulders—round, yearning little blossoms that sprang from arid soil to seek the sun, fragile yet hardy, independent yet needy. An impulse came over him to sweep her into his arms and crush her against him, to press her fragility to his body. "You ask too much," she whispered.

And then to his shock she began to weep, not in great bitter sobs but softly, moving Jakál's heart all the more for the weeping's delicate sweetness.

"I have upset you," he said.

She lifted her tearstained face. "No, my Lord, you have not upset me. I am so alone! I have no one!"

"You are not alone," he said, dismayed at the emotional burst. "Summer Rain, you have—" He almost said, "me," but quickly changed it to, "Quetzalcoatl, the Lord of the Breath of Life. He is here. You live in his divine presence."

Her upturned face was awash with tears, and it tore his heart as she said, "My people shun me. They have cast me out of their midst. I am alone in the world and I cannot bear it."

Jakál knew loneliness. The *tlatoani* of Center Place, Lord Jakál from the Place of Reeds, Guardian of the Sacred Plume, Watcher of the Sky had felt the same cold wind blow through the empty chambers of his heart, had felt the tightness in the throat, the sad yearning that consumes all who are alone on earth. And he realized once again how alike they were, the Lord and the peasant girl.

Without thinking, he pulled her to him, not crushingly but gently, and she pressed her face upon his shoulder. As they stood within the protective shelter of the pavilion's gossamer walls, no one saw the supreme leader of the land hold the commoner in his arms, her slender body shuddering with each sob. He felt his heart break in two. Jakál kissed her hair and made soothing sounds. He pressed his lips against her vulnerable head. Never had he felt so violently protective of one thing, one person. He wanted to lash out, but he did not know at whom or what.

His struggle with himself became a physical one. He wanted to take pleasure with her in that moment, to demonstrate with his body and virility that she was not alone, that she was wanted and desired. But with his own tongue he had declared her *tiacápan* so that she was forbidden even to the Lord of Center Place.

The moment held and stretched, as if time itself were constricting, as if the gods wished to preserve this instant for themselves, greedy for the passions of the man and the girl, wishing to reminisce about their own earthly incarnations of long ago when they were flesh and knew the pleasures of the flesh.

Jakál inhaled the pine-scent of her hair. Hoshi'tiwa dug her fingers into the sinews and muscles of his arms, as if she clung to a great ancient rock that would harbor her and shelter her from all evil. She opened her heart to him as she would her body. The struggle between desire and obedience grew so great that she made a sound of desperation so that, with great effort, Jakál pushed her from him, gently, so that he held her at arm's length, and he cursed the space and air that separated them. He was astonished at the words that next tumbled from his mouth, but he could not stop them as they poured from his heart and not from his conscience. He hated himself as he said, "At the Autumn Equinox, when you have brought rain, you will be free to go home." Hated himself because he thought it would kill him to lose her now that she lived in Precious Green where he could luxuriate in a glimpse of her now and then, now that it was permissible for him to talk to her and she to him, now that a relationship of sorts was allowed. This flower-faced girl who had sprung from common blood who inflamed and infuriated him at the same time, and who made his heart spin like a whirlwind.

He didn't want to lose her, but her pain cut him to the core and in his desire to relieve that pain, he would have said anything, and thus a fateful promise, regretted the moment it left his mouth, was spoken.

Forty-seven

CAPTAIN Xikli scratched his armpit and thought: Does Jakál truly think that offering a few beating hearts to Blue Hummingbird is going to placate the god of war? Is Jakál so besotted with the rain-girl that he does not see the dangerous imbalance he is creating, the holy war he is inviting?

The drone of another man's voice brought Xikli out of his vengeful thoughts. Copil the tax collector was kneeling before him, reciting a litany of the Jaguar Captain's achievements and virtues. Xikli sighed. A boring man and a tedious situation, but one that had to be suffered all the same. In his gradual and secret campaign to bring supporters to his side, it was necessary for Xikli to tolerate the presence of such men and, worse, listen to their endless requests. Because, for each request he filled, he gained a new ally.

Finally Copil got around to the reason for this audience. He was dissatisfied with being a mere tax collector and wished to obtain the post of Superintendent of the Marketplace—a post that made the holder of it wealthy and powerful, but a post that, sadly, was already occupied.

Nonetheless Xikli asked, "If I arrange this appointment for you, what will you do for me in return?"

Copil raised solemn eyes. "Anything, great Captain."

Xikli weighed the value of this man, as well as his many worthy connections due to his office as a tax collector, and said, "I will help you."

The next morning, in the crowded plaza, Xikli found Oquitzin, Superintendent of the Marketplace, squatting in the shade and receiving a line of merchants who came with favors to ask, complaints to air, and bribes. The Superintendent looked bored, and the moment Xikli strode up with a grin on his face to challenge him to a friendly game of *patolli,* Oquitzin was instantly on his feet and shooing away the supplicants.

They chose a spot at the edge of the plaza, away from the merchants' mats displaying wares, out of the way of foot traffic, in a relatively quiet place between the kivas of the Wood Carvers' Guild and the Feather Weavers. Games always attracted onlookers, but when the combatants were men of wealth and power, it was not to be missed, and so as soon as Xikli's *patolli* mat was spread upon the paved ground and the two opponents squatted down to face one another, a large crowd gathered.

The game was played by rolling beans marked with white dots and moving one's pebble according to the number of dots rolled. Each player had three pebbles, one played red, the other blue, and the object was to move along the fifty-two squares until one managed to get three pebbles lined in a row.

The play began light and merry, with small wagers such as pieces of jade or a plump turkey. Xikli called for a scribe who came running with his kit. The man dropped to the ground, crossed his legs, and spread a fresh sheet of bark paper on his knees. With brush and paint, he hastily drew symbols and numerical figures. As the beans were rolled and the pebbles went round and round, as games ended with alternating winners, as the sun rose and the crowd grew, and the atmosphere intensified because more than sky-stone and gold was at stake—the reputations of the players themselves—the scribe's hand flew over the paper, adding more treasure to the growing jackpot: Xikli's leopard-skin armor, Oquitzin's collection of copper bells.

Around and around the pebbles went, chasing each other across the board in the four directions of time. The beans rolled. The day grew hot. Oquitzin impatiently called for shade, and his servants came running with four poles and a cotton awning. After a brief break for tortillas and beans, the game progressed, the air growing charged now as men in the crowd placed wagers among themselves, the faces of the two players set in intense concentration, each watching the other man's moves, trying to determine his hidden strategy.

Oquitzin rolled the beans, and as he surveyed the board to determine his best move, Xikli drew a noisy gulp of *chocolatl*. The Superintendent of the Marketplace tried to mask his annoyance. The Captain was employing dishonorable tactics, but there was nothing in the rules against distracting one's opponent. Oquitzin himself could use a few to unnerve Xikli, if he could just think what those tricks might be.

A break was called so that the players could retreat behind the main wall to relieve themselves. Two of Xikli's men accompanied Oquitzin, and two of Oquitzin's accompanied Xikli to ensure no cheating, while a ring of men guarded the board, their eyes on one another.

The game resumed and the sun sank into the west.

As word of the contest spread through the valley, more gamblers arrived, milling about the edge of the plaza, asking for progress and laying bets. Hearing about the competition, Lord Jakál sent men to watch and report back to him, as he could not watch the game himself, his presence being too disruptive in the marketplace. Moquihix had also heard, and sat with Jakál, making friendly wagers with him, first betting on Xikli, then on Oquitzin.

The moon rose and the two men were brought mugs of *chocolatl* to keep them alert. Torches were set out. In the flickering light, Xikli and Oquitzin, no longer relaxed and friendly, resembled two mountain rams locking horns.

Toward dawn they finally arrived at a game where there was nothing left to wager—all of Xikli's wealth and all of Oquitzin's wealth, including his villa, were in the pot. This would be the deciding game. One man would walk away wealthy, the loser impoverished.

The enormous crowd listened and watched without a sound. Early morning light crept across the canyon as dawn breezes caused the torches to sputter and wink out. Onlookers were tense now as their own wagers would be decided—whether a man had bet a feather or a gold bracelet.

It was Oquitzin's turn to throw the beans. He did so, and as he moved toward victory, lining up his three pebbles, without warning Xikli shot to his feet and bellowed, "You cheated!"

Oquitzin looked up. "Captain?"

"You dare to cheat in a game with me?"

Oquitzin's face was blank. "I did not cheat, Captain, surely you—"

The onlookers drew back, grasping the gravity of the moment. Before the commencement of any game of *patolli,* be it between two farm boys or two of the most powerful men at Center Place, the contestants always prayed to the patron god of the game, promising to play honestly and without deceit. To cheat at the game, therefore, was to commit sacrilege.

And there was only one punishment for sacrilege.

"But how—" Oquitzin began, his throat constricting in sudden fear as he stumbled to his feet, his hands outspread.

Xikli bent to snatch up the beans and held them out in his palm for all to see. "You switched them!"

Jaguars and friends of the Superintendent bent forward to examine the beans, as every man knew how to recognize a gaming bean that had been altered so that it always rolled a specific number.

It was plain to all that the beans had been tampered with.

Oquitzin turned gray and his Adam's apple went up and down. "I did not do that," he whispered. "I have never seen those beans." Frantically, he searched the floor and the game board, but found no other beans.

To the onlookers he said pleadingly, "You all know me. I do not cheat." But the looks on their faces told him he was doomed. Belatedly

Oquitzin realized that the crowd consisted of merchants who were now recalling steep bribes they had had to pay to him for a good spot in the marketplace, men who had been denied a space and as a result had lost trade. Oquitzin's gaming integrity was not even considered. Old grudges decided his fate.

In a swift move, before Oquitzin could react, Xikli yanked a club from one of his Jaguars and brought it down upon the Superintendent's head.

Oquitzin yelled in pain, and the crowd retreated.

Again and again the club came down, as Oquitzin fell to the paved floor of the plaza, trying in vain to protect himself as the blows sent blood spattering, as his cries of pain grew fainter until he finally lay still, his brains seeping out onto the paving.

The onlookers had first watched in shock, and then with indifference, for the punishment was due and just, and a few were secretly pleased that this pompous man who had fattened himself on their ill-afforded bribes should meet such an end.

Xikli looked with dispassion upon the corpse of his erstwhile friend. A loyal comrade for years, the man had outlived his usefulness. Oquitzin had nothing more to offer Xikli and therefore his death would be a useful stepping stone.

Although such coveted appointments were the purview of Moquihix the High Minister, he could not act alone but must listen to the counsel of other nobles and officials, and so it was that, after gold and sky-stone had crossed numerous palms, Moquihix was persuaded to name Copil the tax collector to the enviable post of Superintendent of the Marketplace.

Once again Copil abased himself at the feet of Captain Xikli, brimming with gratitude and heaping the blessings of the gods upon his benefactor.

Xikli remained silent, satisfied that he had done well. And all it had cost him was a percentage of the winnings in payment to the priests of Five Flower, the patron god of *patolli*. And the man who had given Xikli the trick beans, which Xikli had tucked beneath a bracelet for just the right moment, had been handsomely paid and could be counted on to keep silent. It had taken a day and a night of his time, but Xikli counted the expense worth it.

Pressing his forehead to the floor, Copil vowed allegiance forever. "I am your slave, day or night."

"When the time comes," Xikli murmured. "When the time comes."

Forty-eight

G OOD day to you!" the young man called out as he reached the top of the ladder and hoisted himself onto the terrace.

Distracted from her work, Hoshi'tiwa squinted in the morning sun and saw that the visitor was a water-carrier, a large water-skin on his bent back, the familiar tumpline across his forehead.

He looked up and down the terrace, at the vacant doorways, empty thresholds, then he settled his eyes on Hoshi'tiwa, who sat alone at her labors. "Everyone's at the Morning Star festival," he said cheerfully, "but not you?" As he drew near, he saw what she was doing and said, "Ah, you are the rain-girl everyone speaks of."

The Autumn Equinox had come and gone. The Evening Star had gradually grown brighter until it was so brilliant, it cast shadows on a moonless night, and Hoshi'tiwa, sitting on the uppermost terrace of Precious Green, worked on a new jar.

She worked alone and separate from her sister potters who, in their workshop, labored over jars large and small, plain and beautiful. Hoshi'tiwa worked with renewed passion because summoning the rain no longer had to do with her people or her family: She was doing it for Jakál.

He had said she could go home. And so she would. But before she did, she would give him a gift. She would give him rain.

Swinging the heavy waterskin from his back and decanting water into a gourd that hung from his waist, the young man said, "For free. All I ask in return is a smile."

Hoshi'tiwa looked at the proffered cup, then up into the stranger's charming grin and, noting the Bear Clan tattoo on his cheek, gratefully accepted the drink. She drank modestly, thanked him, and returned the gourd. With a flirtatious wink, he turned and made his way back to the ladder. While Hoshi'tiwa thought what a pleasant man he was, unlike the majority of water-carriers who grumbled about their lot, the young man was thinking that this would be a good place to carry out his assignment.

His name was Bone Snapper, and he had been hired to break Hoshi'tiwa's back.

Forty-nine

L IKE all men whose job involved decisions of life and death, Bone Snapper was highly superstitious.

He could have executed his assignment that morning on the terrace, while the girl was drinking from the water gourd. But he had seen that she was making a rain jar and he dared not desecrate so sacred a task. He had decided to wait and watch, knowing that the moment would come when the jar was finished and the girl's usefulness to the gods at an end.

That moment was tonight.

In a hut adjacent to the barracks, where he lived with others of his race who served Xikli and the Jaguars, Bone Snapper scoured the sweat and dirt from his body, prayed to his personal gods, and called upon the spirit of the protective token he wore around his neck.

The plan was to render the girl unconscious by a grip at her throat. And then, with his knee pressed into her lower back, crack her spine and lay her at the foot of a stairway, arranging rubble around her. She would not remember what happened, and might even believe it was an accident—that she had broken her back in a fall.

Bone Snapper had been brought to Center Place as a child and put to work as a boy-helper to the Jaguar knights. His recollections of home were meager: a settlement near a river, a mother and father, an uncle who performed comical dances. He did not recall their names but he did know his clan totem and understood the significance of the tattoos on his cheeks. He also knew that he belonged to the People of the Sun.

But he served his Toltec masters with pride.

Bone Snapper did not know where his pleasure of inflicting pain came from, but the roots lay in his early days in the barracks, doing the soldiers' bidding, helpless and without control over his own life and body. From that boy's silent rage stemmed a need to lash back. He never questioned a task put before him, nor did he ask who was requesting his services. He was now the one in control, and therefore Bone Snapper complied cheerfully and with true dedication to his calling.

His body clean, dressed in a fresh loincloth and mantle, the young man struck off into the bright afternoon, whistling a pleasant tune. He knew where the girl was and that she was nearly finished with her task. After that, it would be time to execute *his* task.

The Evening Star had vanished into the setting sun and the time that the Lords feared the most—the Eight Days—had begun, when Quetzal-coatl looked into the hearts of his people and judged their deeds to determine if they were worthy of his return as the Morning Star. After Lord Jakál had been at his sacred vigil on the promontory above Center Place for seven days to watch for the first sign of the Morning Star, Hoshi'tiwa's jar was ready for the final stage.

Late afternoon sunlight bathed her shoulders as she chose the yucca brushes and moistened the paint. As she began to lay the first stripe upon the clay, she thought of Jakál, how he had held her when she had cried in the colorful pavilion, the feel of his arms around her, the firm chest and deep voice that brought consolation—the excitement and forbidden hungers the feel of him had ignited.

O Quetzalcoatl-Pahana, she silently prayed now, pour your holy grace into this paint that my rain jar might invite the Cloud Spirits to Center Place.

Without conscious thought, her mind focusing on the repeated chant, she dipped the brush into the dye and drew a line on the jar. She knew what she would paint: a symmetry of clouds and sky and rain, not graphically realistic but in symbols that the gods would recognize.

O Quetzalcoatl-Pahana, pour your holy grace into this paint that my rain jar might invite the Cloud Spirits to Center Place.

She drew a curved line, a dot, a spiral. She dipped her brush again and her hand moved on its own.

O Quetzalcoatl-Pahana, pour your holy grace into this paint that my rain jar might invite the Cloud Spirits to Center Place.

She stopped hearing the wind, stopped feeling the sun on her skin as the brush went into the dye and returned to the smooth, curved surface of the jar.

O Quetzalcoatl-Pahana, pour your holy grace into this paint that my rain jar might invite the Cloud Spirits to Center Place.

And suddenly, unbidden, a voice from the past whispered its way into her somnolent mind: "The Dark Lord has chosen you for himself," her mother had said as they were huddled high up in the cliff house. "He will join his body with yours."

Her hand moving on its own, Hoshi'tiwa recalled the long walk afterward, shackled to other slaves so that she could not run away, Noseless complaining that now he had the added burden of guarding her virginity, and Hoshi'tiwa the whole while dreading the moment when she would be taken to the Dark Lord to be an instrument of his pleasure. She had thought then that she would rather die.

And now she thought that if she did *not* join with him, she would die.

Her thoughts shocked her. They were impure and impious and not to be entertained while she was about her sacred task. Yet try though she did to suppress these ideas, she could not, for as soon as one was tamed, another bubbled to the surface.

She focused her thoughts, repeated her silent chant until she moved trancelike at her task, moistening the paint, dipping the brush, drawing the lines, not seeing the swirls and dots and circles as the brush caressed the clay, covering every surface of the jar in patterns and symbols and design.

And so lost in hypnotic thought that she was oblivious of an observer on the terrace below, the young water-carrier who now watched her with singular attention.

When the final prayer was recited and the last symbol painted, Hoshi'tiwa brought herself back to full awareness and set her brush aside. Straightening her aching back and unfolding her pained legs, she realized in shock that the sun had set and night was coming. She had had no awareness of the passage of time. And then she saw the design on the jar and her eyes widened in astonishment.

It was like nothing she had ever seen.

The pattern was not the one she had intended. In fact, it wasn't a pattern at all, but something ugly and chaotic. She gasped in dismay. How could she have painted it without knowing? Had a spirit guided her hand? Had she been in a trance? And what a terrible design. The Cloud Spirits would despise it!

But there was no time to remedy the error. The kiln in the Precious Green kitchen had been in readiness for hours, and she had wanted to offer the new jar to Lord Jakál upon the first rising of the Morning Star.

Hurrying downstairs, past a young man waiting in shadow, she slipped her jar into the stone oven and whispered a prayer. As she waited for the fire to give life to the clay, her eyes went up to the promontory, where she saw Jakál holding vigil for the appearance of his god, just as she now held vigil beside her baking jar.

Many people of Center Place watched the eastern sky for the first glimmer of the Morning Star. Even such nonbelievers as old Pikami and Yellow Feather looked out of their hut at the cool, dying night, anxious that the star would appear so that they would know the world was still in harmony, that the heavens would roll on as they always had, that those things which people had depended upon for generations could still be depended upon.

White Orchid, cradling a magic snake in a box on her lap, sat tensely in her garden, praying that a man named Bone Snapper was successful

tonight; Xikli stood with his Jaguars, ready to cheer or to revolt; Moquihix gnawed his lip while a new slave girl waited for him on his sleeping
mat; Yani glanced over her shoulder as she stole in the darkness toward a
secret destination, unaware that Chief Physician Nagual followed.

And Bone Snapper, waiting outside the kitchen door for the rain-girl
to retrieve her jar from the kiln, smiled in anticipation.

Hoshi'tiwa gently fanned the flames so that the heat remained high,
but not too high that the clay might explode, until finally she let the fire
die, slipped the wooden tongs into the warm ash, and brought the new
rain jar into the torchlight. As she had planned, the vessel was more
beautiful than any she had made, than any she had ever seen, the background the color of golden spring poppies, the painted design a deep
bloodred.

She frowned in dismay. Patterns on pottery were intended to symbolize the balance of nature, its harmony. *This* design was chaotic. There
was no balance, no harmony. It was certainly something she would never
have painted.

It frightened her. Had an evil spirit possessed her while she painted?
Was this impossible design meant for black magic?

As the valley watched and waited in pre-dawn silence, as Bone Snapper hidden in shadow grew tense and watchful, Hoshi'tiwa stared at
what she had unwittingly wrought, and suddenly she saw in the perceived chaos what was clearly a four-legged creature.

She blinked. The more she stared, the more she realized that, yes, it
was an animal of some sort. A mountain sheep or a dog. And then she
saw what might be a tree. And another symbol depicting water. Here, a
star.

She began to tremble with excitement.

The design she had painted was not chaos after all! Not random lines
and swirls and dots but actual objects in a cosmos filled with objects.
And then she realized that out of each object—whether a tree or a star
or an elk—other symbols grew, lines connected, forming a web that en-
compassed the entire jar, connecting all things with all things.

In an instant her heart burst open and her mind yawned wide, as if shackles had been severed, tightly bound ties had been cut—her thoughts, her emotions, and her spirit shot up to the starry sky like doves released from a cage.

She ran to the kitchen's threshold from where she could see all of Center Place, and even though she was seeing it as she had been seeing it since her arrival—the fields and paths, huts and villas—she suddenly saw the valley in a different way—crisper, clearer, as if a layer of fog had been lifted. Hoshi'tiwa saw how connected it all was, like a giant cosmic net, the paths connecting the houses, the smoke spiraling up to connect with the sky. She looked toward the road that had brought her from her settlement in the north, and she suddenly saw how it ultimately connected her to the clan. She felt no longer plucked from her family, to live separately from them in a distant place because she knew that if she put one foot upon the terminus of that road, here at Center Place, it would be as if she were setting foot upon its terminus at the other end, in front of her mother's adobe house.

Lifting the bear claw from under her dress, she looked at it in the moonlight. Ahoté had given it to her, and thus the claw connected her to him as surely as all the patterns on the jar were connected.

She closed her eyes. *Everything intermeshed, from a woman's joy to the fluttering of a butterfly's wings to the piquant spice of chilies.*

Trembling with joy, she looked up at the silhouette standing on the promontory and suddenly needed to tell Jakál.

With the warm jar in her arms, Hoshi'tiwa ran from the kitchen, across the plaza where a few people stood watching Jakál, and started up the steps carved into the limestone cliff. She did not know that a man followed her. Was unaware that he fell silently into step behind her, that he grinned when he saw her start up the stairs because she was making his job easy for him.

But when she had gone part of the way, she stopped and turned to peer into the dark shadows pooled at the foot of the stairs. "Who is there?" she called softly.

He pressed against the wall and held his breath. When he saw that she still carried the rain jar, he frowned. He had not planned for this. He must make certain it did not break when he rendered her unconscious.

Hoshi'tiwa continued to search the darkness at the foot of the stairway. Her senses were heightened, her intuition sharp. She could swear that someone was down there, watching.

"Who are you?" she whispered. "What do you want?"

Bone Snapper slowly released his breath, then slowly inhaled, holding himself as still as the stone wall that hid him, his mind calculating. The moment she turned and started back up the stairs, he would take three steps in stride, seize her throat and—

He froze. His eye caught something in the starlight he had not seen before. An object that lay against the white cotton of her tunic.

His eyes shot open. It was a bear claw! Just like the one he himself wore, because he was Bear Clan.

Bone Snapper froze in indecision. The girl was Tortoise Clan; the tattoo on her forehead was clear. Yet she wore a Bear Clan talisman. What did it mean?

His thoughts flew—Tortoise Clan girl wearing Bear Clan token, and the job he was supposed to do tonight—until finally his shoulders slumped. There was no doubt. He dared not touch her. Though Tortoise Clan, the girl was protected by the spirit totem of his clan. And for as long as she wore the talisman, he could not harm her.

Slowly Bone Snapper backed down the stairs and dissolved into shadow, and Hoshi'tiwa, thinking it had been a trick of the eye, turned and resumed her ascent on the stairs.

When she reached the top of the mesa, she emerged onto the ledge reserved for the Prince of Toltecs. While Lord Jakál remained transfixed, his face toward the east, the humble corn farmer's daughter waited and watched in anxious anticipation, clutching the still-warm rain jar to her as if she had caught a falling star, and she prayed with all her heart that the Morning Star return to Center Place.

And then . . .

A spark on the horizon. A dot of flickering light.

And Lord Jakál, humble servant of the Lord of the Breath of Life, lifted his arms and cried, "He is risen! The god is risen!" And those gathered below erupted in cheers, Jaguars thumped their shields, trumpets sounded.

Jakál turned abruptly to see Hoshi'tiwa standing there. And his moment of ecstasy was complete.

"Look, my Lord," she said, approaching him, holding out the ceramic fresh from the kiln.

Night still hung over the mesa, but there was sufficient starlight to see the details of her handiwork. "It is beautiful," he said, puzzling over the strange design, wondering why she had brought it.

"I have something to tell you, my Lord," she said, looking up at him, a strange new courage filling her as she felt bold enough to speak, to say anything that was in her heart, to the supreme ruler of Center Place. "I believe I was brought to Center Place to create a rain jar, but *not* to bring rain, to receive an illumination."

He took the warm ceramic from her, and as he turned it round and round, making no sense of the pattern painted upon it, a small entourage emerged onto the mesa from the top of the carved stairs—Moquihix and the priests of Quetzalcoatl. Seeing their Lord with the rain-girl, standing close and speaking quietly while the Morning Star winked brilliantly upon the horizon, Moquihix quickly recovered from shock and gave hasty thought to the situation. When the girl had first been brought to Center Place, a shooting star was seen at sunset in the southwestern sky. The Star Readers had declared it a dire omen—but of what, no one could say.

Moquihix wondered now if that omen were a message, because this was the second time the girl had walked upon consecrated ground at the first sighting of the Morning Star. And the god had not stricken her dead.

Although his mind wanted to have her arrested and punished, his heart told him there was more afoot here than mere mortals could discern. This was now in the hands of the gods. Turning on his heel, the High Minister of Center Place, his heart heavy with foreboding and doubt, led the entourage back down the cliff and wondered if this new day was going to begin the end of the world.

"Illumination?" Jakál queried softly, not having seen Moquihix and the priests depart, unaware of celebrations going on in the valley, not knowing that a new and different dawn was in fact about to break over Center Place. All he was aware of was Hoshi'tiwa's face, turned up to him, her eyes shining in the darkness.

"We are living in the Fourth World, my Lord," she said passionately, "what your people call the Fifth World. Before this, we lived in other world cycles, which we have forgotten. Each time, in order to survive, the people retreated underground. When we lived in the previous worlds, humans knew the nature of life and the cosmos, we possessed secret wisdom. But then calamity struck and the world was destroyed. While we lived underground, we forgot that wisdom. We remember the destruction but not the wisdom of our ancestors, whom we call the Ancient Ones."

Jakál already knew all this, but he listened nonetheless, rapt, watching her moist lips as words tumbled from them.

"After we climbed out of the earth and into this world," she said with zeal, "we were no longer unified but had separated ourselves from the gods and the animals. We thought of ourselves as isolated from everything around us. Before I made the jar, I gathered clay, temper, water, vegetable dye. What I did not realize, my Lord, was that *I already had the jar*. It simply waited for me to give it form! The sky is also in this jar," she said as she laid her hands on the ceramic, which he still held, placing her small hands beside his larger ones, as if the two together held the world between their palms, "because the sky's wind dried the clay. Sunlight is in the jar, because the sun baked the clay. Fire is in the jar, because fire hardened the clay. All these things are in the jar."

She spoke softly but urgently, as the eastern horizon grew pale and priests thumped drums in the plaza far below, and Jakál listened to her excited voice as he looked down at the slender fingers touching his.

"My Lord, this jar *is* the cosmos, and the design which I painted upon it as a spirit moved my hand, represents what my people call *suukya'qatsi*—the Unbroken Oneness."

Jakál watched as her tongue moistened her lips, and her eyes sparkled with excitement, and the dawn wind toyed with errant strands of her long hair.

"*Suukya'qatsi* is a very ancient word, my Lord. It comes not from the language of the People of the Sun but from distant memory, a word that swims in our blood before we are born. I heard it for the first time when I brought the jar out of the kiln and saw its design. *Suukya'qatsi*. I understand now that I am no longer alone, my Lord! Nor are your people if Tollan has fallen. You are afraid of being cut off from your race if your city falls, but how can you be cut off when all things are connected?"

Although she had posed a question, she gave him no time to respond. "My Lord, I have experienced the most glorious opening of my spirit. I was one with all of nature. The stars touched me."

And Jakál, infected by her ardor, his head swimming with her intensity and nearness, thought: If stars can touch her, then surely so can I.

"I see it all now, my Lord. As you must prepare for the coming of Quetzalcoatl, my people must ready themselves for the return of Pahana. They must be prepared for his return and the new golden age. I must teach them what I have learned tonight—"

Hoshi'tiwa stopped suddenly, filled with awe and wonder as she realized in that instant that she was indeed the Tortoise Clan girl foretold by Yani's grandfather's grandfather. In the next instant she was aware of Jakál's nearness, as they both held on to the rain jar, the intensity in his eyes as he looked down at her, his tall form backdropped by dark sky and stars, while behind her the sky was growing pale. A lump formed in her throat and she suddenly had difficultly speaking. "My Lord, you and I together will prepare the way for our white brother who will return and bring about the new world."

"The new world," he murmured, "yes," as he took the rain jar from her hands and gently placed it on the ground. When he straightened, his eyes bored into hers. Hoshi'tiwa could not breathe. While the world celebrated the return of the Morning Star, she saw only this man whom she had once feared and hated, whom she had called Dark, but who now confused her and filled her with strange, exciting emotions.

He suddenly seized her by the shoulders and, bending his head, pressed his lips to hers. His mouth stifled her cry. She felt as if she had been struck by lightning. Electricity shot through her. Hoshi'tiwa flung her arms around Jakál's neck to bring him closer. Their bodies came together.

As the celestial manifestation of Quetzalcoatl rose in the east, in a bright winking light that future generations would call Venus, the Lord of Center Place crushed the humble rain-girl to himself, he could not kiss her hard enough or long enough, his hands greedy for her flesh, while Hoshi'tiwa clung to him as if he were an oak in a monsoon, holding on to him to keep from being swept away.

He thought he had never felt so alive. She thought she was going to burst into flame.

For the Eight Days vigil, a small pavilion had been erected on the mesa. Jakál drew Hoshi'tiwa into it now, into the privacy of colorful cotton walls and roof, to lay her down on soft buffalo hide blankets. His kisses were gentler now, and he went slowly, even though Hoshi'tiwa urged him to hurry, hungry for more. And then she experienced another kind of connectedness, the complete joining of man and woman, and she felt not only his flesh bonded with hers, but his soul as well.

She cried afterward, but only from an overwhelming flood of emotions. She smiled as she cried, and touched him here, there, rubbing her nose to his in the kiss of the People of the Sun.

Lifting himself up on an elbow, Jakál traced a fingertip over her eyebrow and said, "The first time I held one of your golden jars in my hands I felt a connection to you that I could not explain. It was as if I were holding *you* in my hands. And we were bound together in that moment. Our two destinies became one."

She watched his lips as he spoke, marveling at the exciting way the Toltecs kissed. Marveling at so much else—the feel of his masculinity, his power, and the ease with which she had welcomed him into her body. No longer the girl in the cottonwood forest who preferred to think of cooking suppers for her husband rather than imagine making love to him.

"Come live with me, Summer Rain. I will elevate you higher than before. I will make you the first handmaiden of Quetzalcoatl at Center Place."

"Yes," she said. "I will live with you." Silently she added: And I will love you. But once again, as long ago among cottonwood trees, she was unable to utter the words. However, the day would come when she would tell him freely what was in her heart. "We will teach my people about *suukya'qatsi* so that they will be ready for the return of Quetzalcoatl-Pahana."

"Granted!" he said with a soft laugh. Other women might ask for sky-stone or gold at such a moment, but Hoshi'tiwa thought only of gods.

"And please, my Lord, may my people be allowed to practice their ancient rites?"

In that moment, as sunlight broke over the mesa, bathing it in a golden sea, he would have granted her anything, even personal posses-sion of the moon were it in his power. "I see no harm in it, Summer Rain. With more of your people coming to Center Place, it will mollify them to follow their traditional ways."

As he bent to kiss her again on the lips, she moved her head to the side and gave him a puzzled smile. "*More* of my people coming?"

"To build my pyramid," he said with zeal. "I will need many work-ers. And when Quetzalcoatl sees the magnificent temple I have placed atop the pyramid, he will come!"

She blinked. "But Quetzalcoatl-Pahana does not need a temple. He will come in the cornfields, he will walk along the rivers and down from the mountains."

Jakál caressed her shoulder, desiring to make love again. "Men have always built monuments to the gods," he murmured.

"The gods don't need man-made monuments, my Lord." Feeling a sudden chill sweep into the pavilion, Hoshi'tiwa shifted away from Jakál and sat up, drawing a buffalo blanket over her nakedness. "There are monuments everywhere—the mountains, the desert, the prairie. You don't need more of my people to build something artificial. You don't need to take more of my people from their farms and homes and ances-tral lands and make slaves of them."

She fell silent, and when she saw a quizzical look in his eyes, she finally gave voice to the forbidden thought she had been suppressing for so long: "It isn't right."

He remained puzzled. The will of the *tlatoani* wasn't a matter of right or wrong, it simply *was*. He said, "But already Jaguars are marching to the four corners to bring back an army of workers. The farms and settlements are to give up all men who are able-bodied. Even small boys will be needed, for they can carry water and run with messages. Once the foundation is laid and the first level is under way, the construction will fill the valley with the glorious sound of industry. Summer Rain," he said, reaching for her, "your eyes will be astounded by what they will see. A magnificent pyramid, rising to the sky, with hundreds of steps climbing to a glorious temple, and—"

She recoiled, a look of horror on her face. "It is wrong," she protested.

"It is not wrong. Your people will be building a monument to the glory of Quetzalcoatl. They will be honored in the afterlife."

"They want to be honored in *this* life," she said, shaking with shock and a sudden feeling of betrayal, made all the sharper by his having told her this news *after* they made love. "Be like a father to my people, my Lord," she pleaded. "Please do not bring more of my kinsmen to Center Place."

Taking her by the shoulders, he said, "You claim that you hope my god returns. You say that you pray for the return of Quetzalcoatl. And yet you will do nothing to help me build my pyramid. Your mouth speaks one thing—your heart speaks another."

What my heart speaks, you will never know! Hoshi'tiwa silently cried as she pulled herself from Jakál's grasp, struggling to her feet, tears of disappointment filling her eyes. Day had broken over the plateau, and when Jakál also rose to his feet, she saw before her a stranger, tall and forbiddingly handsome, but no longer the man to whom she wished to give her body and her heart—a conqueror who thought only of his own selfish aims at the sacrifice of her people.

She looked down at the things she had worn when she came up to the mesa, and she was horrified at the rich cotton dress, the luxurious mantle, the leather sandals. She thought of her room on the fifth tier, the slave who cooked and cleaned for her, and she recalled her sister potters throwing her gifts into the dust, the resentful looks of her kinsmen as they toiled on the foundation of the pyramid.

Shafts of golden sunlight shot across the mesa, illuminating parched brown brush against the orange-and-red landscape, and Hoshi'tiwa thought: I have been living in a dream.

"What are you doing?" Jakál said as she turned and walked out of the pavilion. He gathered up his loincloth and hastily wrapped it around himself. But Hoshi'tiwa did not get dressed. Instead she let the buffalo blanket fall so that she stood unclothed in the morning light. The sight of her nakedness, the full breasts, narrow waist flaring into wide hips, caused the breath to catch in his throat.

And then he saw the angry look on her face as she stripped off her sky-stone and gold bracelets, throwing them to the ground until all that was left was a humble bear claw suspended on a leather thong between her breasts.

"I know my destiny," she said with challenge in her tone. "And it is *not* joined with yours."

Jakál was speechless. Her skin glowed like golden honey in the new dawn. Her body was lush and desirable. Desire and fury clashed within him. He had never been so immobilized.

Retrieving the rain jar, Hoshi'tiwa said in a defiant tone, "This I will keep, for it belongs to my people. To them I will carry its message since you have rejected it."

He opened his mouth, but no voice came out. Emotions marched across his features—confusion, anger, regret. He pointed to the blankets where they had known ecstasy. "And what was that?" he asked softly.

Now it was her turn for emotions to traverse her face, and they were the same as his. "You took pleasure with Summer Rain," she said, her lip trembling, her voice tight as she suppressed a sob. "But I am Hoshi'tiwa, of the People of the Sun."

With her head held high but with her heart shattered with grief and disappointment, she turned and walked away from him, purposefully, even though her feet wanted to turn her around and run back to him—over the orange-and-yellow sand she strode, to disappear into a brace of stunted cottonwood trees, leaving Lord Jakál, ruler of Center Place and the most powerful man in the land, to stand alone beneath the cloudless morning sky.

BOOK FIVE

Suukya'qatsi

Fifty

WHERE was everybody?

Yani nervously wrung her hands as she waited near the entrance of the secret cave, watching for members of the cult to arrive. She had spent the morning preparing for the Winter Solstice ritual, and it was soon to begin. But so far only a few worshippers had shown up.

The number of believers in the secret kachina faith was growing. People of the Sun who were denied their ancestral ceremonies, and who were revolted by the violent gods of the Toltecs, were finding comfort and solace among the benevolent spirits recently arrived from the south. Soon, Yani thought in deep satisfaction, we will outgrow this cave and will have to find another secret venue to hold our rites.

But she had expected so many more on this important day that was sacred to both People of the Sun and Toltec. Even now, as the sun carved its arc in the winter sky, drums and flutes and rattles could be heard throughout the valley as the priestly brotherhoods emerged from their rising-splendors to gather at the main plaza for the day's celebrations. Yani and her companions also had drums and flutes, and burned sacred incense. Soon, the spirit named Cold Sun would emerge from the hidden chambers at the back of the cave to lead the celebrants in an uplifting chant.

But more people should have arrived by now. Had the whereabouts of this cave been discovered, and her friends were staying away out of fear?

A girl came running in then, the embroidery on her shift identifying her as a member of the Basket Weavers' Guild. "The others will not be coming today," she said breathlessly.

"Why not?" Yani cried in dismay, and those gathered in the cave murmured nervously.

"They are going to the sacred Sun Dagger. There is to be a traditional ritual there! Oh, Yani, isn't it wonderful? Who would dare to stage such a thing?"

Yani knew. Hoshi'tiwa. And it was not, as the girl thought, a "wonderful" thing.

Although several in the valley had witnessed the shocking spectacle on the mesa on the morning of the first Morning Star—when Lord Jakál was seen embracing and kissing the rain-girl Hoshi'tiwa—none knew what had transpired afterward (although most suspected that Jakál had taken pleasure with her and Hoshi'tiwa was no longer a virgin). Therefore what followed, in the days afterward, had further shocked and baffled everyone: The girl had appeared in the valley, suddenly and with no warning, dressed simply, barefoot and carrying a breathtakingly beautiful rain jar, and had begun visiting people at their work or at their hearths, to deliver a message of wisdom and simplicity. She had given up her Toltec name, material possessions, and her residence at Precious Green to take up a life of itinerant wandering and preaching.

It baffled Yani. Her own benign kachina cult was being persecuted. Already, a few followers had been tortured and executed. But Hoshi'tiwa, with her seditious talk of a faith that did not need priests or stone idols, was free to go about in the sun.

Yani suspected it was because of Lord Jakál. Although he had surprised everyone with his edict that the girl Hoshi'tiwa was forbidden to leave Center Place, he had taken no further steps to quell her new teachings, which were a blatant admonition to ignore the Toltec ways and return to those of the ancestors. What, therefore, *had* happened up on the mesa that fateful morning? And why was Lord Jakál now so furiously about the work of laying his pyramid's foundation that he was acting like a man obsessed? The whole valley was abuzz with gossip about the *tlatoani*'s new tireless energy as he stepped up work and demanded more slaves and even insisted that construction be done at night when spirits walked the land.

Yani suspected the root of this new furious energy. He doesn't know what to do with Hoshi'tiwa, she thought as she stepped out into the cold, pale sunlight and squinted toward the eastern end of the valley. She could not see the Sun Dagger, but she could picture it—the tall column of ancient butte, striated and majestic, at the foot of which lived the old Sun Watcher priest, even though his office had long since been outlawed.

Hoshi'tiwa was there now, the basket weaver explained, and a number of People of the Sun were with her, praying with the old Sun Watcher and holding vigil as the sun slowly cast its shadow upon the sacred carvings that had been etched into the rock generations ago.

Yani had heard Hoshi'tiwa's new message. One day, in a corner of the marketplace, Yani had seen a small knot of people paying rapt attention to something, or someone, in their midst. Yani had reached the perimeter of the small group just as Hoshi'tiwa was saying, "We must unite as a people again. You remember as children, those of you who grew up on outlying farms, how the rain came when all the clan prayed together. Here at Center Place, the People of the Sun do not pray together. You observe ceremonies in the plaza, but you are not part of them. Our grandfathers held rituals at the sacred Sun Dagger four times a year, and all the people prayed together. We were united. It is in united prayer that the world is kept in balance and harmony. We must be connected again, as we are in the design on this jar. Sky-spirits and sun- and earth-spirits guided my hand when I painted this. It shows us the way."

"But our old ways are forbidden," a women had said in a low voice, and Yani recognized her as the newest member of the kachina cult. "We are punished if we perform the rites of our ancestors."

"And that is why the rain stays away," Hoshi'tiwa had said in a voice that was tinged, Yani could not help notice, with a new strain of maturity. Where had Hoshi'tiwa suddenly found the courage to be so outspoken? Yani realized that a subtle transformation had taken place. The previously shy and modest Hoshi'tiwa was speaking with passion, and Yani wondered if Hoshi'tiwa's encounter with Jakál on the mesa had somehow set her free.

"We must find the strength in our hearts to live the way we have lived for generations, not as the overlords live," Hoshi'tiwa said with conviction. "We must respect the spirits of nature, for we are connected to them. Sky-spirit and sun-spirit and earth-spirit are not made of stone. They are the sky, the sun, the earth. Nor do they have names as people do, but are called Sky, Sun, and Earth. And we honor them by paying respects to them each morning, thanking them for taking care of us. In this way we will restore balance and harmony, and Pahana will return. He will come to prevent the end of the Fourth World. But he will not come if we live as we do now."

Yani had walked away with her heart racing. Several in the group were members of her cult, and it appeared Hoshi'tiwa was winning their hearts away from the kachinas. But Hoshi'tiwa was the girl prophesied to unite the People of the Sun, not to divide them! If only I could bring her to a kachina ritual, Yani thought. But the problem was, Yani didn't know if she could trust Hoshi'tiwa.

What really happened between her and Lord Jakál?

Feeling a chill at the mouth of the cave, Yani drew her cloak tighter about herself. Noting the position of the sun, Yani turned back inside and said, "The hour draws nigh. Though there are fewer of us, we will honor the spirit Cold Sun so that he grants us a new year and sends the sun backward on its course toward summer."

But silently, to herself, Yani said: I must find a way to steer Hoshi'tiwa from her erroneous path, bring her to the kachinas, and fulfill the ancient prophecy.

Fifty-one

T H E day of the magic serpent arrived.

White Orchid had coddled and nurtured the exotic creature with constant care and attention, feeding it live mice and as much water as it wanted despite the increasing shortage in the valley. She had consulted with two astrologers to determine the most auspicious date for giving the gift to Lord Jakál, and then she had had to wait for the snake to be in the right phase of its yearly cycle, when the Caravan Master had said the venom would be at its sweetest and most potent.

The day was at hand.

As she dressed with care, applied cosmetic, and selected her jewelry, White Orchid thought about the recent chain of events that had upset her world: Bone Snapper failing in his mission so that Hoshi'tiwa was unharmed and able to walk; the shocking spectacle high on the promontory on the first dawn of the Morning Star—Jakál kissing the girl; and then, to White Orchid's surprise, the girl appearing in the valley, plainly dressed and going about preaching, according to the kitchen slaves, a doctrine of ancient wisdom. "She is a holy woman," White Orchid's cook had said, herself born to the People of the Sun.

And now, Lord Jakál's perplexing obsession to step up the work on his new pyramid.

His schedule for building had grown frenetic, even to the point of work being done at night, filling the valley with the light of a thousand blazing torches. Long lines of men labored day and night beneath whips to form the first level of the pyramid, spreading the sand, laying the bricks. Jakál barely ate or slept, it was said.

What was the cause of this new driven behavior? White Orchid wondered. It did not matter. Once the magic venom had done its job, she would not have to worry about the rain-girl ever again, and she would have Jakál and, through him, connection to a bloodline once more.

As White Orchid neared the colorful pavilion at the edge of the construction site, she heard voices within, Lord Jakál saying, "Why have you not wiped out this seditious cult?"

And Chief Physician Nagual, responding in an even tone, "I am not lax in my diligence, my Lord. But they keep changing the secret locations of their meetings. These canyons and ravines are riddled with caves. We find one, and the cultists move to another. But if I may venture, my Lord, perhaps we should not be as concerned with the kachina followers as with the rain-girl who is freely preaching—"

"Enough!" snapped Jakál, cutting him off.

A moment later, Nagual emerged from the pavilion, a thunderous expression on his face.

The guard posted outside signaled for Lady White Orchid to enter. Jakál was not an easy man to gain audience with these days, because, despite his obsession with the new pyramid, he still must see to his regular duties as governor of Center Place. She stepped around the bright red cotton wall that was a windbreak and saw building plans drawn on bark paper strewn everywhere. When White Orchid saw a sleeping mat in one corner of the pavilion, it surprised her. Jakál even slept here.

He was alone, dressed in a loincloth the color of sky-stone and a scarlet cloak knotted at his neck. He was frowning over a large square of bark paper bearing symbols of measurement and quantity. When he looked up, it took him a moment to register recognition. "Lady," he said with a nod.

White Orchid tried to hide her shock over his appearance. New lines etched his face, shadows encircled his eyes, and there was gauntness to his cheeks that had not been there before. "I bring you a gift, my Lord," she said and held out the gaily decorated box.

He looked at it, a furrow forming between his brows, as if no one had given him a gift before and he didn't know what to do.

She extended the box and he took it, staring at it as he held the ornately carved mahogany in his hands. The palms of his hands were callused, White Orchid noticed, which was not normal for a *tlatoani,* who had others to do work for him. In his new heated obsession with his pyramid, she reasoned, he must be laboring with the workers. It was not unheard of. The gods were known to appreciate a man who toiled on their behalf.

"Open it, my Lord," White Orchid said, "but only look in. Do not put your hand inside, as it is a live creature from the jungles far to the south."

When the lid came off, Jakál looked for a protracted moment at the reptile inside. As he did, White Orchid held her breath. *"Just one strike,"* the Caravan Master had warned. *"As soon as the snake bites, withdraw it at once, for a second bite will be lethal."*

She kept her eyes fast on Jakál, his head bent over the box as he stared at the small red snake, and her heart thumped wildly as she silently prayed that, unable to resist, he would reach in to touch the creature's slim, scaly body. One strike, she thought, and you are mine, and the terrible truth of my birth can be forgotten. . . .

But Jakál was not thinking of the snake or wondering if he should touch it, nor were his thoughts upon his gracious visitor with the delectable perfume. He was thinking of Hoshi'tiwa, hating her, aching for her, wishing he could banish her to the sky-stone mines, wishing he could summon her to his sleeping mat. And yet he could! She could be his. All he had to do was stop bringing more men to build his pyramid, for that was her price. A simple choice, he thought bitterly: Take Hoshi'tiwa as his lover, or build his pyramid. He could not do both. He must choose between the woman and his god.

What a fool he had been, allowing himself to be misled by a face like the moon and lips like bruised berries. How she had stood naked before him in the Morning Star's dawn, defiantly, as if to say: Feast your eyes upon what you will never have again.

He had wanted to strike her. He had wanted to kiss her. Even now, as his eyes came into focus and he found himself holding a wooden box with a tiny jungle creature inside, the two halves of his warring soul clashed.

"You may stroke it," White Orchid urged, mistaking his hesitancy for fear. "But carefully . . ."

Jakál lifted a hand and brought it down to the box. White Orchid braced herself. She would seize his wrist as soon as he was bitten, and pluck his hand out of harm's way. But, to her surprise, when Jakál reached in, it was not tentatively as another man might do, but boldly, sliding his hand under the snake to lift it out of the box.

To White Orchid's horror, the snake immediately curled itself around his wrist, forked tongue flickering in and out. "My Lord," she began, frozen with fear. With the snake thus wrapped around Jakál's forearm, how could she prevent it from striking twice?

And then, to her further surprise, the snake did not strike Jakál, nor did he seem afraid of it.

"I was told," she said with a tightness in her chest that she thought was going to make her faint, "that the snake possesses magical qualities."

Jakál lifted his wrist so that his eyes were level with those of the serpent. "The snake is one of Quetzalcoatl's earthly incarnations," he murmured. "When I was a novice in the priesthood back in Tollan, we handled many snakes, poisonous and benign. I had one just like this as a pet, and I carried him about with me curled on my wrist like a bracelet." His smile was bittersweet with recollection. "I liked to chase girls with it."

White Orchid's heart thumped wildly against her ribs. "Some snakes are poisonous, my Lord. I was—" The lie made her stammer. "I . . . was assured that this one is . . . not."

Jakál shook his head. "This little beauty is the most harmless of creatures. The gods created her to please the eye, not to terminate life."

"Then—" White Orchid licked her red lips. "Then it will not bite?"

"Never," he said, replacing the snake in its box. He offered White Orchid a sad smile. "It is a pleasing gift. I am touched."

But his eyes did not meet hers as he said this, focusing instead upon a point above her head, as if he envisioned someone else standing there, and White Orchid was suddenly filled with fury. The Caravan Master had tricked her! She remembered now that the old herbal peddler had said the snake with the aphrodisiac venom was *green,* and this one was red. The Caravan Master had not sent men into the jungle on a dangerous reptile hunt but had most likely plucked a harmless snake from his own garden. He had preyed upon her obvious desperation, pretending to bring a magic snake and taking her entire shell collection in trade. And he had clearly invented the so-called special phases in its life cycle so that he could be sure to be well away from Center Place before she gave the snake to Jakál and learned the truth.

As she left the pavilion, with Jakál absently thanking her for the gift and returning to his diagrams, White Orchid thought of the witch, the terrible crone who lived deep in the canyons, neither Toltec nor People of the Sun. *Her* magic, it was whispered, never failed.

But, White Orchid had heard, such magic came at a terrible price. . . .

Fifty-two

"I AM *the blood and you are the clay,*" Jakál had said in her dream. But in real life he had told her of his plan to enslave more of her people.

Outwardly, Hoshi'tiwa appeared to be serene and at peace, but inside she was in turmoil. Was it possible to love *and* hate? She had lain with Jakál, surrendered her body and soul to him, and then he had betrayed her. How could pain and ecstasy reside in the same heart?

"Here we are," Yani said, and Hoshi'tiwa found herself at the mouth of a cave. "You must promise not to tell anyone what I am about to show you."

Hoshi'tiwa pulled herself from her thoughts and looked at Yani, whose graying hair, coiled like a crown on her head, was wrapped in ribbons the color of sky-stone. Yani had appeared that morning at old Pikami's hut, where Hoshi'tiwa was living now that Yellow Feather had found a man to take care of her and her baby, to whisper a confession: "I am the leader of a secret cult."

Hoshi'tiwa had readily accepted Yani's invitation to observe a kachina ritual. Spirits and faith were foremost on Hoshi'tiwa's mind—when she wasn't wrestling with her feelings for Jakál—ever since the morning she had walked down the stairs carved into the mesa, wearing nothing but Ahoté's bear claw and carrying the new rain jar.

After defiantly turning her back on Jakál, to walk away from him and a beautiful future with him, Hoshi'tiwa had found a small copse of cottonwoods tucked away off the ravine, and there she had spent the day crying in bitter disappointment. Despite the cold temperature, because it was the middle of autumn, she remained hidden there, without food or water or comfort, with no company except for the mythical animals and people decorating the golden ceramic, and when night fell she had made her way, unseen, across the valley to Pikami's hut. There she fasted and prayed and purified herself with sacred herbs and incense. When she was done she dressed in a simple white shift, her hair plainly coiled without colorful ribbons or adornment, and, with no sandals on her feet, she had struck out into the valley carrying the rain jar to spread the message of the Old Ones.

She preached to whomever would listen, and she would tell them that a new world was coming. She had seen the new world and had painted it on her rain jar so that others might see it. In humble dwellings she found small idols of Toltec gods. She heard prayers recited in the language of the south, meant for the ears of foreign deities. People of the Sun attended rituals in the plaza that they did not understand. They did not protest when their kinsmen were led to the altar of blood. They did not raise their voices when Toltec men used their women and discarded them.

As she went about the valley, urging her brothers and sisters to return to the ways of the ancestors, people fed her and gave her shelter, sharing what little they had. She wasn't welcomed at all hearths. Some drove her away, saying, "We are taken care of by the Lords."

As Hoshi'tiwa now followed Yani into the secret cave, her thoughts returned to Jakál, because he had her heart no matter how much her mind and spirit denied it. She knew they could be lovers. But it would be at the expense of her people. If she gave up preaching in the valley, she could live with Jakál and it would be a life wonderful beyond imagining.

But the golden jar had spoken to her, and now *she* must speak to the People of the Sun.

The air inside the cave was thick with smoke from burning pine pitch and incense. Torchlight flickered, creating eerie shadows on the uneven, rocky walls. People smiled and nodded welcome as Hoshi'tiwa took a seat among them. She looked around in curiosity, noting the wooden figurines lined up on stony shelves and standing in niches: dolls dressed as humans but with inhuman faces. Some of the figurines held cornstalks; others held bowls or arrows. They were gaily painted, carved in intricate detail, and dressed in miniature clothes.

Yani sat cross-legged in front of the gathering and began a chant. The others picked it up until the vaulted cavern was resonant with a sacred prayer. Hoshi'tiwa waited and wondered.

Presently a figure emerged from the deep shadows at the back of the cave. Hoshi'tiwa could not tell if it was a man or woman, because the person wore a mask similar to those on the wooden dolls—a black face with two large yellow eyes, the mouth a rectangle edged in red showing bared teeth. Hoshi'tiwa surmised it was a representation of a woman, as the hair was in a woman's style, although it was done up in a whorl on one side but hung full length, untidily, on the other. She wore a long black dress with a black cape over it. A quiver of arrows was slung over her shoulder, and she held a rattle in one hand, a bow and arrow in the other.

Hoshi'tiwa watched spellbound as the spirit began to dance, and as the movements became recognizable and pronounced, Hoshi'tiwa realized that a story was unfolding.

Yani explained in a soft tone, "She is Héhewuti, Warrior Woman. She was putting up her hair when her village was attacked and that is why only one side of her hair is done. She threw on her clothes, which is why she is so untidy, and she grabbed up her bow and arrows to help defend her people."

The masked figure danced, gyrated, mimicked anger and distress. And then from behind the mask came a high-pitched, terrifying song.

"She is imitating the distressed cries of her people," Yani said quietly.

The spirit danced in and out of the torchlight, fell to a crouch, then jumped to her feet. She brandished the bow and shook her rattle. She spun about on one foot, her disarrayed hair flying, until finally the story came to an end, Warrior Woman vanquished the enemy and disappeared back into the shadows of the cave. Yani rose and assured the cult members that once again Warrior Woman was in their midst and would always be ready to defend her people.

As the participants blessed one another and left, Yani explained to Hoshi'tiwa that the kachinas had come from the south with the caravans. "But they are not Toltec. Their origins are far in the south."

Leading Hoshi'tiwa to the wooden dolls, she said, "And they are not *all* new, for here is Crow Mother, whom you know," pointing to a doll with a blue face and a headdress of black wings. "And this is Masau'u," who had big red protruding eyes, a colorful cape, and feathers rising from the top of his head. "And when we sing, it is in our own language, and we chant the familiar prayers of our grandfathers."

Yani explained that when she had first been introduced to the kachina cult, she had been skeptical that such a new faith would be of any concern to her. "But I discovered that the spirits brought me an inner peace that I had not felt since before my daughter's execution. Since then I have been an ardent follower, and I have brought more followers into the faith."

When Hoshi'tiwa saw the expectant look on her friend's face, she said, "I am not looking to worship new gods, Yani."

"But we do not worship the kachinas," Yani quickly replied, "they are mere representations of everything in the real world. Kachina spirits are our partners, not our gods. I was hoping you would join us. I was hoping you would see yourself in Warrior Woman and be inspired to follow her example."

When Hoshi'tiwa started to protest, Yani held up a hand and said, "I have watched you from the moment you first arrived at Center Place, and I have waited for the right moment to bring you here, to show you the path you must take. While you were living at Precious Green as a Toltec lady, my heart was heavy and anxious, because I feared you might be seduced by the Lords and lose your way altogether.

"But I see now, Daughter, that it was a time of test and trial for you, like a vision quest, and that it was up to you to find your own path, to eventually turn your back on the ways of the Lords, their riches and their gods made of stone. And this you did! But now you must open your eyes and your heart, Hoshi'tiwa, for *this* is the message you were born to bring to our people." Yani stretched out her arms to encompass the cave with its curious wooden idols. "Not until our people have embraced the kachina spirits will balance and harmony be restored. And not until then will Pahana return and bring about the new age."

Hoshi'tiwa took her friend's callused hands and said, "Thank you for sharing your new faith with me. The kachinas are indeed wondrous and benevolent spirits. And I am glad they bring you and your friends peace of heart. But I walk a different road."

Yani felt her panic rise. This was not to have been the outcome of Hoshi'tiwa's visit to the kachina cave. In fact, it could not have turned out worse. Now it seemed Hoshi'tiwa was more determined than ever to lure *more* people away from the kachinas.

Hoshi'tiwa went to the cave's entrance, where she paused to turn to Yani and say, "I cannot join you, but I will keep your secret."

As she started to leave, Yani put a hand on her arm and said, "You have changed."

Hoshi'tiwa's eyes flickered. "I discovered the wisdom of the ancients."

But Yani shook her head. "There is something else. Daughter, I saw you with Lord Jakál on the mesa."

A look of uncertainty clouded Hoshi'tiwa's face. She bit her lip.

"You are troubled," Yani said quietly.

Hoshi'tiwa looked over her shoulder at the trail heading down to the canyon. She scanned the limestone walls of the cave. Then her gaze came to rest on the calm, wise face of her friend. "My heart is burdened," she confessed at last, speaking quietly even though they were alone. "I thought . . . I felt love for Lord Jakál. And I thought he felt the same for me."

Yani's lips tightened. It was what she had dreaded.

Hoshi'tiwa looked down at her hands; then she brought her head back up and met Yani's eyes. "He betrayed me. I gave myself to him, Yani, and then he told me he is going to enslave more of our people. That is why I preach *suukya'qatsi*. I must fill my heart with something other than anger and resentment. Oh, Yani, is it possible to love and hate at the same time?"

Yani took the girl's hands and said, "Your heart is only beginning to discover the troubled road that life can be. I have no answers. You must find them yourself. But if *suukya'qatsi* brings you no comfort, you are always welcome here."

They embraced, and as Hoshi'tiwa delivered herself into the sunlight and made her way along the hidden path back down to the valley, she was unaware that she was being watched, that she and Yani had been followed when they came to the cave earlier: Yellow Feather, hiding among boulders, congratulating herself once again for her cleverness and thinking how quickly fortune can change, how unexpectedly bad luck can become good.

She thought most especially about her smart seduction of a young man at Blue Hummingbird, who was now taking care of her. An aide on the staff of Chief Physician Nagual.

Fifty-three

TENOCH glowered at the ghost standing at the foot of his bed and said, "Go away, First Tenoch. You weary me. I am no longer afraid of your hauntings."

When the ghost did not reply, Tenoch sat up and squinted into the darkness and remembered that the form at the bottom of his bed was his old combat uniform—padded armor, leggings, and helmet—displayed upon a wooden clothes tree.

He slumped back and stared up at the ceiling. The hour was late. Once again, White Orchid had not come to kiss him good night. They could not go on like this. The house was as silent as if it were unoccupied. He knew about the magic snake, his daughter's crushing disappointment. He was sorry and wished a thousand evil curses upon the head of the Caravan Master. But Tenoch could not abide a house out of balance. Each day he sent for White Orchid, and each day the servant came back to say that the Lady was indisposed.

Could she go on forever this way, not speaking to him?

Because he could not walk but needed servants to carry him, Tenoch was at her mercy. And so each day he sat in his bedroom waiting for her to come and pay respects. Did White Orchid know how much she was hurting him? Of course she did! But the truth of her birth should not matter if she would just remember all the times he had been a father to her—when she fell and cut her knee and he kissed it better and gave her sweets to stop her from crying. So many memories!

When tears sprang to his eyes Tenoch clamped his jaw firmly shut. He was the father, the head of the house. She must come to *him*.

And then came the day when he himself was in pain and in need of kisses and sweets, at the cremation of his beloved Omaya, who had died after a demon laid an egg in her breast. Tenoch had been inconsolable. But White Orchid had been at his side throughout his days of grief and suffering. Had it not been for her, he would have ended his life.

"Please," he whispered in the darkness. "Please, my precious daughter, come and talk to me. . . ."

White Orchid, wide awake on her sleeping mat, listened to the silence of the night. She missed her father's company. If only she could think of a way to reconcile with him. She accepted now that he had been acting out of love, because Omaya had been a wonderful woman and White Orchid did not blame Tenoch for wanting to grant her every wish. And who knew? Perhaps White Orchid had been abandoned as a baby, or orphaned, and Tenoch and Omaya had committed a kindness by rescuing her. And what wonderful parents they had been. White Orchid suppressed her tears as childhood memories played behind her eyes, to remind her of the love and care the two had given her. What did bloodline matter? Tenoch *was* her father, and she loved him.

But she could not go to him, could not take the first step toward reconciliation. White Orchid was crippled by pride and a stubborn streak, preventing her from going to Tenoch's room and asking his forgiveness.

Bitterness filled her mouth. How had her life, once perfect, come to this? She had even been the victim of an unscrupulous Caravan Master.

And she never found the witch.

White Orchid had discovered that, although everyone talked about the dispenser of potent magic, and stories of her miracles and wonders circulated throughout the valley, and her existence seemed to be common knowledge, not a single soul knew where the evil crone could actually be found.

Or perhaps they were afraid to say, for to know where the woman lived implied that one had made use of her vile services. Of course, White Orchid had not been able to ask directly, as that would let the world know that she wished to purchase black magic, and so she had been circumspect in her inquiries, which had produced no results, wasting precious time in a futile search for something that, she realized now, most likely did not exist.

Suddenly she heard a strange sound outside her door. A queer scraping, lurching sound.

She held her breath and listened. Now there was only silence.

And then the sound again, accompanied by gasping. Followed by another spell of silence. Now thumping and moaning!

Had an animal had gotten into the house? Wounded, perhaps, or with its leg trapped.

White Orchid struggled to her knees, her eyes wide with terror, and was about to call for a servant when she heard a tapping on the doorjamb, and a voice whispering, "Daughter, are you awake?"

She ran to the doorway and, drawing aside the tapestry, saw her father on all fours, looking up at her.

He had crawled across the house to her bedroom.

"Oh, Father," she cried, reaching for him. But there was nothing she could do. Tenoch needed to go the last distance on his own, and it broke her heart to watch as he lurched on the stumps of his legs, causing himself great pain, pulling his stocky body along by his still-powerful arms.

When he reached her mat, she went to his side and threw her arms around him. "I am so sorry," she sobbed. "I should have come to you. It is not right that I made you do this."

"And I am sorry, too," he said, holding her tight, "that I lied to Lady Corn. I *wanted* to record the truth of your birth, but I could not. In my heart, I somehow thought that recording our names with the goddess would make you truly our daughter. And we never thought of you otherwise. Your mother and I, over time, came to believe you had truly issued from Omaya's womb. Can you forgive me?"

She pressed her face to his neck and soaked his nightshirt with her tears. "You must forgive me first, for I have acted without honor."

He stroked her hair. "I should never be forgiven for the terrible luck I brought upon my house and upon you."

White Orchid drew back and, in darkness lightened by starlight, smiled at her father. Their faces both glowed with the dampness of tears. "Let us forgive each other. And let us forget the past, forget bad luck. A new dawn will break soon, with a new sun on the horizon." She bit her lip. "I know," she said softly, "that there are things we must speak of. Important things. The magic serpent . . ."

Tenoch let her tell him about it, even though he already knew through the grapevine of servants' gossip.

When she was finished, he took her damp face between his callused hands. "Forget the serpent and the Caravan Master. You cannot be blamed for the guile of an evil man. Now listen to me, Daughter, for my daughter you are. You *must* marry. But now it is not because of Tenoch's bloodline. That has come to an end. I have accepted that, and my ancestor haunts me no more. But there are other reasons you should marry. I will not live forever. Once I am gone, you will need a man's protection.

"Precious Daughter, there are unscrupulous men who will find ways to take your house from you and all your wealth and cast you out alone and without so much as sandals on your feet. You know this. Captain Xikli is a powerful man, *and* he is the son of Moquihix the High Minister. Marry him and you would be wealthy, secure, the envy of all the women in the valley."

But White Orchid had other plans.

When Bone Snapper had failed to carry out his task because he could not touch Hoshi'tiwa while she wore the protective bear claw, White Orchid had ordered the young guard to see that the necklace was removed. To her surprise, he had said that he could not.

Apparently, White Orchid thought in disgust, men will do anything as long as it did not imperil their own souls.

So she would have to do something about Hoshi'tiwa herself.

But things had changed. Was it Jakál who dispelled Hoshi'tiwa from Precious Green, or did she leave on her own? And what was she up to, with her new humble act? Was it another ploy to win Jakál? Jakál was a religious man. Perhaps Hoshi'tiwa thought she could seduce him by being publicly pious. But then there was the curious decree that Hoshi'tiwa was not to leave the valley, and anyone helping her would be punished. Strange, White Orchid thought. He kept her bound to him by this decree.

So the girl was still an obstacle to White Orchid's plans.

This time, however, she was not going to hire spies, or others to do her work. From now on, anything that needed to be done, White Orchid would do herself.

Not far from Five Flower, in a fallow field between two derelict farms, Hoshi'tiwa sat beneath the meager shade of a dead cottonwood, talking quietly to gathered listeners. The day was so hot and dry that the thirsty audience shared fragments of a prickly pear cactus, sucking on the thick spiny leaves.

Hoshi'tiwa showed them her golden-orange rain jar and said quietly, "Nothing dies. I will show you how I know this. You know that the lights in the sky do not stand still. And so it is in nature: Nothing stands still, not even a stone, for it is constantly changing. Everything in the universe is continually transferring from one phase to another, changing without ending. Our thoughts and our souls are always moving, changing, transforming, even though they remain connected to all things. Therefore nothing dies. If a loved one has passed from this world, he or she is not lost but has simply joined the stars and the rocks and all of life."

A woman seated near Hoshi'tiwa was weeping softly. She was the Master Potter Red Crow, who came from a clan that had dwelled in the east, near a body of water called Big River. Red Crow had been brought to Center Place against her will, when she had been rounded up along with others of her clan by Jaguars. Red Crow had been a new bride then, those many summers ago, and she had watched as her husband of only a few months had been slain when he resisted capture. She never saw her family again, and it was rumored that her clan, like other people in outlying settlements, had scattered and now hid in the wilderness to escape the reach of the Lords. Red Crow had long since given up hope that she should ever see her kinsmen again.

"Do you see?" Hoshi'tiwa said to Red Crow, handing her the rain jar. "The great web of All Things, even souls and hearts and minds? How can anything, or anyone, be separated or lost? They are not, but with us still, in a changed condition."

Red Crow closed her eyes and felt warm comfort flood her heart. Not even the kachinas had brought such solace, because she could see on the jar that her lost clan, her young husband, were there still, somewhere in the Oneness.

Old Pikami, sitting at the periphery of the group, having come out of curiosity, gave thought to Hoshi'tiwa's words and wondered if it was possible. Did the clan she had exterminated through a single thoughtless act still exist somewhere in the Oneness? Was it true that nothing really died? Although the last surviving member of the clan had forgiven her, Pikami could not forgive herself. And so she resisted the succor that Hoshi'tiwa's new words brought.

Nonetheless, she found them compelling, as did others in the group—farmers, artisans, soldiers, even the widow of Oquitzin, the assassinated Superintendent of the Marketplace—a mixture of Toltec and People of the Sun, rich and poor, young and old, each having come for different reasons and finding the rain-girl's words irresistible. To this varied group a newcomer now arrived, a Toltec noblewoman with a handsome deep blue mantle covering her hair and shoulders.

White Orchid held the hem of her mantle to her face, to protect it from the unusually hot wind that was blowing sand and grit into her eyes. The dryness prickled her skin. All moisture had been sucked from the air. And the branches of the dead cottonwood clattered like old bones.

She came to a halt at the edge of the group, her sharp eyes watching Hoshi'tiwa. To make herself less conspicuous, the noble lady sat on the ground, slightly apart from the others, within the protection of her slaves. Her mouth dry with thirst, White Orchid withdrew a small skin of water from beneath her mantle and, when no one was looking, took a long drink, quickly secreting it back beneath her cloak before others could see and beg for a sip.

Then she settled her eyes on Hoshi'tiwa and began thinking of ways to separate the girl from her bear claw necklace.

Fifty-four

T HE valley thirsts," Hoshi'tiwa murmured as she turned her face into the hot dry wind.

Although the Vernal Equinox, a time of planting and hope, lay but days away, the winter rains had been absent. Hope was thin. A few farmers and craftsmen had tried to leave Center Place, attempting to escape with their families under the cover of night. Jaguars had followed and dragged them back, to make examples of them by offering their beating hearts to Blue Hummingbird.

Hoshi'tiwa had hoped to hold another ritual at the Sun Dagger, for the annual spring rite, but already people were telling her that they were too afraid to take part, even though in their hearts they yearned to return to the traditions of their ancestors.

As she lived among her kinsmen, she saw their increased misery and suffering as the Cloud Spirits continued to stay away. She saw people shaking handfuls of grass over blankets to catch the bitter but edible seeds, which were ground into a paste or eaten raw. Dew traps dotted the valley in the hundreds, lined with shiny ceramic that attracted night-time moisture. Scorpions were roasted and eaten after poisonous tails and claws were pinched off. Dogs vanished. Snakes grew rare. And turkeys had all but disappeared from the valley—a sorrowful sign because the People of the Sun ate their turkeys only when times were desperate, for once a turkey is eaten, it can no longer provide the eggs and feathers everyone so loved.

Hoshi'tiwa stood on the baked earth of a failed squash farm where no life grew and the farmer and his family were starving. She looked up and down the valley, at the rising-splendors—twelve magnificent stone and mortar centers with plazas and kivas and priests—thriving and plentiful, and the houses of the rich where such water as trickled along the ancient riverbed was diverted by dams and channels to slake the dry throats of such as Lady White Orchid and her father Tenoch the Hero.

She squinted up at the stark cliffs rising vertically from the canyon floor to end in majestic flat mesas overhead, their crowns bristling with dry brush and stunted trees. Her eye traveled along the ancient geologic strata that gave the cliffs their beautiful striations of orange and gold and red, and she remembered a large reservoir of water, cradled in the bosom of a taboo canyon, reserved for the nurturing of one small glade verdant with plants and flowers.

Calling to the farmer and his neighbors, she instructed them to bring jars and waterskins and follow her.

They followed, not knowing where she was leading, gathering others along the way, telling farmers and workers and wives to bring anything that could hold water, a growing mob that was strangely peaceful and orderly, following the young woman in the plain white shift as she led them across the valley to the mouth of a forbidden ravine carved into the cliff behind the Five Flower rising-splendor. Musicians and dancers, well-fed and wearing fine clothes, interrupted their practicing to watch the ragtag procession flow by, like a river of cast-off humanity. Old women hurried alongside small children. All carried whatever vessel they had been able to lay hand to.

When they reached the reservoir that was like a small lake, the people cried out. They gasped, they stared in shock at the sight of so much water, and many ran forward, falling into the joyous abundance of life-liquid.

They rushed to the edge with their pots and baskets and leather pouches and filled them to brims. They threw themselves prone and pushed their faces into the water to drink and drink and drink.

Unlike the government reservoir higher up the valley, this small water supply was unguarded because it was sacred, and so it was unthinkable that anyone should desecrate it. But the thirsting people did not think of gods or sacrilege as word spread down the valley so that more came running. When the perimeter of the small lake was packed with thirsty people, Hoshi'tiwa marched to the earthen levee and smashed it with rocks. She demolished the wooden sluice gates. She broke down the stone dams so that water gushed into channels built a century prior, when the reservoir with its runoff from mountain rain and springs was used in times of drought to irrigate the farms. The water flowed once again down channels and dusty irrigation ditches not used in a hundred years, to spread out along man-made arteries, among farms and villas, like blood through veins, fresh rainwater spilling over clod and weed as people came running from their shacks and shelters to scoop up the precious "blood" and sprinkle it on their struggling crops—and to wonder what, or who, had caused this miracle.

Behind the high wooden walls of the Jaguar barracks, Captain Xikli was receiving bad news with a sour expression. He had sent a scouting party eastward to learn why the latest shipments from the sky-stone mines had not arrived.

"The mines are no more," said the scout, the only man from the party to survive, a wounded and bloody Jaguar who had barely reached Center Place alive. "The foreign raiders, who come from the far north and who speak an unholy language and pray to evil gods, have slain all who work at the mines. These raiders are fierce, Captain, and fearless. They fight without honor but strike like snakes and kill in cowardly ways. They roam the country in a lawless way. They are a terrible scourge, Captain. No one is safe who sojourns in the east."

Although a Toltec knight and the son of aristocracy, the man was on his knees before Xikli, his forehead pressed to the ground. That he had escaped the fate of his fellows was a disgrace to the Jaguars and to his family in Tollan. When Xikli had heard enough, he raised a club and bashed the man's head in. As he was about to order his guards to drag the body out, Xikli heard shouts beyond the barracks wall. "What is going on?" he asked his lieutenant.

And when Xikli was told, he seized his spear and ran out.

Moquihix was in the marketplace, sitting cross-legged beneath a shade bower of twigs and branches, listening to the complaints of the new Chief Tax Collector, who, filling the office that Copil vacated, had found much corruption and was now informing the High Minister that portions of the tribute collected from the outlying settlements—hides, seashells, copper, corn—had not found their way into the administrative coffers.

Moquihix was not listening. His eyes were fixed upon the progress of Yellow Feather as she made her way through the crowd, pausing to look over the wares of a seller of medicine bags and magic bones. She had grown plump. Moquihix had heard she was now the woman of Chief Physician Nagual's young aide, a man whose duties were to care for diagnostic seeds and healing charms and to make sacrifice daily to Nagual's personal gods. From the look of her lush thighs and large breasts, Yellow Feather was not starving. Moquihix wondered if the food was in trade for sexual favors alone, or if she was trading for something else, such as information, as she had once traded with him. If so, what secrets was she channeling to Nagual through the aide?

Moquihix was eyeing the infant riding her hip, a healthy boy now a year old—his son—when the orderliness of the marketplace was disrupted by a commotion at its edge. People shouting something about sacred water . . .

Hearing of the remarkable water miracle, Yani had run from the potters' workshop, along with the others, and when she arrived at the frenzied scene at the end of a narrow canyon she had never visited before, just moments before the Jaguars arrived with their spears and clubs, she was stunned to realize what had happened. She recalled her own words of nearly two years prior, when Hoshi'tiwa had sighted the reservoir across the valley and asked about it. "That is a catchment built by the Lords for their private use," Yani had warned. "That water is for the gods, it is not for us to touch."

Hoshi'tiwa had led the people to the reservoir and was now letting them fall upon the sacred water with their profane gourds and jars and goatskins. And she was setting the water free!

The Jaguars will slaughter us all, Yani thought, trembling. And in that moment she arrived at a terrible, frightening decision, one that could no longer be ignored. She knew what must be done.

Lord Jakál was the last to know.

Everyone in the valley was in an uproar over the release of the sacred water—either in ecstasy as one of the thirsting People of the Sun, or in outrage as a privileged Toltec—but no one, even though orders were given, had the courage to deliver the devastating news to the *tlatoani* of Center Place. Therefore it was up to Captain Xikli, arriving at the construction site of the pyramid, to find Jakál in his colorful pavilion, going over plans for the south-facing stairway. Xikli was not afraid to deliver the news.

And when he heard, Jakál was so stunned with disbelief that he made Xikli repeat the report.

When the Captain had arrived at the reservoir with a contingent of Jaguars, he had found an obscene pillaging of the sacred water meant for the gods. The people scattered at once. The Jaguars caught a few, and before having their throats slit, they divulged the identity of the one who had committed this desecration. Hoshi'tiwa the rain-girl.

"My Lord, we must launch a search for her," Xikli demanded. "We must use every soldier and guard to scour the valley and root her out."

Jakál felt as if he had been kicked in the chest. "When you find her, bring her to me."

"And then?"

Jakál had not objected to Hoshi'tiwa arranging a Winter Solstice celebration at the Sun Dagger. He had even admired her for her courage to stage a forbidden practice. Jakál understood religious devotion and was in fact proud of her for honoring her gods, knowing that with such defiance she placed herself in great danger. However, the water reserved for the sacred glade was another matter. This was the most serious sacrilege, and the transgressor must be punished in the most extreme way.

"I will make that decision when she is brought to me," Jakál said.

"And how will you decide?" Xikli said in disgust. "With your brain or perhaps somewhere below your waist?"

"Mind your tongue," Jakál snapped. "Or I will offer your beating heart to Blue Hummingbird."

Xikli curbed his tongue. He had not yet enough support to topple Jakál. Many were still loyal to this man who, by a word, could have Xikli slain on the spot.

The Captain left—with Jakál calling for his seers, astrologers, the Star Readers, and Quail, asking for the Book of Fate and the Book of Dreams, demanding sacred incense and the many tools of augury and divination to be found in the twelve rising-splendors—and Xikli found outside the pavilion a gathering of nobles, *pochtecas,* officials, and priests all demanding an audience with Jakál. A regiment of guards was necessary to keep them out. Up and down the valley, mayhem was erupting as the People of the Sun lavished their pathetic farms with water stolen from the gods.

Xikli looked grimly upon the scene and came to a decision. He would give a special order to his Jaguars: Find the girl and bring her to *him*.

Fifty-five

HOSHI'TIWA was in old Pikami's hut, preparing herself for the arrest.

Both were surprised when Yani arrived, agitated and afraid, saying, "You must save yourself, Daughter. You must hide."

But Hoshi'tiwa said, "I will go with them when they come for me. I will not hide. I will stand before Lord Jakál and tell him that the world must be brought into balance again."

"Daughter, you do not understand! There will be no chance for you to stand before Lord Jakál. He has ordered your instant death. When the Jaguars come, they will slay you on the spot."

Hoshi'tiwa stared at her. "It cannot be."

"There is a bounty on your head. A wealth of sky-stone will be given to the man who finds you and slays you and lays your body at Jakál's feet."

When Pikami began to wail and beat her withered old breast, Hoshi'tiwa wondered if what Yani said was true. Had she finally gone too far and enraged Jakál to even his limits?

Realizing that she might have put Pikami and the boy in danger by coming here, Hoshi'tiwa seized her plain cloak and the rain jar—as its presence in the hut would connect innocent people to her—and said, "You are right: I must leave. I wish no harm to come to my friends. I will go away and wait for Jakál's anger to die down."

"I will hide you," Yani said, and together they fled from the hut.

Having learned that their last hiding place had been discovered, Yani and her followers had found a new secret cave at the extreme western end of the valley, not far from the limestone overhang where she had shown Hoshi'tiwa the pictographs prophesying her arrival at Center Place.

As they hurried along the path, hearing trumpets blaring at all rising-splendors, mingled with shouts and calls to action—the releasing of the sacred water had caused more of an uproar than Hoshi'tiwa had foreseen—they ducked behind large boulders, pushed through thick dry brush, and frequently glanced over their shoulders to make sure they were not followed.

Neither Yani nor Hoshi'tiwa saw Chief Physician Nagual stealthily make his way along their trail, concealing himself behind rocks and in shadows whenever they looked back.

Inside the dim cave, Yani caught her breath, considered her next words and said in a low voice, "Daughter, what I am about to tell you is very dangerous information. The secret I am about to reveal could mean death for some of us. I reveal it to you now only out of dire necessity, not by any wish to do so."

Outside, unbeknownst to the two in the cave, Chief Physician Nagual moved quietly along the rocky wall. He paused to listen, heard voices within. Quietly, he slipped inside.

Her eyes large, her voice timorous, Yani said, "Hoshi'tiwa, you are living under a gross misconception. You need to know the truth."

Yani collected herself and her thoughts, and said in a steadier voice, "You believe that Lord Jakál is a reasonable man. That, once his furor dies down and he is calm, he will listen to your case when you state it before him. But, Daughter, that man does not exist."

Hoshi'tiwa frowned. "What do you mean?"

"When your betrothed, Ahoté, who had committed sacrilege in the sacred glade of the gods, was brought before Lord Jakál, and you stood up to the *tlatoani*—"

"Yes," Hoshi'tiwa said, a strange coldness creeping into her veins. She did not want to hear what Yani was about to say.

"You and I, and all the people of Center Place believed that Ahoté was set free by Lord Jakál and allowed to go home. But, Hoshi'tiwa, this did not happen."

A fluttering sound came from the back of the cave where, in deep shadows, something with wings was trying to get out.

"What—?" Hoshi'tiwa asked, her heart suddenly thumping. "What do you mean?"

"In his private chambers, out of the eye of the populace, Lord Jakál changed his decree."

"I don't believe it." Hoshi'tiwa's chest grew tight. The fluttering at the back of the cave grew louder, more desperate. Something was trapped. It could not find its way out.

"Ahoté was not allowed to go home," Yani said, and Hoshi'tiwa saw in the older woman's calm, sorrowful gaze that she spoke the truth.

Hoshi'tiwa put a hand on the rocky wall to steady herself, braced for what she knew was coming. "Tell me," she whispered.

"Lord Jakál believed that his decision to let the boy go free would anger the gods and destroy harmony. So he sent Jaguars after him and they picked him up on the road. From there he was sold to a miner of sky-stone, and taken east to the sky-stone mines to live out the rest of his short life in forced labor."

Hoshi'tiwa closed her eyes. She felt the cavern swim and sway around her. The fluttering in the shadows had ceased.

"There is no doubt, my Lord," the Star Reader said, his black robes streaked with years of dirt and grime, his long fingernails gnarled and curled. "The arrival of the rain-girl and the shooting star herald a coming eclipse."

"An eclipse of what?" Jakál asked as he had asked two years prior in the Star Chamber.

"We do not know, my Lord."

Jakál paced the width and breadth of the pavilion while all the wise men whom he had summoned stood around him in their colorful robes and impressive feathers and strings of beads, bones, and teeth. Even Quail was there, his hands bloody from an inspection of a tiny fluttering bird's heart.

Jakál plunged deep into thought. An eclipse need not necessarily be a celestial event; it could be symbolic. It could mean perhaps that some*thing* was ending. And if something was ending, he reasoned, then that meant something else was beginning.

The prophecy had begun with Hoshi'tiwa, and today's monumental sacrilege, which had set every Toltec on his ear and every farmer happily dancing in the mud, had been caused by Hoshi'tiwa. All puzzling events in the past two years were also connected to her. It was as if she were at the nexus of a great, imminent cosmic event. But what?

When Hoshi'tiwa opened her eyes and the cave stopped swaying, she took a deep breath and thought: It cannot be. Lord Jakál is a man of honor, a man of his word. It is Yani who is misinformed. She has been fed lies by an enemy of the *tlatoani*. Ahoté is back home with my family, happily reciting the events on the Memory Wall.

"You do not believe me," Yani said.

"Lord Jakál would not break his word."

"He is a Toltec. His people rip beating hearts from men's chests."

"How do you know he changed his decree?" Hoshi'tiwa said in a challenging tone. "Surely you were not present when Lord Jakál gave the order?"

Before Yani could respond, the sound of footsteps came from the direction of the cave entrance, and then a shadow loomed over them. A tall man with a magnificent cockscomb on his shaven head, and dressed in handsome blue cotton, looked at them with hooded eyes.

Chief Physician Nagual's lips curved in a cryptic smile.

"The priests of Tlaloc are overseeing the repair of dams and gates at the reservoir, my Lord," Moquihix reported to Jakál, who paced back and forth. "And Captain Xikli has dispersed soldiers and guards throughout the valley with promises of a rich reward to the one who brings the girl back alive—"

Jakál stopped suddenly and faced Moquihix, whom he had summoned in urgency after Quail had posited a startling conjecture, a message he had read in the tiny quivering bird's heart. And Jakál repeated now to Moquihix what Quail had asked: "Are we so sure, my friend, that what Hoshi'tiwa did at the sacred reservoir is *in fact sacrilege*?"

"My Lord!" Yani whispered as the Chief Physician stepped all the way into the cave. "You startled me. I did not know you would be here."

"I did not want Hoshi'tiwa to see me. I did not want to frighten her." He turned to Hoshi'tiwa, who was staring at him with her mouth open, and said in a deep voice, "Yani knows about the changed decree, about Ahoté being sent to the sky-stone mines, because I told her."

Hoshi'tiwa was too stunned to respond. Why was the Chief Physician here? Why did Yani address him with such familiarity?

"I was present," he added somberly, to drive his point home, "when Lord Jakál gave the order."

Hoshi'tiwa continued to look at him in confusion. "I don't understand," she said, finally turning to Yani. "I thought," she began. Enemies, her mind whispered. Their children were found taking pleasure together; the girl was sacrificed, the boy died on his way to Tollan.

"Calm yourself, Daughter," Yani said gently. "We are in no danger from this man. He is, in fact, the leader of the kachina cult."

Hoshi'tiwa caught her breath.

"The dance that you witnessed," Yani went on, "the Warrior Woman kachina. Do you remember?"

Hoshi'tiwa nodded, too dumbfounded to speak.

"This man was that dancer. Nagual is a kachina priest. In fact, it was he who brought the kachina cult to Center Place when he arrived with Lord Jakál."

Hoshi'tiwa looked at the Chief Physician, whose face remained impassive. Then she turned to Yani and said, "So . . . you are *friends,* and not enemies?"

"More than that," Yani said with a smile. "Nagual is my husband."

The priests, seers, dream-readers, astrologers, and Quail all arrived at two agreed-upon conclusions: that an eclipse was coming, and that the gods, for some reason, were allowing Hoshi'tiwa to commit sacrileges without punishing her. Which could mean only one thing: that they were not sacrileges. Not if she were indeed *tiacápan,* the chosen one of the gods, as Jakál himself had once declared.

Therefore, the wise and learned men reasoned, if she were chosen by the gods, then it was permissible for her to interfere with the sacred reservoir, and that in fact she might be working as an instrument of the gods.

Jakál paced again, his body tense, snapping as he spun about to march back and forth, his mind so focused on Hoshi'tiwa that he almost spoke out loud to her, as if she were there in the shade of the colorful pavilion. He saw her in all her incarnations—the frightened girl in tattered clothing as she marched with the harvested humanity from the north to Center Place; the curious girl who stood in the pre-dawn as Quetzalcoatl rose in the east; the defiant girl who stood in the plaza demanding that her beloved be set free; the girl who had wept in his arms because she was so alone.

The woman she had been, in his arms, high on the mesa beneath the stars.

Hoshi'tiwa, changing as the seasons changed. And himself, he could feel it, no longer the man he was two years ago. And suddenly—he knew!

Jakál turned to Moquihix. "Summer Rain," Jakál said, "is the chosen one of the gods, as these wise men have concluded. She is *tiacápan*. Therefore she is part of the eclipse that was foretold."

Moquihix did not like where Jakál's thoughts were leading. He was rationalizing, twisting sacred canon to suit his carnal desires. Moquihix thought of Captain Xikli's outrage and once again the High Minister felt conflict pierce his heart. Whom should he follow? His son, or the man who was going to turn Center Place into another Tollan?

Before Moquihix could speak, Jakál hurried on. "The eclipse is merely symbolic! It is not in fact an ending but a *change*. I see that now. Quetzalcoatl, Lord of the Breath of Life, has illuminated my soul! He has shown me that the time has come for one way of life to end and another to begin!"

Moquihix, in his very fibers, did not like change. He did not even like the word. "My Lord," he began.

"Summer Rain is to be the instrument of the new beginning," Jakál continued as he turned in a circle, looking at each man, meeting their eyes, searching for doubt and defiance but finding none. The interpretation of omens was vague at best, and if Quetzalcoatl had shown Jakál the way, these men were not about to protest.

Moquihix, on the other hand, was not afraid to speak up. "My Lord," he began again, wanting to be heard before the final words were spoken, because Jakál's word was supreme law and once an edict was uttered, all must obey without question. "My Lord—"

"We have been living as two races," Jakál said, cutting him off, "with two sets of gods who are constantly at war. And when gods are at war, there can be no rain—everyone knows this. That is why we suffer this drought. That is the meaning of the shooting star and the eclipse foretold and the summoning of Summer Rain to Center Place. The gods have been speaking to us and we have not been listening!"

"My Lord—"

"It is so clear to me now!" Jakál said triumphantly. "Center Place must be united. The gods must be united, and the way for that to happen is for the *people* to be united. My dear friends and advisers, I am going to take Hoshi'tiwa as my wife!"

Hoshi'tiwa stared at Nagual in disbelief, and then at Yani. "Your husband!" she blurted. Although Toltec nobles were known to choose sexual partners from the People of the Sun, marriage was forbidden and punishable by death. Had not their own two children suffered that very fate?

"Promise me you will tell no one," Yani said urgently.

Hoshi'tiwa thought back and realized that her observations of Yani's body language, whenever the Chief Physician was nearby, had been through naïve, inexperienced eyes. In retrospect, she saw that the trembling was due to passion, and what Hoshi'tiwa had thought was a look of fear on Yani's face had been in fact a mixture of awe, respect, desire, and love.

"I will tell no one. But," she began. "How—?"

"It was our shared grief that brought us together," Yani said, looking at Nagual, her eyes filled with tender devotion. "After my daughter was executed, and his son was sent away, whenever we encountered each other in the marketplace, when we exchanged looks, it was as if our hearts were reaching across to touch and to share the grief. Nagual came to me one night at the workshop. He needed to talk about his son, and I needed to talk about my daughter. We spent many nights thus in talk, and in mutual consolation, until the same love that had existed between his son and my daughter came to life again in us. We did not fight it, did not question it. We fell in love and accepted it."

Hoshi'tiwa looked at the formidable Chief Physician and was startled to see his eyes damp with tears.

"But listen, Daughter," Yani added quickly, "as long as no one knows Nagual and I are married, as long as no one knows he is a priest of the kachina cult, we are safe. Everyone believes that Nagual is the sworn enemy of the kachina cult, and in this way he keeps us safe, for people who spy on us go to him with their information. Yellow Feather found our last cave and reported it to Nagual. He rewarded her and then told her to leave us alone lest her spying give her away and make it harder for him to ferret us out and punish us. So now we have no further fear from Yellow Feather. In this same way, Hoshi'tiwa, we can protect you from Jakál's decree."

Yani's motives to help her friend, however, were not so much about saving the girl as saving the cult. With Hoshi'tiwa joining the kachina faith, she would bring many more followers, all the people in the valley she had been preaching to, until their numbers were so large that even Jakál dared not attempt to stamp them out. Therefore Yani felt justified in speaking a lie.

Jakál was filled with rapture. Summer Rain was to be his! They would be free to love and there would be no more obstacles between them, not even the pyramid.

To Moquihix he said excitedly, "My architects have been telling me that a pyramid is not feasible in this canyon. That it cannot be done. That we have not the manpower or the resources. I have come to agree with them! I shall not insult Quetzalcoatl by promising what I cannot deliver. Therefore I shall build instead a temple, modest and humble as would suit the Lord of the Breath of Life, but hold rituals every day to make up for the prosaic building, and sing his praises and glorify him every morning, noon, and night."

The High Minister said nothing because he, like the others standing under the pavilion like stone statues, was too shocked by Jakál's marriage announcement to utter a word. He wanted to say, "Xikli was right. It is not your *mind* that you are thinking with." But he held his tongue.

Jakál smiled now, as the new idea blossomed in complete perfection and beauty in his mind. How happy Summer Rain was going to be when he told her he was not going to enslave more of her people, that he had decided it was wiser to leave them on their farms to continue to produce food for Center Place. He would be, as she had begged, like a father to them.

"Find her!" he commanded the priests and seers and astrologers. "Find Summer Rain and bring her to me!"

Hoshi'tiwa thought her heart would break in two. Jakál had sent Ahoté to the mines. She believed this now, because it was Chief Physician Nagual who had told her so. Jakál had betrayed her. And now he had put a price on her head, and was at that very moment planning to offer her heart to his bloody gods.

"I must go after Ahoté," she said at last.

Yani blinked. "What?" She exchanged a glance with Nagual, who said, "Did you not hear what we said? The boy was sent to the sky-stone mines in the east."

"And I will find him," Hoshi'tiwa said resolutely, steeling her heart against the waves of emotion that washed over her. *I will cry later, after I have found him.*

"But, Daughter, no man survives the mines beyond a few months, and Ahoté was sent there a year ago!"

"Then I will find his body," Hoshi'tiwa said firmly. She did not yet understand her motives for this decision, that it had less to do with Ahoté himself than with Jakál's betrayal of their trust. She would find Ahoté—dead or alive—and bring him back to show the people of Center Place the deceit of their leader.

Yani wrung her hands. "If you do this, you can never come back to Center Place, for if you find Ahoté and bring him back, you will both be sacrificed on the altar of blood. Daughter, listen to me! If you defy Jakál's order, he will have you hunted down and all your family slain. Leave Ahoté to his fate and to the gods, and stay here, Hoshi'tiwa, with us. Jakál will never find you. My husband has much power at Center Place, powerful friends. And with you as a member of our cult, more people will come, for they listen to you."

In one last effort to dissuade the girl from this madness, Yani said, "It is rumored that the mines are no more, that fierce marauders roam the lands to the east, savage men without laws or gods. You would not survive!"

But Hoshi'tiwa said she must go, and Nagual, not wanting to force her to join them against her will, held private council with his wife, whose face was stricken with panic and disappointment, and then, kissing Yani gently on the lips, offered to lead Hoshi'tiwa from the cave by an exit in the rear, and place her on a path back to Center Place so that she could travel unseen.

Retrieving the rain jar from the shelf where she had placed it upon entering the cave, Hoshi'tiwa held it out to Yani and said, "Where I am going, I cannot take this, for it might encumber me. I entrust this treasure in your care, my dear friend, for there are good spirits in the clay. Protect them as you would have protected me, and they will be good to you in return. And perhaps someday, when you share your kachina spirits with others, you will share my message of Oneness and *suukya'qatsi.*"

Even as she spoke, her thoughts were racing forward. Hoshi'tiwa would wait until nightfall before collecting supplies and weapons, and anything else she might need for the long trek. She would not tell anyone where she was going. For their own safety, she would not say goodbye to Pikami or any of the new friends she had made in the past few months of teaching the message of *suukya'qatsi.*

Yani and Hoshi'tiwa embraced one last time and wished each other luck and then, as was their practice after secret meetings, Yani waited until Nagual's and Hoshi'tiwa's footsteps faded before she herself turned to leave the cave by the front entrance. And there she saw, in the sunshine, Yellow Feather, not bothering to hide the fact that she had been eavesdropping.

And Yani's blood ran to ice when she saw Yellow Feather's mouth slowly curve in a sly, vindictive smile.

BOOK SIX

Daughter of the Sun

Fifty-six

HOSHI'TIWA'S arms and legs screamed with pain.

She had been crouched in a clump of sagebrush since early morning, when she had stumbled upon a marauders' camp. Fearful of making a sound and thus giving herself away, she had squatted unseen, to wait for them to move on. But they had stayed and now her body was in agony.

She had not thought they ranged this far west. The Invisible Ones had told her the raiders' territory lay beyond the Big River, and as the river was difficult to cross, the raiders stayed on the other side.

Yet here they were, sitting at a campfire and feasting on rabbits roasting on spits—lean men wearing only breechclouts despite the cold spring weather, their hair long and adorned with beads and feathers, their bodies covered in black paint. Hoshi'tiwa had been told they were lawless men without honor who fought among themselves, stole from their brothers, and cursed the gods. And so she stayed low, bided her time, and waited.

Sixteen days had passed since she left Center Place, and the sorrow of her departure was still sharp in her breast.

After leaving the secret kachina cave with Chief Physician Nagual, Hoshi'tiwa had found a place where she could remain hidden until nightfall, as Jaguars and soldiers and regular citizens searched for her. But activity had dropped with the onset of night, for even Jaguars respected the evil spirits that walked in darkness, and Hoshi'tiwa was able to return to Precious Green, where she slipped into the back of the main kitchen through a narrow corridor.

While the chief cooks and servants slept, Hoshi'tiwa went through the stores and took what she needed for the journey. The mines, Chief Physician Nagual had said when he led her out of the cave, lay far to the southeast, across rugged terrain, beyond the reach of the Toltec empire. So she knew she would need weapons for defense and hunting, and other supplies, including food and water.

She took a spear, a knife, and a digging stick, but no bow and arrow, as she was not skilled in their use. Loops of twine made from agave fibers. Copper fishhooks. Goatskins filled with water. The most precious commodity she took was dense bundles of *huemac,* which would sustain her should she find no food along the way.

Huemac was made from thin slices of lean deer meat dried over a fire and then ground between stones. Dried berries and melted fat were added to the mixture, which was then stuffed into sheep bladders and intestines. These were left out in the sun so that as they dried and shriveled, the meat-berry mixture was compressed and sealed, making the food concentrate easy to carry, nor did it spoil, and a small amount sufficed as a meal.

Keeping her eye on the men at the campfire, she eased her body into another position to relieve her aching muscles and slowly shifted her carrying bundle from her shoulders to the ground. Her stomach growled. She wished she could slice off a chunk of *huemac* and eat. She also wished there were a way around the men at the campfire, but unfortunately they had chosen a spot at the edge of the sky-stone trail, and there was no other way to the mines.

When Nagual led Hoshi'tiwa from the kachina cave, he had told her where to find the beginning of the sky-stone trail that would take her, after many days, to the mines. He had also given her a small protective spirit: a little wooden kachina that fit in the hand. The spirit had protected him, he said, during his long journey northward from Tollan, and he hoped that it would help Hoshi'tiwa on her own perilous journey. To her surprise, the Chief Physician, one of the most powerful men in the world, kissed her on both cheeks and blessed her.

Later, when she had her supplies, weapons, and a goat-hide cloak, and was ready to strike eastward, Hoshi'tiwa had paused beneath the stars to look down at the valley that had been her home for two years. Most dwellings were dark and silent as people slept and dreamed while spirits walked the land (although she saw men's shadows as soldiers went furtively from homestead to homestead in search of her). But Jakál's colorful pavilion was ablaze with torchlight beneath the night sky, alive with activity as people came and went, their voices drifting up to the stars. She had even heard music as Jakál no doubt prepared for her execution.

He is making a merry event of it, Hoshi'tiwa had thought bitterly, her heart in her throat.

Then, forcing the man she had loved—still loved—from her mind, she had strengthened her resolve, straightened her body, and turned her back on Center Place. Walking in darkness, alone beneath the stars, had at first been terrifying, as she imagined supernatural beings everywhere. But as the crisp night air blew against her face, and she planted her bare feet firmly on the cold ground, her goat-hide cloak wrapped about her, the carrying bundle on her back, along with spear and digging sticks, Hoshi'tiwa had felt a curious sense of freedom steal over her. As the canyon that embraced Center Place fell behind her, and all sounds and lights of humanity, and she saw the starry canopy hang low over the mesas and canyons, she felt her fear strangely vanish to be replaced by a sense of rightness.

It was as if she had been born for this journey.

Shortly before dawn, she came upon the head of the sky-stone trail, where a counting station stood—a small stone edifice with several rooms and one kiva. But no one was there, all was in darkness. Setting her feet upon the beaten path, and marking the stars that Nagual had said would be her guide, she began her long walk.

As Hoshi'tiwa followed the trail, walking by day and making camp by night, the topography changed. Gradually the deep canyons and sheer cliffs, carved by wind and water for countless millennia, gave way to rolling hills and valleys the color of a mountain lion, dotted sparsely with brush and trees. She crossed rugged arroyos and trickling streams. As she climbed in elevation, she struggled for breath but after a while grew accustomed to the thinner air. She subsisted on edible juniper berries and piñon pine nuts. Mountains rose in the near distance, purple and lavender. Hoshi'tiwa walked noisily, beating her path with a stick to warn rattlesnakes and scorpions, to give them time to slither away. She spoke calmly to coyotes and gray foxes and bobcats, assuring them she meant no harm, and showed them she carried no bow and arrows. But she set traps for rabbits and plovers, and collected eggs when she could. Occasionally she would pause to let a striped skunk have right of way, standing at a respectful distance until the squat little body had passed without odiferous incident.

She did not walk alone. Jakál was with her every step of the way, in her thoughts, in her heart, and, at night as she slept beneath fitful dreams, in her flesh. She longed for his embrace. She loved him still. And she hated him. Her anger and feelings of betrayal infused her bones and muscles with strength. But her heart was troubled and conflicted. When emotions threatened to overwhelm her, when she felt weak and thought she might turn around and go back to Center Place, back to Jakál, she forced the feelings down and focused on her mission: to find Ahoté.

On the tenth day she encountered the Invisible Ones.

She had come upon abandoned campsites along the way, where the sky-stone traders had paused in their many journeys between the mines and Center Place. But at each site she found only cold ashes and no signs of recent habitation. What had made the traders cease the journeys that they had been making for generations? Had a calamity befallen them, and Ahoté as well?

But on the afternoon of the tenth day, a blustery spring day with enormous white clouds rolling across the blue sky, and red-tailed hawks noisily defending their territory from squawking ravens, Hoshi'tiwa found an abandoned campsite that would turn out to be like no other.

Deciding to stay there for the night, as boulders and cottonwoods provided shelter from the wind and nighttime dew, she untied her cloak and spread it on the ground—she would later use it as a bed and blanket—and then she removed her belt from which tools and a knife hung, and prepared to light a fire using mineral shavings she had taken from the Precious Green kitchen. But as she struck a flint with her knife, to spark the magnesium shavings, the feeling of being watched came over her.

Hoshi'tiwa looked around and saw nothing but stunted oaks, juniper bushes, mossy old boulders. Had some marauders ranged this far east? she wondered.

Keeping her actions minimal, to appear as nonaggressive as possible, she fanned her small fire, sipped from her waterskin, and cut off a small chunk of *huemac* to chew thoughtfully.

The day died, the sun dipped behind mountains, temperature dropped. Hoshi'tiwa drew her goat-hide cloak around herself and kept her eyes on the campfire flames. The feeling of being watched intensified. Strangely, she felt no fear.

When a human figure materialized in the light of her fire, long after the sun had set and the stars were out, she looked up at a remarkable person. His body was covered in the red-orange dust of the region, his hair adorned with twigs and leaves, and about his waist hung a grass skirt instead of a loincloth. It was camouflage, Hoshi'tiwa realized. The man looked as if he had stepped from the landscape, and should he retreat a few steps, he would vanish again.

Without rising, Hoshi'tiwa held out a bladder of *huemac,* made eating gestures, and smiled.

Others materialized—women and children this time—disguised the same as the man, in dust and twigs and grass. An elder came forward and shyly accepted the offering.

They sat with her, delicately sharing the *huemac* and finding it a treat, and presently Hoshi'tiwa learned something astonishing. Although her companions spoke an unfamiliar dialect of the People of the Sun, they were able to communicate that they lived high atop a nearby mesa and survived by blending in with their surroundings. They called themselves simply "the People," but Hoshi'tiwa privately named them the Invisible Ones. Neither the Toltecs nor the raiders knew of their village, where they lived a peaceful existence. Nor had the sky-stone traders been aware of them, for the Invisible Ones had seen that the traders were not men of goodwill but rather were exploiters, and so did not show themselves.

But what Hoshi'tiwa soon learned, and what astonished her, was that these people did not all belong to the same clan. In fact, as she studied their faces in the firelight, she began to realize that a variety of identifying tattoos decorated their cheeks, foreheads, and chins. Outside of Center Place, she had never heard of different clan members living together in one community. As she remarked on this, the elder of the group explained that they had not started out as a communal group but were refugees from clans escaping the abductions of the Jaguars. The elder himself was the last of his people, having run and hid when the Dark Lord's soldiers came to his settlement long ago to snatch away girls, youths, women, and men.

These people were refugees, Hoshi'tiwa learned, who had found one another in hiding, had stayed together for protection, and had since formed a community that was safe from the Jaguars, resigned to the fact that they would never again see members of their own clans.

After a spell of companionship, the elder thanked Hoshi'tiwa for sharing her bounty and said they were in her debt. Then they left, disappearing as soon as they stepped from the light of the campfire.

Now, sixteen days out of Center Place, Hoshi'tiwa was crouched in sagebrush, watching the small band of raiders whom the Invisible Ones had warned her about, saying that their reputation for being savage and ruthless stemmed from the fact that they were nomads; these men neither built settlements nor grew crops, but existed by stealing from others.

Finally, to her relief, they picked up their bows and arrows, their carrying bundles and buckskin blankets, and struck off northward. Hoshi'tiwa waited until their voices faded, their campfire had burned down, and the sun dipped into the west. When she was sure the raiders were not coming back, she slowly unfolded herself, her joints creaking as she did so. She left her hiding place without pausing for food or water, and hurried on toward the southeast, intent upon putting as much terrain between herself and the savage nomads as she could.

Four days later, after a trek through springtime country where she found game and water in plenty but no other human beings, the skystone trail ended, as she had known it would, at the Big River.

Wide and curving, its sandy banks lined with cottonwood trees, clumps of cattails and reeds growing in marshy places along its edge, with silver minnows glittering in the shallows, Big River was the largest body of water Hoshi'tiwa had ever seen. She thought of the drought at Center Place, the children dying of thirst, and wished she could summon them all to this glorious place.

As she pondered this new obstacle, Hoshi'tiwa did not know that future generations would call this river the Rio Grande. She did not know that this mighty pathway of water originated in mountains far to the north in Colorado and emptied in the south into what would one day be known as the Gulf of Mexico.

Hoshi'tiwa knew only one thing: that because she did not know how to swim, she must find a way to cross to the other side.

Fifty-seven

THE night Hoshi'tiwa had left for the sky-stone mines, Chief Physician Nagual gave her two things: directions to the mines, and a protective kachina spirit.

Wishing her well and uttering a prayer of blessing and protection, he left her in a place of concealment where she would wait until it was safe to collect supplies and weapons from the Precious Green kitchen before leaving Center Place.

Nagual had then gone to his quarters to retrieve his medicine bundle and a goatskin of water. He was needed at Blue Hummingbird, where the wife of the Chief Archivist was suffering from evil spirits in her stomach. But as Nagual left Precious Green, he paused and looked down the canyon where late afternoon shadows stretched long and dark over sand and shelter. Soldiers and guards were combing the canyon for the whereabouts of Hoshi'tiwa. He knew their search was futile, and wondered what Xikli would do when she could not be found. Would he send Jaguars out into the countryside, possibly even along the sky-stone trail?

But Hoshi'tiwa was no longer Nagual's concern.

Turning his gaze toward the far western edge of the valley, he thought about Yani, whom he had left in the kachina cave. He was worried about her, his beloved, secret wife. When he and Hoshi'tiwa had left her, Yani was in a terrible emotional state, and looking so woebegone that Nagual could not put it from his mind. Deciding to let the archivist's wife suffer awhile longer with her stomach pains, Nagual struck off on the path to the western end of Center Place.

He arrived at the secret cave to find Yani still in an agitated state, even more so, he thought, and wondered why. She was frantically removing the kachina idols from their shelves and niches and tucking them at the back of the cave where they would not be found. "But Yani," he said, perplexed by her behavior, "we will need them for the Equinox celebration."

She turned a shockingly white face to him. "We have been found out."

"What do you mean? The cave?"

"Everything!" she cried, her voice echoing in the limestone cavern. "The kachinas, that you are the head priest, that you and I are married!"

His hand shot to his chest. "How?" he whispered.

"When you left with Hoshi'tiwa, I found Yellow Feather at the cave entrance. She overheard our entire conversation."

Nagual carefully set down the waterskin and his medicine bundle—a large swath of cotton fabric wrapped around diagnostic tools and healing supplies—and took Yani by the shoulders. "Do not panic, my love. Yellow Feather is a greedy girl. We can pay whatever she demands."

Yani shook her head. "This is not about payment. It is about revenge. She reminded me of the day I banished her from the potters' workshop and she said that now I will be sorry for what I did."

Nagual frowned, deep in thought. When the girl had come to him the month before, to report finding the heretics' kachina cave, and he had rewarded her and told her to leave the cultists alone, he thought he had heard the last of her. But now Yellow Feather knew much more, and this time it was dangerous information. "She did not demand payment?" he asked incredulously.

"She demanded nothing. She smiled a wicked smile and walked

away. By now she is already talking to High Minister Moquihix, or perhaps to Captain Xikli. It is only a matter of time—" Yani's voice broke.

Drawing her into his arms, Nagual held her tight and made soothing sounds. There was nothing he could say. Despite his lofty station, he knew that they were powerless in the face of their crimes. Xikli, he knew, would use them as an example, and as a stepping stone in his climb to power.

Their time together had come to an end, Nagual knew. But only Yani would be sacrificed, for he was too powerful, and too vital. He knew that Jakál would find a reason to spare his life.

"They will not execute you," she said, thinking the same thoughts, "they will say I bewitched you. But they *will* demand my sacrifice."

Nagual drew back, holding her by the shoulders, and said with passion, "Then we will run away together. We can go where they will never find us."

Yani smiled sadly and laid her hand on his face. "If we do that, the kachinas will perish. They need you to keep them alive."

"I cannot live without you!"

"My dearest, the kachina spirits are more important than our earthly time together. You must live so that the people can embrace the kachinas."

"Then *you* must run, save yourself."

She shook her head. "Nor could I live without you. I will stay, Nagual."

Tears dampened his eyes. "They will execute you."

"And before they do I will stand up and tell our people about the kachina spirits."

Nagual thought about this. He knew that a holy war was brewing between Quetzalcoatl and Blue Hummingbird—that only Xikli or Jakál could be the victor. He also knew that such a war could destroy the kachinas altogether. Although Yani was right, that they needed their human guardian and therefore he must stay and see to their care, Yani must not be allowed to speak up to Jakál.

"If you do this," he said, "then our cult will be hunted down and stamped out. You must say nothing."

Pressing her lips together, she nodded in agreement. She was to go to her death in silence. A dishonorable end.

"What I will do," he said in tones that he hoped comforted her, "I will allow the kachina spirits to sleep so that they come to no harm. When peace has been restored in the valley, when one god triumphs over the other, I will resume the kachina rituals and I will show our people the comfort and solace these benevolent spirits bring."

Taking Yani's square, handsome face in his hands, he bent his head and kissed her gently on the lips. And he felt himself die inside. He could not bear to lose this woman who had restored his life.

When his son was caught taking pleasure with the daughter of a potter and was ordered back to Tollan as a reprimand, Nagual had thought life could not be bleaker until word came back that the boy had died en route, under mysterious circumstances and possibly by suicide. Nagual felt that he, too, had died. This man of impressive bearing and such power as to control life and death at the altar of blood, had moved through his days and nights like one made of stone.

And then came a day, as he dwelled in personal darkness, when he glimpsed across the marketplace the potter named Yani, whose daughter his son had loved. Nagual's initial impulse had been to hate the woman, to blame her and her daughter for the boy's destruction. But as their paths continued to cross, as they must with the potters' workshop being in such proximity to his own quarters in Precious Green, he started to notice the shadows on her face, the haunted look, the listless way she walked, and he had thought: She is in the same pain as I.

After that, he contrived to cross her path, to accidentally encounter her in the marketplace. He invented excuses to visit the potters' workshop and make eye contact with this woman he could not stop thinking about. And she, too, like Jakál's curious fish-shaped Guiding Stone, seemed to point always to Nagual, walking nearby in the plaza, materializing in his view with increasing frequency.

After their first halting conversations and furtive meetings, they discovered the powerful bond of shared grief.

Then he remembered the kachina spirits he had brought from Tollan (where they were already an old, secret cult). After finding a hidden cave, he asked Yani to help him waken the spirits. There, amid incense and torchlight, she had watched the dance of Crow Mother and had felt the stones of bitterness she had built up around her heart start to break away and fall. When she broke down and cried, Nagual, no longer in Crow Mother costume, comforted her in his arms. He no longer hated or blamed her, but was falling in love with her.

Together, with the help of the kachina spirits, they worked through their grief and loss, the benevolent beings assuring them that the cycle of life was inevitable and good, that the brief sojourns on earth of Nagual's son and Yani's daughter had been part of the cosmic plan and that the souls of the two enjoyed the peace and bliss of afterlife with the Great Creator.

"Let us honor the spirits one last time," Nagual said now as he opened his medicine bundle and retrieved the goatskin of water. He turned his back to Yani so that she could not see how his hands shook.

He filled two small gourds with water, sprinkling a sacred herb into one of them, stirring it with his finger until the herb was dissolved.

He turned and held out the cup.

Yani looked at it, saw the quivering surface that meant his hand was shaking. She smiled and took the cup. "We told too many lies, my love, to protect the kachina spirits and to further our own ends," she said, thinking of the lie she had told Hoshi'tiwa and wishing now she had not.

She drank, tasted the bitterness, and drank again. Nagual sipped from his cup, his hooded eyes heavy with sadness. Yani looked up at him and marveled that a man so handsome, with such regal bearing, had looked upon a humble Daughter of the Sun with favor. And with love.

She drained her cup and handed it back. The air in the cave grew heavy, even though it was late winter and the day was cold. She felt the kachina spirits swimming around her in their ethereal sea, whispering in her ears, holding out their arms like protective wings. She remembered her first kachina ritual, when Crow Mother had danced—a figure dressed entirely in white, and singing a beautiful, haunting song. Yani had been so mesmerized by the ghostly spirit that she had forgotten her grief and anger and had allowed the spirit to enter her heart. And when Crow Mother had picked up a basket of corn to symbolize the eternal cycle of life, and her people's connection to the earth, Yani had broken down and cried.

She did not feel like crying now. Instead, a strange lightness entered her soul. The cave seemed to grow bright, even though they had not lit any torches. And a sense of such utter peace stole over her that she had to suddenly sit down. She said, "My love, have I drunk from the cup of death?"

He swallowed with difficulty. "You have. I will not let them offer your beating heart to their bloody gods. I will not let them make a spectacle of you, and shame you before your people." He knelt at her side. "Your passing will be painless, I promise."

"Then promise me this as well," and she pointed to the golden jar that Hoshi'tiwa had left in the cave. "Give the rain jar to Lord Jakál."

When Nagual gave her a quizzical look, Yani said, "Hoshi'tiwa loves him and I suspect that he loves her, but their two worlds keep them apart as our two worlds stand between us, as they did between our children. Hoshi'tiwa would want Jakál to have the golden jar, for I think there is more to the inspired message painted on its body than the guidance of spirits. I believe it was Jakál, although Hoshi'tiwa does not know it, who inspired such a treasure. He will keep it safe."

Her vision grew dim. She reached for Nagual, and his arms went quickly around her. "I have not regretted a moment of our time together," she whispered.

"Nor I," he said, his tears splashing onto her cheeks.

They kissed again, long and deep, until Yani's final breath filled Nagual's lungs.

She died in his arms, and although he wanted to sit and hold her and pray for the peaceful release of her spirit, he knew that Jaguars would be coming. So he carried her to the far end of the cavern and gently laid her down in a deep, hidden niche, placing stones over her body so that it would never be found. And then he gathered the kachinas to carry them far from this place, and as he did so he wept bitterly. For the second time in his life, Chief Physician Nagual had died, and yet he still lived.

Fifty-eight

HOSHI'TIWA stood at the edge of Big River and looked over the water in stark terror.

Long ago, when her father had traveled to another village to trade jars for blankets, he had taken little Hoshi'tiwa with him, and along the way they had encountered a mighty river. It was there Hoshi'tiwa tasted her first fear of a body of water, and where she had seen, at its edge, the hidden depths and currents to which she would later compare Lord Jakál. But she and her father had not crossed that river. And the stream that trickled past her family settlement in the north was a small ankle-deep channel that had been easily traversed on stepping stones.

Looking to the left and right, upstream and downstream of the great flowing water, she saw no place where she could cross, no narrow, shallow place, no convenient boulders that would carry her to the other side.

How had the sky-stone traders crossed?

She spoke gently to the river-spirit, trying to hide her fear as she explained her urgent necessity to cross its body, asking if there were some way it could help her.

There was no response.

As the day was dying, she made camp in the shelter of tall reeds and boulders. In case raiders were nearby, she did not light a fire, but sated herself with cold *huemac* and then wrapped herself in the goat-hide cloak and fell into a fitful sleep, worrying about the river, fearful of drowning.

She dreamed of Grandfather Tortoise, who had once saved her life. In the dream, he spoke to her but no sound came from his throat. And as he had no hands, he could not make himself understood through gestures. When she awoke before dawn, she puzzled over the meaning of the dream.

Breaking camp and hoisting her carrying bundle onto her back, Hoshi'tiwa followed the river downstream, noting that it grew wider and calmer. Despite its placid surface, however, she sensed strong undercurrents, reminding her of Lord Jakál and his mercurial moods, how treacherous he had been, and how treacherous the river could be, so that her heart rose in her throat as it had when Yani told her of the price Jakál had placed on her head. This river could kill her as surely as Jakál wished to.

Yet she must cross it.

Her stomach grumbled, reminding her that she had not eaten in a while. Walking away from the water's edge, she approached the dense inland vegetation, and as she scanned the area for edible berries and seeds, wanting to preserve her store of *huemac* for as long as possible, she spotted something in the muddy soil.

Animal tracks.

Bending close, she noted the oval-shaped pads and five little toe-points. They looked familiar. But more distinctive was the line drawn between them, the distinct mark of tail drag. And when she saw the drops of dark green scat, she almost cried out in joy.

She followed the tracks as they moved parallel to the river, and then turned toward the water. She lost them occasionally as they entered wet sand and the prints were nearly obscured, and she twice went in the wrong direction but picked up the trail again so that at midday, she came upon the large desert tortoise, placidly nibbling on vegetation near the river. And lying nearby on the sandy bank was a large dead tree, its roots dry in the air, its trunk blackened by lightning strike.

Hoshi'tiwa smiled and whispered, "Thank you again, Grandfather Tortoise," and proceeded to remove her tunic and skirt and wrap them, with everything else, in her waterproof goat-hide cloak.

Tying the bundle to her bare back, she pushed and dragged the log until she got it to the water's edge, where she paused to pray to the river-spirit, and to pray to her personal gods for inner strength and courage. Then, with her heart pounding and her mouth dry, she waded into the water, which was cold from winter snowmelt, plunging in waist deep and pulling the log with her. She waded out as far as she could until the swifter undercurrent began to tug at her legs. She clambered up onto the log and, frantically wrapping her arms around it, clinging for dear life, she rode it downstream.

Knowing from the Invisible Ones that she must not let the river carry her too far south or she would miss the mines altogether, she began to paddle with her hands to turn the log, fighting the current, making a little sideways progress. Then she stopped and rested and rode the river downstream again, trying not to think of the vast expanse of water all around her, that she was out in the middle of it, far from land, at the mercy of its tides, before paddling once more with all her might, muscles straining against the water, using her legs as rudders to fight the current. Fear fueled her; terror infused strength into her fatigued muscles. Thus did she cross the Big River in an arduous zigzag fashion that left her exhausted and panting on the opposite bank, thanking the gods for helping her safely across.

When she recovered and was able to dry and dress herself, she paused first to thank the spirit of the river for carrying her safely across. But now she was deep in the territory of the savage marauders, and Hoshi'tiwa knew she must not let her guard down for even an instant. Therefore she did not light a fire, she ate only enough *huemac* to sustain herself, and then found a safe sleeping place among boulders and brush.

In the morning she woke to landscape that was hilly and rugged, with scrubby vegetation and occasional dense stands of trees. She advanced cautiously now, listening for voices, pausing frequently to look around. But she heard only birds, and small creatures rustling in the growth. If there were men nearby, they were being quiet.

On the third day she entered a cluster of cottonwood trees, moved stealthily through, but when she emerged into sunlight, the ground suddenly gave way. In a quick reflex, she grabbed a low-hanging branch and clutched it as sand and rock fell beneath her. Pulling herself up and scrambling back onto solid ground, she looked down at a wide hole in the ground, dropping into a deep, black vertical shaft.

She had almost been swallowed by the earth.

Placing her hand on her chest, recovering her breath, and feeling her heart slow to a normal rate, Hoshi'tiwa scanned the area more carefully and realized in horror that the ground all about was dotted with dangerous openings into which she could plunge and have no way of climbing out.

She had found the mines.

She felt her way now with the tip of the spear, punching the ground as if she were planting corn, jumping back when the earth gave way, or proceeding if it were solid, until finally she came upon a flat clearing that was obviously a main camp. Or had been. Grass shelters still stood, and blackened rings of stones indicated where cook fires had burned. She found tools scattered everywhere—stone hammers and axes, antler picks, mauls and chisels, leather buckets with head straps. But the miners were nowhere to be seen.

She continued her exploration of the eerily silent place until she came upon what must have been the main pit mine—a vast hole nearly the diameter of the main plaza at Precious Green—and when she peered in, saw that it plunged to such a depth that the bottom could not be seen. The sides of the pit mine were lined with notched ladders, clearly what the miners used to scale up and down with leather tool belts and buckets for rocks.

The pit was dark, silent and deserted.

With a growing dread—where was Ahoté?—she returned to the

main camp. There was no evidence of recent campfires, or of any human habitation in the last few months. She found a few bleached rabbit and armadillo bones, picked clean, but they had been there a long time.

The cold, eerie wind picked up, whistling mournfully through the trees, and the back of her neck prickled as she sensed danger. Clutching her spear in both hands, ready to strike in defense, she moved through the trees. In a clearing on the other side she found the ground littered with bewildering objects. It was not until she crept closer that she realized they were human bones and skulls.

Crying out and tracing protective signs in the air, she looked in horror upon the hundreds of scattered remains, bleaching in the sun. Then she saw the arrowheads and tips of spears, ends of stone axes that had come off, and she knew that a terrible slaughter had taken place here.

As she crossed the clearing, murmuring prayers while she did so and asking for blessings upon the slain men, she again plunged into dense trees and when she came out the other side, found what had obviously been the compound where the slaves were kept. Here, too, she found skeletons whitened by the sun and picked clean by scavengers. These men had not even been able to fight back, for the skeletons were still tethered to posts in the ground, as she had once been tethered during her forced march to Center Place.

And then her eye caught something that was neither bone nor rock nor arrowhead. Bending close, she recognized the fat little owl body she had fashioned from clay, the pointed owl ears, the big comical eyes she had painted on the face. The figurine was still attached to the string she had made for it, the string still looped around a neck that was now a row of tender white bones connected to a fleshless skull.

She slumped to the ground. She had found Ahoté.

Fifty-nine

As White Orchid hurried through the marketplace, she eschewed her carrying chair, as she did not wish to be recognized—she felt herself driven not by her earlier fears and desperation, but by a strangely emotionless resolve.

"We cannot wait any longer," her father had said that morning. "Today I will send for Captain Xikli and we will seal the marriage contract. I am sorry, Daughter, but it is for your own good."

As she threaded her way among vendors of rabbit pelts and copper bells, she saw that most customers looked but did not buy. A thriving economy, everyone knew, depended upon rain. The drought had caused a shortage of crops, which led to a shortage of goods, and such goods as were for trade were too expensive.

Crime was on the rise, as desperate people turned to desperate measures. In her own household, White Orchid suspected her slaves of stealing. And when she had come home from the kiva one afternoon to discover her pet monkey missing—a species prized for its fur and meat—her servants had hung their heads and said the animal had simply run away.

And now this growing rivalry between the two major gods of Center Place.

Captain Xikli and his Jaguars were becoming bolder and more vocal in their insinuations that Lord Jakál and his god were responsible for the drought. While keeping their words short of being treasonous, they fomented discontent among the masses. Their message was this: Blue Hummingbird will restore balance and bring rain, but the god of war demanded that Quetzalcoatl and his weak leader be deposed.

Wily merchants, seeing an opportunity for profit, created emblems for the two factions, and called out over their wares: "Let the gods know whom you honor!" The symbols were turkey feathers—blue for Blue Hummingbird and green for Quetzalcoatl—and so hastily dyed that the color rubbed off on the buyer's hands. The feathers had triggered an unexpected chain reaction as each camp grew increasingly bold in publicly averring their support for this god or that.

White Orchid's thoughts returned to her father, who had said, "I love you more than the sun and the moon, my sweet child, but I am thinking of your safety. You know this, do you not?"

"Yes, Father," she had said, kneeling to kiss him. She understood his concerns. With the continued drought, the land upon which their villa stood was becoming increasingly more valuable due to the small artesian well that gave forth a trickle of brackish water. A path was being beaten to Tenoch's door by the feet of men eager to marry his daughter and take ownership of the property. White Orchid and her father both knew that he had not many years left and that once she was a woman on her own, she would be defenseless against ruthless men who would stop at nothing to steal everything from her. And so she knew she must be married.

But she was going to make sure it wasn't to the odious Xikli.

For the first time, White Orchid's was not a mission of seduction. She wore no cosmetic, had not reddened her teeth, and had dressed plainly. She even arrived unescorted, and when she announced herself to the guard at the main entrance of Precious Green, he initially dismissed her as a commoner. But a few sharp words from her in Nahuatl, with the ease of one used to giving orders, and he vanished inside.

White Orchid had not sought Jakál at his pavilion near the site of the new pyramid, because everyone knew he had abandoned the project. Plunged into an inexplicable torpor, the Lord of Center Place had retreated to his quarters at Precious Green, where he received few visitors and rarely ventured outside.

Few knew the reason for Jakál's depression: Hoshi'tiwa's disappearance. Even fewer knew of his impulsive plan to unite the two races by making intermarriage legal—with the Lord of Center Place setting an example by being the first to openly wed a girl of the People of the Sun. But White Orchid knew all of this through her spy, and now she hoped to use Jakál's vulnerable state to her own advantage. I will make Jakál strong again, she thought in firm resolve, and together we will restore peace and harmony to Center Place.

The guard returned and said, "I am sorry, my Lady. You cannot go in. Lord Jakál is accepting no visitors."

"You cannot continue like this, my Lord," Moquihix said, spreading his hands in a gesture of helplessness. For that was how he felt. With his Lord in a torpor, the running of Center Place had been left to him. If Moquihix, as a young man, had once aspired to be *tlatoani,* that dream had long faded.

Along with his virility, he thought bitterly. Hoshi'tiwa might be gone from Center Place, and her enchantment over him no longer effective, but his old problem had returned and he feared now that he would never regain his manhood. With increasing frequency he was dreaming of Tollan, the city of his youth and sexual prowess. And the yearning to go home grew within him like the irrepressible desire for an unreachable woman.

But if he could not go home, then he would settle for a Toltec city here at Center Place, starting with the pyramid that Jakál had abandoned.

Lord Jakál did not respond, but sat on his throne carved from mahogany and inlaid with jade and sky-stone, oblivious of the attention of the young dancers from Five Flower, deaf to the twin flute players, and without appetite for the platters of food and mugs of *chocolatl*.

He was reliving over and over the morning that Captain Xikli had come to him to report that Hoshi'tiwa had left Center Place.

"There is a girl, Yellow Feather," the Captain had said, "who used to be a member of the Potters' Guild—"

"What about her?" Jakál had been short with him. He had spent all night waiting for his men to bring Hoshi'tiwa to the pavilion, a night spent in eager anticipation of her surprise and delight when he told her of his plan to marry her and his vow to enslave her people no more. But by dawn they had not found her, and Jakál had been left sick of spirit and body.

"Yellow Feather is a friend of the rain-girl," Xikli had said. "She told me the girl has left Center Place."

"Why would she tell *you*?" Jakál had asked suspiciously. "Why did she not come to me, knowing that I was searching for Summer Rain?"

"I do not know, my Lord. Perhaps she heard that I offer generous rewards for important information."

"But why would Summer Rain leave?" Jakál had cried.

"People are saying that Hoshi'tiwa," Xikli said pointedly, to remind Jakál of the girl's real name, "feared your wrath."

"My wrath? By the gods, I want to marry her!"

Jakál could not accept that Hoshi'tiwa was gone, and had refused to give up hope of finding her and marrying her. Yet, with each day of fruitless search, his hope dimmed. Finally, Chief Physician Nagual had come to Jakál with information that corroborated what Xikli had said: that Hoshi'tiwa and the Overseer of Potters, a woman named Yani, had fled Center Place together. Nagual's advice had been to forget her. It would not be worth the time and manpower to search for her, especially with discontent rising in the valley and the Jaguars needed to police possible insurgents. "It is Xikli's doing," Nagual had said. "His men are encouraging people to take sides, to choose which god they honor. He is working to create a schism at Center Place."

Unlike the Captain of the Jaguars, Nagual was a man Jakál trusted.

The physician had made the long journey up from Tollan with him; they had spent many nights along the way in conversation and company. And Nagual was a follower of Quetzalcoatl. He had even taken to wearing a green feather.

So it was true. Hoshi'tiwa was gone.

Moquihix now pursed his lips and saw that his words fell upon deaf ears. What could be done to waken his Lord out of this strange melancholy and get back to the business of government and building the pyramid?

When a guard from the main entrance came in to announce that Lady White Orchid was requesting an audience, and Jakál said, "No," Moquihix thought quickly. He suspected the reason for her visit. It was no secret that Tenoch was eager for her to marry. And Captain Xikli, it was said, was Tenoch's choice.

Since his own prodding had come to no avail, Moquihix wondered if a time-honored persuasion might work—the wiles of a woman?

Hastily excusing himself, with Jakál barely noticing, Moquihix hurried after the guard and arrived at the entrance as White Orchid was turning away. "My Lady!" he called. When she faced him, he fabricated his best smile—although it pained him to expose yet another gap where a tooth had once been—and said, "The guard is mistaken. Lord Jakál would welcome your company."

Her nonexistent eyebrows rose, and then she read a message in the aging High Minister's eyes—tacit approval of her purpose there—and went inside.

She was filled with urgency. Tenoch had sent for Xikli; perhaps they were already speaking at that moment. Even so, White Orchid reassured herself, if she could return home to say that she was to marry Jakál, her father would annul any arrangement he had made with the Captain.

Jakál looked at her in mild surprise when she entered.

After making proper obeisance, she said quietly, "My Lord, I have come with a proposition."

When he said nothing, she gave him a significant look. Jakál flicked his wrist, and the dancers, musicians, and servants left the room.

Once they were alone amid incense and flickering torchlight, she knelt at his side and said, "Your power is weakening, my Lord, everyone says so. Xikli intends to rule in your place."

He hardly stirred as he said, "He cannot depose me."

His listlessness startled her, even though she had heard of the depression that claimed the Lord of Center Place. "Perhaps not, my Lord, but without the support of the Jaguars and all the nobles and officials, you would be too weak to rule. You might remain *tlatoani,* but it would be in name only, an empty title."

His expression was blank, and it frightened her. She spoke quickly. "My father wishes for me to marry Captain Xikli. Xikli knows that by allying himself to the house of Tenoch the Hero, he gives himself new prestige and stature. He will also inherit my father's many friends and allies. This marriage would tip the balance in Xikli's favor. In Blue Hummingbird's favor," she added with emphasis.

Jakál finally looked down at the beautiful, aristocratic face. Even without cosmetic, she was an alluring woman. But her face was not like an upturned flower. She did not stir his heart and loins as Hoshi'tiwa had. Nonetheless, she *was* a noblewoman, and she spoke with urgency, reminding him of his position. "You said you came with a proposition?" he asked, although it was without interest.

"That you and I wed," she said abruptly, and hurried on before he could protest. "You would be allied to the house of Tenoch the Hero, and reap the benefits of such. The people love my father, and he is a follower of Quetzalcoatl. Were you and I to marry, many who now wear blue feathers would exchange them for green."

She paused to let this sink in, and when he seemed to be considering her words, she added, "If you do not wish to think of your own position here, then think of Center Place, of the chaos that is brewing, and of what a holy war would do."

When he continued to say nothing, White Orchid pressed on, "At least think of Quetzalcoatl, for whom you are building a magnificent pyramid."

He finally said, "The temple . . ."

Rising to her feet and standing before him, she drew open her cloak to expose her dress underneath, and Jakál's eyes widened in surprise.

Stitched carefully into the white cotton, so that it looked as if it were part of the fabric itself, was a flawless, shimmering green quetzal feather, elegantly long and delicately curved, from the collar to below the waist, a bold and striking statement that she, Lady White Orchid, daughter of Tenoch the Hero, was a follower of the Lord of the Breath of Life.

"It is lovely," he said softly. But that was all. She had expected the sight of it would stir him from his morose state.

White Orchid bit her lip in disappointment. She had labored for days over the feather, working it into the cotton, using the finest thorns and threads, praying over her hands as they stitched, burning precious incense and calling upon all the gods of Center Place to infuse their blessings and magic into the masterpiece.

And then suddenly, as she looked down at the man garbed in the finest cotton, his bronze forearms heavy with gold and sky-stone, the topknot of his long hair elegantly intertwined with scarlet, blue, and green feathers—this man she had desired and admired and loved—she suddenly saw him as weak. And she was filled with disgust.

"So you will let Xikli defeat you?" she asked archly, forgetting her place. If it were in her nature, she would have spat at his feet.

"Leave me," Jakál said wearily.

"I had not thought you so easily vanquished," she said, her sudden contempt overriding common sense and self-preservation. White Orchid's barbed words verged upon treason.

Yet even these did not stir the man on the throne. And in that moment White Orchid felt all the disillusionments and disappointments of her life come to a head. No one on earth could be trusted or counted on. Men pretended to be fathers, or to be strong rulers, and women masqueraded as mothers, or as preachers of a comforting new faith. Ultimately, everyone White Orchid had turned to for help or comfort had let her down. Even Hoshi'tiwa, although the girl herself did not know it. While White Orchid had initially gone to Hoshi'tiwa's gatherings to find a way to separate her from the bear claw necklace, White Orchid had listened to the message of connectedness, that no one was alone, and the words of hope had lodged in White Orchid's hardened heart until she had felt a small easing of her private agony. Forgetting her contract with Bone Snapper, White Orchid had decided to become a follower of the new creed. And then Hoshi'tiwa had run for her life, abandoning her followers.

I will never trust anyone again, White Orchid thought bitterly as she drew her cloak over the quetzal feather and said to Jakál, "Very well, my Lord, I will leave you. Xikli has won. And it did not take alliances and powerful friends, or wealth or a distinguished marriage. All he had to do was put a bounty on that common girl's head and he won!"

Jakál's head snapped up. "What did you say?"

White Orchid looked down at him, saw the sudden life and interest in his eyes. "You did not know?" she said. "Captain Xikli has offered a generous reward to whoever brings the girl to him."

Jakál rose slowly to his feet and White Orchid felt a resurgence of his power. And then she realized: Here was the key to awakening him. She had had it all along, but had not known! "It was why the girl left Center Place," she said quickly, seeing the fury rise in his face, his body tighten, his jaw clench, and deep color infuse his neck and cheeks. "Xikli said the reward would be paid whether she was brought dead or alive."

"By the gods!" Jakál bellowed, and guards from the outer corridor came running.

When Jakál began to shout orders to summon a regiment, that Captain Xikli was to be arrested and brought before the throne of Center Place, White Orchid calmly stopped him and urged caution until, grasping the wisdom of her counsel, he retracted his orders and dismissed the guards.

"Do not act rashly, my Lord," White Orchid said. Her hand, lying on his arm, trembled. She had brought him back to life. Now she needed to channel his newly born rage in the right direction. "Xikli is more powerful than you know. To confront him now might not mean a victory for you. If you wish to punish him for sending the girl away, you must move carefully and with a plan."

"I want more than mere punishment," Jakál growled, his heart thumping in joy—Hoshi'tiwa had not fled because of *him*!—and rage. "I want Xikli to suffer. I will have him tortured—"

"My Lord," White Orchid said quietly, glancing toward the doorway covered with but a woven hanging, inviting eavesdroppers. "Let us work together. I have the same ambition for Xikli as you. Together, you and I will be stronger than he. Together," she licked her lips, "we will punish him."

Jakál immediately grasped her meaning. He looked into the calm, calculating eyes of this aristocratic woman, thought of another pair of eyes that reminded him of pebbles in a stream, and understood what he must do. As long as Xikli's bounty was on her head, Hoshi'tiwa would not come back to Center Place. The only way to lift that bounty was to vanquish Xikli. And to accomplish that, Jakál needed power. The unpleasant and inescapable fact was that, to bring Hoshi'tiwa back, he must marry this woman. "Very well," he said, knowing that by speaking these words the chance to marry Hoshi'tiwa was forever out of his reach. "Tell your father that I will marry you. As soon as possible."

Jakál had finally spoken the words White Orchid had long dreamed of hearing. Yet, strangely, they brought no joy. He would always yearn for Hoshi'tiwa. White Orchid knew this now. The rain-girl would always have his heart. And so the noblewoman arrived at a cold decision. If he never loved her, it would not matter. She would have the man, his title, his power, and his children.

She would be the mother of a new and noble bloodline.

Xikli was pleased with himself. He had gone to the house of Tenoch the Hero armed with four weapons: a scribe, two witnesses, and a gourd of the strongest *nequhtli*. He could not possibly lose.

And now, everything was finally falling into place. The throne would soon be his.

Along with a report on Hoshi'tiwa, Yellow Feather had told him about Nagual and his illegal marriage to the Overseer of Potters. A useful piece of information that Xikli would not yet act upon, but choose a time when it would be most beneficial to himself. He would allow Nagual to falsely think he and his illegal wife, and their heretical cult, were safe. The day would come when Nagual, too, joined Xikli's supporters.

For now, he had Tenoch the Hero in his camp.

Their transaction was done. The scribe had recorded the agreement on paper, a contract that included not only the promise of marriage to Tenoch's daughter, but also the relinquishing of his lands and water rights to Captain Xikli. The Captain knew that Tenoch preferred his daughter marry Jakál and might still back out should she return to say that she and Jakál were to be wed. (It was no secret where White Orchid was at that moment.) The presence of two witnesses precluded such a possibility—powerful men whose word would not be questioned: the Superintendent of the Marketplace and the Chief Archivist, both of whom owed their high positions to the Jaguar Captain, both of whom had painted their marks on the contract.

Xikli and his entourage were emerging from Tenoch's bedroom when White Orchid came home. Their eyes met and locked across the atrium, where plants wilted in the late spring sunshine. White Orchid knew by the look on the Captain's face that her father had agreed to the marriage. But she lifted her chin and said, "You have wasted your time, Captain. Lord Jakál and I are to be wed."

Xikli showed her the contract drawn up by the scribe, pointing out its terms, ending with the personal marks of Tenoch, Copil, and the Archivist. "It is all legal and indisputable," Xikli added, folding the paper into accordion fashion so that it would fit on a shelf in the Blue Hummingbird archive.

She would not be cowed. "Lord Jakál will nullify the agreement. He has that power, once my father agrees to it."

"*If* your father agrees."

"He will," she said. Xikli might intimidate every man at Center Place, but Tenoch was not one of them.

"And what do you think Jakál will do when I tell him where the rain-girl has gone?"

White Orchid blinked.

"You see, my Lady, I am in possession of a certain piece of valuable information. I know where the rain-girl can be found."

White Orchid held her breath and waited. She knew what he was doing; she refused to take the bait.

"So far," he finally said, "I have said nothing to Jakál about the girl's whereabouts, for how would that benefit me? However, should you not honor this agreement between me and your father, I will divulge her location. What do you think will happen to your own agreement with Jakál then? Do you think he will even know your name when his head is filled with plans to fetch the girl back to Center Place?"

White Orchid's eyes narrowed. Xikli spoke a horrible, inescapable truth. Nonetheless, she said, "We shall see," making a gesture of dismissal. She would talk to her father. When he learned that Jakál had agreed to marry her, he would nullify this contract. Let Xikli tell Jakál where the girl was; Jakál was a man of honor. He would hold to his word and they would marry. And if he wanted to send men in search of the girl . . . well, there was still Bone Snapper.

Xikli strode past her, stopped suddenly, and leaning close, said with onion-breath, "I look forward to our wedding night."

White Orchid watched him go and wished she could take a bath. Instead, she would smoke his touch and his nearness out of her skin in the kiva. But first she must talk to Tenoch and persuade him to go at once to Jakál and void his contract with Xikli.

To her horror, she found her father lying passed out on his mat. Next to him, an empty gourd not familiar to her, and when she sniffed it, she realized Xikli had brought a gift of very strong *nequhtli*.

"Father," she said sharply. "Father."

White Orchid swallowed down her fear. "Father," she said more sharply. When he did not stir, she shook his shoulder. The skin felt strangely cool. "Father?"

When she shook him more vigorously, his head lolled to the side and she saw the blue lips, the strange pallor to his skin. Frantically she felt for a pulse at his neck, then pressed her ear to his chest.

Tenoch had no heartbeat, no breath.

"Father!" she screamed, and Xikli, who had taken his time walking down the path from the villa, laughed.

Sixty

HOSHI'TIWA was filled with rage.

Ahoté was dead, and one man was to blame. A man who had kissed her with his lips and joined his body to hers, taking pleasure with her, asking her to live with him, while Ahoté was in this terrible place.

Hoshi'tiwa had come on this journey to bring him back to Center Place, to show the people, to show Jakál himself that such treachery would not be tolerated. But now she had no Ahoté to bring back, only the little owl figurine.

But as she buried Ahoté's poor bones and said a prayer over them, keeping the figurine and hanging it next to the bear claw beneath her tunic, a new idea began to germinate in her mind, and the more she thought about it, the stronger it grew.

The Invisible Ones. Remnants of once-powerful clans, forced into hiding because of Jakál's demand for slaves. She would take *them* back to Center Place.

Filled with new purpose, knowing that the task was going to be a challenge—would the Invisible Ones even want to go to Center

Place?—and finding fresh vigor in her heart (where she nurtured a secret, fragile hope that what Yani had told her about Jakál had been untrue, that the man she had loved, and loved still, was not dishonorable), Hoshi'tiwa struck westward upon the abandoned sky-stone trail.

Sixty-one

MANY miles to the south, and many months prior, one hundred strong and brave warriors set out from the city of Tollan, heading north. They climbed mountains, forged rivers, hacked their way through jungles, survived extreme heat and cold, dying off one by one from poisonous snakes, wild animals, fever and sickness, so that only one man made it to Center Place, and he was on the brink of death when he was discovered and brought to Lord Jakál.

The man uttered but a few words before he expired: "The city has been burned to the ground—all the beautiful temples and pyramids and palaces destroyed—by our enemies. Tollan is no more."

And now it was the day of the Summer Solstice. Because Lord Jakál and his high officials, including Captain Xikli, kept the news of the collapsed empire a secret, keeping secret also the fact that no more caravans were coming, the main plaza of Precious Green was a-bustle with music, dancing, horn blowing, and chanting. And the People of the Sun, eager to please the gods so that they would bring rain, crowded the plaza and the valley.

As he readied himself for his entrance into the plaza, with four slaves dressing him and two scribes recording every word he uttered, Lord Jakál said to High Minister Moquihix, "Mark this day, my friend, for it will be remembered in years to come."

He was no longer morose. Learning that Hoshi'tiwa's flight from Center Place had not been because of him, but due to Xikli's bounty on her head, had infused him with renewed vigor and spirit. Throwing off his depression like a discarded cloak, Jakál had vowed to restore his power at Center Place, to build his temple to Quetzalcoatl, and to find Hoshi'tiwa and bring her back to be his bride.

"Captain Xikli might believe he can win," Jakál said to his High Minister, "but I am still *tlatoani,* and Xikli is soon to be painfully reminded of that fact."

Moquihix was not convinced. Was Jakál truly blind to the power Xikli had built for himself? Did he not see the profusion of blue feathers among the people, with only a few green here and there? Blue Hummingbird had all but won the bloodless holy war. Even now, out in the plaza as the populace waited for the Solstice ritual to begin, it was the statue of Blue Hummingbird that dominated, while that of Quetzalcoatl was not even to be seen.

Moquihix said quietly so that the scribe could not hear, "My Lord, we must leave this place."

Jakál held out his arms as a bright yellow ceremonial robe was draped over his shoulders. "I will not leave."

Moquihix glanced nervously at the slaves. "Everyone knows that when the gods abandon a place, the people must also leave. Thus it was with the great Teotihuacan, and so it was with Chichén Itzá, and now our own Tollan. We must do as we have always done—find a new place to build a city and start anew."

But Jakál shook his head. His was a vision of hope, not surrender.

Grimly, Moquihix said, "It is the girl. You wait for her. But she is never coming back."

"No," Jakál said with confidence. "She will return."

After White Orchid had told him about Xikli putting a bounty on Hoshi'tiwa's head, and that was why she fled, Jakál had been furious, wanting to slay Xikli on the spot. But White Orchid had cautioned care and planning, and part of that plan had been for Jakál to marry White Orchid and ally his house with hers. But then Tenoch signed a marriage contract with Xikli, and died shortly after. Such a contract, bearing Tenoch's mark and witnessed by two Toltec nobles, was unbreakable, and so Jakál was released from his promise to marry White Orchid.

With so noble a lady as his wife, Xikli now believed himself to be the most powerful man in the world, and he waged an evil, insidious war, encouraging internecine fighting among the erstwhile peaceful People of the Sun. Four men wearing blue feathers had been caught after raping a woman who wore the green. But as Jakál sat on his throne for a morning of judgment, the offenders were not brought before him. The Jaguars who had held the men in a stockade could not account for their escape. But when the family of the abused woman took justice in their own hands, attacking and killing two blue-feather men, the entire family was led to the altar of blood and sacrificed. Blue-feather merchants refused to sell to customers wearing the green feather; betrothals were broken when the families chose opposite sides; neighbor turned against neighbor; brother against brother.

It had to stop. Jakál must restore order and do away with the rivalry between the gods, restoring Blue Hummingbird to his rightful place as god of war, nothing more, and raising Quetzalcoatl to be the father god of Center Place. But because he had allowed his power to wane, and because marriage to Lady White Orchid was now out of the question, Jakál had only one recourse.

He was going to kill Captain Xikli.

It was still within his power to do so and not incur reprisal from the Jaguars. They had all sworn oaths of loyalty to their *tlatoani,* and as knights they were men of honor, men of their word. Jakál would then replace Xikli with his first lieutenant, a less ambitious man and one who placed honor above even his own life.

Jakál chose today for the act because the Summer Solstice was the most sacred day of the year to both People of the Sun and Toltec. Xikli's death would be symbolic and sacrosanct. The Jaguars would then obey Jakál's command to scour the four corners of the earth for Hoshi'tiwa, and bring her back for a wedding celebration such as Center Place never had seen.

The trumpets sounded, the procession lined up, and Jakál began to move toward the plaza. Before him went the priests of Quetzalcoatl, dancers and musicians, high officials, and Moquihix. In the sunlight, they fanned out and took their places facing the populace. And when Jakál emerged into the light of day, the thousands in the valley fell to their knees and pressed their foreheads to the ground.

Only those waiting to have their hearts cut from their chests did not kneel, for it was their right to remain standing in this last hour of their lives.

Jakál turned to where Xikli stood on the plaza with his Jaguars. The two rivals exchanged a slight nod, a signal that the ceremony was to begin. In a ringing voice, Jakál ordered the people to rise to their feet.

In the crowd of commoners, Yellow Feather, her fat boy riding her hip, watched in eager anticipation, while Pikami squinted with her old eyes and told her grandson to report what he saw. On the plaza, Chief Physician Nagual stood by the altar of blood, ready with the sacred drink, while across stood the priest with his obsidian knife. Standing among the highest-ranking nobility in their colorful finery was Lady White Orchid, known to all in the valley as the bride of Captain Xikli. Despite heavy cosmetic, those nearby saw the lines of bitterness and defeat etched into her features.

All eyes were upon Lord Jakál, who strode toward the waiting throne, where Xikli was to meet him and hand him up into the chair, a centuries-old gesture of the Jaguars' loyalty to their *tlatoani*. What no one saw, not even Moquihix and certainly not Xikli, was the dagger clasped tightly in Jakál's hand beneath his ceremonial robe.

The Captain strode forward, spear in one hand, club in the other, as emblems of his high office, and of his own personal oath to defend Center Place against all enemies. As he and Jakál reached the throne at the same time, Xikli raised his club and bashed it down on Jakál's head.

With a brief look of surprise on his face, Jakál's body dropped lifelessly to the ground.

The crowd fell silent. The nobles and Jaguars stood in frozen disbelief. The only sound to be heard was the snapping of pennants in the breeze. After a moment, a priest rushed forward, remembering himself and his duty, for he was the Soul-Sender priest, whose task it was to see that the ghost of a recent departed knew to fly away to the afterlife. Without this priest's special prayers, a dead man's ghost could linger and haunt the valley.

As the formidable man loudly intoned a prayer over the prone body of the fallen *tlatoani,* Xikli's defiant eyes scanned the faces of the nobles, officials, Jaguars. No one made a move to challenge him.

Smiling grimly, he stepped over Jakál, climbed up onto the throne of Center Place and, with a dramatic pause and then an exaggerated flourish, seated himself upon it, declaring in a loud voice, "Lord Jakál is dead! All pay homage to the new *tlatoani* of Center Place!"

Sixty-two

WHEN Hoshi'tiwa came again to the Big River, it proved no obstacle, for she found the rope hand-bridge that the sky-stone traders had used, and by this method was able to safely pull herself across to the other side.

She continued her westward trek along the abandoned trail, where already weeds obscured the path. The Spring Equinox had come and gone, snowmelt delivered refreshing streams with plentiful fish. Flowers bloomed everywhere. But Hoshi'tiwa was too heavy of heart to savor life. She had not known how desperately she hoped to be reunited with Ahoté until she realized she had come too late.

She came at last to the camp where she had encountered the Invisible Ones. Building a fire, she brought out the last of her *huemac*.

And waited.

She dreamed about the rain jar.

It came to her in hues of gold and orange and deep red, like a rich sunset splashed across the western sky, and etched with symbols and stunning imagery. Her message of *suukya'qatsi.* The Eternal Oneness.

When she awoke, she lay for a long time listening to the night. Although she could not see them, she sensed the Invisible Ones nearby. And she thought how peaceful it would be to stay and live among them, where there was no bounty on her head, no threat of execution, where she could live out her life in harmony and safety.

When dawn spilled over the mountains, Hoshi'tiwa saw a man standing at the edge of the encampment, covered in red dust, his hair disguised with twigs, a grass skirt about his waist. He was the elder with whom she had once shared *huemac,* the last surviving member of Snake Clan, he had said.

"Come with me to Center Place," Hoshi'tiwa said as the elder and his people sat with her, sharing food and conversation.

She had not forgotten the price Jakál had placed on her head, that she was to be brought before him dead or alive. She knew that by leading her people to the water reserved for the sacred glade she had overstepped her bounds and had finally incurred Jakál's wrath. How much greater was that wrath now? she wondered. It did not matter. If the bounty was still upon her head, if she returned to Center Place to face execution, so be it. She would not run away and hide. She would return with her head held high and with a message to her people: that the Lords were not invincible. That they did not govern life and death for the People of the Sun. That it was possible to stand up to the masters and show them the pride and spirit of the people who had been here long before the Toltecs came.

And she would deliver the message with these refugees at her side.

But the elder looked at her in astonishment. "Why should we go with you? We are safe here. There is game and water. We eat well. What is in Center Place for us?"

"Your families are there. Those who were taken from you are in Center Place."

"They are dead," growled a young man scarred with Badger Clan tattoos. "Those who were taken from us are dead."

"A few perhaps, but many live there and thrive. Our people belong together," Hoshi'tiwa said with passion. "We must pray together, and hold the rituals of our ancestors together. Otherwise we are scattered like seeds on the wind. Someday our people will vanish entirely."

"We will all be killed if we go there," cautioned a Wolf Clan woman.

"No, you won't," Hoshi'tiwa said.

"How do we know this girl speaks the truth?" asked another.

Soon they were murmuring among themselves, shaking heads or nodding. The elder held up a hand to silence them. "Our families were taken from us to be sacrificed to the gods of the Lords," he said to Hoshi'tiwa.

"Some, yes," she conceded. "But not all. I was taken from my home in the north and brought to Center Place to make rain jars. I am still alive, am I not?"

"Rain jars?" the elder said, eyes narrowing.

Hearing the spark of interest in his tone, Hoshi'tiwa stared at the tattoo on his jawline and suddenly remembered seeing another like it. "In fact," she said in excitement, "I know a member of Snake Clan. She works in the Potters' Guild and is a respected woman. Her name is Red Crow. So you see, you are not the last of your clan."

The elder's face remained unreadable as he digested this information.

The Wolf Clan woman interjected: "If our families are alive, why did they never return to us?"

"It is not so simple," Hoshi'tiwa said. "The way is long and dangerous. Many would not survive the trek back. But also, some of your kinsmen became servants of the Lords, and they are watched, and punished if they try to run away. But there are those who married and settled down, because they were told that their families here in the east are no more."

She addressed the elder. "Red Crow, the potter who is Snake Clan, told me that her entire clan was massacred, that she saw them slain before her eyes. What was there for her to come back to?"

The elder continued to consider her words, and then, slowly rising, he turned to address his group: "I believe this young woman. I believe that some of our families are still alive. And if they are, we must reunite with them."

"And be killed!" cried Wolf Clan woman.

"They will not kill us," Hoshi'tiwa said quickly. "The Lords are trying to bring more People of the Sun to Center Place. They need us to build their temples and raise their crops and manufacture their goods. Even now, Jaguars are scouring the settlements to the north and west to bring more people to the canyon. They will welcome us," she said, knowing it was an exaggeration but finding it necessary in order to convince these timid hearts, "and so will your long-lost family members! Think of the brothers and sisters, sons and daughters, cousins and aunts and uncles who have been in your hearts all these years and with whom you would be reunited."

As she spoke, it occurred to Hoshi'tiwa that she was once again preaching *suukya'qatsi,* except that this time it was a connectedness of another kind—the bonds of love and home. This, too, she realized in wonder, was a message in her rain jar.

Finally she said, "Return with me to Center Place. You shall be invisible no more."

But they did not immediately strike westward upon the sky-stone trail. When the elder told Hoshi'tiwa of other refugees living in hidden camps in the many canyons and valleys, she said, "Then we will find them, and bring them also back to Center Place."

Sixty-three

T H E priestess did not at first see the ominous cloud approaching Center Place.

Bent over her labors on the mesa above Lady Corn, she was inspecting long strips of bark paper that had been left in the sun to dry, and when she straightened to look out over the plain that spread southward and eastward to distant mountains and canyons, she blinked in the noon sunlight. A great cloud of dust rose up from the desert. She rubbed her eyes and looked again. The cloud was following the ancient sky-stone trail.

A caravan!

She wrinkled her brow. No . . . not a caravan. An army? Not an army either. But definitely people—many people, dressed in different ways, men, women, and children, carrying burdens, with dogs loping alongside.

Hiking up her long skirt, the priestess flew down the stairway carved into the cliff, down to Lady Corn, where without ceremony, she cried, "Someone is coming! People! Many people!"

By the time the multitude entered the valley, the westering sun burnished cliffs and mesas in brilliant gold. Hoshi'tiwa was in the lead of the great mass of varied humanity, who looked this way and that in wonder at the rising-splendors, the farms, the many houses, shacks, and cook fires filling the canyon.

Not only the Invisible Ones walked with Hoshi'tiwa. Accompanying them were people Hoshi'tiwa had found in hiding when she had searched for other scraps and remnants of disrupted clans and families. Sitting with them in their camps and speaking to them as she had to the Invisible Ones, the message of reunification, and the promise of finding loved ones, she had convinced them to join the westward migration.

The Invisible Ones no longer wore the disguises that had allowed them to blend into nature. Gone were the twigs and dust and grass skirts that had made them invisible, and in their place were buckskins that had been stored away, fringed leggings not worn in years, agave-fiber tunics and skirts, and with faces washed, the clan tattoos were visible once again: Snake, Wolf, Cloud, and Sweet Water. From infants to the elderly, people with red skin and copper skin, speaking different dialects, sporting the many tattoos of their clans, and bearing upon their shoulders their worldly goods, they followed the Tortoise Clan daughter.

As they passed through fields, farmers straightened from their toil, wives emerged from huts, children ceased their play. And as they stared at the new arrivals walking past, some saw familiar faces, or recognized clan tattoos. Digging sticks and tortillas were forgotten as men and women ran to the crowd to embrace long-remembered loved ones, aunt embracing niece, father embracing son. Laughter erupted, and tears, and exclamations of wonder.

The procession underwent changes as people splintered off, going to farms and shelters with newly discovered loved ones, while others, residents of Center Place, dropped what they were doing to join the crowd heading to the main plaza. One man, the elder of the Invisible Ones, saluted Hoshi'tiwa and struck off to the potters' workshop, which she had pointed out to him.

He filled the open doorway of the workshop and called in a booming voice, "Where is the one called Red Crow?" He stepped inside, a man in buckskins and looking fierce. "Red Crow!" he shouted.

All heads turned to where she sat in the corner, coiling clay. Red Crow brought her head up, a look of surprise on her face.

Her eyes widened, then narrowed, then widened again. "Running Elk?" she whispered in disbelief. Quickly tracing a protective sign in the air, she said, "You are a ghost! I saw you slain!"

He stared down at her, his eyes wide with wonder. "Red Crow?"

She slowly rose to her feet and took a faltering step forward. "Are you real?"

"I was not slain," he said, remembering the day many years ago when the Jaguar's spear had felled him. But he had recovered from the wound only to discover he was the last of Snake Clan.

Until now.

They flew into each other's arms and wept with joy.

Hoshi'tiwa proceeded to the plaza, where Jaguars were hastily mustering, and officials and priests were coming out to see what the commotion was.

When he saw the throng that was advancing toward the plaza, Moquihix sent a Jaguar back into Precious Green with a message for Xikli. Then he waited as the mass of newcomers came to a restless halt before the plaza. He watched in amazement as people embraced and laughed, wiped tears from their eyes, or searched anxiously this way and that. A strangely diverse mob, yet cohesive in a curious way.

He eyed the rain-girl at the head of the crowd. Her return, he knew, portended disaster.

A moment later the Jaguar returned to whisper something to Moquihix, who rapped his skull-topped staff on the paving stones and shouted for silence. "All show respect and obeisance to the Lord of Center Place!"

When Xikli strode out from Precious Green, wearing the official robes and feathered headdress of office, many in the mob fell to their knees. Others stood and stared. Hoshi'tiwa looked at the Jaguar Captain in confusion.

When Xikli said nothing, coming to a standstill at the edge of the plaza to look down at her, and the moment stretched until not a sound was heard up and down the canyon, Hoshi'tiwa finally called out, "Where is Lord Jakál? I demand to speak with Lord Jakál."

"Don't you know?" muttered a peasant at her side. "Jakál was killed by Xikli."

Hoshi'tiwa gave the man a startled look.

"Clubbed to death before the eyes of all the people. Now Xikli is Lord of Center Place. And since then, many beating hearts of our people have been offered to the Toltec gods."

Hoshi'tiwa stared up in shock at the former Jaguar Captain standing at the edge of the plaza, looking down at her with a triumphant look on his disfigured face. So it was true, she realized in fear. Xikli had finally realized his dream of attaining the throne.

What Hoshi'tiwa did not know, as she and her new adversary locked eyes in the late afternoon sunlight, was that Xikli's ambitions did not end there. Once the throne of Center Place had become his, a new ambition had sprouted in Xikli's heart: to found a new dynasty. No sons of his would call themselves the progeny of Moquihix, but rather would tell the world that they were the sons of the great Xikli, who had founded a new Toltec empire. His name would be carried down through the ages, people would speak his praises and he would be remembered, like the great princes who had lived generations ago and who were still honored. He had already taken possession of the foundation for Jakál's pyramid and planned to build there a pyramid dedicated to Blue Hummingbird. Xikli had also commissioned sculptors to chisel his likeness in stone—something no *tlatoani* at Center Place had ever done—and he would place the taller-than-life statues of himself at the base of the pyramid steps.

He smiled with satisfaction over the mob of fresh humanity Hoshi'tiwa had delivered to him. Tomorrow, they would all be inducted into his slave workforce. *After* he had put the girl on public display in the plaza.

He shouted an order for her arrest.

Hoshi'tiwa was too stunned to move. But when Jaguars came toward her, she turned to the crowd and shouted, "Find your families! Go to your homes! Hurry!" and then the Jaguars dragged her away.

Sixty-four

THE cage was small and foul-smelling, and abutted the wall behind the Precious Green kitchen where the compound of the Jaguars' barracks stood. As night fell and the stars came out, Hoshi'tiwa shivered with fear and cold, wondering what went wrong.

What happened while she was away, to change things at Center Place so drastically? How could Jakál be dead?

She curled her fingers around the wooden poles that imprisoned her, and shook them. But this cage had held stronger prisoners than she. Crouching, she examined the base of the pole-wall, searching for loose foundations. But the poles were sunk deep and lashed together with unbreakable twine. The top of the cage was covered with a lattice roof through which she could see the stars, but it was beyond her reach and she could find no handholds or footholds to use for climbing.

Only one soldier guarded her, and he stood sleepily at his post. She wondered if she could bribe him to set her free. But what could she offer?

When she heard footfalls on the path approaching the cages, she ran to the wooden bars and peered through. Had Xikli come to torment her? To gloat over his victory? She saw a cloaked figure emerge from the darkness to exchange a few mumbled words with the guard, who first shook his head, and then extended his hand, as if receiving a bribe. To Hoshi'tiwa's surprise, the guard left at a trot, to run back down the path and disappear.

The cloaked figure approached swiftly. Hoshi'tiwa backed away from the cage door. The door swung open and the stranger reached her in three strides, throwing back the cloak to reveal his face, and then to pull her into his arms and kiss her hard on the mouth.

"You came back," Jakál said, pressing his lips to her hair and holding her tight.

She trembled in his embrace, wondering if she were dreaming. "I thought you were dead."

He stepped away and, taking her by the wrist, led her from the cage, saying, "Hurry!" in a harsh whisper.

She followed, knowing where they were going as they slipped through a narrow doorway behind the kitchen of Precious Green, along dark corridors and past covered doorways through which no light shone. When they reached his apartment, familiar to her now, Jakál turned and pulled her to him, to press his mouth to hers again, but in a slower, more tender kiss.

She drew back, filling her eyes with the sight of him. "They told me you were dead," she said once more, electrified by his nearness, his touch, stunned to realize how desperately she had missed him.

"I am," he said in a sorrowful voice. "I was killed and now I am dead, and no man may speak to me. I am *makai-yó,* Hoshi'tiwa."

Throwing off his cloak, Jakál strode to a low table set with food and cups. Hoshi'tiwa watched him as he poured water from a pitcher, taking in the plain white loincloth, the absence of sky-stone and gold, his hair hanging loose and unadorned, and she thought he was all the more beautiful for his plainness.

He offered Hoshi'tiwa a cup, and she took it, drinking gratefully.

"Why did you leave?" he asked, watching her.

She drained the cup and delicately wiped her lips. "You placed a bounty on my head. Your soldiers were searching for me."

"The bounty was Xikli's. I placed no price upon your head." He took a step toward her. "Where did you go?"

"To the sky-stone mines."

His thick black eyebrows arched. "Why did you go there?"

"You know why," she said, her face upturned to his.

"No. Tell me."

"To find Ahoté. You sent him there."

Jakál frowned. "That is not so. I told him he could go home. Did he not?"

"Someone told me," she said cautiously, omitting Yani's name to protect her, "that you had changed your edict and sent Ahoté to the mines."

"You were told a lie. The order to send the boy to the mines must have been Xikli's."

Hoshi'tiwa frowned. Why would Yani and Nagual lie about such a thing? *They wanted me to stay at Center Place, to join the kachina cult.*

"The night that I left, it was your soldiers who were searching for me."

"Yes," he said with passion, "because I had decided to marry you."

Her lips parted in a small gasp.

"The night you left Center Place, Hoshi'tiwa, I pronounced an edict declaring interracial marriage legal at Center Place. I had hoped to unify our two peoples, and I was going to set the first example by wedding a Daughter of the Sun."

Incense burning in a shallow bowl suddenly filled Hoshi'tiwa's nostrils. Her head swam. The torchlights seemed to blaze more brightly, and the room grew suddenly warm. The chamber's two occupants looked at each other in the realization that everything had changed— their worlds, the laws, even the gods.

"I did not know," she whispered. All this time, hating him, thinking he had betrayed her, but loving him also, her heart divided in painful conflict.

And then she remembered. "Why are you *makai-yó*? Why do they say you are dead?"

"It is but a symbolic death. Xikli struck me with a ceremonial club made of soft cactus wood, for not even the power-drunk Xikli would dare to assassinate a *tlatoani*. A symbolic slaying was sufficient. He had known the blow would not be lethal, but enough to knock me unconscious so that I had to be carried from the plaza. And then, in front of all the people, the nobles and priests, with the backing of the Jaguars and his powerful friends, Xikli declared himself the new Lord of Center Place. And no one challenged him."

Jakál took the empty cup, refilled it, sipped first, and then handed it back to her. "When I regained consciousness and realized what had happened, I knew I had not the power to retake the throne, for Xikli has gathered many powerful men on his side. As well as the Jaguar army. And then he married Lady White Orchid, to make his power complete. Through his ties to the house of Tenoch, there is not a Toltec in the valley who would raise a sword against him."

"I thought Lady White Orchid wanted to marry *you*," Hoshi'tiwa said softly.

"She chose Xikli and now she carries his child. For that more than anything Xikli will fight to hold on to his power—for his heir. And so, dear Hoshi'tiwa," he said with a sigh, "I am symbolically dead. Xikli would like to make it real, and perhaps someday he will. My movements are restricted. I am watched. Xikli will make sure that I cannot rebuild my power and challenge him."

"But you were the *tlatoani*!"

"Not a very good one, I think," he said with a sad smile. "It is the way of the world, Hoshi'tiwa, for the strong to take over the weak. And perhaps this was meant to be. Since Tollan is no more, then perhaps Toltec power has shifted to Center Place and the gods chose Xikli because he is strong and a leader of warriors. He will build and expand here, create a new heart of the empire. So it has always been, and so it always will be."

Suddenly overcome—Jakál was alive, he had not betrayed her, and he had kissed her—Hoshi'tiwa looked around the chamber that she had visited before, and when her eyes fell upon the golden jar standing on a pedestal, she cried out. "Yani gave it to you?" she asked as she picked up her old familiar friend.

His look darkened. "Yani vanished the same night you left Center Place. Rumors say she is dead."

"Dead! How?"

"I do not know," he said, taking the delicate jar from her.

"And what of Chief Physician Nagual?" she asked, wondering if they had been spied upon in the cave the day before she left Center Place.

"It was Nagual who gave me the rain jar," Jakál said, wondering why Hoshi'tiwa would inquire about the Chief Physician. "I have kept it against the day of your return. And now," his voice fell to a throaty whisper, "here you are."

"Yes," she whispered.

Jakál set the jar aside and turned questioning eyes upon her. "So . . . you left Center Place because you thought I had put a price on your head? How could you have believed that, after we shared such joy together?"

She turned away from him, away from his penetrating eyes and power over her. She needed to tell him what was in her heart. "Yes, we enjoyed physical pleasure together. But then, afterward, when you told me you were bringing more of my people to Center Place to build your pyramid, I felt betrayed. I was hurt and angry. But . . . I was in love with you. And that made me feel even more betrayed."

"I am sorry," he said softly. "I had decided against conscripting more of your people, but you did not know that."

Her eyes flickered to the doorway. "What will happen now? What will Xikli do to me?"

He turned her to face him. "I won't let him touch you, Hoshi'tiwa. You are safe with me."

Looking up into his dark eyes, she knew it was true.

"Did you find the boy?" he asked.

She saw a beseeching look in his dark eyes, a yearning to hear only one answer. But she had to say, "I found him."

Jakál bent his head so that she now saw the new lines on his face, the traces of worry and grief and despair that must have engulfed him these past months. "And are you still," he said quietly, "his betrothed?"

Hoshi'tiwa was silent for a heartbeat. And then a second. And a third and fourth until her heart raced and she could not keep count. She was lost in the dark warmth of Jakál's eyes, and intoxicated by his nearness. "No, my Lord," she whispered. "I am not."

As worry melted from his face, to be replaced by a look of love and yearning, Jakál lifted a hand and touched a fingertip to her forehead, to tenderly trace the three vertical lines tattooed there, evidence of her bravery and endurance. "Do not call me 'Lord,'" he murmured. "Say my name. I want to hear you say my name. . . ."

She turned her face up to him, parted her moist lips, and whispered, "Jakál."

He took her by the shoulders and bent his head to kiss her hard, pulling her to him, Hoshi'tiwa surrendering.

They were up on the mesa again beneath the star-splashed sky, awaiting the first sighting of the Morning Star. But this time they were free to love. There were no boundaries, laws, or gods to separate them. When Jakál gently kissed her, Hoshi'tiwa thought that the force of Big River was as a trickling stream compared with the rush of passion that swept over her. The golden chamber grew bright and hot, but Hoshi'tiwa was aware only of the feel of Jakál's hard body against hers, his own hot skin beneath her fingertips. His forceful kiss stopped the breath in her throat.

He broke away only long enough to lift her into his arms and carry her to the woven mat, clearing a space among the books and plates of fruit and pitchers of precious water. He still could not believe she was real, that she had returned to him after all this time, after he had given up. For the first time since the hour of his birth, Jakál, formerly Lord of Center Place, felt complete.

Sixty-five

As they lay together on the reed mat, Jakál lifted himself up on one arm and looked down at the miracle woman in his arms. There were no shadows of melancholy in his eyes, none of the sadness and loneliness Hoshi'tiwa had so often seen. His dark eyes beneath thick brows were warm now, glowing like embers in a winter campfire.

"Why the gods have favored me, I do not know," he said softly, stroking her hair, the coils having come undone, her ribbons lying on the mat, "for all my life I have been alone. I grew up in a palace with many servants and many friends, yet I always felt alone."

He gently touched the places on her shoulders and breasts that were still tender from the traveling pack she had carried over hills, through deep gorges, across a mighty river. Then he kissed each raw place, softly, one by one, so that Hoshi'tiwa sighed in deep pleasure.

"I confess, Hoshi'tiwa, that I did not know an undercurrent of sadness flowed within me until I knew the happiness of a moment with you. And now it is as if a cloud has moved away from the sun and I am seeing life for the first time. Though we come from different worlds and worship different gods, we are together now and shall never be apart. I want to make you happy. I *will* make you happy."

He removed a pendant from around his neck and placed it over her head. "As I once told you, this *xochitl* is very old and very sacred, and possesses great powers because it contains the blood of Quetzalcoatl."

The talisman was beautiful, a tiny gold flower nestled in the palm of her hand, reflecting the torchlight that flickered in sconces. Hoshi'tiwa loved the detail in the fine metalwork, the exquisite craftsmanship. But more than that, she loved Jakál.

She looked into the eyes that were peering into hers. There was mystery there, and excitement. Lying with Jakál was exquisite, and she wanted it to go on forever. Yes, whispered her delirious mind. I will stay with you. I will marry you. I will give you sons. . . .

She reached for him and he drew her to him again, his mouth meeting hers, and she bent to him as she believed she always would, believing, too, that this was the moment of her destiny, the moment for which she had been born.

They awoke the next morning to a strange sound on the wind.

"What is that?" Hoshi'tiwa asked, starting to rise from the sleeping mat.

Jakál listened. "Preparations for a ritual," he said.

"What ritual?"

"I do not know."

The adjoining chamber opened directly onto the plaza. Covering her nakedness with a cloak, Hoshi'tiwa tiptoed to the doorway and peered out into the pale early morning light.

Gathering on the plaza, erecting the pedestals of the gods, were priests and soldiers. Out on the plain, a vast crowd was collecting, people answering the trumpet calls. And then she saw the victims, tethered ankle to ankle, being led onto the plaza.

She froze in shock.

In the light of the breaking dawn, Hoshi'tiwa saw that the sacrificial victims were those she had brought to Center Place, the scattered refugees whom she had collected and led to this canyon—and at the head of the line was the elder of the Invisible Ones, Running Elk, who was married to Red Crow.

She rushed back inside. "There is to be a sacrifice on the altar of blood!"

"It has become Xikli's practice," Jakál said with a dark look as he reached for his clothes.

"You must stop him! It is the people I brought here! I led them to a slaughter."

Jakál hastily dressed, his features cast in worry; then he turned to Hoshi'tiwa. "We cannot stop Xikli."

"But we must!"

He took her by the shoulders. "Hoshi'tiwa, listen to me. I am no longer the *tlatoani*. I have no powers."

"Then *I* will stop him."

"Xikli will slay you where you stand."

"But I led them here—"

"Hoshi'tiwa," he said more firmly, "the fate of the victims has already been decided. You and I cannot change it."

Her lip trembled. "Is Xikli's power so complete?"

"Believe me when I say that it is. Hoshi'tiwa, I governed Center Place and my own life according to the laws of the gods. But there are other laws, those of men. And that is Xikli's way. I did not know he would be so bold as to strike me down in front of the people. I suffered a shameful and dishonorable defeat. But that was because I did not understand the depth and breadth of the greed for power that can exist in a man's heart. I had thought that even a man like Xikli respects the gods first. But he does not. I was naïve, Hoshi'tiwa, as you are now. But my eyes were opened, as I wish to open yours. You cannot stop him."

She stepped away. "I will not stand by while my kinsmen are slaughtered."

"We do not have the power to stop it. You and I are but twigs on a raging river. Hoshi'tiwa, if you and I go out there now and stand up to

Xikli, he will kill us on the spot and his victory will be complete. Do you not see that?"

When she did not respond, a sad smile played at his lips and he said, "You have always followed your heart, Hoshi'tiwa, you have always been impulsive. I beg of you now to listen to your mind. What is your conscience dictating?"

Throwing down the cloak, she snatched up her tunic and blouse, hastily dressing. "That there must be a way to break Xikli's power."

"There is no way. Even if we somehow defeated Xikli, another man would rise up and take his place. Do you not see? It is not Xikli himself that you are fighting, it is Toltec power. The grip my people have on this canyon will never be broken. This is what I learned when I regained consciousness after Xikli struck me down. That there is hunger for power in the hearts of men, a hunger I myself never knew, and perhaps that is why my power was so easily taken from me. The Toltecs will never leave Center Place."

"Then what would you have me do?" she cried.

"Stay with me, Hoshi'tiwa. Live with me. We can be happy together."

She looked into his dark and troubled eyes and knew that everything he said was true. And she agreed with him. How could she, one girl, fight such a formidable force? For an instant, she teetered on the brink of indecision: to stay, or to march out onto the plaza and stand before Xikli. "I love you, Jakál," she finally said in a tight voice. "And I want nothing more than to spend the rest of my days with you. But not this way. Not at such a high price."

He took her by the arm and said, "You choose strangers over me?"

"I choose life!" Hoshi'tiwa's eyes filled with tears as she looked down at the strong hand gripping her arm.

And she heard the pain in his voice as he said, "Why could you not have returned to Center Place when I was in power? Why are the gods playing cruel tricks on us? I beg of you, do not go out there, Hoshi'tiwa. You will never come back."

"Then come with me."

"Then we shall *both* never come back! Hoshi'tiwa, what good will your death serve your people?"

Pulling her arm free, she gave Jakál one last look, felt her heart rise to her throat when she saw the sadness and anger in his eyes, then she turned and headed for the plaza.

"Wait," he said.

She turned.

"You are determined to do this?"

"Yes."

"And there is nothing I can say or do that will change your mind?"

"Nothing," she whispered.

Taking her by the shoulders, he looked deep into her eyes. There was fire in his voice as he said, "The day you stood in the plaza when that boy was to be condemned, and you offered your life in place of his, I did not know what to make of it, and it has haunted me since. I have never known such love, such devotion. I have never risked my life for anything. Hoshi'tiwa, you have more courage in one strand of hair than I have in my entire body. You have made me feel ashamed, my love, and for this I thank you, for Quetzalcoatl does not look with favor upon a cowardly man."

"What—"

"I cannot lose you, Hoshi'tiwa," he said in a strangled voice. "Not this way. I will go with you. Together we shall face Xikli." He ran a dry tongue over his lips. "Perhaps Nagual will help us. And I have a few supporters still among the nobles and Jaguars. . . ."

Hoshi'tiwa looked up into his dark eyes, transfixed by his power, and realized he did not believe his own words. There was defeat in his tone. *He knows he will be killed.*

Suddenly she saw the terrible mistake she had made. She thought of the many victims who had fallen to Jaguar spears, who had died at the hands of the priests at the altar of blood, and her mind shouted: No! Not Jakál as well.

She could not let him be slain a second time. Could not lead him to a *real* death.

Her thoughts raced.

When she hesitated, he said, "What is it?"

"Yes, we will go out there together," she said in a tight voice. "But . . ." She licked her lips. "You . . . look like an ordinary man. The people out there . . . they might not recognize you. You would stand before Xikli and the Jaguars like a commoner."

Jakál looked down at himself. It was true. No one had ever seen him so plainly attired.

"You need to show them who you are," she said rapidly, trying to remember the procession of the Golden Mask when Jakál had arrayed himself as a high priest of Quetzalcoatl. Where were the ceremonial trappings kept? *On the fifth tier of this rising-splendor.* It would buy her time.

"Xikli would laugh at you like this," she said. "Is there something . . . a staff, a headdress perhaps . . . ?"

"My priestly robes," Jakál said, marveling at her cleverness. "If I were to appear in the plaza wearing my priestly robes, and carrying my holy scepter, people would listen to what I have to say."

"Yes," Hoshi'tiwa said, knowing that while the people might listen, Xikli would not. He had already killed a *tlatoani.* Why would he stop at a priest?

Jakál glanced over his shoulder. "But I cannot wait for servants. There is no time." Taking her hand and pressing his lips to the palm, he said, "Wait. I will be back."

"I will wait," she said, and she did wait until he had hurried from the room. And when his footfall faded down the corridor, she whispered, "Good-bye, my love," and turned toward the grand entrance onto the plaza.

Xikli had been informed that Jakál released Hoshi'tiwa from her cage. It did not matter. They could not go far. As he took a seat on the throne in the plaza, to commence the ceremony of sacrifice, Xikli decided he would plan a special amusement after the girl was recaptured.

White Orchid took her seat next to her husband and looked over the crowd, the Jaguars and officials, the trembling victims. No one knew the turmoil that went on behind her placid gaze.

White Orchid had tried at first to find a way out of marrying Xikli. But he had the contract signed by her father and he would have taken her villa, her wealth, and even, as Tenoch had warned, the sandals off her feet. For survival, she had capitulated. But living with the murderer of her father proved intolerable. She had feared that she could not survive it without taking her own life. Only one thing kept her alive, her desire for a child.

Therefore she had suffered Xikli's nightly assaults and humiliations, and now she was pregnant. The child she had longed for slumbered in her belly. She had a bloodline once again.

Xikli must pay for what he did, White Orchid thought again as she waited for the ceremony of human sacrifice to begin. After Tenoch's cremation, she had taken the empty *nequhtli* gourd to Pikami and asked if she could identify the residue White Orchid had found at the bottom. As if the old woman already understood White Orchid's couched meaning, she had taken one look, sniffed the contents, then said, "Deadly nightshade. Lethal."

Once she knew the method, White Orchid had only to select the time. But she had wondered if she would have the courage to carry out her plan, and worried that she might never do it.

But now she was thinking of the spectacle she had witnessed the day before, when a remarkable procession had passed by her villa, with Hoshi'tiwa at its head. Word had spread swiftly through the canyon that these were the remnants of clans and families which the Jaguars had for years terrorized, and Hoshi'tiwa had gathered them all together to bring them to Center Place.

So the girl had not run away after all, as White Orchid had thought when she had felt all the disillusionments and disappointments of her life come to a head on the day she had proposed a marriage contract with Jakál, when she had believed no one on earth could be trusted or counted on. Listening to Hoshi'tiwa's message of connectedness had brought White Orchid a measure of surcease of her private agony, but then Hoshi'tiwa had run for her life, leaving her followers alone and wondering what had happened, and White Orchid to feel disillusioned once again.

But Hoshi'tiwa was back, and the sight of her walking proudly at the head of so large a multitude, with joyous reunions taking place, had renewed White Orchid's faith in the human spirit. And it had renewed her faith in her own spirit as well, so that she knew now she had the strength within her to change her own life.

From inside the safety of Precious Green, Hoshi'tiwa surveyed the plaza.

Along the periphery stood the Jaguars, important nobles, and officials, while Xikli himself sat upon the throne that had once been Jakál's, the erstwhile Captain attired in the regalia of office—a feathered cloak and plumed headdress. Seated next to him was a woman Hoshi'tiwa recognized as Lady White Orchid.

Hoshi'tiwa was startled by the profusion of soldiers. They were everywhere, their clubs and shields ubiquitous in the crowd. She saw more guards, too, than she had ever seen at Center Place, all fitted with spears and shields. And she realized that, in her absence, the world had become *naqoy'qatsi*—war as a way of life.

When the first sacrificial victim was brought to the altar of blood— the proud elder named Running Elk—Hoshi'tiwa stepped from the shadows, uncertain what she was going to do, knowing only that she could not stand by but must act. Sunlight suddenly stabbed her eyes so that she had to shut them against the brilliant glare. And all in an instant, behind her closed eyelids, she saw a vision so glorious that it took her breath away—more than a mere image, but an *experience,* that made her feel and hear and smell, as if she were actually living it.

The People of the Sun leaving Center Place.

So vibrant and grand was the vision, that Hoshi'tiwa fell against the wall, as yet unobserved by anyone, held enthralled by what she saw: her people finding new land and settling down, families staying in one place, growing large and strong, no longer needing to build cliff houses as the Jaguars were gone and there was no more living in fear. The vision shouted of prosperity, fields of golden corn, fat babies, mothers no longer seeing sons marched away, husbands no longer torn from wives. Hoshi'tiwa saw that all the corn the people grew, all the rain jars they made, all the blankets they wove and the flutes they carved, stayed with the clans who made them. No more sending tribute to the Lords of Center Place. No more world out of balance—*koyaanis'qatsi*—but oneness and harmony in its place.

The *suukya'qatsi* she had been entrusted to bring to her people.

And then her mother's voice, as crisp and clear as the day Hoshi'tiwa heard these same words two and a half years ago, saying, "You were born to a special purpose. I do not know what that purpose is, only that you cannot turn from it. You can be brave. I know this."

In that instant a new idea came to Hoshi'tiwa: We will fight back.

Hoshi'tiwa did not know that she was the first of her kind to think this way, nor did the thought come easily to her. It was an idea that, unbeknownst to her, had been germinating since the day Yani had shown her the pictographs in the limestone overhang, and now it burst forth like something forgotten but always known.

In her new mental state, which had heightened her senses and wit, she surveyed the plaza and the crowd in the valley once again, and this time her keen eyes detected what they had not seen before: tension among those gathered to observe the sacrifice. But it did not come from the People of the Sun. The ill-ease was among the Jaguars and nobles and officials, and it occurred to Hoshi'tiwa, who knew nothing of politics and economic alliances, that a shaky truce existed between them and Xikli. She knew that the knights were men of honor, and she wondered now if they were troubled by Xikli's dishonorable coup. Perhaps Jakál's overthrow had not been met with approval of all, maybe some Jaguars did not wish to serve Xikli, or spoke of restoring Jakál to the throne. Among the nobles, too, and high officials there might be dissention, she reasoned in her new wisdom, and among the priests, too, who would fear the wrath of the gods for what Xikli had done. To steal the throne of a *tlatoani* . . .

The young and naïve girl Hoshi'tiwa had once been would never have thought of all this, nor would she have known how to use this insight to her advantage. But she had lived much and learned well in two and a half years, and now she reasoned with maturity and vision. And new courage.

Without another thought, she strode out onto the plaza and, raising her arms, called for a halt to the sacrifice. A stunned silence fell over the valley. Even Lord Xikli, on his stolen throne, gaped at Hoshi'tiwa in disbelief.

"That man is not the Lord of Center Place!" she cried, pointing to the stupefied Xikli.

A murmur ran through the crowd and among the soldiers and priests and officials on the plaza.

"He rules with lies and dishonor!" Hoshi'tiwa said, turning slowly so that her eyes met those of the brilliantly attired men and women, the Jaguars in their padded armor, the special guards in their wooden helmets. And she saw the fine cracks in their unified façade as a few shuffled their feet, exchanged looks, frowned.

"Jakál is alive!" she cried.

Xikli shot to his feet and shouted, "Seize her!"

A few Jaguars ran forward, but then stopped and looked back at their comrades who had not moved.

"You know that man is a false *tlatoani*," she said to the Jaguars aligned on either side of the throne, encouraged by their hesitancy, hoping that she had calculated correctly that all that was required was a wedge between them and Xikli, and his power would be toppled. "You know he laughs in the faces of your gods."

"Stop her!" Xikli screamed.

"Do you think Blue Hummingbird will welcome the beating hearts of those men," she asked, pointing to her tethered kinsmen awaiting sacrifice, "when he knows they were offered in a ritual tainted with sacrilege and desecration?"

Seizing a club from the nearest Jaguar, Xikli strode across the plaza.

The murmur in the crowd that spread from the base of the plaza out into the valley grew to a dull roar, with a few brave shouts: "Leave her alone!" "She speaks the truth!" "Sacrilege!"

Hoshi'tiwa stood her ground as Xikli advanced, a savage look on his face. From the corner of her eye she saw nobles in their colorful cloaks and feathered headdresses move uneasily. Guards stepped hesitantly forward. Jaguars, whose former Captain was now an illegal *tlatoani,* turned to one another in indecision.

She held her head high and faced him with courage. Even if she were to die right now, she knew that she had set doubts and uncertainties into motion that would lead to the usurper's downfall and the freedom of her people.

As Xikli came so close that Hoshi'tiwa could see the madness in his eyes, the perspiration on his scarred forehead, a sharp rock came sailing from the crowd, missing Xikli's head by a whisper, to crash on the paved floor of the plaza.

Xikli stopped and spun around. "Who threw that?" he shouted.

Hoshi'tiwa, too, looked out at the crowd in surprise. She had not expected one of her own kinsmen to act.

White Orchid watched events unfold in cool detachment as another stone came flying, also missing Xikli, and more shouts erupted from the crowd: "Get away from her!" "Assassin!" In that moment, calmly and serenely, White Orchid knew that her opportunity had come.

Rising to her feet she held up her arms, drawing attention to herself, so that for an instant all eyes were upon Xikli's wife. White Orchid took a deep breath for courage, and said in a ringing voice, "Jaguars! Noble knights of the empire! Hear me! That man who shamed us all when he slew our beloved Lord Jakál in front of the people—the blasphemous and dishonorable Xikli—also murdered my father!" She pointed at her startled husband. "He slew Tenoch, Hero of the Empire!"

When the Jaguars, who had been displeased with Xikli's overthrow of Jakál, his dishonorable clubbing of the *tlatoani* in front of the commoners, heard this—ignoble assassination of one of their own, a hero!— they broke ranks and charged at Xikli, spears and clubs held high.

Before Hoshi'tiwa's horrified eyes, before the startled faces of Copil and Nagual and the Overseers of the guilds, before the shocked people in the crowd, and the nobles seated high on the walls and terraces—before the eyes of the world, the knights who had once blindly followed their Captain without a second thought engulfed Xikli in a rain of clubs and spears, bludgeoning him until his blood ran red and thick over the paving stones, until his screams of outrage and protest fell silent, until his pulpy body no longer writhed at their feet. Then they stripped him of his clothes and jewelry and *tlatoani*'s headdress and dragged his body by the heels while Jaguars scaled a wall and reached for the naked corpse, pulling it up to display it upside down before all the valley.

High Minister Moquihix looked on with sadness. After Jakál's symbolic slaying, he had been of mixed opinion about the unexpected attack. On the one hand he was proud of his son for pulling off such a brilliant coup—Jakál had not seen it coming. But on the other hand, Jakál so deeply represented to Moquihix the homeland and the Toltec empire that such a swift and brutal overthrow was a foreshadowing of greater falls to come. And now his son had met a dishonorable death for assassinating a Hero of the Empire. Moquihix's heart was so heavy with remorse that he made no move, gave no command as order began to break down.

Running Elk, having been freed from his bonds for the sacrifice, ran to the nearest statue and pushed with all his might, toppling the stone figure of Blue Hummingbird so that it shattered into a hundred pieces. When the Jaguars saw this, they bolted after him. He turned and fled from the plaza, dashing through the lines of nobles and officials to disappear into the mob. As soon as the Jaguars entered the crowd, they were set upon by the starving and thirsty and impoverished who had nothing to lose and whose bellies and hearts were full to bursting with bitterness and hatred and despair.

Hoshi'tiwa stood in frozen shock—this was not what she had intended! She tried to call them to order, running to the edge of the plaza, crying, "No, do not harm those men! There has been enough killing!" They did not listen. The Jaguars were swallowed up by the sea of her suddenly violent kinsmen, and before her horrified eyes chaos erupted.

A few swarmed up onto the plaza, where the nobles huddled together and Jaguars ran at the people with spears, but the majority of the mob turned away, toward the villas of the rich.

"Stop!" Hoshi'tiwa shouted in a useless attempt to stem the rampage. Her people were suddenly out of control. They ran this way and that, mindless, impelled by a primal instinct to kill and destroy. Men ran into villas and came out with their arms laden with goods. The screams of women pierced the air. Fires broke out.

Hoshi'tiwa looked on in numb horror and thought: What have I done?

She threw herself into the mob and tried to stop the mayhem one person at a time, but all she saw were twisted faces and angry fists. Up and down the canyon the violence spread.

Yellow Feather had been at the front of the crowd to watch the blood sacrifice, her eighteen-month-old son on her hip with his thumb in his mouth. When the first rocks flew, and fists rose in anger, she felt herself pressed on all sides, as the rising fury and tension of the mob made people move where there was no room to move. Squeezed until she could not breathe, Yellow Feather forced her way through and had almost made it to safety when Running Elk plunged from the plaza into the crowd, Jaguars in pursuit.

As bodies swarmed around her, people shouting and hissing, pushing blindly this way and that, Yellow Feather's hold loosened on her son. When he dropped to the ground, she cried out. She fought those around her as they attacked the Jaguars, unaware that their feet were trampling a small child. Yellow Feather was carried away on the tide of angry humanity, able only to look back and see the bloody little form lying lifelessly in the dust.

Old Pikami was in her hut when the riot broke out, as she refused to witness the blood sacrifice of her kinsmen, even though Xikli had passed an edict that anyone not attending would be arrested. Hearing shouts and the stampeding of many feet, she emerged from her hut to see that looting, pillaging, and destruction had gripped the valley. Old grudges were suddenly remembered. Women and possessions that had been coveted were now set upon. And People of the Sun, using for weapons anything they could lay hand to, turned on their Toltec masters.

Pikami did not panic. No one would burn her humble hut or come to rape her. Like a boulder in the middle of a stream, she stood in complete safety as the mob swarmed around her, flowing past in a heat of rage and blood lust. She kept her arm around the shoulders of her lame grandson—who was not really her grandson but a baby she had found abandoned because of his withered leg—and held him tight, telling him he had nothing to fear.

She watched the human river flow to the western end of the canyon where Star Readers had emerged from the Star Chamber to see what was happening. As their concern was with the heavens and not with beating hearts, they never attended blood sacrifices. "Tell me what you see," Pikami said to the boy, whose eyesight was sharper, and he said, "People are killing the priests."

She nodded and drew him back inside the hut, where a kachina of Grandmother Spiderwoman protected them.

Hoshi'tiwa followed the enraged mob to the Star Chamber, where people had set upon the Star Readers and beat them to death with stones and fists. Someone threw a firebrand into the air, igniting the dry wood of the great kiva's roof. As it took flame, the angry crowd swirled and swarmed around the circular observatory—like angry wasps around a nest, Hoshi'tiwa thought, wondering how she was going to get them under control. Jaguars had come, too, trying to break up fights, but starting them as well, so that the cracking of skulls sounded in the air.

Frantic to stop the carnage, Hoshi'tiwa clambered to the top of the circular wall, carefully avoiding the billowing smoke and flames, and called for attention. She had not meant to trigger a riot. Her people were going to destroy everything, and themselves in the doing.

Waving her arms and shouting over their heads, she was able to bring those nearest to turn to her, but fighting on the periphery continued, ugly shouts and epithets continued. "Please! Calm yourselves!" she shouted. "This is wrong!"

And then suddenly someone shouted, "Look!" pointing to a place behind her. Another cried out, and a third shouted, "It is the gods!"

A hush fell over the mob, Jaguars stopped fighting, and all faces turned toward the Star Chamber. Wondering what they were looking at, Hoshi'tiwa turned to see a figure emerge from the subterranean corridor beneath the Star Chamber, smoke billowing behind him, flames licking out as he walked to the rim of the great stone wall and stood before the people.

Mouths fell open, eyes stretched wide. None but a few knew of the underground corridor. It was a device used for secret initiations and mystery rites, to create the illusion that a god had emerged from out of nowhere.

They had seen this god before, on the day Lord Jakál dedicated the ground of his new pyramid. The god's face was made of hammered gold, his teeth carved from ivory, eyes fashioned from jade, and his hair comprised a hundred long brilliant green quetzal feathers shimmering in the sun. The god's robe was a blinding rainbow of colors, sweeping from his neck to the ground as thousands of quetzal, parrot, and hummingbird feathers glittered scarlet, yellow, and blue. The stunned crowd did not know that the god's tallness was due to platform slippers beneath Jakál's feet, that the shoulders had been broadened by a yoke beneath the cloak, that the fingers were not solid gold but merely gloved in supple gold-leaf.

Stepping close to Hoshi'tiwa, Jakál said quietly so that only she could hear, "I told you there was no way to break the Toltec hold over your people. I was wrong. There *is* a way."

Facing the mob, he raised his arms and called out in a tremendous voice, "The spirit of Quetzalcoatl has filled me. He is here! He has returned to us!"

So brilliantly did the god shine, so beautiful and magnificent did he tower over their heads, and so convincing was his regal voice that the Jaguars dropped their weapons and fell to the ground to press their foreheads to the dust. To see the powerful warriors prostrate themselves so, the people followed, falling to their knees and cowering before the majesty of Quetzalcoatl incarnate.

"Hear me now, listen to the words of the Lord of the Breath of Life!"

All were silent; all listened. And Hoshi'tiwa watched in awe.

"You must cease this fighting! The gods are displeased. I, Quetzalcoatl, am displeased!"

People began to tremble, their faces pressed to the earth, their bodies shaking with fear.

As the wind picked up, stoking the fire on the burning kiva roof, building up great clouds of smoke, the god's commanding voice boomed: "I will return someday to my people. And I will return to the People of the Sun as Pahana!"

A unified gasp filled the valley. And Hoshi'tiwa's heart swelled with love, knowing in that moment that she would follow Jakál to the ends of the earth, that she would stay with him forever.

"But I will not return until there is harmony and balance in the world. I cannot create my new golden age while men fight and steal and lie. Learn from the detestable acts of Xikli! Do not follow his example! Return to the ways of your ancestors! Now you must pray, every one of you, with your hearts, Jaguar and farmer alike, father and child, all who draw breath in this valley, pray to your gods for the restoration of peace!"

He lifted his arms higher, revealing a stunning scarlet tunic beneath, belted in gold, and cried: "Now all of you rise and pay homage to me!"

Thunder filled the valley as the vast throng struggled up from the dirt and found their feet. "Toltecs, hear me! Tollan has fallen. Your countrymen are vanquished. Go back and find your families. Your days here are done."

Jakál paused to survey the transfixed people spread out and away beneath him; then he turned to Hoshi'tiwa and said quickly, "My love, I go to join the Morning Star. When you next see Quetzalcoatl rise on the horizon, know that I am with my god."

And then before her horrified eyes, Jakál turned toward the burning roof and, with arms outflung, head held back, he hurled himself into the flames as his god, Quetzalcoatl, had done a thousand years before when he walked the earth as a man.

Sixty-six

THE day of the full moon approached—the Day of Leaving. The cremations and burials for those who had perished in the riot (with the exception of the traitor Xikli, whose corpse still hung on the plaza wall, although no longer recognizable as ravens had picked the bones clean) were done, and now the two peoples prepared for the exodus from Center Place: one group to follow Hoshi'tiwa north, the other to go with Moquihix south.

When Hoshi'tiwa had stood on the rim of the Star Chamber and watched Jakál disappear into the flames, the feathered cloak catching fire, the quetzal plumes igniting and flaring, the golden mask melting, she had stood immobilized for only an instant, and then she had flung herself forward to follow her beloved into the inferno. But two powerful arms had seized her and pulled her back.

"He did it for you!" Moquihix had cried above the roar of the fire. "Do not make his sacrifice an empty gesture."

Sobbing, shocked with disbelief, she had turned and looked into the solemn face of her former enemy. "You knew he was going to do this!"

"I did not. I would have advised him against it."

"But did he have to kill himself?"

"He had to throw himself into the fire because otherwise he was simply a man dressed as a god. This way, the Toltecs were convinced he *was* the god, and so they will leave. But now the gods will also leave Center Place. The world here has come to an end. I will take my people home. And you must lead yours to a new home."

Heaving with sobs—*He did this for me, for my people*—Hoshi'tiwa had then turned to face the thousands who stood in stunned silence so that the only sound on the wind was the crackling of flames and a lone hawk crying overhead. Their hollow faces and ragged clothing pierced her heart. And the lost look in their eyes—they were like children. They had no direction, no leadership.

Lifting her eyes to the hawk that soared on air currents, Hoshi'tiwa had seen the clear blue sky with not a cloud from horizon to horizon, the treeless landscape and the barren riverbed cutting through the canyon, and she had known that what Moquihix said was true. The gods were no longer here. And where there were no gods, humankind must not dwell.

Lifting her arms, although her heart was breaking and she wanted to weep for Jakál, Hoshi'tiwa had cried out in a commanding voice, "My brothers and sisters, it is time for us to leave. Center Place is *makai-yó*. We must find new homes in the north and the west. You are free to go south with the Toltecs if that is your wish. But do not go eastward, for inhospitable tribes dwell there."

She did not know where her courage came from, or how she was going to take responsibility for so many people, but the vision that had blinded her in the plaza, when she had *seen* the People of the Sun thriving in peace and balance and harmony, infused her with new vigor and decisiveness.

"On the first day of the full moon, we shall depart," she said. "Take with you all that you have, collect food and water where you can find it. At noon on the first day of the full moon, we shall walk northward and southward from this valley, and we will not look back. We will never speak of this place again."

Her voice broke. The silence held. Hoshi'tiwa had seen that the Jaguars did not retrieve their weapons. And she had known then that the holy war was over, the world of master and slave was at an end. Jakál had known his charade as Quetzalcoatl would have this effect, that the Jaguars would obey his command and allow her people to leave. He had known that his own self-sacrifice was the only way to save the People of the Sun, and so she said to them, mustering breath and voice though she was on the verge of weeping, "Lord Jakál came to us as the great god Quetzalcoatl and sacrificed himself to set us free. Therefore we will let the Toltecs go in peace. We are no longer enemies."

Hoshi'tiwa spent the afternoon and evening in prayer, staying by the walls of the charred kiva that contained the remains of her beloved Jakál. She had spoken to his spirit, prayed to his god, and then, wishing she could stay there forever to grieve and mourn, but knowing that her people needed her, she had turned her back on the symbol of human strife and self-sacrifice and proceeded among her people to ready them for the great trek northward.

It was not an easy task. Many had been born at Center Place, as had their parents; some were the descendants of those who had lived in the valley before the Toltecs came, and these were the hardest to persuade to leave. But Hoshi'tiwa kept at it, undaunted, tireless, following her new vision. She spoke with authority to each family, assuring them that though they had lived here for generations, it was no longer good luck. And they believed her. Had she not had the vision to gather up all those scattered refugees and bring them home? Therefore, they would follow her to a new destiny.

But families were torn. Brothers wanted to go different ways, women wished to follow Toltec men with whom they had fallen in love, Toltec women sought a more peaceful life among the People of the Sun, and everyone argued about gods and which was supreme and who should inherit the family grinding stone or the buffalo hide blanket or the children. Many cooperated as well and came together to pool resources and promise to look out for one another on the journey north, for they would be in strange lands and encounter foreign people and gods.

As she walked from hut to hut, camp to camp, alone on the dusty paths through dawn, noon, and sunset, Hoshi'tiwa spoke silently to Jakál. She thanked him for setting her people free. And she promised him she would love him all the days of her life.

Gradually, under her persuasion, a massive breakdown of camps and shelters took place and people divided up and shared their goods, deciding whom to go with and where.

Hoshi'tiwa went to Precious Green and requested a visit with Chief Physician Nagual, whose assistants were stripping his apartments of his implements of divination and diagnosis, healing herbs and ointments, magic amulets and charms, and books containing healing spells and incantations. Thanking the physician for the small kachina spirit, she handed it back, but Nagual asked her to keep the little wooden figurine, saying, "He is the spirit of ponds, lakes, and rivers. He will help you on the journey."

In wonder, for she remembered her ordeal at Big River, Hoshi'tiwa said, "He has already helped me. Therefore I will keep the spirit safe and honor him." She paused and the cryptic, hooded eyes watched her. Finally, Nagual said, "Yani is dead. But it was a peaceful passing and she spoke your name with love."

In the twelve rising-splendors, priests, officials, and residents gathered up all that they owned, arguing and agreeing over what belonged to whom, who was responsible for this god or that, squabbling over whose burden was lighter or heavier. At Precious Green, Moquihix climbed to the top tier and opened the cage that housed the exotic birds, setting them free. It had been Jakál's last command.

When Jakál had returned to his chambers with the priestly robes and scepter, he saw that Hoshi'tiwa had already walked out onto the plaza to stop the sacrifice. He was too late. Chaos had erupted. Pandemonium filled the valley. And Jakál had known then the only recourse left.

Before donning his Quetzalcoatl costume and making his way to the Star Chamber for his dramatic emergence from the subterranean corridor, he had sent slaves to search for Moquihix and bring him back. "My friend," Jakál had said as he hurriedly dressed, "our empire is no more.

We are without King, city, people. Return to our land in the south and find what remnants of our scattered race you can. Take all the sky-stone and feathers, all the wealth we have accumulated here. And lastly, my friend, release the caged birds. Perhaps they will fly south with you."

"Are you not coming with us?" Moquihix had asked in alarm.

Jakál had smiled, laid a hand on his friend's shoulder, and said, "I walk another path."

That path had been one of flames, and with Jakál's death Moquihix had felt a loss as keen as that of his loss for Xikli. Jakál had symbolized home. Jakál was Tollan and the Toltec empire.

With a heavy heart, having lost son, friend, and empire, Moquihix had overseen the packing up of all the sky-stone and feathers, salt and silver that would be borne on the backs of a hundred slaves to form a final caravan home, and now, after watching the parrots fly skyward in flashes of brilliant color, he paused to look across the canyon where the charred ruins of the Star Chamber smoldered. He thought of the girl who had caused this ending to happen. Daughter of the Sun, a commoner, born to a corn grower. Yet he, noble Moquihix, shared one thing with her: their deep love for Jakál.

Climbing down to the plaza, for it was time to join his people who were gathered, in an irony not lost to him, near the sacred Sun Dagger to begin the journey southward, Moquihix glanced northward, where a similar mass of humanity had gathered just beyond the now-deserted Five Flower, ready to begin *their* journey.

Many had dismantled their wooden shelters and bore the sticks and poles upon their backs, for who knew what building materials they would find in the new land? Everyone carried something; even small children had the responsibility of holding on to gourds and bowls and light sacks of grain. Babies were strapped to mothers, and the elderly and infirm who could not walk were tied to the backs of strong men.

White Orchid's villa was not one of the houses that had been set afire in the riot, but it had been looted. As White Orchid wrapped her few remaining goods in a blanket, she wondered which way she should go: north or south.

Clasped in her hand was the pale pink stone, rounded and flat and sanded smooth, that she had worn all her life. Placed about her neck by—her mother? the stranger who brought her to Tenoch?—the amulet was incised with a symbol that White Orchid had not been able to decipher. Curling her fingers now around the talisman, she closed her eyes and silently asked: Which way should I go? Whom should I follow?

The People of the Sun.

Opening her eyes, she scanned the chaos that filled the valley, families uprooting, tearing down shelters, gathering goods and children together, and she saw through the haze of doused cook fires and dust kicked up by so many busy feet, the old herb peddler struggling outside her hut. Thinking of her unborn child, and that to travel with a healer and a midwife would be beneficial, White Orchid shouldered her bundle and struck off toward Pikami's hut.

As Pikami carefully packed her precious herbs, roots, and seeds, she recalled another day when her life had taken as dramatic a turn as this. The day she had caused Rainbow Clan to vanish from the face of the earth.

Young Pikami had been the hope of Rainbow Clan. No one knew why bad luck afflicted them, but the clan had been shrinking, with members dying from injury or illness, women failing to bring babies to term. When Pikami finally became pregnant, and then delivered a healthy baby girl, all looked to her and her new child as the hope and future of their people.

The fateful day had been like any other. Pikami had gone down to the river to bathe. She had placed the infant in its basket on the riverbank, not too close to the water's edge, and she had turned her back for a brief moment. But when she turned again to pick up her baby, it was gone.

She had been frantic. She examined the ground for paw prints. Had a mountain lion carried the infant off? Perhaps a wolf, a fox?

And then she saw them. Human footprints, larger than her own.

She had run, but the kidnapper had run faster. Pikami never caught him, never knew who had snatched her baby when her back was turned for just an instant. After that she could not bring more children to term, so that the clan one by one died out and she was the last of the Rainbow Clan. No one ever blamed Pikami, because babies were stolen, by thieves or animals, but Pikami never forgave herself.

Recalling that long-ago day, as she collected the herbs she would take on the long journey out of Center Place, Pikami hoped her daughter had not been killed, that she had been placed with a kind family, and that she had been protected all these years by the magic amulet Pikami had placed around her neck, fashioned of pale pink stone and inscribed with the symbol of the Rainbow Clan.

Hearing footsteps approach, she emerged from her hut and saw a Toltec noblewoman coming along the path. Lady White Orchid, widow of the late *tlatoani*. "May I travel with you?" the Lady asked. "We can help each other. I am strong and," White Orchid laid a hand on her stomach, "I am with child."

Pikami rubbed her neck, where the skin was wrinkled and sagged so loosely that lost in the folds was the tattoo of Rainbow Clan: two curved lines, like arches, suspended above five dots. She was happy to travel with a pregnant woman. Pikami loved babies, ever since she lost her own. It was why she had invited Yellow Feather and her newborn to live with her. Now another newborn would enter her life. "I will give you healthful herbs to help your baby," she said, feeling a curious joy lift her old heart. "And when the times comes, I shall deliver you of your child."

With the lame boy helping Pikami, they headed to the western end of the canyon, where a massive gathering of humanity was preparing to depart. "Will you be returning to your family, Old Mother?" White Orchid asked, because she had heard that the migration would be traveling to settlements in the north where people would find kinsmen.

"I have no family," Pikami said. "Sadly, I am the last of Rainbow Clan. But you also do not return to a family. Your family is far to the south," she said, wondering why the Lady chose to go north instead of south with her own people.

White Orchid said nothing as she relieved the old woman of one of her bundles. Who her family was, White Orchid had no idea. She had been afraid to show anyone the amulet around her neck for fear that, if it was not Toltec, how would she explain wearing it? And discreetly surveying facial tattoos in the marketplace, and even among her own servants, had produced no match. But now that she was traveling with the People of the Sun, she would perhaps have a chance to learn its significance. Not right away, but after a while, when she and the old woman had become familiar with each other—already, White Orchid was feeling a small sense of family as she walked with the old herb peddler and her lame grandson, three generations, and the promise of a fourth, bonding together as they walked toward the unknown—White Orchid would show Pikami the pink stone with its three lines arching above five dots, and maybe she would find her bloodline in a distant settlement at last.

As Moquihix emerged from Precious Green, to watch the exotic birds fly up and away into the sky, he saw hollow-eyed Yellow Feather sitting on the edge of the deserted plaza. She had placed her little boy on the funeral pyre of Copil the Superintendent of the Marketplace in the hope that Copil would take care of the little child-spirit in the afterlife.

Moquihix looked down at Yellow Feather and, as he recalled the first day she had come to his house and he had felt a stirring of life in his loins, now, too, he felt a stirring, not of lust but of his heart. He sympathized with her loss. He himself had lost an infant daughter years ago when she had been dropped by a careless servant.

He reached down and lifted Yellow Feather to her feet. She wordlessly fell into step at his side and, joining the group at the eastern end of the canyon, they began their long journey to the south.

Before taking her place at the head of her people, Hoshi'tiwa went one last time to Jakál's chambers, where she found the rain jar. She would not take it with her but leave it there, believing it would comfort the lonely spirit of Jakál as it haunted Center Place. Removing the *xochitl* he had placed around her neck, the golden flower that contained a drop of Quetzalcoatl's blood, she placed it inside the rain jar.

Finally, the once young and naïve Hoshi'tiwa, now empowered by the spirit of *suukya'qatsi,* proceeded to lead her people out of Center

Place. Behind her, Running Elk and Red Crow walked hand in hand. Among the vast throng that slowly wound its way along the ancient trail walked Nagual with his group of kachina supporters, carrying their sacred wooden spirits.

As they began their long walk, Hoshi'tiwa thought: Ahoté's death was not in vain. Had he not come to Center Place, and then been taken to the mines, these people would not now be reunited with their loved ones. And so Ahoté was with her still. He was in her heart, and his spirit was in the bear claw and owl figurine she wore around her neck. And she would remember him for all the rest of her days.

As the Lords and priests and Jaguars started homeward, the unified clans of the People of the Sun followed the Tortoise Clan daughter northward toward their unknown future and destiny among the mesas in the West.

DAUGHTER OF THE SUN

by Barbara Wood

In Her Own Words

- A Conversation with Barbara Wood
- About the Author

Historical Perspective

- "Where Did They Go?"
  An Original Essay by Barbara Wood

Keep on Reading

- Recommended Reading
- Reading Group Questions

For more reading group suggestions
visit www.readinggroupgold.com

 ST. MARTIN'S GRIFFIN

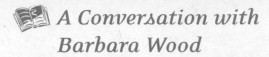

A Conversation with Barbara Wood

Can you tell us a bit about your background, and how you decided to lead a literary life?

The facts will tell you that I grew up in the San Fernando Valley outside of Los Angeles, California, but personal memory tells me differently. Looking back, I see that I spent my formative years in a tenth-century harem in Cairo, for a while at least, before moving on to the French court at Versailles on the eve of revolution. When I got tired of that, I took off for tropical climates and sailed the seas with Captain Blood (who bore a remarkable resemblance to the dishy Errol Flynn), learned the hula from Queen Liliuokalani, and experienced high adventure in the untamed Australian Outback. My body might have been in Tarzana, California, but my spirit was elsewhere and elsewhen.

"My childhood escape became my adult profession."

All kids fantasize, I suppose, but for me it was a way of life. I was a foreigner in a culture that did not forgive foreignness. This was pre-Beatles and I had arrived in America with a Liverpool accent that was the butt of many sixth-grader jokes and taunts. Those taunts did not bother me because I had many wonderful places to retreat to where people did not laugh at me, where I was in fact a queen floating on her barge down the Nile, or a "lady" pirate finding treasure in the Caribbean.

My family moved a lot. I don't know why. Once we hit the U.S. with our green cards and accents, my mother could never find a place that satisfied her as England did, and so we had many changes of address, and my brother and I attended many schools. This did not foster close attachments to

friends my age. I was always the new kid in the class, and often the loner. But who cared? In my alternative world I was well known and loved as the inventor of fabulous medicines and cures, as the woman who wrote the first printed book, or who discovered the headwaters of the Nile.

As I got older, fantasy turned to curiosity and I became thirsty for facts. The local library became my home away from home as I devoured books on geography, travel, exploration, and history. The accumulating knowledge fired the imagination so that my fantasies became rich in detail and I began writing them down. Thus was my love of research born.

Today I still retreat into other epochs and take on the lives of past people, I create their stories and fill those stories with fabulous detail. My childhood escape became my adult profession.

What inspired you to write Daughter of the Sun?

A visit to Chaco Canyon in 1992, when I walked among the ruins, listened to the wind whistle down the cliffs, and felt the hot sun on my face. They say that if you listen carefully, Chaco Canyon actually hums. I never heard the hum, but I sensed great spiritual power there. I have felt it before, in Egypt—not at the Great Pyramids but in a small upriver temple called Philae. This is the sense of the Spiritual—the powerful, unseen world that we try to explain through religion and the paranormal. I am a believer in sacred places on earth, and Chaco Canyon is one. My visit there prompted me to do some reading, and when I learned of what historians call the Abandonment, I needed to know more, and when no answers came, I decided I had to come up with an answer of my own. That answer is in *Daughter of the Sun.*

Were any of the characters in Daughter of the Sun based on you?

I suppose all writers put something of themselves in their books. We can't help but want to be part of the story. I am not, however, the heroine in this case. There are two wise teachers who shape Hoshi'tiwa's destiny: Yani, a fellow pottery maker, and Pikami, an elderly healer. Between the two, they guide young Hoshi'tiwa, even though it really is Barbara Wood doing the guiding.

Do you have a favorite character in the book?

I fell in love with Lord Jakál even though I had no intention of doing so. As he evolved and grew in the book, and presented his belief in the return someday of his Savior God, Quetzalcoatl, as his passion came through, along with his devotion and dedication, I grew to love him. I think he reminded me of a Catholic priest I was drawn to a long time ago. The combination of deep faith and personal charisma is very attractive.

The subject of cannibalism among the Anasazi is a touchy and controversial issue. Can you take a moment to talk about why, and how, you dealt with it in Daughter of the Sun?

I think cannibalism goes far to explain the reasons behind the Abandonment. Since the modern-day Hopi say that the inhabitants of Chaco Canyon were their ancestors, and since today's Hopi do not practice cannibalism, it stands to reason that the practice must have been brought to the region by

"I like to live vicariously in history, through reading and writing."

outsiders. There is a theory among some historians and anthropologists that Toltecs came from Mexico, perhaps from as far away as Chichén Itzá in the Yucatán, and established trade with the indigenous people of Chaco. It makes sense to me that such violent invaders would invariably force the more peaceful natives to pick up stakes and leave.

Where does your fascination with the indigenous people of North America come from?

I love their belief in the connectedness—the Oneness—of all things. A man does not own land, he is part of it. He is not superior to animals, he is their spiritual equal. Man is connected to the cosmos as well, to the heavens and to the unseen world, a concept I discovered when I wrote *Sacred Ground,* my account of the history of Southern California beginning with the Indians. The Navajo believe that an unkind act, or evil thoughts, will have far-reaching effects and cause bad things to happen. So thoughts, too, are connected to everything else, material and spiritual. This happens to be my own basic belief, ever since I discovered the world of quantum physics which, for me, has explained so much while offering even deeper, more wonderful mysteries.

In writing about an ancient civilization, what modern-day conveniences do you appreciate the most?

Certainly modern medical practices. I love history, I like to live vicariously in history, through reading and writing. However, when asked if I would ever like to go back and actually live in a past era, I find the prospect horrifying. People died young of the most innocuous of causes—an infected wound, a broken leg, an abscessed tooth, a high fever, childbirth. Infant mortality rate was high. Diet was poor. Surgery, of course, was out of the question, as were antibiotics or even the most rudimentary understanding of anatomy and disease. In *Daughter of the Sun,* I have the Chief Physician diagnosing an ailment by sprinkling seeds into a bowl of water and watching how quickly they sink. This was an actual diagnostic tool among the ancient Toltecs! The doctor rarely even looked at the patient. It was all magic and luck, and so people died young.

"I would like to meet the unsung heroines of the past."

You are a spiritual person. Were you raised in any formal faith?

I was raised Roman Catholic but drifted away when I did not feel that my personal needs were being met. Like many who have left Catholicism, I explored the world of religion, faith, and beliefs. Many I rejected, some I have embraced. I think that religion and spirituality are not necessarily the same thing. The former never brought me comfort while the latter definitely does.

If you could meet any writer, alive or dead, who would it be, and what would you talk about?

Without a doubt, that would be Mika Waltari, a Finnish author who wrote a book called *The Egyptian.* I was twelve when I read that book, my first adult novel, and it so grabbed me from the start, so transported me to another land, another age, that it was a life-altering experience. I had always intended to write Mr. Waltari a fan letter but never got around to it until I read his obituary years ago and felt awful. So if I could speak with him now, I would thank him for inspiring a young

girl to come out of her shell and discover the greater world. I was so amazed by how vividly he brought ancient Egypt to life that I found within myself a need to do the same. I thought: If this man can do it, so can I. Since then, I always strive to attain Mr. Waltari's high level of superb writing.

Are there any special women in history that you wish you could meet?

Aside from the obvious ones, such as Marie Curie, I would like to meet the unsung heroines of the past. The women whose inventions and ideas and discoveries were credited to men, usually husbands or fathers, because the scientific world refused to acknowledge such accomplishments from a woman. Women who broke barriers, such as the first female medical students in the late nineteenth century who, when they showed up for class, were physically picked up by the male students and thrown out of the room. Pioneer women who crossed two thousand miles of hostile territory in rickety wagons, taking care of husbands and children, fighting illness and starvation, giving birth, blazing the way for those who came after— women who have no trails, no forts, no mountains named after them.

The smart, inventive, creative, outrageous women whose names are lost to us—these I would love to meet.

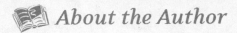

BARBARA WOOD is the internationally bestselling author of sixteen novels. In Germany, she is a bestselling American novelist and her sales on a single title are consistently over one million copies. She lives in Riverside, California.

Photo credit: Volker Corell

Where Did They Go?
An Original Essay by Barbara Wood

Daughter of the Sun is based on several unexplained mysteries found in the American Southwest.

All the significant locations mentioned in the book exist today and can be visited and explored: the rising-splendor called Precious Green is known today as Pueblo Bonito and the Star Chamber is called Casa Rinconada, to name a few. We do not know who built these great pueblos, or why. The "safe house" carved high in the cliff over Hoshi'tiwa's home settlement is typical of such mysterious cliff dwellings found all over the Four Corners region of the Southwest. No one knows who built these strange, inaccessible fortresses, or for what reason. Likewise, the wide, straight paved highways exist today, and experts cannot agree on their original purpose. Kivas are found in modern-day Hopi pueblos as well as in Anasazi ruins. Thousands have been discovered and, again, experts cannot determine what their original purpose was.

Rock art (in petroglyphs and pictographs) offers little in the way of explanation. The prophetic wall of symbols that Yani shows to Hoshi'tiwa exists today at the eastern end of the canyon. Many believe it records an astronomical event that took place in the year 1054 A.D. when a star went supernova and could be seen all over the world. Others who have studied the pictograph believe it is merely a representation of Venus in the night sky at the time of the crescent moon.

Finally, there is the mysterious event historians call the Abandonment.

We know that, a thousand years ago, Chaco Canyon was the center of a thriving civilization, and the nexus of a vast network of trade routes. We believe that the Great Houses (the rising-splendors) were used for religious and administrative purposes. But who, exactly, lived there we do not know, or why, after centuries of living in the canyon, the entire populace suddenly vanished, almost overnight. The fact that intact pottery, tools, and clothing have been found in the ruins leads us to believe that the departure was unplanned and hurried. We also do not know where those Chaco Canyon inhabitants went after they left. A deeper mystery is why, after a thousand years of habitation, building a rich cultural center, did they never return?

The modern-day Hopi say that the Anasazi were their ancestors and that after they left Chaco Canyon, they went west to settle on today's familiar mesas. Yet the term "Anasazi" is in fact a Navajo word meaning "ancient enemy." No one knows the origin of the term, why or when it was first coined, and so we are brought back to the question: Who were the inhabitants of Chaco Canyon?

All of these elements, existing today and accessible to visitors and explorers, are combined in *Daughter of the Sun,* like pieces of a puzzle, to form a picture of what might have happened there long ago.

> *"A thousand years ago, Chaco Canyon was the center of a thriving civilization."*

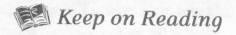 *Keep on Reading*

Frazier, Kendrick.
People of Chaco: A Canyon and Its Culture.
W. W. Norton & Company, 1999.
One of the absolute best references for those just
starting to explore the subject.

Gabriel, Kathryn.
*Roads to Center Place: A Cultural Atlas
of Chaco Canyon and the Anasazi.*
Johnson Books, 1991.
A remarkable work. The reader gets so caught
up it is hard to put this book down.

Lourie, Peter.
The Lost World of the Anasazi.
Boyds Mills Press, 2003.
This book contains breathtaking pictures of
Chaco Canyon. They are the next best thing to
being there.

Roberts, David.
In Search of the Old Ones.
Simon & Schuster, 1997.
Poetic, lyrical, beautifully written. Draws you
into the mystery so that you don't want to let go.

Vivian, R. Gwinn, and Hilpert, Bruce.
The Chaco Handbook: An Encyclopedic Guide.
University of Utah Press, 2002.
An in-depth reference for the truly interested, and
in a convenient format. Absolutely everything you
want to know about the Chaco phenomenon.

Waters, Frank.
Book of the Hopi.
Penguin Books, 1963.
If the Hopi are indeed the descendants of the
Anasazi, this book provides a rare window into
what their ancestors were like.

*Recommended

Reading*

 *Reading Group Questions*

1. Historians and archaeologists still do not know why Chaco Canyon was abandoned. The drought in *Daughter of the Sun* is one theory. Can you think of other reasons a people would pick up and abandon a thriving settlement, never to return?

2. The Toltecs and the People of the Sun did not believe that anything happened by accident. Everything is part of a great cosmic design and we can read our fate in the stars. Does this still leave room for free will?

3. If you had access to a time machine and you could visit any period or event in the North American past—but only one—what would you choose, and why?

4. What is the significance of dreams in *Daughter of the Sun*? Do they foretell the future? Do they bring messages from the gods/God, as Lord Jakál believed? Or are they merely the random misfirings of a sleepy brain?

5. What was the purpose of the Anasazi roads? The people of Chaco Canyon did not have beasts of burden, they did not have the wheel. So why did they need wide, straight highways?

6. Regarding White Orchid's secret adoption: Why is bloodline so important? Can love make up for not being related to one's parent? How important is it to know where one came from?

7. Hoshi'tiwa was willing to die for her beliefs. Is there anything you would give your life for? And how is self-sacrifice different from the human sacrifice described in the book?

8. The final battle in the book is sparked by a single act of defiance—a person from the crowd throws a rock. A simple gesture producing profound consequences. Can you think of a time in history when other such simple acts had such a powerful influence?

9. Hoshi'tiwa believes that nothing dies, that there is constant change in the universe. When a person dies, he or she is not lost but joins the stars, the rocks, and all life. What do you think?

10. Hoshi'tiwa's mother tells her she "was born to a special purpose." Are we all born for a special purpose? If we believe this, then how does this tie in with the belief in a cosmic Oneness, that all things are connected, that we are part of a universal design and that nothing happens by accident?